Battlefield China

Book Six of the Red Storm Series

By

James Rosone & Miranda Watson

Copyright Information

Disclaimer

This is a fictional story. All characters in this book are imagined, and any opinions that they express are simply that, fictional thoughts of literary characters. Although policies mentioned in the book may be similar to reality, they are by no means a factual representation of the news. Please enjoy this work as it is, a story to escape the part of life that can sometimes weigh us down in mundaneness or busyness.

Table of Contents

Chapter 1

Winds of Change

April 16, 2019

Fort Meade, Maryland

National Security Agency

"Here's your change," the cafeteria cashier said to Katelyn Mackie, the President's Chief Cyberwarfare Advisor.

"Thank you," she replied, swiftly shoving the coins into her wallet. Then she grabbed her morning cup of joe and bagel with cream cheese. Had Katelyn not been in such a hurry to get to work, she probably would have stopped at a Dunkin' Donuts for her staple macchiato and veggie and egg white sandwich.

Walking down the hall away from the cafeteria, she swiped her access card, which let her into the secured side of the building. After a couple of minutes of wandering down a hallway that was surprisingly crowded for that hour of the morning, she eventually reached the elevator bank in the center of the cavernous building. Rather than hitting a button to travel to one of the various floors like the others around her, she walked past the gaggle of government workers and sauntered up to a door being guarded by two United States Marines.

She smiled as she saw the familiar faces. One of the Marines at the door had lost a leg during the first days of the war in Korea. The government had issued him a prosthetic limb and sent him right back to work—this time guarding the nation's utmost secrets.

"Good morning, Corporal Daniels, Lance Corporal Tips," she said cheerfully.

"Good morning, Ma'am. Got your breakfast and a new haircut, I see," replied Corporal Daniels. He had a mischievous look that almost seemed to say that if they'd met at a bar, he might ask her out.

"Come on, Corporal, you know the world runs on caffeine and adrenaline," she said lightheartedly, eliciting a laugh and nods from the two sentinels. Katelyn presented her NSA credentials for them to read and then ran her coffee and brown-bagged bagel through the security scanner. She placed her JWICS-capable Blackberry in one of the locking metal phone boxes next to the guards and smiled as she walked through the scanner.

Seeing nothing out of the ordinary, the Marines returned her smile and let her pass. She then entered an access code into a keypad, which turned on the two biometric verification devices next to the door. She placed her right hand on the flat panel, which quickly lit up and carried out a scan of her five fingers and her palm, verifying the match. Seconds later, the iris scanner just above the panel turned on. She leaned in and looked directly at the soft blue light. Moments later, there was a soft beep and a hiss as the locked door popped open, allowing her to enter the nerve center of a very secretive office space tucked away inside the building.

As she walked toward her private office, adjacent to the operations floor, she was greeted by the duty officer and a few of her colleagues.

One of her male counterparts sidled up to her as he approached her office. "New haircut—you have a new boyfriend I should know about?" he asked playfully, an eager smile on his face.

Katelyn shot him a disapproving look. "No, Tyler. I just wanted to change things up. I'm visiting the White House a lot more lately, and I want to make sure I look professional and presentable in case I'm asked to speak to anyone outside of the National Security Council."

Tyler held his hands up in mock surrender. "OK, OK. If you don't want to talk about it, that's cool with me."

Sitting down in her chair, she immediately started to log in to her numerous computer terminals, emails and accounts. Tyler plopped down in the chair across from her desk.

"Seeing that you're still here, I presume you have something important you needed to talk to me about?" she asked, continuing to type her passwords into one system after another.

"You did get my text message, right?" he asked, his left eyebrow raised quizzically.

"You mean the message you sent me at 1:09 a.m.? Yeah, I saw it. That's why I'm here thirty minutes early."

"It's happening," he said. "It's finally happening, Kate."

"Lightning Wing?" she asked, swiveling her chair around to face him.

"Yeah," Tyler answered. "Our source in the PLA Air Force sent a coded message an hour before I sent you that text. He didn't know exactly when, but he said it was happening and soon."

"Did you and the rest of the team make sure everything on our end is set? That we're ready when this happens? I need to know we're prepared before I call the

White House," she said cautiously. She hoped everything was going to work out.

Tyler nodded. "I double-checked the code myself. It's ready to go. Once they start things, they'll have no way of knowing we're mirroring everything. *If* they ever did find out, they'd have to replace every drone to completely get rid of the firmware in them—not an easy task."

Katelyn leaned back in her chair, looking nervously at the ceiling. What they were about to do could totally screw up the economy, but it would probably win the war. "*God, I hope we're not making a huge mistake,*" she reflected.

Katelyn took a deep breath and let it out. "OK," she said. "Inform the Director that it's happening, so the agency can begin to prepare for it. I need to let the National Security Advisor know."

With the decision made, Tyler stood and exited her office, leaving Katelyn to inform her own masters in D.C.

She turned her SECRET Tandberg on, which would provide her a secured video connection, and dialed Tom McMillan's line, hoping to catch him in his office. It rang three times. Then the screen opened up and she saw Tom sitting in his chair behind a stack of folders.

"Good morning, Katelyn. I suspect you're about to give me some bad news, calling me first thing in the morning like this," he remarked, getting up from his desk to close his office door before sitting back down.

She sighed. "I'm afraid so. You remember during the summer, we provided you with a brief about a Chinese operation called Lightning Wind? The one that entailed the use of those new UAVs and the disabling of the Allies' commercial satellites?"

Tom thought for a moment, then his entire demeanor changed. "I thought you guys said the Chinese would probably not tamper with the global commercial satellite systems. Are you saying something has changed?"

She nodded. "We received a coded message from our source. He told us they're moving forward with the entire plan, and soon."

Tom looked concerned. He turned away from her and looked at something on the wall for a few seconds, obviously collecting his thoughts. "This is going to change everything. I need you here to brief the President. I'm sending a helicopter to pick you up. We don't have time to waste with you stuck in the morning commute. Be ready to meet your ride at the helipad in ten minutes," he ordered. Then he disconnected the call without saying goodbye.

Katelyn was not offended by the abrupt ending. She knew McMillan had to get the President's schedule cleared, and a lot of other people needed to be brought up to speed on what was about to happen.

****

White House

President Wally Foss was sitting outside on the upper portico of the White House, which overlooked the front lawn and the city. The morning rush hour was in full swing, complete with the periodic honking of horns, the bumper-to-bumper traffic, and the sidewalks bustling with people heading to their places of work.

He reached down and grabbed another slice of duck bacon as he thumbed through the morning headlines on his tablet. He didn't have time to read all the articles, but he liked to get caught up on the initial morning bullet points to get a sense of where things stood with the public. He'd have his morning intelligence brief in another half hour, and that would get him up to speed on the behind-the-scenes stuff the public seldom knew about.

Just as Foss polished off his second piece of duck bacon, Josh Morgan, his Chief of Staff, opened the door to the portico and walked up to him. "Sorry to disturb you, Mr.

President," he said, "but an urgent matter has come up that you need to address."

Foss looked up and examined his friend's face, which registered a mix of anxiety and anger. This was obviously serious. The President scooped up a quick mouthful of eggs and grabbed the last piece of bacon before following him down to the working level of the White House.

They skipped going to the Oval and went straight to the Presidential Emergency Operation Center, deep underground. The PEOC had essentially become Foss's war room after the President had sought to separate the duties of the war and domestic affairs by holding the meetings for each in separate rooms on different levels of the White House.

When Foss entered the room, Tom McMillan cleared his throat, silencing everyone at the table. "Katelyn should be here momentarily, Mr. President, but I can go ahead and get you up to speed on what's happening."

Foss nodded and reached for the pen sitting next to the pad of paper in front of him. "OK," he answered. "Let's get going, then, but don't get too far ahead of Kate. I suspect this is going to be more of her show once she arrives."

Tom nodded. "This past summer, we briefed President Gates about a secret Chinese Air Force program forming up at that time that could radically impact the landscape of the war. The PLA had developed several new UAVs—drones that will most certainly change the face of modern warfare."

The tension in the room thickened. Foss and the others shifted in their seats a bit, but everyone held their tongues for the moment.

"Their new UAV weapon platforms appear to be at least a decade ahead of ours. Each design has a specific mechanism for countering our defenses."

Tom brought up an image of a very sleek-looking fighter drone. "This image was captured and smuggled out of China at great expense. It's the first of the UAVs, though there appear to be two versions of it. It's called the Long Huo, or Dragon's Fire. DARPA has been developing a similar capability with Raytheon and General Dynamics for nearly fifteen years. It's a hunter-killer drone—in many ways, it's similar to our Reaper drone or the Russians' Zhukov, but these are much more advanced."

He pulled up some more detailed schematics of the drone to display on the screen. "The key difference is that, unlike other UAVs, this one operates much like a fighter plane. Without a pilot, the PLA was able to eliminate a lot of safety and redundancy systems a manned aircraft would naturally have, which means this aircraft can outfly and outmaneuver anything we've ever built. The UAV is large, almost the size of an F-16, with a wingspan of nine meters. It's built like a fighter plane, and in reality, it *is* a fighter plane. It's jet-powered, with a flight range of 550 kilometers fully loaded and a ferry range of 3,900 kilometers.

"As I said earlier, there are two versions of this UAV. The first image I just showed you was the fighter version. On each wingtip is an air-to-air missile, and underneath the UAV is an internal weapons bay that we believe can hold either six or eight additional air-to-air missiles. Our source was not able to get us the full schematics of the aircraft, only parts of it.

"I don't have much further information to give other than what I've just shown you. There's a small group at DARPA who can provide more detailed specifics. What I *can* share are the few specs we have on the ground-attack version of this beast."

He pulled up another image of a similar UAV—though the shape was slightly different than the fighter version, more squatted with wider wings. "The ground version isn't nearly as aerodynamic as its sister, and from what DARPA's been able to extrapolate from the information on it, it's also a bit slower. They estimate its speed to be around 720 kilometers per hour, with a flight range of between 350 and 400 kilometers when fully loaded. We have no idea if the UAV is armored, or what its full payload capacity is. We *do* know we've spotted it once or twice in use in Vietnam, but we were never able to get any video or pictures of it. We only knew about it from stories some of our ground assets were able to relay to us. We're still learning a lot about this UAV. Again, DARPA can probably provide more information on it than I can."

The Air Force Chief of Staff jumped in. "Do we know where this UAV is being constructed? Perhaps we can try to target where they're building them and reduce the likelihood of seeing any sort of swarm impacting us on the battlefield."

Admiral Meyers took this question for Tom. "I spoke with the same people at DARPA Tom has been consulting with, along with our guys at NSA and DIA. They told us a large part of the Chinese aerospace industry was actually located in Shenyang, the city we nuked during the opening hours of the Korean War. Last we heard, most of the aerospace industry had been moved down to the city of Guangzhou and the surrounding area. It's pretty heavily defended, and just far enough inland that it would require a large-scale ground invasion for us to attack them there."

The President chewed on that for a moment. "If this is where the Chinese are building their new superweapon, then perhaps it's where we need to focus our efforts," he asserted, pausing to let out a deep breath before he turned back to his generals. "Look, I know President Gates was all for invading the Chinese mainland and bringing the fight to the enemy, but after the most recent Chinese raid on our B-2 and B-1 bomber bases, I'd say they nearly knocked our strategic bombing ability out of consideration. We've lost 65% of our B-2s since the start of the war and nearly 50% of our B-1s. We're burning through cruise missiles faster than we can make them."

Before the President could continue, the outer door to the PEOC opened and Katelyn Mackie walked in. The room grew silent as she headed to her seat, next to McMillan's. "Sorry I'm late. My ride from Fort Meade was a few minutes behind schedule," she said, looking at the slide McMillan had just finished briefing. She immediately knew from the looks on everyone's faces that she had just interrupted an important discussion, so she stayed silent, waiting to be called on next.

The President commented, "All I'm saying is that, in light of what Tom's been discussing and what I'm sure Katelyn is going to bring up, I just have some serious reservations about the upcoming offensives, that's all." He gestured for the cyberwarfare advisor to take the floor. "Please, Katelyn, bring us up to speed. I can continue my discussion with the generals later. Besides, I have a feeling what you're about to tell us is going to change a few plans we already had in the works," the President said with a slight wink. He liked Katelyn; she was incredibly smart, and somehow wise for someone so young. She was an out-of-the-box thinker, and he knew Gates had thought she would be one of the key people in helping the US defeat the Chinese.

"Yes, Mr. President. Again, sorry for my tardiness," Katelyn said. She pulled her NSA-issued laptop out of her small carrying bag and swiftly hooked it up to the overhead projector. "If I may, Mr. President, I want to use some illustrations and videos to demonstrate the next UAVs and our plans for countering them. Before we go down this road, I want to take a moment to let you know that as grave as these new weapons sound, we do have a plan in place to respond to them."

While the President seemed skeptical, she could hear several of her counterparts breathe a sigh of relief. She smiled. It was nice to have such a vote of confidence in her abilities. Of course, her programs had already wreaked havoc in Russia, and the attack on the Indian transportation sector had sent that country's economy into a tailspin. Her actions might very well be the impetus for the Indians to end the conflict with the Allies.

She continued, "At the beginning of the war with Russia and China, all sides went after each other's military and spy satellites. They also went after the global GPS system with a DDoS attack, as you'll recall, though that issue has largely been fixed. Within a week, the major global powers established a détente to leave the civilian satellite infrastructure alone; the interruption in the GPS system caused such an immense worldwide disruption that I think even the Russians and Chinese had to face how heavily dependent they had become on these systems. Once all parties realized that everything from transportation to logistics to weather had been affected, a compromise was put in place, and the agreement still stands today.

"All sides have done their best to move critical aspects of communications networks and other military functions onto the civilian satellite grid, surreptitiously coopting control of many of the satellites in certain cases. Everyone knew this was going on, so the Chinese went to work on devising a way around it. They couldn't wipe out the civilian satellite grid without wiping out their own grid, so they found a way to do it without crippling themselves."

She pulled up the slide of the newest UAV. "This little guy is called the Y'an, which translates to *The Eye*. The Chinese have been building these giant UAVs to act as a nationwide 5G umbrella to compensate for the inevitable loss of their civilian satellite network. While this new network won't replace all of the satellites' functions, it'll provide them with consistent real-time ground surveillance and high-speed digital data and communications, ensuring their civilian population isn't left in a data or communications blackout," Katelyn explained.

The President held up a hand. "Excuse me if you will. What you're saying is that at this juncture in the war, the Chinese are going to go after the global civilian satellite network in an effort to blind and cripple the Allies right before our major ground invasion?"

All eyes turned to look at her and Tom, who clearly knew more about this than anyone else in the room. Tom tipped his head toward her to take the question. "Yes, Mr. President, that's what I'm saying," she responded.

The President snorted. "So, if they can't win, they're going to make sure no one else does either," he said, disgusted that the war was stooping down to a new low. It wasn't enough to inflict the horrors of war on each other's militaries, now they wanted to spread that discomfort to as much of the world's population as possible.

Katelyn quickly brought up another briefing slide. "If I could, Mr. President, there's more you need to know."

He signaled for her to go on. He might as well rip the Band-Aid off rather than prolong the inevitable.

"Sir, this is going to be bad, but it's not completely unexpected. We've known this was a possibility for nearly nine months, so we've been taking measures to prepare for it. In the late 2000s and early 2010s, the US Army in Iraq and Afghanistan was trying to tackle a major data communications problem of keeping the ground forces out on patrol in contact with their bases. The lack of infrastructure and the mountainous terrain of Afghanistan made it nearly impossible for our guys to transmit high volumes of data and maintain steady communications. The DoD came up a solution they termed 'the last tactical mile,' which utilized two systems to solve this problem.

"First, they placed 4G communications equipment on static aerostat blimps high above the bases, which provided a twenty-to-thirty-kilometer 4G bubble. They also explored ways of integrating 4G capability into UAVs that could be flown over the ground forces. Ironically, it was Facebook that took the latter program on and really ran with it. Mr. Zuckerberg had plans to leverage this kind of capability to bring Facebook to even the remotest parts of the world.

"When we first caught a whiff of the insidious Chinese plan to cripple the civilian satellite network, we reached out to several technology firms to discuss a plan B. SpaceX, Facebook, Microsoft, and Google all signed on to a classified program we established just six months ago. When the Chinese *do* begin to destroy the civilian satellite network, we have the ability to deploy aerostat blimps in 300 cities right now. That number will continue to increase by 50 cities a week at our current production scale. While this is still going to leave an enormous gap across the country, it won't leave us completely blind. We've also been working with the broadband providers to be ready to pick up the data slack, which will be huge.

"For the military, SpaceX and Facebook have developed several drones that will be able to stay aloft continuously running on solar energy. That network will be able to provide 5G communications and data capability to our naval, air and ground forces in the war zones."

She took a deep breath. "Mr. President, while the loss of the civilian satellite network will obviously hurt our economy, this development is actually going to be the key to defeating the Chinese."

The President's left eyebrow rose in incredulity. Several others leaned in closer, hanging on her every word.

"If I can, I want to give you a little background on this next piece. It'll help you understand our plan better. During World War II, the Germans developed the Enigma cipher machine, which at the time was a foolproof communications system—at least until the British Navy was able to capture a German U-boat and seize an intact Enigma and the codebook. Once they had these two components, they were able to essentially read the entire German military communications system for the duration of the war, giving the Allies an enormous leg up.

"In our case, once we became aware of this Chinese program, we inserted a code into the firmware of a critical component used in the Y'an communication UAV. Once the Chinese activate the Y'ans and switch all their communications over from their encrypted satellite and radio systems to the 5G system on the UAVs, we'll have complete access to their entire communications infrastructure. We'll be able to see everything they're transmitting on that network." Her lips curled up in a devilish smile.

Someone in the room let out a low whistle. The President leaned forward in his chair and a smile spread across his face. "This is huge, Kate. You should've led with this. That said, I can't help but wonder how this is going to impact things here at home. The level of chaos it's going to cause when the satellite systems begin to go down isn't something I'm even sure we can monetize, Tom."

Foss turned to his NSA. "We're going to have to have an emergency meeting with DHS, Treasury, and Commerce to see how bad this is going to be."

McMillan scribbled a note on his paper. "Yes, Mr. President. I'll make the calls as soon as we're done here."

Turning to face the SecDef, the President said, "Jim, I think this goes back to my original hesitation about the ground invasion. If we're going to invade, then perhaps we should focus on going after the factories producing these new UAVs and the Chinese financial enclaves. In light of these new developments, my concerns about a wide-ranging ground war are only increased. What are your thoughts?"

The Secretary of Defense paused, adjusting his tie as he mulled over the options. Finally, he turned to Katelyn. "Ms. Mackie, does your source know for certain that these UAVs are ready to be deployed now? And do we know how many of them are currently ready for use? Lastly, what if the Chinese suddenly decide not to take down the global satellite infrastructure at all but to keep things as they currently are?"

Katelyn pulled up some other information she had on her laptop. "Sir, up to this point, the information our source has provided has been nearly 100% accurate. He wasn't able to tell us how many of these fighter UAVs are currently available for use, but clearly, from both the source in Vietnam and our guy, we know it's real. As to your last question, if the Chinese suddenly develop cold feet about taking down the global satellite network and they opt to not use the Y'an UAVs, then we'll have to keep fighting them the way we have been. We almost need to hope they take down the satellites, so we can gain access to their military communications systems."

The SecDef, Katelyn, Tom, and the Chairman of the Joint Chiefs bantered back and forth for another fifteen minutes while the President listened silently. As they spoke, Foss grew more and more concerned about the current invasion plan. A ground war in mainland China would be messy, no matter how they looked at it.

"OK, people, I think I've heard enough," the President finally asserted. "I know this is going to ruffle some feathers, but we're going to change our current tactics. Instead of launching diversionary invasions in southern China and an offensive drive on Beijing, I want us to focus on going after Guangdong Province. That will disrupt their aerospace manufacturing base and interrupt their collection of tax revenues.

"Next, I want to go after China's piggy bank. We need to attack Shanghai and the surrounding area—that will take down their financial *and* tech sectors in one fell swoop. I was just reading a white paper written by the Institute for the Study of War that emphasized the strategy of depriving the Chinese government of the ability to pay for the war and disturbing the manufacturing base needed to sustain the PLA. I know this kind of throws a wrench into your plans, Jim, but what are your thoughts?" the President asked. He surveyed the faces of his military leaders and tried not to be amused when he observed that most of them were just doing their best not to look irate that their Commander in Chief had just thrown out their yearlong invasion plans.

Jim didn't say anything for a moment. He put his index fingers together and leaned into them, thinking it all over. "Mr. President, you're the Commander in Chief," he finally said. "If you want us to revamp our invasion plans, then that's what we'll do. I haven't read that same white paper, but I believe I know who wrote it—a retired colonel, Kyle Buller, if I'm not mistaken. He had worked many years in the Pentagon's procurement program and at DARPA. He's a smart fellow. We hadn't initially looked at that angle under President Gates since he favored a more direct attack strategy against Beijing, but I can also see the merit in considering the path you just outlined. If I may, would you allow us a few days to give this a good study and see how feasible it would be? We've spent a lot of time positioning war stock for the original plan, so I need to evaluate whether we would need to shift most of that war stock around, or if we could still use it in its current positions."

The President nodded his approval. He knew he couldn't spring a major change like this on the military without allowing them a chance to look at its viability. "That's fair enough, Jim. And, yes, it was Kyle Buller who wrote the white paper. I believe it was written maybe four months ago. I'll give you some time to look into it all, but

I'd like an answer within a week. If we're going to make this change, then we need to do it quickly."

With that said, the meeting broke up. The various parties went to work on getting the country ready for the eventual loss of satellites and preparing for a possible change in the invasion strategy.

Chapter 2
Calmer Heads Prevail

Chennai, India
Ripon Building

At 0830 hours, the air was already hot and muggy as General John Bennet, the Supreme Allied Commander for Asia, walked into the central meeting room of the Ripon Building. As soon as he entered, he was met by Major General Alan Morrison, the Australian Commander of Allied Forces in India. Behind him waited a small cadre of staff officers as well as Rear Admiral Shelley Cord, the commander of Task Force 92, the naval fleet supporting the ground operations. The new Secretary of State, Philip Landover, was also seated at the table along with several of his staff. When General Bennet walked in, Secretary Landover walked over to Bennet and heartily shook his hand.

The pleasantries were short, even by military standards. They had a lot to discuss. Once everyone was seated, General Bennet started the meeting. "All right, General Morrison, I'd first like a quick update on the disposition of the Allied forces in India," he announced.

General Morrison stood. "General Bennet, five days prior to your arrival, we successfully offloaded the remaining Allied units and supplies for our next offensive campaign. As of right now, Operation Jade Tiger, which will capture Bengaluru in the center of the country, is still ready to launch when you give the order. I have two Australian divisions, one New Zealand brigade, one British armored division, and two American mechanized infantry divisions ready to move.

"To cover our right flank and ensure the continued occupation of Chennai, I have a Canadian light infantry brigade, a French brigade and a German tank brigade, along with numerous other support units. If the Indian government doesn't want to pursue peace, then we're still ready to prosecute the war until they will," General Morrison said, a full grin on his face.

General Bennet smiled too. It was obvious the man before him was truly loving his position as the Allied commander in India. After all, within the last month, he'd gone from having a small contingent of 32,000 soldiers to over 73,000, with more on the way.

Secretary of State Landover inserted himself. "I've read over your progress up to this point, General—very impressive. You've certainly succeeded in humbling the Indian government."

"General Morrison, please excuse Secretary Landover," said General Bennet, shooting a scornful look at Landover. "I have a few more military matters to discuss before we move to politics." He didn't like being interrupted. This was his turf.

"My apologies, General," said Secretary Landover, his cheeks a bit red. "I was getting ahead of myself. I'll wait until we're ready to discuss tomorrow's meeting."

Bennet turned his attention back to the Australian. "General, I'm pleased with your progress up to this point. You have done a superb job with the forces given to you. You managed to pull off some impressive wins. Chennai was captured with very few casualties and very little civil unrest, which is fully attributed to the way you had the Army carry out its initial seizure of the city and the port.

"I spoke with President Foss, who has spoken with your Prime Minister, and they've accepted my recommendation that you be given a third star and continue to remain the overall Commander of Allied Forces in India. I have multiple divisions en route to Asia from Europe, and depending on how tomorrow's meeting goes, I may have those divisions placed under your command for you to widen the war in India. I hope that doesn't happen, but if it does, then we'll begin discussing additional objectives beyond Operation Jade Tiger."

General Bennet paused. "OK, then, Secretary Landover, it's over to you now."

Secretary Landover stood. "Thank you, General. My objective tomorrow is simple: get the Indian government to agree to a complete and unconditional surrender. If they don't, the war will continue as planned. You've shown me that you have the supplies and the forces needed to keep the war going, and frankly that's the major reason I wanted to meet with you today. I do have one question—may I inform the Indian prime minister that if he doesn't agree to our terms, our victorious European armies will now be directed to India?"

General Bennet thought about that for a moment. Under normal circumstances, he would never want to advertise his position like that to an enemy, but at the same time, if that information could lead the enemy to surrendering, then it'd be worth it. "If General Morrison has no objections, then neither do I," Bennet asserted. "We need this Indian theater wrapped up sooner rather than later. Once ground operations start in mainland China, we're going to be hard-pressed to keep India fully supplied for heavy offensive actions."

"I have no objections," Morrison confirmed.

The meeting went on for a bit longer as the military and political sides were discussed, then everyone broke for an early lunch and a nap. Between all the flying and the time zone changes, the sudden shift was wreaking havoc on people's mental alertness, and they'd all certainly need that the following day.

****

En Route to Ripon Building

Prime Minister Vihaan Khatri was both enraged at the situation he now found himself in and greatly ashamed that he had allowed it to come to this. He knew India should have stayed on the sidelines of the third great war, but he had permitted himself to be convinced that joining the Russian and Chinese grand alliance would position India for future greatness. America had been on the decline—everyone had said so for years. Even the President prior to Gates had publicly acknowledged it. Khatri clenched his fists. "*I should've known not to count America out*," he mourned.

The scene was filled with juxtaposition. Khatri sat in the leather chair of an Embraer Legacy 600 luxury jet, and yet, the members of his parliament were ready to throw him out of office. After such horrific humiliation and loss of life suffered under his leadership, even his partner in crime, President Aryan Laghari, had begun to side with the growing antiwar movement sweeping across the country. The absolute slaughter of their militia forces at the naval airbase outside of Arakkonam had shaken the population to the point of nearly collapsing the government. The people were furious that these largely underequipped and poorly trained militia forces had been thrown against a battle-hardened enemy because the government had not accepted the Allies' first peace offer to end the war. Now, the people and parliament had demanded that he settle the matter, or they'd replace him with someone who would.

When Khatri's jet flew over Chennai, he immediately noticed the sheer size of the military buildup on the outskirts of the city. He didn't need a military general to tell him the Allies had landed many more divisions of fresh troops in his country. They were obviously gearing up for a major offensive should his talks fail. Moments later, his plane, which was being escorted by a pair of Australian F/A-18s, landed at the Chennai International Airport in full view of rows of helicopter gunships and Allied warplanes. Once his jet had parked and the engines were shut off, the outer door was opened, and he was greeted by an Allied military honor guard.

At the end of the line of military members stood the American Secretary of State, Philip Landover, the American general currently in command of Allied forces in Asia, and an Australian general, the man Khatri recognized as being in charge of the Allied armies currently invading his homeland. Lifting his chin up in pride, he stepped off the plane and walked past the military members arrayed before him.

"Prime Minister Khatri," Landover said cheerfully, extending his hand, "I'm Secretary of State Landover, and this is Supreme Allied Commander General Bennet. It's good to meet with you. If you would please come with us, we have a room set up nearby for us to talk."

Khatri followed his hosts to the small room that had been set up. Some stewards offered everyone cold water and other assorted drinks. After some obligatory small talk, everyone began to take their seats. The mood was somewhat somber. Khatri realized that the decisions reached in this meeting would determine whether calmer heads would prevail or whether thousands more men and women would die in a futile attempt to resist the Allies.

Opening the discussion, Secretary Landover said, "Mr. Prime Minister, it's sad that world events have led us to this meeting today. I truly hope that today, you and I can put this matter behind us and allow our nations to move forward together in peace."

Khatri was a bit taken aback by the statement but quickly recovered his composure. He wondered what sort of terms he was going to have to accept to bring about the peace his nation demanded he achieve.

"I agree, Mr. Secretary," Khatri offered. "It was unfortunate that our two nations, once strong trading partners and friends, found ourselves on the opposite sides of this terrible war. Now it's time for us to set aside our differences and work toward peace."

Landover nodded. General Bennet, who appeared unmoved by the Prime Minister's statement, continued to stay silent. Secretary Landover shuffled a few pieces of paper in front of him. "I agree, Mr. Prime Minister. Let us begin then," he said. Landover seemed to find what he was looking for and composed himself. "Many months ago, President Foss offered your country the opportunity to end the war and leave the Eastern Alliance. The terms of surrender were generous. The terms I am authorized to present to you now are much less generous, since your continued war against the Allies, and in particular America, has caused us great harm. Your nation's cyberattack on our financial institutions cost the jobs of hundreds of thousands of people in our country and destroyed the wealth of millions."

Khatri shifted uncomfortably in his chair. The PM had been hoping his nation would be presented with the same terms of ending the war as they had been offered prior to the cyberattack on JPMorgan and the ground invasion of India.

"The terms being offered are this—complete and unconditional surrender of your armed forces and complete denuclearization of your country. You may retain your nuclear power capabilities, but your weapons labs and current nuclear inventory up to this point will have to be surrendered. Upon the acceptance of these terms, the 91,000 prisoners of war we're currently holding will be released back to your country."

Khatri swallowed uncomfortably but said nothing.

Secretary Landover continued, "Just as in the case of Russia, a small occupation force will remain in your capital and here in Chennai to ensure your government is honoring the terms of the surrender. Your nation will also no longer be allowed to continue war production or provide any sort of economic or financial support to the Eastern Alliance."

Landover sat back in his chair. "Are you ready at this time to agree to these terms, Mr. Prime Minster?" he asked.

Khatri had felt like an hour had passed as the secretary read the terms of surrender. The bile in his stomach slowly made its way up his throat to the back of his mouth. By the time Landover had finished, he wanted to vomit. What had been presented was a long list of humiliations he'd have to accept if he wanted to end the war. Khatri reached for the glass of water in front of him. He needed to calm his stomach before he responded and buy himself a few moments to think. After taking a couple of gulps of water, he shook his head as he looked up at Landover.

"Mr. Secretary, I'm afraid some of these terms are not acceptable," Khatri finally said. "While I can concede the points on providing financial and economy aid to the Eastern Alliance, I can't abide by the dismantling of our nuclear deterrent. India has not threatened to use these weapons against the Allies, but these weapons are imperative to our national security and protection against the Pakistanis, who also have nuclear weapons. If we're forced to hand our weapons over, we will be subject to attack from our unfriendly neighbors to the north. That's simply unacceptable." Khatri puffed his chest out defiantly. He felt he'd made a strong case.

General Bennet, who had remained quiet up to this point, spoke up. "Mr. Prime Minister, with all due respect, I know where your nuclear weapons are at this very moment. If I have to, I'll order their complete destruction and be done with it. *If* your government opts to use them against my forces, I've been authorized by the President to turn your country to ash. These terms are not up for negotiation—these are the terms being offered, and either you will accept them, or within the hour, I'll order my armies to begin tearing your country apart. I have many more divisions from Europe heading this way, and I can occupy your country before the end of summer if I choose to. Secretary Landover is giving you an opportunity to save tens of thousands of lives before it's too late. Please don't force me to destroy your country."

Khatri recoiled. "We are a nation of over one billion people, General. You cannot occupy our country like you can Russia—there are too many of us," retorted Khatri.

"And how did that mighty civilian uprising you proclaim work out for the militia forces at Arakkonam? Your armies have been defeated. Please don't force my men to slaughter untrained and ill-equipped civilian militias," General Bennet shot back, anger and determination burning in his eyes.

Raising his hands to calm everyone, Secretary Landover stepped in. "Gentlemen, please. Arguing and threatening each other isn't going to resolve this situation." Turning to look at Khatri, he added, "You're correct, Prime Minister. The Allies, America, can't occupy your country like Russia. I personally don't believe that's either necessary or required. However, the President is clear that India can't retain its nuclear weapons as part of the unconditional surrender. President Foss does recognize the unique security challenge your country faces with Pakistan; as such, he is willing to make the same security guarantee to India that we made to Russia. India will fall under the protected nuclear umbrella of the United States, and we will make that publicly and privately known to the leaders of Pakistan. A nuclear attack on India will result in a nuclear response against the attackers by the United States. Just as we agreed to in Russia, America will sign a twenty-five-year military defensive guarantee to that effect."

Khatri returned Landover's gaze. "What happens when we move past the twenty-five-year mark? Our issues with Pakistan are deep and long-standing. These issues may still remain well past your security agreement. Will India be allowed to openly pursue a nuclear weapons program then, or are we going to be under continued military threat if we move in that direction?"

Landover had known this might be a problem. He had mentioned it to the President prior to flying out here. However, no one had had a really good answer for him. "Prime Minister, let's hope that twenty-five-years from now, nuclear weapons will be a thing of the past." He paused. "I wasn't given specific guidance that India *couldn't* acquire nuclear weapons at the end of the agreement, so I believe that it would be safe to say your country would not face any threat from the United States if it pursued that course of action at that time."

Pausing for a moment, Landover asked, "Do you need a few moments to confer with your advisors?"

Khatri shook his head. He knew he wasn't going to get better terms. As humiliating as the offer was, part of him was just glad the US wasn't seeking financial reparations in addition to the dismantling of their nuclear arsenal. "How many Allied forces would remain in my country, and what would be the process of ending the fighting?" he finally asked, deflated and defeated. More than anything, he just wanted the killing to stop. So many young people had already died in this pointless war.

General Bennet leaned forward to take his turn to speak. "I will order the fighting to cease across the Allied lines immediately, and I request that you order your military to do the same. A forty-eight-hour cooling-off period will go into effect to make sure everyone in the field knows what's going on. Then I'll ask that the head of your armed forces meet with General Morrison here to work out the details. For the time being, we'll leave four divisions of Allied troops in India until the war in Asia is over. Once we can be assured that there will be no further problems within your country, and there are no overt acts of aggression being made by the Pakistanis toward India, we will look to draw down further Allied forces. *If* we detect any increase in military forces by the Pakistanis near your border, then I'm going to request that you agree to a redeployment of Allied forces to your shared border and allow our forces to be given any support and assistance they require. Our Air Force may also need access to your northern airbases as well."

While Khatri felt like he was drinking from a firehose, he was pleasantly surprised to see how quickly General Bennet had gone from threatening to reduce his nation to rubble and ash to aggressively defending the territorial integrity of his country should they be threatened by Pakistan. While he hated the terms of the surrender, he felt some peace now that Bennet appeared to be an honorable general and sincere in his effort to end the killing and honor the terms of the agreement, even if that meant fighting the Pakistanis.

"Mr. Secretary, General, I agree to your terms of surrender," Khatri said, calmly and in a calculated tone. "If we may, I would like to invite you both to New Delhi in forty-eight hours, where we can formalize the end of this terrible war. Would you do my nation the honor of holding a public signing ceremony to formally end the conflict between us? I believe it will greatly aid in the healing process between our two nations." He hoped he could at least manage this meager face-saving act before his parliament and people.

General Bennet looked a bit uneasy with the commitment, but after a moment prodding by the Secretary of State, he reluctantly agreed.

****

Following the meeting with the Indian Prime Minister, General Bennet held a separate meeting with his generals. They needed to iron out the details of the occupation and which units would be staying on. While they had to make sure they left sufficient combat power in country to keep the Indian government honest, they also needed as much firepower as they could muster for the coming summer offensive into China. The President had given him clear guidance that he wanted the war over within the next twelve months. Like his predecessor, Foss didn't want the war to be a deciding factor in the coming 2020 election. If he didn't win reelection, he didn't want another president changing the course of the war and eroding the gains they had made.

Chapter 3
Mongolia

Ulaanbaatar, Mongolia

Standing on top of the highest elevation above Ulaanbaatar, General Tony Wilde looked off to the east of the sprawling capital of Mongolia. Most of the snow had finally melted, though traces of it remained on peaks off in the distance. Warmer air was finally moving in from the Gobi Desert, drying everything out, which was good, considering his army would need to get moving soon. His grand army was spread out across a number of camps, and as he observed the men and women from afar, they looked like a well-organized troop of ants as they rushed about, completing their morning physical training. Others hurriedly worked on repairing and maintaining the immense number of vehicles and equipment needed to support such a large force. He put his hands on his hips and leaned back, straightening out his spine, admiring his soldiers like a beekeeper marvels at the inner workings of a beehive.

Turning to look back at the city, General Wilde saw the railyard. It was as busy as ever. Soldiers and local nationals steadily unloaded fuel and other necessary supplies. Next to the main yard was a series of new track lines his engineers had built, filled with flatbed train cars that were fully laden with a battalion of tanks, Stryker vehicles, munitions and fuel trucks. These flatbeds were going to be one of the key ingredients to capturing his next set of objectives.

Having seen what he needed to, General Wilde turned to his driver and signaled that he was ready to head back to his headquarters. It took them nearly thirty minutes to navigate the twisty turns of the road, and Wilde did his best not to admit that the journey made him just a little carsick.

The nausea subsided fairly quickly once he had his feet on the ground and could breathe fresh air again. He strode over to his office, a cavernous room that had been commandeered from the international airport. As he walked in the door, he was met by the familiar sight of the large map board hanging on one of the walls. On it were the outlines of the camps spread out around the Mongolian capital, color-coded supply lines, and arrows marking the most likely approaches they'd need to take to capture their overall objective, Beijing.

Next to the map stood a Dutch colonel, freshly arrived from the European front. "It's quite the logistical challenge, isn't it, General?" asked the colonel matter-of-factly.

Raising an eyebrow at the newcomer, Wilde replied, "That's an astute assessment of the situation. You must be my new logistician." The corner of his mouth curled up in a half-smile.

The colonel stuck his hand out. "Yes, Sir, I am," he said warmly. "The name is Colonel Johan Willem, and it's a pleasure to finally meet you. I've heard great things about the man who defeated the Indian and Russian armies of Siberia."

General Wilde nodded approvingly. "Colonel Willem, General Cotton sent me an email a week ago about your transfer to my Army group," he responded. "He told me you were one of the most capable officers he'd ever worked with. He said if anyone could handle this logistical quandary, it would be you." He paused for just a moment, then his tone changed. "I'm eager to get things moving, and we don't have a lot of time."

The two of them turned back to the map board, and Wilde brought him briefly up to speed on what he had done up to that point.

Colonel Willem scratched his chin in thought as he absorbed the information. "If I could, General, I believe your biggest challenge is going to be keeping the Army group properly fueled and maintained," he offered. "Armored vehicles unfortunately need a lot of love; they tend to break down if they're not properly taken care of, and this harsh environment out here will make maintaining them a lot harder."

Wilde nodded.

The Dutch colonel seemed to suddenly remember something. "Last night I took an unannounced tour of the railyards, and I must say I'm impressed. Having your engineers build a series of rail lines off the main line and loading them up with flat cars to move your heavy armor is brilliant. I'm not sure I would have thought of that. If I may, what is your objective with them? How do you plan on making use of the rail lines? I have to assume the Chinese are actively sabotaging them, no?" Willem inquired.

"You would be correct on that count, Colonel. I have near-constant drone cover of the rail lines, and we routinely hit small raiding parties with drone strikes. As a segment gets blown up, we replace it quickly." Wilde sighed. "The road infrastructure in Mongolia is crappy at best. I can't move most of my armor across these roads without further destroying it. My goal is to use the rail lines as much as possible to move my army as close to the front lines as I can."

The general pointed on the map to the city of Baiyinchaganzhen. "Right now, my goal is to capture this city, just across the border in Inner Mongolia, China. It's a major railhead connecting the two countries. Once we take control of this city, we'll be able to start transporting my Army group across nearly seven hundred kilometers of empty wasteland. I've had Baiyinchaganzhen under surveillance now for five months—the Chinese have it garrisoned with a mechanized infantry battalion and a battalion of light infantry. I don't believe the Chinese think we're a threat because of how far away we are, or they would have started to build up some defenses. Heck, they haven't even torn the railyard up."

Colonel Willem nodded in approval. "This is brilliant, General, but how are you going to seize the railyard and the city before the garrison destroys it?"

"I spoke with General Bennet about this problem. What I need is an airborne force. Sadly, I cannot currently have any of the airborne forces from Europe or elsewhere in Asia. He's got them committed elsewhere. However, now that the Indians have officially surrendered, he's granting me control of the 2nd Battalion, 75th Rangers for the mission.

While he won't let me keep the battalion for long, he said we can use them to capture the city and the railhead. My question to you, Colonel, is how should we have the Rangers capture the city? Should we have them go in overland or through a direct airborne assault?" Wilde had his own views, but he was interested to see things from a logistician's perspective.

"Does the enemy have a lot of air assets or air defenses in the vicinity?" asked Willem.

"Nothing of note," Wilde responded. "There's a handful of antiaircraft guns and a couple of SAMs in the area, but we'd take them out in advance of the attack."

"I'd do both, then," Colonel Willem asserted. "Have some of the Rangers parachute in behind the city and set up on this ridge here. That would draw the enemy out, away from the railhead and the border. Then you can have some of the Rangers move in overland here, dashing in quickly to secure the railyard and this major road junction. If you can arrange for some good air support for them, they should have no problem holding the position long enough for additional reinforcements to arrive and relieve them. I would make sure you move one of your Stryker units to be within at least a four-to-six-hour drive of the city. The Strykers can move relatively fast, so that would be my choice of units to send in first."

The two of them turned away from the map board and made their way toward Wilde's enclosed office. They took seats next to each other on the chairs in front of his desk. "Colonel, keeping this army supplied, fed and fueled is going to be a nightmare," explained General Wilde, running his fingers through his hair as he often did when he didn't like a situation. "I'm not even sure we can do it and remain a combat-effective fighting force."

"Hmmm," was the only answer Willem offered at that moment.

"Despite the challenges, General Bennet and the rest of the Allies are depending on us to at least *appear* to be a credible threat to Beijing. If the PLA believes us to be a legitimate fighting force, then they will divert much-needed forces away from defending Beijing to confront us. The more enemy forces we can tie down in our area of record, the better chance our forces will have of defeating the main PLA Army in the east."

"What's my timeframe to get everything ready?" Colonel Willem asked.

"I've been given the order to capture the city by May twelfth. We have a little less than a month to get everything in place. Do you think you can do it?"

"It's a tight deadline, but I think we can make it happen," said Willem. "I've got a Dutch logistics unit arriving later today. These are my go-to guys. We'll make it work."

Chapter 4
Decisions

Zama, Japan
Camp Zama Army Base
Allied Headquarters, Asia

General John Bennet sipped on his Green Beans coffee as he readied himself for the big meeting, one that would decide the fate of millions of people. Today was one of the final strategy meetings to end the third great war. While former president Gates had been involved in many of the strategic decisions of the war, the current president, Wally Foss, was content to let his generals execute the war. Secretary of Defense Jim Castle had taken that extension of the leash and fully intended to let his generals do whatever was necessary to end this war quickly.

The door to the briefing room opened, and the SecDef walked in, followed by several of his aides. Bennet had insisted on using a long boardroom-style table for the day's meeting. He'd wanted everyone to be able to sit opposite each other. He had his ground, air and naval commanders at one end and the SecDef and other support groups at the other.

Everyone's faces looked weary. They had already met all day yesterday. In the morning, they'd gone over the disposition of the current People's Liberation Army ground, air, and remaining naval forces, which had taken several hours. In the afternoon, they'd examined the key rail and logistics networks the enemy was using, as well as the likely routes enemy reinforcements would use depending on where the Allies launched their next attacks. Then, in the evening, they'd discussed the disposition of the Allied forces up to this point, and where they had built up supplies and logistical support. It was all relevant information to build a successful strategy, but everyone had grown weary of PowerPoint slides and printed dossiers at this point.

Despite the obvious lack of enthusiasm, by 0750 hours, all stragglers were present and ready to begin the meeting that had been scheduled for 0800 hours. Even in boredom, military punctuality reigned supreme. Besides, the President had given them a twelve-month window to defeat the Chinese, and they intended to meet their objective.

Once everyone was present, the doors were closed, and a guard was placed outside to make sure they weren't interrupted and that the information being discussed inside remained secret from any potential prying ears. Bennet stood, walked over to the large wall map, which measured three meters by two meters, and rapped his knuckles on the board to get everyone's attention.

"Good morning," he said with as much gusto and gravitas as he could muster. A broad smile crept across his face.

"I'd like us to pick up where we left off. We went over a lot of information yesterday, and today we'll be going over a lot more. This is the day we decide on how we're going to defeat the People's Republic of China." He paused for dramatic effect. "Without further ado, I'd like to hand things over to Secretary Castle."

The bulldog of a secretary stood up and walked over to General Bennet, nodding as he took his place at the center of the map. "Listen up, people. The President has given us the objective of defeating the Chinese by May of 2020. He wants the war to be largely wrapped up before the fall of 2020, so the outcome or course of the war doesn't become a political decision." Walking up and down along the map like a schoolmaster, Castle continued, "Secretary Landover has told the PRC our terms for ending the war, and as you can guess, they summarily rejected them."

A few snickers escaped.

Secretary Castle continued, "I also need to make you all aware of a key piece of intelligence—up to this point, it's been closely held, in hopes that the information wouldn't be needed. Unfortunately, the Chinese are going to move the war in a new direction, and I'm afraid it's not going to be good for us. In the near future, the Chinese are going to begin going after the global civilian satellite network."

A few people gasped. Castle seemed undeterred and plowed on. "Their aim is to bring down our ability to communicate, navigate and fight. In doing this, they know we'll be responding in kind against their own civilian satellites. To compensate for the loss of those satellites, they will be switching their entire communications network over to a fleet of low- and high-altitude UAVs that will encompass their country and their army."

Despite the fact that the room was secured, Castle leaned forward and spoke in a softer tone. "What the Chinese don't know is that the NSA has inserted a code into the firmware of the UAVs that will allow us to decode and transmit a copy of everything they're saying. It's like the PRC decided to use the Navajo language to transmit all its data and we suddenly have a willing translator to help us interpret it all. With this access, we'll know in advance what units are being arrayed against us, where and when they plan to attack us, and the disposition of their current air, naval and ground forces. I'm not going to lie and say losing our own satellites isn't going to hurt us. It is. But in exchange, we're going to gain complete access to their communications network, allowing us to anticipate their moves. With this information we're going to crush them."

Admiral Lomas, the Pacific Commander, held up his hand. "Excuse me, Sir, if I may. If the Chinese disable our satellite infrastructure, how are we going to compensate for that? For example, I don't think the new MQ-4C Tritons the Navy acquired for targeting and surveillance for the carrier strike groups could handle the bandwidth and data load required on their own. How are we going to offset this loss without crippling our own capabilities?"

Crinkling his eyebrows, Castle explained, "There's no other way to say this—this situation *is* going to suck. Fortunately, this problem was considered last summer, and a small contingent of people in D.C. have been hard at work figuring out a workaround. Between SpaceX, Google and Facebook, they've developed several types of UAVs that will essentially address our last tactical mile problem. At the front line, we're going to make heavy use of our RQ-4 Global Hawks. Slightly further behind the RQ-4s will be a layer of Google/SpaceX high-altitude UAVs. Intermixed within this layer will also be a series of E-8 Joint STAR planes until Boeing is able to refit roughly three dozen 737s with midair refueling capability and additional communications equipment and a power plant to run it. While this *will* be tough on us, we will adapt."

He cleared his throat. "I believe I've spent enough time on this issue," he asserted. "Let's move on to some of the changes the President just made to the rules of engagement."

Castle pulled up a new PowerPoint slide. "The first major shift is for the Air Force and Navy. If your fighters or analysts find a target of opportunity, they are cleared to engage it. No more seeking higher-level authority, just execute and report what you hit and why. Second, no more restrictions on attacks, regardless of whether there's a high probability of collateral damage. The Chinese have figured out that if they move something important near a civilian target, we won't attack it. Well, that's now changed. No more hiding behind a school and operating with impunity. Your guys are cleared hot to take 'em out. Third, we have been authorized to carry out any necessary strategic bombings of Chinese cities and industrial parks."

He held up his hand. "Before anyone gets up in arms over this, let me explain what I mean. If we spot a PLA brigade using a small city or town for cover to launch attacks on our forces, then we are cleared to use our strategic bombers to flatten the city in an attempt to destroy the enemy brigade. This does *not* mean we will carry out blanket carpet bombing of cities like what happened in World War II. It just means we won't allow the enemy to hide behind civilians and kill our men."

A strange murmuring echoed through the room. General Bennet surveyed the faces around him; some were obviously pleased with the changes, while others were less than thrilled.

"We've already gone over the changes in the ground invasion," said Castle. "What we need to talk about now is the logistics of it all and how we're going to make it work. With that, I'll hand the meeting back to General Bennet."

Bennet walked back up to the front. The conversation turned to the minutiae of the supply situation. Since the liberation of Taiwan, the island had quickly become a massive supply depot, and the Marines continued to build up their forces there in preparation for the next move. The Army was regrouping and preparing their fuel stores in Korea and Mongolia. Many maps were displayed, and a plethora of war scenarios were played out, but at the end of the day, they all left realizing that the next few months would see some of the heaviest fighting yet.

****

Red Sea

Aboard the HMS *Albion*, Sergeant Neil Evans held a new cigarette to the nearly burnt-out one he had in his hand, managing with some effort to light the new one before tossing the butt overboard into the waters of the Red Sea.

The ship was passing through the Suez Canal now. Sergeant Evans's eyes drifted toward the horizon. Not too far away, a number of security patrol boats moved along the shore, keeping pace with them. He chuckled. Even from where he was, he could tell that the men on the patrol boats were bored and tired.

One of the corporals walked up behind him. "Can you believe twelve days ago we were strolling through the streets of Moscow, and now we're being shipped off to Asia?" he complained. Evans didn't mind his corporals grumbling to him, so long as they didn't share their criticisms with the men below them. Complaining always goes uphill, not down to your subordinates.

"Come on, Corporal, you know you love a good fight," Sergeant Evans replied lightheartedly. "We'll find that when we get to Asia. Besides, we can't let the Aussies or Kiwis show us up. They've already been fighting the

Chinese and Indians—hell, it was an Australian general who forced the Indians to surrender. What have we done in this war?"

Evans was trying to keep the conversation good-natured, but he wondered to himself how Great Britain would fare after the war. "*Those politicians have really bollocksed things up*," he mourned. Fighting with the US, then pulling out, then reentering the war again—it was enough to make any person's head swim.

"I suppose you're right, Sergeant," said the corporal. Then he chuckled. "I wonder if they're going to make us fight with those wannabe Marines."

Evans snorted. "You mean the American Marines?" he mused. "I have no idea, but I can tell you this—they've seen more fighting in a month than the Royal Marines have seen this entire war. It's about to change though, you'll see. We'll get a crack assignment; we just need to be ready when it comes down."

The two of them talked for a bit longer before they resigned themselves to going back below decks and checking on their men. The ship had nearly completed its passage through the Suez.

******

Sergeant First Class Conrad Price watched as Major Fowler stepped around a couple of the sleeping soldiers of the 2nd Battalion, 75th Rangers before plopping down next to him. Price tensed up a bit as the CO sat next to him. He had a pretty good idea of what was coming next.

"Sergeant Price, we haven't had much of a chance to talk since the end of hostilities with India and the battle back at the airfield," Fowler began. "I need a no-BS assessment from you. How's the platoon holding up?"

Price thought about that question for a moment before responding. The battle he was referring to was really nothing more than a massacre. It had broken many of his men, but he wasn't sure if they just needed some downtime to rest and recover, or if they truly couldn't fight anymore. Finally, Price asked, "What did Martinez say?"

"I spoke with him, and he said he has some concerns about a few of them. He said you know which ones he's talking about—you're the platoon sergeant, and I want your input."

Price let out a short sigh. He looked around him to make sure none of the soldiers he was going to mention were within earshot. *Not that you can hear much in the cargo hold of a C-17 anyway, but still,* he thought.

He leaned in closer to Major Fowler. "There's at least six of the guys in the platoon that I would recommend not sending on any new missions right away. I'd like to think they could still be salvaged, but I know at least one of them is never going to be back to 100%. The other five, I think we can get back to the front lines at some point but, Sir, you're going to have to let me place them in a noncombat role for a few weeks, maybe a month. Hell, if we had access to a shrink, I think we could get them better faster, but I'm not sure that's in the cards."

Major Fowler took the information in and leaned back. He looked like he had just been punched in the gut.

Turning back to look at Price, he replied, "Thank you for being honest and upfront. I know you want to protect your guys, and I appreciate that. I wish you'd brought this issue up sooner, maybe to the sergeant major, but you're right—we need to deal with it. I'm not sure what kind of medical support we'll have when we land in Mongolia in a few hours, but I'm going to make sure to find out. If they have a combat stress clinic, then I'm going to order them to be seen daily by the docs there, and we'll find them a support position in battalion headquarters or something. I'll try to pull a few guys from the other platoons to get you back up to strength. We've got another ballbuster of a mission ahead of us. I'm going to need my best platoon ready for action."

****

Seoul, South Korea
International Airport
FedEx Flight 9102

This was George Tailor's fifth flight from Minneapolis, Minnesota, to Seoul, South Korea, in the last ten days, and he was beaten down physically and mentally. The lack of good sleep, decent food and contact with his family was making him irritable.

Since the conflict in Asia had begun, his plane had ferried munitions or other war supplies to Seoul once or twice a month. The first few flights had been harrowing; he could see the heavy fighting taking place across the border. Explosions had ripped apart the forested ridgelines a mere twenty or thirty miles away.

While George didn't mind the excitement of flying near a combat zone once or twice a month, the uptick in tempo of the last two months had been horrendous on the FedEx crews. Each time they'd landed in Minneapolis, he'd thought they were finally caught up on delivering war supplies, only to see the nearby warehouse had been completely restocked, waiting for delivery to Korea again.

George's job was for the most part simple. As the flight's engineer, he was responsible for making sure the maintenance was up to par. He also oversaw the loading or unloading of hazardous materials, which in this case happened on every flight into Korea.

Perhaps it was because he'd never been in the military, but the one thing he just couldn't fathom was the number of artillery rounds he'd been charged with carrying to Korea on each flight. When one of the DoD contractors had climbed aboard his plane, after he'd finished signing the receipt to acknowledge receiving the newest batch of rounds, George had finally said, "Hey, Tim, I have a question—you know my crew and I have been flying these artillery rounds from the factory near Minneapolis to Korea now for over a year, right? We bring in close to five thousand of these bad boys a trip. I've got to know, if for no other reason than to satisfy my own curiosity—how fast are you guys using these things up?"

The contractor had looked at him quizzically for a second, as if trying to decide if he would be breaking some sort of protocol by answering him. He'd finally grunted and replied, "George, at the outset of the war, the Army and

Marines were burning through five thousand rounds every couple of hours. We were practically running out of ammunition to use before you guys from FedEx and UPS started making deliveries. We're caught up now, and we're building up our supplies for the next big battle, but you guys are probably the reason the Chinese aren't in control of Korea."

The contractor had taken his signed papers, shaken George's hand, and then left to go supervise the offloading of another five thousand 155mm artillery shells destined for the front lines.

One of the pilots had overheard part of the conversation and walked up behind George. "Can you believe that? Five thousand rounds an hour?"

George had shaken his head. Somewhat stunned by that information, the two of them had watched for a moment as eight other FedEx DC-11s were offloaded. All of them had been carrying artillery shells from Minnesota. Looking past the FedEx planes, they'd seen half a dozen UPS planes also being unloaded. "What do you suppose UPS is moving?" asked George.

Shaking his head, the captain had replied, "I have no idea. Maybe tank rounds or rifle bullets, or maybe those MRE things the soldiers eat. Who knows? All I know is, as soon as we're offloaded and refueled, we're supposed to head right back to Minneapolis and do this all over again."

The two of them had gotten off the plane and headed toward the crew entrance to the terminal. At least they had time to get themselves a decent meal while the ground crew worked on getting them ready to be turned back around.

Chapter 5
South China Sea

Bunguran Island, Indonesia
PLA Garrison

Sitting in the underground bunker, Colonel Yi Xiaoguang was under no illusion that his forces would soon be locked in mortal combat. This was the fifth day the Allies had bombed his position, and his last remaining surface-to-air missile or SAM site had been destroyed two days ago, leaving them with no way to defend against the enemy planes or cruise missiles that relentlessly pounded his men.

Small amounts of dirt and dust drifted down from the ceiling as yet another explosion shook their bunker. Colonel Yi looked out at the faces of the men around him. They couldn't hide the fear in their eyes. They seemed to be questioning him with their eyes, asking, "Are we going to make it out of this alive?"

He had no idea what to tell them other than the standard party line—that they were winning against the Americans and to stay strong. Deep down, he knew that to be a lie. With the defeat of their fleet, the PLA had no way of keeping their myriad of island bases supplied. They were being left to die on the vine, just like what had happened to the Japanese soldiers when they were trapped on their island fortresses across the Pacific.

Turning to one of his lieutenants, Yi asked, "Have we spotted any enemy ships yet?"

"Negative, Sir. They don't look to be making any landings anytime soon."

The men nearby seemed dejected by the news rather than relieved. "*Most of them would rather just get on with it*," Colonel Yi realized.

For over a year, all they had done was build fortifications and wait, secretly hoping the war would be won before they were forced to defend the island. As the months had dragged on, the men had grown weary. Then Indonesia had been invaded, and the government had collapsed. The Indonesian major who commanded the small contingent of soldiers on the island informed Yi that he had been ordered to surrender the island to the Allies if they came for it.

Colonel Yi obviously couldn't let that happen. Seeing that the Indonesian soldiers wouldn't carry on the fight if it came down to it, he'd ordered them stripped of their weapons and allowed them to leave. He saw no reason to keep them on the island eating through his supplies if they wouldn't aid his men in its defense. Nearly all the civilians on the island had left at that point. They knew a fight was coming, and their only concern now was for their families.

Colonel Yi yawned. Despite the ongoing barrage, he and his men still needed to get some sleep.

"Well, if no ships have come in, we might as well rest up," Yi announced.

"Yes, Sir," said the men nearby. A few of them left to disseminate the order, and soon, those that were able to sleep through the noise and trembling had entered the world of slumber.

****

Early the next morning, Colonel Yi was roused from his sleep. "Colonel!" shouted one of the lieutenants rather loudly.

"What is it, Lieutenant?" asked Colonel Yi groggily.

"They're here. Enemy ships have been spotted off the coast, Sir," the young officer said in an excited voice.

"*I know my men have been weary of waiting, but I'd somehow hoped this day wouldn't happen,*" he thought. He quickly pulled his pants on and slid his feet into his boots.

"Have you woken the rest of the garrison yet? Are the men heading to their fighting positions?" Yi asked. He finished putting his uniform on, grabbed his body armor, picked up his rifle, and followed the young officer to his underground command bunker.

"Yes, Sir, the men are ready," answered the lieutenant.

Yi followed the young officer to the underground command bunker. Once there, he looked at the wall-mounted video display, which showed him a commanding view of the shoreline below the capital city of Ranai. On the video feed, he could easily count at least thirty ships. He had to admit he really had no idea what all the types of ships were, but regardless, he knew they would offload thousands of enemy soldiers bent on killing him and his men.

Colonel Yi turned to look at his deputy commander, a man by the name of Major Shin Hu. "Have the men wait to engage the Americans until they get ashore," Yi ordered. "If we give away our positions too soon, their destroyers and gunboats will take our bunkers out."

Major Shin nodded, then quickly picked up a phone to send the message out to the various fortified bunkers they had built around the city. They knew they couldn't stop the Americans from landing, not since their anti-ship missile systems had been destroyed a week earlier. Their only hope now was to bloody them up once they got ashore.

"*Hopefully, the enemy will lose too many men to keep trying to land more and just bypass us,*" thought Yi, almost willing it to happen.

Minutes turned to hours as they watched more ships arrive. Then the gunboats and destroyers crept closer to the shore, looking for targets of opportunity. When Colonel Yi heard gunfire blast from one of the bunkers toward the enemy ships, his stomach sank. "*What in the world? Do they really think their 152mm Howitzer is going to sink that ship?*" he moaned to himself.

The gunners missed with their first two shots, and the ship took evasive maneuvers. Before they were ready to fire a third round, a pair of missiles streaked in from one of the American attack helicopters, pulverizing the bunker into oblivion. Then, Yi watched in horror as even more missiles streaked in their direction from the choppers that now seemed like an angry swarm of hornets.

Shaking his head, Colonel Yi knew he had less than twenty-four hours to live unless he was willing to surrender the island. While he wanted to surrender and save the lives of his men, he also knew that when the war was over, he'd never be allowed to return to China if he failed to defend the island. "*Perhaps becoming an American prisoner and eventually going to America might be best,*" he thought.

****

Standing near the front ramp of the landing craft utility or LCU, First Lieutenant Ian Slater couldn't help but wonder how the Army had gotten stuck with carrying out an amphibious assault on this island and not the Marines. This was his second such amphibious assault of the war. *"Don't the Marines train for amphibious landings?"* he mused.

Their mothership, the USS *San Antonio* had brought them close to the shore, less than four kilometers away, so their LCU wouldn't have far to ferry them. Fortunately, the water remained relatively calm. At fourteen knots, they weren't exactly traveling fast, but the entire company fit on the landing craft, so at least they'd all land together. Slightly ahead of them were several dozen smaller, faster landing crafts that would drop the first wave of soldiers ashore.

Intelligence had told them that the main PLA garrison and headquarters was located in the nearby city of Ranai, but despite their ever-increasing proximity, Lieutenant Slater still hadn't heard any explosions or the chattering of machine guns. *"Perhaps the Chinese already left?"* he thought wishfully.

Ten minutes went by. One of his fellow soldiers shouted out, "We're nearing the shore. Prepare to disembark!"

Moments later, Slater felt the bottom of the landing craft scraping across the surf. The vessel slowed, and then, without warning, the front ramp dropped, splashing him.

Lieutenant Slater looked to his right and left as he ran through the shallow water. All he saw were hundreds of other soldiers doing exactly as he was, dashing as quickly as possible toward the beach and hoping they weren't about to be cut apart by some hidden machine-gun bunker. So far, there was silence.

Slater continued scanning the horizon around him. Off to the left, maybe a kilometer away, he spotted the top of a large mosque at the base of a mountain. Not far from his position, he saw a small row of houses, surrounded by brush.

He yelled out to the men of his platoon, "Search those houses over there!"

Several soldiers rushed off ahead to follow his order. When Slater finally made it to the first batch of houses, several of his soldiers had already kicked in the door of one of homes and started searching it. One of the specialists exited the building. "There's no one in here, Lieutenant," he announced as the rest of his fire team followed him out.

They quickly moved to the next house. Soon Slater was getting the same news from each of the groups—no civilians or enemy soldiers in these houses.

With the houses cleared, one of his squads started to move up what appeared to be a dirt road, heading toward their primary objective, the Islamic center. Without warning, the lead soldier's head snapped back, and he collapsed in a heap. In a fraction of a second, several machine guns opened fire, cutting down several more of Slater's soldiers before they could react.

"Enemy gun bunker, three o'clock!" yelled one of his squad leaders.

One of their heavy machine gunners laid into the enemy position. *Ratatat, ratatat, ratatat, pop, pop, pop!*

With several members of Second Squad lying either dead or wounded near the dirt trail, First and Third squads came online and directed some heavy fire on the enemy positions. A couple of his grenadier gunners fired their 40mm grenade guns at the bunkers as well.

"Use one of the AT-4s!" Slater shouted to one of his sergeants.

The sergeant then directed one of his soldiers, who quickly got his antitank rocket ready, aimed and fired. The projectile punched through the air with a firm thud and flew flat and true. Unfortunately, although the rocket hit near the gun slit, it had little effect. The steady stream of machine-gun fire paused for less than five seconds.

"Damn! I wish we'd been issued more of the those M141 bunker-buster rockets," Slater said angrily to himself. He looked around for his Fourth Squad leader—he had to move to plan B.

Once he found Matz, he flagged down the sergeant. "Sergeant Matz, I need you to take your squad and try to flank those bunkers. There are two of them, roughly fifty meters apart. Do you see them?" he asked as he pointed in the direction of the two enemy positions. Bullets zipped over their heads, snapping tree branches and underbrush.

"Yeah, I see 'em, Lieutenant. We'll try to move in from over there," Matz responded, pointing to where his guys were going to try and sneak up on the bunkers. "When we get close, I'll have one of my guys pop a smoke grenade. When you see that signal, I need you to tell everyone to hold their fire, so we can crawl up there and toss some grenades in."

Slater nodded, and Sergeant Matz yelled for his squad to form up on him. He briefly explained what they were going to do while Slater went back to seeing if they could try and retrieve their wounded brothers out there on the trail.

While Lieutenant Slater's platoon was fighting it out, the rest of the company started to take fire from a couple of other fortified positions not too far away from the Islamic center. They were well-sighted positions with good fields of fire, and more importantly, they were shooting down into Slater's men from a higher elevation.

Stealing a quick look toward the city to their left, Slater saw soldiers quickly moving through the streets. It didn't look like they were running into any enemy fire just yet.

A handful of minutes went by, and then a purple smoke grenade started puffing away near one of the gun bunkers. "Everyone, hold your fire!" Slater yelled. He had to shout it a few more times to be heard, but eventually, everyone stopped shooting.

Another minute went by, and then Slater heard the telltale crumps of hand grenades going off.

While Slater's platoon held their fire, the remaining enemy bunker continued to shoot at them, kicking up dirt and snapping tree branches overhead. Over this continued noise of battle, Lieutenant Slater now heard the cries of the two wounded soldiers who were out on the trail. With each passing moment, their voices became weaker.

Just as Slater didn't think he could take listening to them anymore, a handful of grenade explosions thumped in the distance, and the last enemy bunker stopped shooting at them. Sergeant Matz briefly stood up near the enemy bunker and waved to them, signaling to Slater that all was clear. Several of the platoon's medics dashed forward and sprinted to the wounded.

Slowly at first, the rest of the platoon got up and crept forward. When they reached the fortified positions, they saw five dead enemy soldiers lying next to each bunker. There were no other foxholes or trenches nearby.

"My money says we'll probably run into more fortified positions like this once we get closer to the mountain at the center of the island," said Lieutenant Slater.

"Forever the optimist, eh, Sir?" Sergeant Matz retorted jovially.

Slater grunted. Looking behind them, he saw another pair of LCUs pull up to the beach and offload eight of their Stryker vehicles. When gunfire erupted off by Third Platoon, two of the Strykers headed off in that direction, looking for a target to blow up.

Two more LCUs pulled up, and Slater saw the first tanks arrive to the island. *"Having heavy armor will certainly help,"* he thought and breathed a sigh of relief. If they ran into any more enemy machine-gun bunkers, he'd be able to call one of the tanks over to help take them out.

His platoon was now less than a kilometer from the outer perimeter of the Islamic center and mosque. They had fanned out into a wide line; First and Third squads moved parallel with each other while he walked in the center with the remaining guys from Second Squad. Fourth Squad followed up as his reserve.

The platoon made good progress until they ran into some thick vegetation that obscured their view. As they got closer to the Islamic center near the top of the hill, the area eventually cleared until they were presented with a very wide 300-meter open space between the edge of the trees where they now stood and the perimeter of the complex. It was not an ideal place to cross; with no cover, his entire platoon could face machine-gun fire the entire way there.

Eventually, everyone came on line with the edge of the trees and the open field. Slater could see the men looking at the open field with caution, hoping he wouldn't order them into such an exposed position. Slater made his way over to Sergeant First Class Starr, his platoon sergeant, then echoed aloud everyone's sentiments. "There's no way we're crossing that field until I know what's on the opposite side of it," he said.

Those who heard his remark nodded, relieved.

Slater grabbed his radio, hoping they could get some armor support or at least have the gunships make a pass overhead. "Ronan Six, this is Ronan One-Six. Over."

Slater smiled. When their battalion had left India, their old battalion commander had gotten promoted and taken over command of the brigade. The new battalion commander was a bit of a comics nut, so he'd had each of the companies pick a call sign based on a Marvel character. Lieutenant Slater had convinced Captain Wilkes to choose Ronan as their call sign. Of course, the battalion commander had picked the call sign War Machine. He was a real hard-charging West Point grad who unfortunately had had the bad luck to be assigned to the infantry officers basic course at Fort Benning for most of the war. He had sadly missed out on nearly all of the action up to this point. When a slot for a combat command had opened up, he'd jumped at the opportunity to get out of the schoolhouse and finally lead soldiers.

A couple of minutes went by before Slater heard Wilkes respond. "Ronan One-Six, this is Ronan Six. Go ahead."

"Ronan Six, we're approaching the main objective. We've come across an open field roughly 300 meters wide. It's too exposed for us to cross alone from our current position. Are we able to get some sort of armor support?" he asked.

"I know exactly what you're talking about. We're looking at a similar situation with Third and Fourth Platoon," said Wilkes. "Stand by. I've put a call in to War Machine for armor support. Out."

"Copy that. Out," Slater replied.

He turned to his platoon sergeant. "Tell the guys to stay frosty. We're going to sit tight and wait to see if we get some armor support. Might as well grab some chow since it'll be at least twenty or thirty minutes or more until we move again."

"Roger that, Sir. I'll spread the word," Sergeant Starr answered, and he turned to go find his sergeants.

Standing next to the tree line, Slater pulled out his pocket binoculars. He zoomed in as far as they would allow and scanned the edge of the perimeter. The field in front of them wasn't *completely* barren of cover. There were small shrubs and bushes, but it was certainly not enough for a platoon of forty soldiers to bound effectively under fire and reach their objective. Looking more closely though at the minarets that dotted the four corners of the mosque, he thought he saw something glint in the sunlight. He spent a couple of minutes examining that spot and waited. A few minutes into his wait, he was rewarded with another glimmer.

"*Gotcha*," he thought. Someone was definitely up in that tower watching them.

"Sergeant Starr!" Lieutenant Slater called out. A few other soldiers echoed his call, and eventually his platoon sergeant came trotting up.

"What's going on, Sir?" he asked in a curious tone. The rest of the platoon had broken out their MREs and were taking a few minutes to recharge their bodies with some much-needed calories.

Slater handed him his binoculars and pointed at the minaret. "There's an observer up there. See the light reflecting off something? What I can't tell is if it's a sniper, a machine gunner, or just someone spotting for mortars or artillery."

Sergeant Starr looked at the minaret for a few minutes until he saw a glint as well. He nodded as he handed the binoculars back. "You're right. There's definitely someone up there." He then turned and yelled out, "Corporal Biggs, get your butt over here!"

A minute later, the lanky corporal walked up to them. "Here, Sergeant," he said calmly.

Corporal Biggs was a rail-thin twenty-year-old from Nome, Alaska. The guy was the best shot in the company and had accordingly been assigned to be their sniper.

"That second minaret to the right looks to have someone in it," Sergeant Starr explained, pointing toward the tower. "Our binos can't pick out if the guy's a sniper or just a spotter, or if they have a machine gun up there waiting to open up on us. I need you to grab that long gun of yours and see what you can see."

"Roger that, Sergeant. Give me just a second to get set up," Biggs replied. He turned around and headed back to where he'd dropped his gear. Six months ago, the Army had started issuing the new Heckler & Koch 417 to replace the older, heavier Knight's Armament M110. The new HK417 had been given the designation M110A1. Not only was it lighter and more compact, it was easier to maneuver with since it was five inches shorter than the rifle it was replacing. The new rifles also hadn't lost any of the range, accuracy or hitting power of the previous model.

Corporal Biggs saddled up next to Sergeant Starr and put his gear down on the ground near the base of a large tree. He unfolded the bipod and did a quick check of his rifle before peering through the scope.

Specialist Hoover plopped down next to him and pulled out his spotter scope, which also had the range finder built in. He did a quick check. "Target 519 meters out," he called.

Biggs made a couple of adjustments on his scope and then peered through, looking to identify the potential threat.

It took him a few minutes of surveilling the minaret, checking over each of the windows to see if he could spot anything in them. When he reached the top one, where the imam would usually announce the calls to prayer, he saw several sandbags had been placed on the ledge. Just past the sandbags, he spotted two soldiers. One guy was lying next to a belt-fed machine gun, while the other guy was looking around the area with his binoculars. The duo was clearly hunting for Americans to shoot up.

He turned to Sergeant Starr and the lieutenant. "Found 'em," he announced. "Looks to be two guys. One's got a belt-fed machine gun up there and the guy next to him is probably the assistant gunner. I'm going to check the other minarets before we engage these guys."

Slater nodded. He was glad he'd waited for armor support and not continued forward.

Over the next five minutes, Corporal Biggs and his spotter, Specialist Hoover, identified seven other machine-gun positions in the other minarets and along the roof of the Islamic center, and they still had most of the windows of the buildings left to check. While they continued to annotate their findings on a notepad, they heard a small commotion behind them.

A minute later, a call came over the radio. "Ronan One-Six, this is War Machine Six, I believe we're near your position with a couple of Strykers. Can you send a runner over to help guide us to you?" asked their battalion commander.

Slater looked at Starr and the two of them shook their heads—neither of them wanted War Machine saddled up with them. Then again, Slater thought, maybe he could help them get some air support to clear their objective instead of using the Strykers. Slater had found very few problems on the battlefield that couldn't be solved with the proper application of explosives.

"War Machine Six, Ronan One-Six. That's a good copy, sending a runner to you now," Slater answered.

Sergeant Starr huffed slightly but then yelled over to a couple of his guys, "Go find those Strykers and lead the soldiers with them to our position!"

Fifteen minutes went by before the two privates returned with the battalion commander, Lieutenant Colonel Isaac Zacharia, and a handful of soldiers from Bravo Company. They sauntered up to their little makeshift observation post.

Zacharia said, "I heard you guys may have found a den of vipers waiting for us."

Slater nodded. "It would appear so, Sir," he answered. "My sniper team has already located seven machine-gun positions in the various windows and minarets of the mosque and Islamic center."

"Make that nine, Sir. Found two more," added Corporal Biggs. He still had his rifle out and he continued to scan the building.

"Well, I'll be damned if we're going to willingly walk into this ambush," Zacharia said. "I'm going to get the rest of the battalion moved over here, and we'll see if we can't get some air support to blast the place before we advance. We'll lead with the tanks and Strykers and then follow in on foot after I get us a couple of JDAMs on that place."

The men around them nodded in approval.

He turned to his radioman. "Put me through to our Air Force TACP," he demanded.

A few minutes went by as the Air Force guys were tracked down. An Air Force master sergeant made his way forward to their observation post and nodded toward the battalion commander. "I heard you have a target you want blown up, Sir?"

Lieutenant Colonel Zacharia smiled. "I sure do," he said nonchalantly. "You see that mosque and nearby Islamic center? Our sniper here and his spotter found at least nine enemy machine-gun positions throughout the building. Every couple of minutes they find another one. I need both buildings leveled. I'm not going to lose any of my soldiers because the Chinese are hiding behind a religious structure."

The master sergeant took a couple of steps forward. Then he leaned down and got next to the spotter. "Can you show me the positions you've found already?" he asked.

"Sure thing, Master Sergeant."

The TACP thoroughly examined the building and the enemy positions. Eventually, he pulled out his map and then got up and walked back to the battalion commander. "Sir, I can take the building out, but could you help me identify the friendly units in the immediate area? I want to make sure when we drop ordnance on that place, our friendly units know how far to stay away."

The group plotted out where the other companies were at in relationship to the rest of the brigade. There was also another brigade of soldiers that was slated to come ashore that evening, and they would need to keep them updated.

Now that he had all the information he needed from the ground level, the TACP got on his own radio and began to identify what aircraft were in the area and what munitions they were carrying. He eventually got a hold of a pair of F-16s who were packing 2,000-pound JDAMs. After giving them the coordinates and making sure they read them back to him, he gave them the green light to hit the building with four of them, one on each corner of the building.

"That should be more than enough to flatten the mosque as well as the nearby building," Slater thought as he listened to the TACP's side of the call.

When the TACP put down his radio, he turned to look at the group of officers. "OK, Colonel, our birds are inbound. They should hit the target in five mikes. I'd suggest we tell everyone to get down and stand by for a really loud boom," the Air Force guy said with a grin on his face.

The minutes ticked by rather quickly until the ground and everything around them shook. Then the blast wave from the bombs going off smacked them with a wave of searing heat. Looking back toward where the mosque had been, Slater couldn't see anything left standing. Now there was just a bombed-out shell with fires everywhere and debris raining down to the ground.

With the building destroyed, Lieutenant Colonel Zacharia ordered the battalion to attack. The four tanks he'd managed to grab lurched forward, quickly followed by their Stryker vehicles. As the vehicles moved forward, the soldiers advanced, leaving their covered positions. The men felt a lot more confident about going into the open field now that the Air Force had blasted the buildings ahead of them and they had plenty of armor leading the way.

An hour after they destroyed the mosque and secured the surrounding area, a small contingent of Chinese soldiers made themselves visible under a white flag. This was the first time Lieutenant Slater had seen a group of Chinese soldiers ever come forward to surrender. He hoped it truly meant they wanted to end the fighting there. He'd already lost three soldiers that day, and another four had been wounded; he didn't want to lose any more.

Two hours after they spotted the Chinese officers with the white flag, the fighting on the island officially ended. The PLA colonel whose unit was in charge of defending the island decided that he'd rather save the remaining lives of his men than fight a futile battle he had no chance of winning.

Lieutenant Slater just hoped this was just the beginning of Chinese forces surrendering. He'd seen enough death and killing for a lifetime; all he wanted now was to go home, get drunk, and not do anything for a long time.

Chapter 6

Complications

Russian Provincial Authority

Kremlin, Senate Palace

Ambassador Ava Hicks was four months into the occupation of Russia. Already, things were starting to fray at the ends. While there was no open revolt against the Russian Provisional Authority yet, there were increasing demonstrations denouncing the occupation and the slow progress of the postwar recovery. Of course, it didn't help that key generals across the military were dragging their feet in helping the Allies maintain law and order.

That was not what was weighing on Ava's mind, however. The Russians' latest request was for them to be allowed to bring their Spetsnaz teams back home from the US and other Allied nations. Since the official end of the war, the ones that hadn't already been hunted down and killed had been lying low in hopes of being able to return home. Ava was conflicted about how to handle this situation. The American people wanted them held accountable for the wanton destruction and deaths they'd caused within the Allied nations—and rightly so, Ava thought.

However, it wasn't a simple one-sided argument. The Department of Defense had reasoned that what the Spetsnaz teams had done was no different than what the DoD had done to the Russians when they had gone after their power grid or the Indian railway system.

It was a tough position Ambassador Hicks found herself in. If she sided with the Russians and the US Department of Defense, then the American people and political establishment would turn on her. If she sided with the Department of Justice and the politicians, then the military and the shaky Russian government might turn on her and the occupation force.

She grabbed a chocolate bar from the secret stash in her desk and munched on it anxiously as she considered her options. Although she wasn't proud of it, she'd gained five pounds in the last month from all the stress. There was a heavy weight on her shoulders.

As if things weren't complicated enough with the issue of the Spetsnaz teams, she also had the far more concerning issue of the "missing" nuclear weapons. There were still almost a thousand nuclear devices that were unaccounted for. She thumbed through the papers on her desk, as if they were going to tell her something new, but she already knew what they said. The Russian Air Force report claimed that three hundred nuclear-armed cruise missiles had been destroyed during several Allied raids in the last weeks of the war. However, the US investigators countering weapons of mass destruction disputed that argument; there was no evidence that these weapons had been destroyed, only of radiation where they had been previously held.

Besides the missing cruise missiles, two Russian ballistic missile submarines had yet to be located. Her Russian counterparts continued to insist that those subs had been sunk during the war, but the US Navy had been unable to verify that claim. She thumbed through more dossiers that didn't tell her anything she didn't already know.

She took another bite of chocolate. It wasn't helping.

Knock, knock.

The sudden appearance of her secretary nearly caused Ambassador Hicks to jump out of her skin. She'd been so deep in thought trying to figure out the ins and outs of the situation that she hadn't seen her approach the office.

"Ambassador Hicks, General Brice is here. Shall I send him in?"

"Yes, please do."

A minute later, General Luke Brice walked in with a couple of his aides in tow. "Good morning, Ambassador.

How are you this fine morning?" he asked. His tone belied his alertness at 0800 hours.

"Morning, General," Ava replied, attempting to feign cheerfulness. "I was doing well when I felt like the Russians were honoring the surrender terms and turning over their nuclear weapons. However, from the reports I'm reading, it would appear that may not be entirely true. Is there something I'm missing?"

The general and his two aides took a seat at the small conference table in her office. General Brice answered, "It's hard to say, Ambassador. The Navy hasn't been able to verify the loss of those two boomer subs—it *is* possible they were sunk, and the Navy just can't confirm it. I've spoken with our counterparts at the NSA and CIA about this, and they're going to assign some satellites and other intelligence assets to try and keep tabs on the Russian Navy and potential locations they could be hiding the subs or areas they'd look to provide them with a resupply. If they're really trying to keep those subs hidden, then it's going to require a long-term sustained effort to keep them supplied."

He held up a hand to stop any potential questions. "I spoke with the Chief of Naval Operations office last night. They said they'd assign a few more hunter killer subs to help search the known SSBN bastions. They'd send more subs but they're heavily tied down in Asia right now supporting operations up there. Plus, our sub force has suffered some terrible losses this last year."

Crinkling her forehead, she asked, "What about the cruise missiles? Is that a dead end as well?"

One of the aides raised his hand slightly, indicating that he would take the question. Ambassador Hicks hadn't really spoken with this aide before but realized from his uniform that he must be a French Air Force officer. "We are bringing in some specialized drones that we believe will be able to help us in verifying the destruction of these weapons," he began. "I'd like to point out that despite the high levels of radiation, there was no actual nuclear detonation at the bunkers. It would appear that several of the warheads must have been damaged during the raid if that is in fact what happened. If that is the case, then that would explain the radiation levels. We'll hopefully know more in a few weeks once the drones arrive."

"What about the smaller tactical nuclear weapons and the large silos?" she asked.

"We're in the process of dismantling the silos now," General Brice said. "Nearly all the warheads have been removed and accounted for. Those are a lot harder to hide and cheat on; it would be too obvious—"

Ava cut him off. "—That still leaves the tactical nukes. Am I correct in assuming there are more accounting irregularities with them as well?"

Shifting uncomfortably in his seat, the general was clearly looking for a diplomatic way to address this question. Sensing his discomfort, Ava pounced. "Just spit it out, General. If we have a serious problem with the denuclearization part of this surrender, then I need to know."

"There are accounting irregularities," he admitted, but he held up his hand to stop her from interrupting again. "I'd also like to point out that we have taken possession of thousands of nuclear weapons so far. I think the Russians are secretly hiding some of them, for what purposes, I'm not sure. Maybe it's national pride, or maybe they just don't trust us. What I can tell you is this—over time, as we build up our human intelligence networks inside Russia and start to build more trust with the local populace, we will find them. If there's one thing I've learned about strategies and deceptions, it's that the more people who are involved in creating them, the harder it is to keep them a secret. Someone will talk, and when they do, we'll find them."

Ava snorted. She didn't like the idea of waiting for these weapons to be discovered later. The Russians had made an agreement, and by Jove, she was going to make them stick to it. Before she could respond though, the other aide, also a colonel, broke into the conversation. "Ma'am, we need to discuss the Russian Spetsnaz units."

Looking at the colonel, Ava noticed the Special Forces tabs on his sleeve. "Colonel, this is a touchy issue domestically," she stated.

"Agreed, but these guys are no different than my own Special Forces teams we had operating behind Russian lines carrying out the same type of attacks."

She quickly retorted, "Except that they lost, Colonel."

Sighing, the colonel decided to take a different approach. "Ma'am, at the end of World War II, during the Nuremberg Trials, Admiral Karl Dönitz was charged with a number of crimes and convicted. However, one of the charges was waging unrestricted submarine warfare against neutral shipping. On this charge, he was found not guilty, because as Admiral Chester Nimitz said, the US had the same policy in the Pacific against the Japanese. Ultimately, Ma'am, over one hundred senior Allied officers sent letters to Dönitz and the court conveying their disappointment over the fairness and verdict of his trial."

He paused for a second, letting that sink in before he continued, "I'm not disputing the actions these Spetsnaz soldiers committed or the loss of life they inflicted on our people. What I am saying, Ma'am, is if these Russian soldiers are charged and prosecuted in America, then how are our soldiers who did the same actions in Russia any different? How are our pilots any different? We've bombed hundreds of cities, and invariably, civilians did die. Remember that bunker-buster bomb that was knocked off course during the opening days of the war here in Moscow? It killed more than a thousand civilians. All I'm saying, Ambassador, is right now we're in a fight to win the peace. The war is over, but if we lose the peace because we want to exact some sort of justice on these enemy soldiers, then we're going to lose the public relations battle we're waging right now across the country. Allowing these enemy special forces to return home would go a long way in helping to heal the wounds of war. It may even help us with finding these missing nuclear weapons."

Sitting back in her chair, Ava had to hand it to him; he did make a good case. She turned and looked outside the window. Spring was in the air and the trees were starting to return to life. Thinking for a moment, she finally made a decision.

****

Three hours later, Ambassador Hicks was sitting across from General Sobolev, the current president of Russia during the transition period. During the past few months, Ava had spent a great deal of time working with the general and had made a point of spending time with him outside of work as well. Sobolev had taken her to a couple of Russian opera and ballet events and shown her some of the better places to eat in the city. Ava knew if she was to be successful in her position, then she'd need to develop deep personal and working relationships with her Russian counterparts.

While this meeting had been scheduled, the tensions between the two parties had been increasing. However, since the meeting was just between her and Sobolev, she hoped she might be able to get a bit more done in such a close personal setting than with a group.

After the usual cursory conversation about family over a cup of tea, she placed her teacup down on the table between the two chairs. "Mr. President," she began, "there are two important items I want to discuss with you."

Sobolev put his own cup down and turned slightly so his body was fully facing hers. "You want to discuss the nuclear disarmament," he said, pulling no punches.

She nodded, knowing this was a touchy issue. "I do. I've also come to a decision on your soldiers who are still in hiding in the Allied nations."

Sobolev raised an eyebrow but didn't say anything. These soldiers were the ones that had been under his command and direction during the war. She knew they meant a lot to him.

"There appear to be a lot of accounting irregularities in regard to your nuclear weapons. It could just be an oversight, and perhaps you'll let General Brice know of a few new locations he should check to find them, but this needs to be addressed."

Smiling at the obvious opportunity she was giving him to turn them over and save face, he nodded. "This is a sensitive issue, Ms. Hicks. I have been looking into it as well and I believe there are a few places I may be able to direct your general to check. I'm still working through some, how shall I call them—personnel issues with the Ministry of Defense right now. Some generals and senior leaders are not very happy with the surrender terms I agreed to. If our remaining special forces soldiers who are still in hiding in America and Europe were allowed to return home…it would give me more leverage with some of these problems."

Ava nodded, knowing exactly who Sobolev was talking about. *"So General Chayko is still causing problems,"* she thought.

"I understand there's still a lot of distrust and animosity between our nations. Emotions are still raw. You and I though, have to get past them. We have to be the ones to push our people past them, so we can collectively pick up the pieces and move forward." She paused for a second as she thought of what to say next, and how to say it in Russian. She was fluent in the language, but trying to figure out the specific translation of certain complex phrases sometimes caused her to have to stop and consider her words carefully. "I'm going to take some serious hits politically back home and amongst many of the Allied nations for this, but I'm going to agree that your Special Forces soldiers and operatives will be allowed to return home to Russia and will not face federal criminal prosecution in the United States. I cannot fully guarantee that other Allied nations will not try to prosecute your men, but we will not. However, this is a major concession I am making for you, Mr. President—I need a much stronger show of good faith on your end with the missing nuclear weapons, particularly the two ballistic missile submarines."

The general sat back in his chair and eyed Ava for a moment. He then turned and looked at one of the paintings on the wall in his office, clearly deep in thought. Without returning his gaze to her, he said, "I *may* know where your General Brice can find some bunkers that may have been mistakenly missed on our nuclear inventory list." He twiddled his fingers. "As to those two ballistic missile submarines…I will have a more direct conversation with General Chayko and my fleet admiral about them. I have been told they were lost during the war. That may be true, but I will investigate further. If I am not satisfied with what I find, then you may notice a series of…personnel changes and early retirements. If that happens, I can assure you, those particular individuals will not be a problem. The sooner my nation complies with the terms of surrender and we are able to move past this occupation, the better it will be for all parties involved."

****

Within days of Ava's decision to allow the enemy Special Forces still hiding in the Allied nations to return, the Allies discovered another large trove of "previously unaccounted for" nuclear weapons at nearly a dozen bunkers hidden across the country. While the mystery of what had happened to the two ballistic missile submarines remained, more than a handful of senior military and government officials had suffered some coincidental heart attacks, car crashes and other freak accidents. While the tensions between the Russian people and the occupying force hadn't gone away, they appeared for the time being to have cooled off as the remaining Russian soldiers returned home to their families.

Chapter 7

Rangers Away

Erenhot, Inner Mongolia, China

The drone of the jet engine on the C-17 Globemaster threatened to lull Sergeant First Class Conrad Price to sleep. He glanced around at the men of Third Platoon, faces painted, parachutes on, weapons and packs ready for their fourth combat jump of the war. He imagined that there were probably some guys from the other battalions who had gotten jealous of the amount of combat his battalion had gotten to see.

"*Maybe they're the lucky ones,*" he thought. Then his mind went back to the handful of guys he'd had to pull from the platoon until they could get their minds and emotions back under control.

"Five mikes!" shouted the jumpmaster.

Price looked out the open side door. It was still dark—a good thing for this jump. It would be dawn in an hour. Hopefully, they'd have the objectives secured by then and the cavalry would be on the way to relieve them.

"Sixty seconds!"

"*Lord, keep me and my men safe on this jump,*" Price prayed silently. It was not uncommon for even the less-than-devout to speak to God before taking a leap into a freefall.

The first Ranger jumped out the door, quickly followed by the man behind him. The line of paratroopers on each side of the plane steadily made their exit to the black abyss below. Seconds later, Price was out the door, his static line yanking him hard as his main chute deployed, stopping his descent with a hard snap.

Looking below him at the city below, he spotted a few lights on, but overall, the dwellers below appeared to be asleep. Then, after a moment of drifting in silence, the sound of an air raid siren sent a shiver down Price's spine. The defenders would all be awake now and anticipating an imminent attack.

"Come on, only sixty more seconds and I'll be on the ground," he said, trying to pump himself up and not expecting anyone else to hear him.

Bang, bang, bang, ratatat, ratatat!

Green tracers reached out into the night sky and a handful of floodlights turned on, illuminating targets for the antiaircraft guns to pick off.

"*Thirty seconds and I'll be on the ground,*" Price thought, unconsciously crossing his fingers.

Just as Sergeant Price was starting to have a genuine glimmer of hope at his chances of making it to the ground, a search light suddenly popped on just below him. Without thinking, he immediately reached down, grabbed his Sig Sauer and fired at the light. He shot six times before the fixture suddenly sparked and blew out.

Unfortunately, although the threat of the light had been neutralized, the noise of his gunfire had given him away. A stream of green tracers reached out as if trying to grab him with monster's fingers, and he heard the bullets from the machine gun whizzing in the air. Using the navigation cords on his chute, Price pulled himself into a tight turn.

A string of rounds tore through his canopy, riddling it with holes. Price got a sick feeling in the pit of his stomach; he was still about a hundred feet from the ground. He did his best to recover control of the rapidly failing chute, hoping not to slam into the ground. A second later, he landed hard and rolled to one side, unable to stop until he'd made two full revolutions.

Zip, zap, zip, zap.

Bullets kicked up dirt and rocks all around him. He fought to disconnect his chute and dashed behind a nearby parked car.

"*Where the hell am I?*" he thought.

Price unzipped his rifle case, which was still strapped to the side of his individual body armor. With his rifle free, he pulled out a fresh magazine and slapped it in place, charging the bolt and placing a round in the chamber.

Bullets suddenly tore into the vehicle that had been shielding him. Shards of glass rained down on him, along with flecks of metal debris. When the deluge paused momentarily, he looked up over the rim of the vehicle's busted window. With his night vision goggles still on from the jump, he could see three enemy soldiers, one of whom was still pointing in his direction. The other two seemed to have turned their attention to the paratroopers still falling from the sky.

Price switched his selector switch to auto and brought his rifle up to his shoulder. He took aim at the guy manning the machine gun and depressed the trigger just long enough to release a three-round burst. In fractions of a second, his mind had willed his body to move the rifle to the remaining two guys, lighting them both up. Before the enemy even had a chance to realize what was happening, Price had dispensed with them.

Searching his immediate surroundings, he didn't see anyone else posing an immediate threat, so he moved forward to grab his ruck. He heard other voices nearby but quickly determined they were fellow Rangers and called out to them. Minutes later, three other paratroopers joined him.

"We thought they got you, Sergeant Price," one of his squad leaders said.

Price shook his head, and then, in a voice that was almost cocky, he answered, "It's going to take a lot more than that to kill me."

They chuckled.

"Where's the rest of the platoon?" he inquired. They needed to start forming up and moving to secure their objectives. There was only so much time left before dawn, and their job would get a lot harder once the sun was up. Night vision still gave them an advantage, and they had every intention of using it.

Boom, BOOM!

An explosion blasted nearby, and they all flinched. More machine-gun fire rattled, and someone shouted over in its vicinity.

"Let's head in that direction," Price said, pointing toward a growing fireball.

Price and the handful of soldiers he'd run into thus far made their way toward some of the heavier fighting taking place near the railyard. In minutes, their little group had rounded up another five friendly soldiers. When they reached the outer edge of the train station, they saw a ZBL-08 Snow Leopard firing away on a cluster of Rangers pinned down on the other side of the trainyard. A handful of PLA soldiers were nearby, adding their own volume of fire at the US soldiers as they looked to flank them.

Price turned to one of his squad leaders. "Have your two antitank troopers try to take that vehicle out," he ordered. "When that's blown up, we can advance from two different angles and take out the remaining enemy soldiers."

The squad leader nodded, and the soldiers quickly went to work, getting themselves in position to execute.

One of the soldiers, who had been carrying a Javelin, made the antitank missile ready. Another soldier with a Javelin stood nearby, waiting to engage any other armored vehicles that might appear. The soldiers signaled to each other that they were ready.

Pop, swoosh.

The missile leapt out of its case and flew the three hundred meters in seconds, slamming into the side of the ZBL-08 Snow Leopard.

Boom!

Sparks and flame engulfed the vehicle and one of the enemy soldiers nearby. The rest of the Rangers nearby opened fire on the remaining enemy soldiers, doing their best to force the Chinese soldiers to keep their heads down while one of the fire teams advanced to close the distance.

Four of the Rangers ran thirty meters across two of the rail lines, taking cover behind an empty flatbed car just as a second armored vehicle they hadn't spotted before pulled around the train station building, firing its 12.7mm machine gun at them. Bullets kicked up dirt, rocks and other fragments around the four soldiers. They did their best to make themselves as small as possible to avoid being hit.

The second soldier with a Javelin popped up from behind his covered position just long enough to get a lock on this new threat. Once he heard the tone indicating a missile lock, he depressed the trigger, and the missile leapt from the tube in a small flash of flame as the rocket motor ignited. In less than two seconds, the second armored vehicle blew up, ending its short shooting spree.

"Now! Everyone forward!" shouted Price.

The remaining Rangers jumped out from their covered positions and advanced in a line with their rifles at the ready, shooting any and all enemy soldiers they spotted as they moved in on the train station itself, clearing the railyard along the way.

"Look out!" shouted a soldier near Price.

He turned just in time to see an enemy soldier poke his head out from behind a cluster of trash cans. Fortunately for Price, he'd turned his rifle with his head. As he saw the eyes of the enemy soldier through his sight, his years of training kicked into autopilot and he reacted without even thinking. He squeezed the trigger just a fraction of a second faster than the PLA soldier did. He watched as his round flew fast and true, hitting the enemy soldier right in the center of his face. It snapped the man's head back, and his body collapsed into a heap.

Turning to the soldier who'd called out the warning, Sergeant Price said, "Thanks, but next time just shoot the guy."

The soldier, a new guy to the unit, just nodded. It was a humbling lesson, and fortunately, Price hadn't had to die for him to learn it.

When their group approached the terminal building, they linked up with another squad from their platoon. The Rangers collectively made their way to one of the entrances. They shot the lock off the door and then proceeded to filter into the cavernous station, moving rapidly through it as they cleared it of any hostile soldiers.

They could still hear gunfire from outside as they continued securing their objective. It seemed to Price that it was starting to move closer to them.

Once they reached the north end of the station, one of the Rangers caught a glimpse through and window and shouted, "Sergeant Price, you need to see this!"

Several of the other Rangers also made their way over, and they all cautiously peered out the window. Through the pane, Price caught sight of three Type 89 armored personnel carriers less than 100 meters away. The back hatches of the vehicles dropped, and out ran nearly forty enemy soldiers.

"Oh, crap, that's a lot of soldiers," Sergeant Price thought.

He immediately signaled to get the attention of his two squad leaders. "Second Squad, take the north side of the building. Third Squad, take the south side. We'll let them walk into our crossfire and wipe 'em out," he ordered.

Sixty seconds went by as the Rangers ran to the opposite ends of the terminal and began to set up their fields of fire. In the meantime, several of the PLA soldiers busted open the front door of the terminal and made their way inside.

Price heard the commotion. "Everyone, hold your fire until you hear me shoot," he ordered through his headset.

Seconds felt like minutes. More and more enemy soldiers filtered into the building, yelling out their own orders in Chinese. Sensing that the most opportune moment had arrived, Sergeant Price closed his left eye and sighted in on a man who was waving soldiers forward and directing them where to go; he was most likely an officer. Price applied pressure to the trigger until his rifle barked. Then he watched as the enemy soldier clutched at his chest and fell to the ground.

As soon as Sergeant Price fired his weapon, the two squads' M240G heavy machine guns and their M27 infantry assault rifles opened fire.

Bang, bang! Ratatat, ratatat, zip, zap, zip, zap!

Red tracer fire crisscrossed from the southeast and northeast corners of the terminal, out toward the main entrance. Their fire completely enveloped the enemy soldiers in a fusillade of bullets that ripped and shredded everything inside the terminal.

Though he couldn't understand the words, Price could tell the shouts from the Chinese soldiers were panicked. The PLA did their best to return fire and counter the ambush they'd walked into, hurling a few grenades toward the Americans.

Bam, BAM!

Sergeant Price grabbed one of the M67 fragmentation grenades from his pouch, pulled the pin, and lobbed it at a cluster of enemy soldiers that had taken cover behind one of the kiosk counters. The grenade exploded with a dull thud and a cloud of smoke, silencing the enemy attackers.

Just as the fire from the PLA soldiers was dying down, the north side of the building erupted in shards of wood, metal and glass. Green tracers tore through the walls of the building and anything they happened to hit. The three enemy vehicles outside had turned their 12.7mm machine guns on the terminal, lighting the entire building up. Price knew they couldn't stay in the building much longer if those machine guns were going to continue to rake the structure with their heavy-caliber slugs—they'd tear the whole place apart.

Price looked around for one of his squad leaders and spotted one of the newer soldiers in their unit unslinging the AT4 he had with him. The young man ran toward one of the windows on the north side of the building. When there was a break in enemy fire near him, he jumped up, aimed the AT4 through the window, and fired.

Sergeant Price heard the usual small popping noise and a sudden swoosh of flame as the rocket flew out of the weapon. It landed squarely against the side of the enemy vehicle, thoroughly decimating it. The young Ranger ducked for cover and sprinted back deeper into the building, but the wall where he had just been standing was swiftly torn apart. A heavy-caliber round hit the soldier in the leg, completely ripping it off. Just as the soldier was about to tumble forward from his own momentum, a second round hit him in the back, nearly cutting the man in half. His body landed with a thud, motionless and suddenly devoid of life.

Before any of them could say or do anything else, two loud explosions outside rattled the entire building, blowing out any remaining glass. Shrapnel pelted the north side of the building. The enemy fire suddenly ceased, and an eerie calm took its place. Cries from the wounded suddenly broke the silence, as both friendly and enemy soldiers called out for medical aid.

"Secure the building!" shouted Price.

He ran to one of the blown-out windows to see what had happened. When he got there, he saw that the last two enemy vehicles had been blown up by something—maybe an Allied plane or drone overhead. In either case, it had saved their butts from certain death.

A few minutes later, the other two squads of the platoon arrived at the station, along with their captain. The next hour was spent securing the railyard, making sure no other enemy soldiers were nearby and then inspecting the tracks for any attempts at sabotage.

It took the Rangers nearly two hours to secure the city, but they had captured the critical railyard, highways and remaining critical infrastructure needed for the main army to arrive on trains. A battalion of Stryker vehicles and a company of main battle tanks arrived, relieving them and taking over security of the city while the rest of the Army group was trucked in by rail and heavy transports.

Over the next several weeks, Army Group One began the process of consolidating its forces in Inner Mongolia and preparing for their backdoor march on Beijing.

Chapter 8

Project Enigma

Taiwan Taoyuan International Airport
Victory Base Complex

The tension in the room was so thick, it felt like it could literally be cut with a knife. General John Bennet and General Roy Cutter exchanged a nervous look as the President's Chief Cyberwarfare Advisor, Katelyn Mackie, finished briefing them and General Cutter's division commanders on the "eyes only" program named Project Enigma. Months of planning for the invasion of mainland China had just changed in the blink of an eye.

General Bennet was the first to speak. "Ms. Mackie, the Pentagon, NSA, DIA and CIA are one hundred percent certain that these new UAVs are being built out of the Guangdong Province? We're about to start our ground invasion of the area shortly. I've already scrapped our old invasion plans to secure this province as ordered by the SecDef—I want to make sure there are no more major changes to our invasion plans."

The other generals stared at her in silence, waiting to hear her response.

"Yes, General Bennet. Our source within the program has verified it," she confirmed. "He's been a reliable source and very accurate. There are a series of manufacturing plants in and around the Guangzhou Baiyun International Airport. The UAVs are being built in the general area of the international airport and over in Shayao District, maybe ten kilometers to the east of it. The capture of this province, General, will in all likelihood knock the Chinese out of the war. It's their industrial heartland and where most of their aerospace industry is located."

"Do we have a firm timeframe on when our satellites are going to go down yet?" asked one of the other generals.

"I'm afraid we don't know the exact date, only that they will, and soon. In anticipation, we're moving forward with deploying as many of our UAVs and contingency equipment as possible."

One of the G6 officers from the group responsible for the ground forces communications systems added, "Fortunately, the Pentagon has kept a large stockpile of older yet still effective communication systems. The older systems may not be able to handle as much data volume, but they will still allow our forces to communicate, coordinate and relay information. I spoke with my counterpart back at the Pentagon, and they're moving a lot more UAVs to our location from Europe. Losing the satellites is going to hurt, but it won't cripple us like it might have two or three years ago, before we figured out a workaround for all the Russian and Chinese jamming and cyberattacks that happened at the beginning of the war."

A few of the other generals nodded. Unlike the Iraqis and Afghanis, the Russians and Chinese had proven themselves to be fairly adept at electronic jamming. However, when the US's military satellites had started to get blown up at the beginning of the war, the American military had quickly switched over to their backup radio systems, so the solution had been proven to work at least once already, even if it wasn't an entirely effective patch to the problem.

The Marine Commander, General Cutter, gruffly added, "My concern is with being able to call in for accurate airstrikes. We need effective communications when the fighting starts hot and heavy. So many of our current systems are digital, transmitting large quantities of data, and I'm worried our older systems may not be as capable of handling the load that's going to be placed on them."

Katelyn Mackie sighed. "Generals, I know this is going to be hard, but let's look at the tradeoff. We are gaining complete access to the PLA's communication system. If the PLA is sending reinforcements or preparing for a massive attack, you're going to know about it in advance. You'll be able to move troops around to deal with them or lay an ambush, knowing exactly where the enemy will be." She paused for a second to let that sink in before continuing. "We can't stop what they're about to do. We were fortunate enough to learn about it far enough in advance that we've been able to prepare for it. Had it happened without our knowing about it, it could have lost us the war. As it is, it may be the very thing that wins it for us."

The group sat there in silence for a moment, thinking.

General Bennet finally broke the stillness. "OK, I accept that I can't do anything to change the crappy situation we're about to find ourselves in. I can't even imagine how badly this is going to screw up the rest of the global economy or our own country, but I have to focus on the military side and do what I can to defeat the enemy and end this war as swiftly as possible. That said, let's talk about what I'm going to need from you."

Katelyn nodded as she picked up her pen, ready to write down whatever he mentioned.

"Ms. Mackie, once the PLA destroys the global satellite infrastructure and we find ourselves listening in to everything they're talking about, I'm going to need a team of folks dedicated to tracking and identifying where China's nuclear weapons are located. I need confirmation of their silos, and I need to know where their mobile launchers are on a continuous basis. There's going to come a point in this war where the PLA leadership will recommend the use of nuclear weapons to save face from a major defeat or surrender. When that decision has been made, we're going to need to know *exactly* where their weapons are located so we can take them out before they can use them."

Katelyn and Secretary Castle nodded. "General Bennet, consider your request granted," she said. Her confident response silenced any further objections.

Chapter 9
Operation Fortress

Jinzhou-Fuxin Line

Private Shane Webster's senses were overrun. The high-pitched shrieking sound of the high-mobility artillery rocket system, or HIMARS, firing another volley of 227mm rockets overhead was unmistakable. Yet another wave of cluster munition and high explosives reached the enemy positions. Intermixed with the piercing shrieks of the rocket artillery was the near-constant thunder of hundreds of 155mm howitzers, adding their own measure of death and destruction to the scene unfolding across the enemy fortress.

Every now and then, Webster and the other soldiers of 2-14 infantry would spot a massive fireball from a secondary explosion, letting them know the artillery got lucky and hit something important. In between lulls in the artillery, ground-attack planes swooped in, releasing a string of bombs or napalm, depending on what they were looking to target. For the newly arrived soldiers of the 10th Mountain Division, it was both awe-inspiring and terrifying to witness such a display of firepower. They all knew that in the very near future, they would have to assault the fortress before them.

Staff Sergeant Sanchez walked up and abruptly broke up the gaggle of spectators. "Enough gawking, privates! I need everyone to head over to the ammo tent and load up. We'll be moving out soon!" he shouted.

Private Shane Webster shook his head as he watched another massive explosion rock the mountain fortress, then he turned to follow the rest of the soldiers in his platoon to the ammo tent. It was a short walk since they were already in the rear of the American lines. When they arrived at the general purpose or GP tent, Private Webster let out a low whistle—the smorgasbord of items before him would make any gun nut salivate with envy.

Webster got in line with the rest of his squad. First, they stopped at a table with crates of 5.56mm NATO rounds packed in twenty-round boxes.

Staff Sergeant Sanchez, who had already seen action in the war, ordered, "Grab twenty-one boxes."

They all dutifully placed the appropriate number in their empty rucksacks. This would give them 420 rounds, or fourteen magazines worth of ammo.

Once the squad had loaded up on the required number of bullets, they moved to the next table. This one had boxes of M67 fragmentation grenades.

"Grab eight," ordered Sanchez.

Again, they put them in their rucks and moved on to the next table.

This time, Sanchez led them over to a crate of M18A1 Claymore antipersonnel mines. "Everybody, take one of these," he directed.

At the next table, a supply clerk stood next to a stack of crates that held four AT4 antitank rockets. Only three of the eleven soldiers were told to grab one. Webster was glad he wasn't one of the guys slated to lug one of those around. *"My ruck is already heavy enough without having to shoulder a fifteen-pound rocket,"* he thought.

The last table their squad leader led them to had tons of ammo cans opened on it. Inside were one-hundred-round belts of 7.62×51mm for the squad's lone M240 Gulf heavy machine gun. They were all to grab one belt of ammo and stuff it in their rucks. Private Webster found himself grateful again, this time that it wasn't his job to carry the machine gun, commonly referred to as "the pig." It was heavy, and it chewed through ammo like a pig at an all-you-can-eat buffet.

Now that everyone was fully laden with the tools of war, Sanchez had them all bunch in close to him. "Listen up, guys. We're going to go back to our tent area and put our magazines and vest loadouts together. Once we've done that and I've inspected everything to make sure you guys are ready, we'll pick up some cases of MREs from supply here and get them loaded into our rucks. Then, and only then, will we get some shut-eye. We move out at 0400 hours for the front."

With their pep talk done, the squad got a move on to the transient tents their company had been staying in the last couple of days since they'd arrived. Walking into the tent, Private Webster and the others plopped their rucks on the floor or their cots and went to work on getting their magazines loaded up.

Private First Class Liam Miller, the squad's heavy machine gunner, tried to make conversation while they got their gear in order. "Hey, Webster, what did you think of that fortress getting the crap pounded out of it?" he asked. Miller and Webster both hailed from the same Ohio city of Akron. They'd become quick friends throughout basic training and had been equally excited to be assigned to the same infantry unit.

Webster looked up at Miller and shook his head. "I don't know, man. It sure looks like we're pounding the hell out of them, but I wouldn't be surprised if they're just riding the bombardment out in some sort of bunker—you know, like the Viet Cong did in the movie *Hamburger Hill*. My dad told me his grandpa fought the Japanese during World War II and he said that's what they used to do, too."

"After the shellacking we've been giving them, I'll bet they're just ready to give up," piped in another private. "I talked to one of the supply guys, and he said we've been pounding that mountain for nearly a week."

"I just hope none of us die in the next couple of days," said another private, who appeared to be holding back some tears. He was clearly scared, and it was starting to show.

"Good God, Private Hodge, are you going to cry again? We're soldiers, grow up!" Specialist Nathan Ryle exclaimed angrily.

"Hey, cut him some slack, Nathan. We're all scared; its normal. Plus, you know his brother died six months ago fighting the Russians," Webster shot back. Several of the other soldiers in the squad all nodded.

Specialist Nathan Ryle came from the mean streets of Compton, California, and had a chip on his shoulder the size of the state he hailed from. A lot of the guys had had some friction with him at one point or another.

At that moment, Staff Sergeant Jorge Sanchez walked back into the tent. "Enough jaw jacking," he barked. "We've got work to do. I want your magazines loaded and your MOLLE gear set up just like mine—use it as an example." He set his pack down on the ground in the middle of the group.

"Pack your rucks the same way I pack mine so you and everyone else in the squad can find the extra ammo, grenades and magazines quickly. I'm going to grab a couple boxes of MREs. When I get back, I expect you guys to be ready for my inspection. Once I'm satisfied, we'll go as a group and get some chow. We have an evening formation at 1900 hours."

With his new set of orders issued, Sergeant Sanchez left the privates to resume their work.

"Why do we have to carry our magazines like this?" asked one of them as he rearranged one of his ammo pouches to match Sanchez's.

"Because this is how the Sarge said he wants it done. Pretty simple if you ask me," replied Nathan, the constant antagonist.

Webster felt the need to add something as he finished packing his last magazine into the front pouch. "We carry the magazines with the bullets facing down so when you reach down and pull one out, it's facing the correct direction to slap into your rifle. It also keeps dirt and debris from getting stuck in the magazine when you go to pull it out. God forbid you ram it home in your rifle full of dirt—you'll jam the stupid thing.

"We carry three packs of two flush against your IBA instead of two packs of three, so they don't protrude as far out in front of our body armor. That way when you hit the dirt, you land relatively flat. It makes sense when you think about it."

Webster grabbed the drop bag next and held it up. "If you're right-handed, this attaches to your vest on the right side, so when you empty a magazine, you drop it in this pouch. That way, when you have time to reload them, they're right there waiting for you, and you're not placing empty magazines back into your magazine pouch and then suddenly finding your gun isn't loaded."

Holding up the pistol holster next, he added, "The Sarge has us carrying our pistol in a leg holster instead of attached to our IBA so we can have room to carry a couple of hand grenades and our first aid kit with the tourniquet."

The privates kind of stood there for a second, looking at their vests and loadouts like a lightbulb had suddenly turned on. It all made sense now why the sergeant was harping on them to wear their gear in a certain way, regardless of how they saw other platoons or companies wearing it.

A second later, Sergeant Sanchez walked into the tent with a couple of MRE boxes and a smile on his face. The others in the tent stopped talking as they watched him walk over to his own cot, placing the boxes on it. When he turned around, he walked over to Webster and placed his hand on his shoulder as he looked at them all.

"I just heard Private Webster explain to you why I have you doing what you're doing. He's 100% correct. It may sound to you like I'm nitpicking, but I'm having you do certain things for a reason. I've seen the elephant and you haven't yet. When the bullets start to fly and your buddies start getting hit, you're going to want to know exactly where your battle buddy's first aid kit or tourniquet is. If you have to search through a wounded or dead comrade's vest or ruck for ammo or more grenades, you're going to want to know exactly where to search, because your life or mine may depend on it."

Sanchez then took a seat on the edge of Webster's cot and motioned for the others to stop and take a seat. "Look, I've been in the Army now for three years. The only reason I'm a staff sergeant instead of an E-4 specialist like Ryle is because all the other sergeants ahead of me were either killed or wounded eight months ago when our unit first encountered this Chinese version of the Maginot Line. During our fourth assault against that ridgeline out there, I got shot for hopefully the first and last time in my life. We were bounding up the ridge from one covered position to another when I caught a bullet in my left arm. As if that wasn't bad enough, when I tried to move back to find a medic, I got shot two more times. One hit me squarely in the center of my back plate. The second bullet hit me in the back of my right shoulder. Fortunately, I was knocked unconscious, so I didn't feel a lot of the initial pain, but I sure felt it when I eventually made it back to a field hospital.

"I spent four months recovering in the hospital. When I returned to the unit, they promoted me to staff sergeant and placed me in charge of Second Squad. I'm telling you all this because I want you guys to be prepared for tomorrow. The captain said our company is moving up for a big offensive that's going to start tomorrow. That means a lot of fighting is going to happen. As a matter of fact, Lieutenant Fallon said I'm to promote one of you guys to corporal to take over for Corporal Ball. Apparently, he had appendicitis, so he's having his appendix removed. He won't be returning back to the platoon for at least a month."

Sanchez pulled a set of corporal chevrons out of his pocket and stood. He handed them over to Private Webster, saying, "Shane, for a newbie private, you seem to have your head screwed on right, and the guys in the squad seem to like and respect you. I'm promoting you to corporal. You're going to be in charge of our heavy machine-gun crew. Congrats."

The rest of the squad congratulated him—everyone except Nathan, who obviously felt *he* should have been promoted. Sure, a specialist and corporal shared the same paygrade, but a corporal was a junior NCO, and therefore carried command authority, similar to a sergeant.

****

Two hours later, the platoon stood in a loose formation with the rest of the company as they waited for their CO to come out and give them a short brief before they would be dismissed for the night. The next day would be busy.

Captain Joel Garcia walked up to his first sergeant, saluted him and called the company to at ease. "Listen up, everyone!" he shouted. "The 2-14 infantry is moving to the front lines tomorrow. The entire division is gearing up to assault that mountain." He gestured toward the fortress that was still getting pounded by air and artillery.

"Beyond that fortress, gentlemen, is a clear shot to Beijing. We punch our way through it and our tanks will lead the rest of the way. We're going to form up at 0400 hours, when we'll road march our way to the front. It's approximately eight kilometers to our new base camp. Once there, we'll find out when they're going to order us up the mountain. As of right now, our forces have secured the lower portion of the mountain. It's going to be our division's turn to finish rolling the enemy up and finally break through this mountain fortress.

"I'm not going to lie to you all and say this'll be an easy fight. It won't. A lot of you guys are probably going to get injured or killed. But know this: once we capture this fortress, we're one step closer to defeating the PLA and ending this war. I want everyone to do their best and take care of each other. You see the enemy, you kill him...I'm going to turn you back over to Top now."

He called the company to attention and then turned them over to the first sergeant, who issued a few other orders before he dismissed them for the evening to get some sleep.

****

Boom! Boom! Bam!

Ratatat, ratatat, zip, zip, zap…

"Take that bunker out!" Sergeant Sanchez shouted over the roar of explosions and machine-gun fire.

Specialist Ryle ducked just as a string of bullets hit a tree stump he was using for cover. He pulled his ruck off his back and unstrapped the AT4 he was carrying. He made sure the rocket was ready to fire and then called out for covering fire.

Private Miller popped up from behind the boulder he had been hiding behind and let loose a string of 7.62mm rounds at the cement machine-gun bunker that was shooting at them. The face of that bunker was dimpled with pock marks from all the shrapnel and machine-gun bullets that had hit it.

Ryle saw this as his moment and jumped up with the AT4 on his shoulder, ready to go. He took quick aim and depressed the firing button.

Pop, whooosssshhh…BAM.

The rocket flew fast and slammed right into the bunker, just next to the machine gun. A ton of sparks flew out in all directions, and the gun fell silent.

"Charge that bunker now! Get some grenades in it!" screamed Sergeant Jacobson, the assistant squad leader. He jumped up and ran toward the bunker, firing his weapon at the gun slits and screaming like a madman.

Webster looked over to his friend, Miller. "Let's go," Miller said as he lurched forward around the boulder they had been hiding behind.

Webster struggled briefly as he tried to catch up to Jacobson, who was nearly to the edge of the bunker. Specialist Ryle was hot on his heels when suddenly the machine-gun bunker returned to life and resumed its killing spree. Ryle was hit multiple times in his chest as he fell backwards, each slug acting like a punch to his chest.

Jacobson ducked to his right just as a string of rounds flew right past where he had just been. Webster ducked to the left behind a large tree stump, maybe ten meters away from the bunker. Looking at Sergeant Jacobson, he saw him signal that he was going to use his M203 grenade launcher on the bunker. "Once I fire it, you charge forward!" he yelled.

Webster nodded as he readied himself to cross the remaining ten meters to the enemy position.

Thump, BOOM.

Webster jumped out from his covered position and ran for all his worth toward the bunker. He jumped past Specialist Ryle, who was still lying on his back, pleading for someone to help him. In seconds, Webster found himself flush with the side of the bunker. He waved to the others below him that he had made it and then grabbed one of his grenades from his vest. He inched around to the front of the bunker and got to just beneath the gun slit. The machine gun was still firing away at his comrades below. He pulled the pin, counted to two, and then shoved the grenade through the gun slit. He felt the grenade fall inside the bunker and heard a lot of frantic yelling before a loud blast assaulted his ears and vibrated the ground around him.

Not trusting the one grenade to do the job, Webster pulled the pin on a second grenade and dropped it in the same slit. A second later, another boom rang out, only this time, there were no more voices to be heard. At this point, several other soldiers ran forward toward Webster and joined him at the bunker.

"How do we get inside this thing?" asked one of the guys who'd joined them.

The bunker had been built into the mountain, so it was tied to a series of tunnels and rooms from the inside. Sergeant Jacobson crawled around the right side of the bunker until he was on top of it. Once there, he noticed a steel hatch on the top.

"In here, guys."

Several of the soldiers crawled around to join him on top of the bunker and saw what he saw. While they were still figuring out how to get inside, the next layer of bunkers several hundred meters higher up the mountain began shooting down on them. They scrambled down the sides and sought cover from the incoming bullets. By now, the entire squad had made its way to their position and had taken cover around them. Specialist Ryle was being treated by one of the medics as a couple of soldiers helped to escort him back to one of the aid stations.

Lieutenant Fallon crawled up to Sergeant Sanchez. "Any thoughts on how we get inside?" he asked. "I'll bet this thing connects to other rooms and bunkers inside the mountain. It could be our ticket to clearing them out."

Sanchez poked his head back up to look at the hatch again. "If we had some C-4 or det cord, we could probably get this hatch open," he answered. "Do you think we could call someone over who might have some? Hey, also—before we do that, we need to get those two bunkers up there taken out, or they're just going to keep shooting at us."

The lieutenant nodded. "Yeah, you're right. Let me see if I can get the rest of the company to head our way and try to take them out."

Fallon sat down below the lip of the bunker and called for an engineer to come up to their position, so they could inform Captain Garcia of what they'd found. Meanwhile, the other platoons pushed past them as they continued to engage the other enemy bunkers further up the mountain.

Boom, boom, ratatat, ratatat, zip, zip, zap!

Bullets flew all around them as they waited for an engineer and their captain to arrive. Explosions rocked the mountain as the other companies and units did their best to root out the enemy, one bunker and fighting position at a time.

Eventually, Captain Garcia trudged up to them with a couple of soldiers in tow. Two of them were engineers. When they got to the bunker, Sanchez explained to them what they needed done, and the two engineers examined the steel hatch.

"Let's try the det cord first," suggested the first engineer.

"Yeah, and if that fails, we'll go for the C-4," the other countered.

A few minutes went by as the engineers pressed the det cord into the cracks and crevices of the hatch until it was neatly packed in, despite the bullets that were snapping all around them while they worked. Once the engineers had done their work, the group moved away from the bunker as they prepared to blow it.

BOOM!

As the dust from the explosion settled, several of the soldiers ran to the top of the bunker to inspect the hatch. To their satisfaction, they found it now accessible.

Sanchez turned to the engineers. "Could you stick around?" he asked. "We may need you to blow open some additional doors once we get inside."

The engineers nodded and smiled. They clearly enjoyed it when explosives were a part of their day.

One by one, the members of Second Squad filtered into the bunker. They fanned out as they moved their way to a rear door, lining up against the walls as they approached it. When they reached the door, they tested it and found that it was unlocked.

Sanchez held his hand up. "Stand by and wait," he ordered.

Stepping over several dead Chinese soldiers, Sanchez climbed out of the hatch. He found the lieutenant and the captain. "There's a door at the other end of the bunker," he said. "We've tested it, and it's unlocked. We didn't open it yet, since we're not sure if its boobytrapped, but I wanted to see if we could get the rest of the platoon or even the company to work with us on clearing it out. Who knows? It might link up to other rooms or levels inside the fortress. If we clear it out, we might be able to silence a lot of these really tough machine-gun bunkers."

Captain Garcia thought about that for a second and then nodded. "OK, Sergeant," he responded. "Lieutenant Fallon, I want your platoon to work on exploring and clearing the tunnels out. I'm going to place a call back to battalion and let them know what we've found. I'll see if we can't get a couple of flamethrowers sent over here to help you guys clear them out. God only knows what's inside. I also want to get the rest of the company in on this. You guys just might have found the chink in the armor of this fortress."

Nodding, the lieutenant signaled for Sanchez to lead the way. The two of them crawled back down into the main gun room. Several of the soldiers had picked the dead Chinese bodies up and stacked them in a pile along one of the walls, out of the way. The rest of the squad was lined up on both sides of the door, ready to go.

Sanchez nodded to Webster to open the door and peer into what lay beyond it. Slowly at first, Corporal Webster opened the door. Small lights had been affixed to the walls of the tunnel every twenty feet or so, dimly lighting the space. The tunnels were like hallways, wide enough for at least two soldiers to walk side by side. They could hear the chattering of machine guns and the occasional voice yelling in Chinese, but the noises were faint, off in the distance.

Webster made his way into the hallway and signaled for the others to follow. One of the fire teams turned right and followed the hallway up a gentle incline, while the group that went left followed the hallway down to the lower levels. Both fire teams made their way further into the fortress to see what they could find. By now, the next squad of soldiers had filtered in and was moving to back them up as well. Slow and steadily, they were advancing further into the mountain fortress.

Even inside the tunnels, Sergeant Sanchez could still hear and often feel the explosions taking place outside. He also heard the chattering of machine guns, though they were softer, muffled by all the rock between them and the outdoors.

After moving maybe five more meters into the mountain, they came to an entrance that opened up into a large cavern. Corporal Webster signaled for everyone to stop and dropped down to one knee. The others did likewise.

Sergeant Sanchez made his way up to him. "What do we have, Webster?" he asked.

Webster leaned in and whispered, "I think we found the ammo depot. It looks like these guys are sorting ammo onto those pushcarts to run them over to different bunkers." He waved his hand forward.

Peering into the spacious room, Sanchez saw at once what Webster had described. The storage facility there had to be at least twenty meters high, roughly one hundred meters in length and fifty meters in width. While it was dark toward the edges and in the tunnels that connected to the main room, there were at least eight or ten overhead lights. On one side of the cavernous room was a table with four PLA soldiers manning several radios and an old-fashioned phone switchboard. Next to them was a series of maps with different color codes on them.

The adjacent wall had a row of maybe twenty cots set up, with wounded soldiers laid out on them. PLA doctors or medics tended to them, and nearby was a military ambulance. The wounded were being loaded onto it, presumably to be taken either deeper in the mountain or out of it altogether. The vehicle was angled toward a tunnel with a sign written in Chinese that probably said *exit*, since there was one other opening maybe thirty meters to the left with the same sign, large enough for a truck.

In the center of the room, dozens of PLA soldiers loaded crates of ammunition onto pushcarts, which were then rushed off down a different hallway, presumably to another gun bunker. Another set of soldiers were loading crates of ammo onto an elevator pulley that would bring additional ammo to another layer of bunkers somewhere above them.

Sergeant Sanchez then heard an approaching truck engine and froze. A pair of headlights crept closer to their position from that second tunnel. Sanchez's heart raced as the noise grew louder and the lights brighter, but the truck stopped. Without seeming to notice any of the Americans, a half dozen soldiers got out and proceeded to help offload more crates of ammo.

Sanchez had seen enough. He knew they didn't have enough soldiers to take this group on, and if they were going to capitalize on this find, they needed to get the rest of the platoon, or better yet, the company over here.

"We could send squads of soldiers down those tunnels and silence the machine-gun bunkers all over this mountain fortress," he thought.

"Webster, let's fall back a bit and hold our position," he whispered. "We need more troops to take 'em out." Webster nodded and scooted back a bit. Sanchez doubled back to go find their lieutenant.

Five minutes went by before Sanchez returned with Lieutenant Fallon and Captain Garcia, who'd brought a platoon and a half of soldiers with them. Captain Garcia sent the other half of the company with the XO down the other tunnel.

Captain Garcia huddled with Sergeant Sanchez further back down the hall. "I talked with battalion before I came in the tunnel," he explained. "They're sending another company of soldiers to help us clear this out. They want a report as soon as we know how big this place is."

"Sir, if I may, when we enter this room, we're going to have to clear it quickly," Sanchez rationalized. "I have no idea if they have an internal alarm system. Once we're in, I suggest we send squads of soldiers down the smaller tunnels, as those most likely lead to other gun bunkers. We can take them out quickly, which will hopefully help our guys on the outside out. But if we're going to try and go down those two vehicle tunnels, I think we're going to need a lot more guys. We have no idea how many other soldiers are down them. They might even lead all the way out to the other side of the mountain."

The captain nodded. "Lead the way, Sergeant."

A few minutes went by; they went over each squad's lane of fire and where they were going to move once the shooting started. With everyone briefed, they were ready to execute.

Corporal Webster was the first soldier to emerge from the shadows of the tunnel. He charged forward, suddenly materializing from the darkness. The first enemy soldier to see him froze in sudden panic at the sight of an American soldier inside their fortress. Webster pulled the trigger once, hitting the soldier squarely in the forehead before he could even react. The man dropped like a sack of potatoes, his body resting in a pile of brain matter.

With the first gunshot fired, the element of surprise was over. Both squads of soldiers systematically shot everyone they saw in the cavernous room while doing their best to filter into the entrance as quickly as possible. More and more soldiers ran into the room to join their comrades.

The shooting inside the large room was intense. Nearly a hundred soldiers on both sides fought to the death in the confined space. With speed on their side, the Americans overwhelmed the defenders.

"Webster! Take your fire team and head down that tunnel," Staff Sergeant Sanchez shouted. He pointed to one of the newly-arrived soldiers and ordered, "Take him with you."

Webster nodded, and the newbie and one of his buddies ran over to join him.

"I was told you guys needed a flamethrower," the young kid said with a wicked smile on his face.

Webster and the other soldiers looked at the two of them with fear and awe. While they had watched the vintage Vietnam-era M9-7 flamethrower being used off in the distance, none of them had ever seen one of them up close, let alone had one of them assigned to their squad.

"Yeah, I guess we do," said Webster with a chuckle. "OK, let's go. We need to move quickly down the tunnel. We have no idea if they just heard this shoot-out or what." Looking at his two new guys, Webster added, "I want you guys in the rear. When we need you, we'll call you forward."

The two guys nodded, not at all put out that they were bringing up the rear. God forbid they should be near the front during a shoot-out; if their fuel tank got hit, it would blow up, possibly wiping out the whole fire team.

Moving down the tunnel, Webster kept his rifle up and ready. About twenty meters in, they reached the first bend. Corporal Webster stopped and pulled a small pocket mirror out of his pocket. He let his rifle hang from his single-point sling and grabbed the bayonet from its sheath.

"What're you doing, Rambo?" chided one of the soldiers behind him.

Turning to look back at the soldiers behind him, Webster held a lone finger to his mouth. "Shhhh, I saw this in a movie. I'm going to make sure no one else is around that corner."

Taking the gum out of his mouth, Webster attached it to the back of his mirror and then affixed the gooey mixture to his knife. He dropped down to his knee and slid the setup past the corner to give him a better angle on what was down there waiting for them.

While the hallway was still poorly lit, with just a small light every twenty feet or so, at the end of the tunnel, he saw something. Squinting a bit, he thought he could make out a pile of sandbags maybe a meter high. He focused his eyes more. On top of the sandbags was what looked to be a Type 67 machine gun on a tripod with a couple of soldiers sitting next to it, looking back at him. He quickly pulled his bayonet back and whispered for one of the other soldiers to do what he had just done and tell him what he saw.

At this point, Staff Sergeant Sanchez had caught up to them, with another six soldiers in tow.

"What's the holdup, Webster?" he asked quietly.

The corporal filled him in on what he had seen and then handed his knife and mirror over for Sanchez to take a look.

Looking at the contraption, Sanchez shook his head. "What are you, MacGyver or something?"

Then he bent down on a knee and used the mirror to look around the corner; it didn't take him long to see what Webster had found.

"Smart, Webster, damn smart. That gun would have killed us all in this tight little corridor," Sanchez remarked. He handed the knife and mirror back to Webster, who proceeded to stuff the mirror back in his pocket and put his knife away. Then he grabbed the gum and put it back in his mouth.

"*No reason to waste it,*" he thought. Plus, it helped calm his nerves.

Sanchez signaled for the flamethrower. "Here's what's going to happen. Harvey here," he said, pointing to one of the guys with the M203 grenade launcher mounted under his M4, "is going to pop out around the corner here and fire one of his HE frags down the hallway to hit that position, and hopefully either kill or wound them. As soon as he does that, I need *you* to haul butt down that hallway as far as you think you need to in order to use that bad boy." Now he was signaling to the guys with the flamethrower.

"If you need to go ten feet or twenty feet, you get as close as you need, and then blast that gun position with your fire stick. Once you've hit it once or twice, then kneel down and step aside while the rest of us run past you and capture the position, OK?"

The soldiers all nodded. Several of them stole a nervous glance at the flamethrower, hoping they wouldn't end up dying in glorious ball of fire if it took a stray round to its tank.

Everyone quietly got themselves ready for the assault. Private Harvey double-checked his grenade launcher, then nodded to the rest of the guys. Sanchez nodded back, then held up a hand with all his fingers spread out. He silently mouthed a countdown as he pulled each finger down into his palm one by one. When he reached zero and his hand had formed a fist, he pointed to Harvey to begin his attack.

Private Harvey moved out around the corner, leveling his M203 at the soldiers at the end of the hallway. Just as he was about to fire, his body was hit with a barrage of bullets—the gun crew must have known they were down there, preparing to attack. Harvey didn't even have any time to react as his body was pounded relentlessly by dozens of 7.62×54mm rounds. They punched right through his body armor, and he collapsed to the ground.

In the flash of a second, everything slowed down as if the world was moving by one frame at a time, one fraction of a second after another as Webster dove for Harvey's now-dead body. He landed right next to him and grabbed him by his MOLLE gear, throwing Harvey's body in front of him like a shield. He grabbed Harvey's M4 with the grenade launcher, and before the gun crew at the end of the hallway could react, Webster fired the high-explosive projectile down the corridor. The round slammed into the wall directly behind the gun crew. Flame and shrapnel hit many of the enemy soldiers.

Instantly, the soldier with the flamethrower jumped around the corner and charged down the hallway like a man possessed, screaming obscenities as he ran. He moved maybe ten feet down the hallway before he stopped and unleashed a torrent of fire on the enemy soldiers who were still trying to recover from the blast that had just wounded them.

Several other soldiers in Webster's fire team ran down the hallway past the flamethrower to capture the enemy position. Looking over Harvey's dead body and past his soldiers, who were charging down the hallway, Corporal Webster saw one of the enemy soldiers screaming wildly, his body completely engulfed in flames. The Chinese soldier shrieked for another minute or so, turning and running down the other hallway before his voice went silent, probably because he had finally collapsed and died.

When two of his soldiers reached the enemy positions, they rounded the corner and a quick firefight ensued. One of his soldiers took several rounds to the chest and fell backwards onto the burning bodies of the dead enemy soldiers. His comrade unloaded the rest of his thirty-round magazine at whatever enemy soldiers they had encountered.

Another soldier joined him and tossed a hand grenade down the corridor.

Crump.

Silence followed. More of the soldiers rushed the position.

Sergeant Sanchez walked up to Webster; he pushed Harvey's lifeless body to the side and took the hand Sanchez offered to help him up.

"It's too bad about Harvey," Sanchez said. After a momentary pause out of respect, he added, "We're going to have to start calling you Rambo, Webster. That was unbelievable. I've never seen anyone move or do something like that," Sanchez exclaimed with a look of pride on his face. "Let's get down there and finish clearing this place out. I can't image them having more internal security positions like this."

The two of them quickly caught back up to the rest of the squad as they moved through the rest of the tunnels. Every few hundred meters, they'd find a metal door leading to a gun bunker. When they found the back entrance to a new bunker, they'd usually throw a grenade inside to stun the defenders and then stand aside for the lone flamethrower guy to do his deed. He'd pop out from around the corner and fire a five-to-seven-second burst of liquid flame into the enemy position. Then they'd slam the door and lock it and move down the hallway to find the next one.

The rest of the day went by in a blur as Corporal Webster's unit moved from one corridor to another, silencing enemy gun positions from the inside. More and more American soldiers filtered in through the new entrances they were opening up in the mountain fortress. By the end of the day, nearly an entire battalion of soldiers had found their way inside the fortress, tearing the enemy stronghold apart. They had transformed a small tear in the enemy lines into a full-blown rip. The way before them now stood clear.

Chapter 10
Operation Sandman

Nonghezhen, China

Lieutenant Colonel Grant Johnson looked at the map one more time as his company commanders filtered into the meeting tent. The air was hot and stifling outside; the sun had broken through some of the morning clouds that had been shielding them from its bright rays. He lifted his coffee mug to his mouth, imbibing the warm liquid. "*I don't care how warm it is outside—coffee is supposed to be hot,*" he thought.

Caffeine now on board, Johnson determined this was as good a time as any to get started. He cleared his throat to get their attention. "At ease. Take your seats. We have a lot to go over before the start of this next offensive."

He turned the map board around to show them what he had been studying and to give the captains and senior NCOs a reference point to refer to while he spoke.

"The commanders from on high have decided that now is the time for us to launch our summer offensive. Some of our infantry units have pushed a handful of kilometers ahead of us and secured a crossing of the Songhua River nearly forty kilometers east of Harbin. *Our* objective is not Harbin—that's going to be handled by the infantry. We've been tasked with going after the enemy armor force further to the south, between the cities of Harbin and Changchun." He used his pointer a few times as he spoke to show their position in relation to where the enemy units were located.

"Right now, intelligence has the PLA 4th Armored Brigade here, roughly ten kilometers south of Harbin. They appear to be in a holding pattern, waiting to see where best to be deployed. Forty kilometers to the south, and just north of Changchun, is the PLA 8th Armored Brigade, along with the 68th Mechanized Infantry Brigade. What concerns us most, however, is the 46th Motorized Infantry Division, which is sixty-eight kilometers to the west of Changchun. If we make a move toward either of those armor brigades, that division could start heading our way."

Captain Jason Diss raised his hand, and Lieutenant Colonel Johnson nodded to allow him to speak. "It sounds like we can handle the armor, but what kind of infantry support do we have to deal with the mechanized infantry we're bound to run into?"

The others perked their heads up, interested to hear the answer.

"We have the 162nd Infantry Regiment that will be moving along with us," Johnson answered. "They're part of the Oregon National Guard. In addition to the guard unit, we'll have the 3-16 AR with us. This'll be a full 2nd Brigade Combat Team move, gentlemen—1BCT is being held in reserve in case we need them, and 3BCT will be to our right. This is going to be a tough fight, but I'm sure we'll be able to handle it."

He paused. "Now, our objective is simple. We're to press the enemy until we obtain a breakthrough, and then drive fast and hard to the outskirts of Changchun. However, we are not going to pursue the enemy into the city. We aren't going to do anything with the city except go around it. Once our infantry forces have caught up, they will encircle the city and deal with whatever enemy units are left.

"Then the Brigade CO wants us to head west. Our next waypoint is a city by the name of Shuangliao. Once there, we'll rally up with the rest of the brigade, figure out what forces we have left, and collect up on our supplies before making our next push.

"If there are no further questions, then I want you guys to stick around and study the map a bit more. Make sure you plot down the various navigational waypoints and note all the call signs we'll be using. As most of you know from our previous conversations and briefings, comms is about to get all sorts of screwed up in the next few days."

Captain Diss and his first sergeant, Bo Adams, looked over the map and the rough distances they'd be traveling. It was a lot of ground to cover and most likely would result in a lot of enemy engagements. They were one brigade, going up against several PLA brigades. Besides this obvious challenge, it looked like it would be difficult to stay properly supplied—the farther out they went, the farther their supplies would have to stretch.

"Air cover is going to be an issue," First Sergeant Adams stated.

"Right, but it doesn't look like the enemy has a lot of air assets in the area to harass us with either," Diss countered.

After spending twenty minutes looking everything over and marking up their own maps, the two of them headed back to their company area to get the rest of the guys ready.

"What's the main priority you have for me, Sir?" asked First Sergeant Bo Adams as the two of them walked toward their bivouac site.

First Sergeant Bo Adams was new to the company. Diss's last first sergeant had died in the Battle of Kursk, so he had been without one for a few weeks. Captain Diss had already decided that Bo was a decent enough guy. He hailed from the backwoods of Mississippi and was no stranger to roughing it. He'd hold things together in the company, and that was all Diss wanted.

Captain Diss thought about Adams's question for a minute. "I think the most important thing, Top, is making sure our supply lines are keeping up with us, and that they know where we are. We're going to burn through a lot of ammo, and we can't be running out," he asserted. "Next, stay on top of casualties…we're bound to take 'em. Focus on the ones that can make it, and mark the ones that can't. Either we'll come back for them, or Mortuary Affairs will get to them at some point."

"Copy that, Captain. I'll make sure we stay on top of those issues. If I need anything else, you want me to go through you or the XO?" he asked.

"Go through me unless I tell you to go through the XO. If things get hairy, that could happen, but let's not start out that way," Diss replied.

First Sergeant Adams nodded and walked off to get his own vehicle and troopers situated.

Captain Diss took a few minutes with his platoon leaders and made sure they knew the big picture of what was happening, as well as how and why. When they broke up a few minutes later, they soberly headed back to their platoons to get their own men ready. Tomorrow was going to be a busy day for them all.

****

The following morning, Captain Diss stood next to the right side of his tank, Warhorse, admiring the sunrise. He thought about the juxtaposition between the beauty before him and the death and destruction that was about to be unleashed.

A voice suddenly intruded in on his thoughts. "Are we good to go, Captain?" inquired his gunner, Sergeant Jesus Cortez. Cortez had been a driver on one of his other tanks four months ago. After continued attrition, he'd been promoted to gunner and taken over for Staff Sergeant Dakota Winters when Winters had taken command of his own tank.

Diss smiled, his way of offering an olive branch to the newbie. "Yup," he answered.

Cortez nodded and, without any further hesitation, climbed up the side of the tank and through the hatch. Diss followed suit.

Despite the fact that he was working with a new gunner, Captain Diss and his team functioned like a well-oiled machine as they followed their training to complete the necessary checks before the coming battle. Before long, all crewmembers of Warhorse had reported ready, and Diss had moved on to checking on the rest of the company.

Everyone called in Redcon One and acknowledged the standard order to begin in a wedge formation, with Blue Platoon in the middle. Diss noticed that the young and previously overly zealous Lieutenant Spade was much more subdued this time around; more than likely, the Battle of Kursk had eroded some of his enthusiasm for combat. Word from the guys was that he had turned into a good combat commander after all.

"If losses stay high, he'll have his own company to command soon enough," thought Captain Diss.

"Roger, Mustangs, begin your movement," said Captain Diss, changing his focus back to what was in front of them.

The platoon of tanks gathered into formation and began their journey. Near the small village of Xindianzhen, they expected to find multiple pontoon bridges that had been set up by the engineers to cross the Songhua River, a formidable body of water and one of China's longest rivers.

As anticipated, when they reached the banks, the engineers guided the tanks across, one at a time. Each tank slowly crossed the first part of the pontoon, sinking into the water until it settled and then rose again as it moved its way across the bridge. With four bridges set up, Diss was able to get one full platoon across at a time.

It took them nearly twenty minutes to get his company to the other side. Once that was completed, they all moved forward half a kilometer and took up a defensive position while they waited for the rest of their battalion to catch up. In the meantime, refuelers drove by and continued to top off their tanks and the other vehicles as they showed up. An hour after Captain Diss's unit had set up their defensive position, they got word that their battalion had fully crossed, and the other tanks were in the process of topping off their own fuel tanks before they moved forward.

Captain Diss reviewed his map while they waited. They had probably close to a hundred kilometers of terrain to cross before they would start to run into any PLA forces. Their last intelligence report was from a small reconnaissance unit screening for the larger brigade of tanks nearby. It was as if someone above them was moving the chess pieces on the board in anticipation of a much larger battle.

"I suppose that's what the men with the stars on their collars do," Diss mused.

The radio in their CVC chirped with the voice of the battalion commander. "All Mustang elements, move out. Begin moving in diamond formation."

Diss depressed his own talk button, adding, "You heard the man. It's time to earn our pay. I want everyone on the move, heads on a swivel. You see a target, call it out ASAP."

Warhorse lurched forward as they took up their position in the formation. Sergeant Cortez, his gunner, searched the horizon for potential targets. Diss reached up and popped his commander's hatch open, lifting it up on the spring and locking it in place. He then used his hands to pull himself up so he could stand in the hatch with a much better view of the terrain they were heading into.

Captain Diss tried not to dwell on the losses they had taken up to this point or the wasted opportunities of the past. They had finally been given permission to do what tankers do best, go kill other tanks and murder unguarded infantry. He nearly let out a sadistic laugh.

"*I love the smell of napalm in the morning*," he thought with a smirk, remembering one of the lines from his favorite movie, *Apocalypse Now*.

His tank rumbled down the side of a two-lane road that was lined with trees, providing a semblance of cover.

While he wanted his tanks to change into a single-file formation and use the trees for cover, he had a sick feeling that this ideally covered road was probably laced with tank-mines and other nasty surprises.

"No, we'll stick to the more open ground, where we can clearly see what we're driving into," he resolved.

Lifting his binoculars to his eyes, he scanned the horizon several kilometers to their front, looking for anything out of the ordinary but spotting nothing. The only thing they had seen in the last thirty minutes was a lot of little kids and old men and women, standing outside their homes or near a road, just watching them drive by. Some waved and smiled at them; others stared daggers, aware that they were the enemy invading their homeland.

Nearly two hours had gone by since they'd crossed the pontoon bridge, and they were just now approaching their first major village, Bin'anzhen. It was a small village of maybe 15,000 people and sat at the crossroads of several major road junctions. Luckily for them, an advance party of military police had arrived ahead of them; MPs were staggered at different turns, bridges and roads to guide them through the village and back into the open fields that would lead them toward the enemy.

By then it was roughly 0900 hours. Their armored chariots rolled down one small road after another as they made their way out of the village. Many of the village inhabitants came out to see them, often lining the roads. Like earlier, some smiled and waved innocently enough. Others stared on in awe, and some oozed hatred at the sight of so many huge American battle tanks. These people had clearly never seen a tank up close, and the size, the creaking noises and the shaking of the ground beneath them gave testament to the awesome power these armored behemoths could project. In Diss's mind, there really wasn't anything close to being as impressive as the sight of several hundred main battle tanks rolling through your city in the middle of the morning. Still, Captain Diss made sure Sergeant Cortez was sitting in the gunner's hatch with his hand on the crew-served weapon, ready in case they needed to use it.

Their next objective was the much larger city of Binzhouzhen, roughly sixty kilometers to the west. With the rest of his company now out of the small city, they resumed their diamond formation and again picked up speed. Despite the faster pace, everyone was on edge, maintaining a high level of vigilance as they moved through more and more farms and possible ambush points.

A squeak over the radio in Diss's CVC helmet let him know someone was trying to break through on their coms. "Mustang Six, this is Darkhorse Six. How copy?" asked the voice, faint and a little garbled but still understandable. It must be their reconnaissance unit.

"Darkhorse Six, this is Mustang Six. I can't hear you the best, but go ahead with your message," replied Captain Diss. He shared a nervous glance with his gunner.

"We're one kilometer from Binzhouzhen City. We've spotted multiple sapper units and missile teams set up on the northeast side of the city. We're going to hit them with artillery. Recommend your unit advance on the city from the southeast side. Darkhorse Three spotted two T-08 IFVs near the edge of the city. Two kilometers to the southeast of the city, Darkhorse Three also spotted twelve Type 96 tanks, hull down with camouflage on top. How copy?"

Diss thought over his options. Missiles and sapper units awaited on the northern side of the city, and heavy armor on the southern side. He had to think a moment before he determined the best course of action.

"Well, we're here to destroy tanks," Diss finally decided. Knowing where the enemy tanks were would made it a lot easier to attack them. Plus, the last thing they wanted to do was run into was a swarm of antitank missiles and

rockets that would force them to have to dismount their infantry.

He hit the reply button. "Darkhorse Six, this is Mustang Six. Good copy on the information. Mustang element will go after the T-96s on the southeastern side of the city. Proceed with artillery strike on missile and sapper units to the north. Out."

Captain Diss switched over to the company net. "Attention all Mustangs, FRAGO follows: we've been given a heads-up by our recon guys on an enemy tank formation, approximately two kilometers to the southeast of our next waypoint. We're going to change formation to a left-facing echelon formation. We're looking for Type 96 tanks, hull down with camouflage on their turrets. If you spot one, identify it, pass it to the rest of the company, and engage it. Good hunting, Mustangs!"

Diss turned his attention to his crew next. "Cortez, when the shooting starts, I'm going to need you to identify and shoot. I'll do my best to help when I can, but I've also got the rest of the company to manage, so you're essentially going to have to run the gun for us, OK?" he asked.

"Roger that, Sir. I got it. Winters told me exactly what to expect and what to do. I can handle it," he replied in a reassuring voice.

Diss took a minute to say a few words to his driver and loader, making sure they felt some love as well, then he switched over to talk with his platoon leaders. He wanted to make sure their platoons were falling in line with the new formation. They were less than four kilometers from making contact.

Less than twenty seconds later, the ground around their tank started to rattle. Then they heard the unmistakable *crump, crump, crump* of artillery rounds landing nearby. Loud pings and clangs rattled their ears as shrapnel bounced off their armor.

"Tanks to our left!" shouted Cortez. He turned the turret to line up with the target he had found.

Diss looked through his commander's sight extension, trying to see what Cortez had found. "There you are," he muttered under his breath as he watched the laser designator light up the turret.

"Tank, 3,100 meters to our nine o'clock. Sabot!" Cortez shouted in an excited voice.

"Sabot ready," replied Specialist Trey Mann, the loader. He pulled up on the arming handle. They'd already been riding with a sabot round in the chamber.

"All Mustang elements, Type 96 tank identified to my nine o'clock. Identify your targets and fire at will!"

shouted Captain Diss. Then he took a deep breath—they were about to go into battle with the People's Liberation Army for the first time.

Finished with his company address, Diss shouted, "Fire!"

"On the way!" Sergeant Cortez yelled. The enemy tank had just crossed the 3,000-meter mark, the extent of their effective firing range, so he dutifully depressed the firing button.

BOOM!

The cannon fired, recoiling back inside the turret. The vehicle rocked slightly but kept right on charging toward the enemy.

Looking through his commander's sight, Captain Diss watched their round slam right into the turret of the enemy tank, causing an epic explosion. Pulling the zoom out a bit on his sight, he saw round after round of his other tankers slam into the exposed turrets of the enemy tanks. Nearly every one of them scored a direct hit.

The three enemy tanks that had survived their first volley fired back. However, they were near the extent of their limited range, and all the rounds that came toward Diss and his soldiers either sailed past his tanks or bounced harmlessly off their superior armor.

Specialist Mann slammed another sabot round into the breach of the cannon and pulled up on the arming handle. "Up!" he yelled.

Delta Company's tanks continued to rumble through the farm fields to the southeast of the city as they closed in on the enemy positions. "Missiles incoming!" shouted Cortez as their vehicle ran over a rough patch of land, jostling them around a bit.

"Black Six, this is Red Four. We're spotting swarms of Red Arrow-12 AT missiles heading toward us from the city to our right flank," explained Lieutenant Spade. "How do you want us to respond?"

"Crap, that's the last thing we needed right now—antitank missiles," Captain Diss murmured.

"All Mustangs, Red Four is reporting antitank missiles swarming us from the city on our right flank. I want everyone to activate your missile countermeasure devices and Trophy systems. Some of these missiles are going to get through the MCD, so let's hope these Trophy systems are as good as the Israelis say they are. In the meantime, I want everyone to shift our movement further southwest into the enemy lines to give us some more distance from that city," Captain Diss ordered.

Crump, crump, crump. Boom!

More explosions vibrated the ground beneath them, this time moving them so much that the company of tanks nearly veered directly into each other.

"ZBDs to our front! 2,200 meters!" shouted Sergeant Cortez. They were less than a thousand meters from the first line of enemy tanks they had wiped out earlier; now they were pressing into the second and third layer of enemy vehicles.

"Loader, HEAT!" shouted Diss. He zeroed in on the newest threat to his command.

Specialist Mann grabbed a round from a different stash this time, slamming it into the opening as fast as possible. "Up!" he yelled.

"HEAT ready!" shouted Cortez.

"Fire!" Diss shouted. Then he immediately began to look for other targets nearby.

"On the way!" Cortez exclaimed. The cannon fired again, and the cabin of the tank was filling with fumes.

"Incoming missile!" Diss shouted seconds after they had fired. He quickly reached over and flipped on the MCD and Trophy system.

"That missile's gonna be close!" yelled Cortez. He grabbed desperately for something, anything, to brace for the impact.

Seconds later, the Trophy system activated, firing out its barrage of ball bearings at the incoming missile. *BAM*…the tank got peppered with shrapnel and pieces of the broken-up missile as its sheer velocity threw the remains of its shell into their armored hull.

"Wow, that Trophy system really works!" exclaimed Specialist Mann. He had the wide grin of a man who has been given a second chance at life.

Sergeant Cortez just shook his head, his face a little white from the near-death experience.

Captain Diss, unaware of his gunner's ghostly appearance, said, "Take over, Cortez, I need to get back on the company net." He looked at his video display of where his platoons were on the map.

"Red Four, this is Black Six," Diss began. "Give me a status on that missile swarm that was headed your way."

A couple of seconds went by before he heard a reply. "Black Six, this is Red Four. The MCD and Trophy system worked amazingly. I lost Red Three, but he was the only one to have taken a hit out of what had to be ten or more missiles fired at us."

"Good copy, Black Six, out."

Next, Captain Diss called out to his FIST team for help. "Black Eight, this is Black Six. I need two fire missions. How copy?"

"Black Six, this is Black Eight. Go for first fire mission."

"Fire mission, fire mission. Grid NC 7642 5642. One round, ground burst HE. Tanks and ZBDs hull down. Stand by for second fire mission. How copy?"

"Black Six, this is Black Eight. Good copy on first fire mission. Go for second mission."

"Fire mission, fire mission, Grid NC 3253 7642. Six rounds, ground burst HE. PLA missile teams hunkered down at the edge of Hatong Expressway. How copy?"

"Black Six, stand by on that last fire mission." A few minutes went by before the FIST team came back on. "I'm getting a negative approval on that last mission. It's in a heavily populated civilian center. Can you readjust fire mission over?"

"Stand by, Black Eight," replied Diss angrily.

He changed channels to his company net. "Red Four, this is Black Six. I need you to contact Black Eight and relay the coordinates you saw that enemy missile swarm originate from. Apparently, the coordinates I gave them are in a heavily populated civilian area. Get them a better grid, and lay four to six rounds on top of them. 1-5 and 1-9 Cav are following right behind us, and I don't want them getting ambushed by that group that hit you. How copy?"

A couple of beeps could be heard on the SINCGARS radio before it synced. "Copy that, Black Six. I'll get them for you. Out," came the reply.

BOOM!

Their cannon recoiled once more as Sergeant Cortez continued to call out targets and Specialist Mann kept loading the gun.

Captain Diss continued the work of managing his platoons until he was stopped by an incoming call. "Black Six, this is Mustang Six. How copy?" It was his battalion commander, breaking his train of thought.

"Good copy. Send," he replied. His mind was racing a million miles a minute just trying to keep track of his platoons and the artillery mission he had just called in. They were quickly approaching the second enemy line of defense.

"Good job on finding a way around Binzhouzhen and the ski resort," Lieutenant Colonel Johnson praised him. "God only knows what the PLA had waiting for us along the highway. I'm going to need you to continue to scout us a way either back on the Tonga Highway or the expressway—

whichever road you think will get us to our objective without taking a ton of losses. How copy, Black Six?"

"Good copy, Sir. I don't suppose it's possible to get a couple of scout vehicles sent up to my position?" Captain Diss asked.

"That's a negative. Scout units are further to our south and north, screening for us. This pocket of tanks and ZBDs your company engaged appear to be the only hostile units in our immediate area. Out."

With his orders adjusted for the time being, Diss pulled up their navigation system and plotted in the new waypoints. Once they were entered, he sent them out to the rest of his platoons so they could sync their systems with his.

They were less than forty kilometers from the city of Harbin. As they got closer to the major population center, their battalion would again swing south to avoid civilians as they pressed southeast using the various Chinese highway and expressway systems. Then they'd race just northwest of Changchun, where they would again avoid the major city.

They stopped for several hours to refuel and rearm before pressing on again. Only this time, they broke west of the city until they came to the outskirts of Bayantalazhen. There they waited for the rest of the division to catch up before they started their next drive. That stretch would lead them around the Jinzhou-Fuxin Line, giving them a clear shot at Beijing.

Chapter 11
Operation Warhammer

Near Mirs Bay, China

Sitting in the wardroom of the USS *Portland* amphibious transport dock, newly-promoted Lieutenant Colonel Tim Long could sense the apprehension in the air from his officers and senior NCOs. They were about to embark upon what would, in all reality, be the bloodiest campaign of the war to date—the invasion of mainland China. After a lot of changes to the original invasion plans over the last six months, it had finally been settled that the Allies would focus on the capture of several key Chinese cities and provinces as opposed to their initial objective of driving on Beijing and dividing the country up. It was hoped that this change in strategy would bring about a much swifter end to the war than the original plan President Gates had approved.

Tim Long was still getting used to commanding a full battalion; six months ago, he had been in charge of a company. Due to attrition in the officer ranks and the continued expansion of the Marines, the Corps had a massive shortage of officers and NCOs to continue filling out the ranks of the new units, and a lot of battlefield promotions had been going around.

Nevertheless, Lieutenant Colonel Long was there in the wardroom, and he decided he'd better make the best of it. He cleared his throat. "This is probably going to be the last time we all meet together for the next few days. It's going to get hairy once the action starts, so I want to make sure everyone fully understands what's expected of them and our overall objective," Long said. His men leaned forward, listening intently.

"Our battalion has been given the task of capturing the Yantian International Container Terminal and the harbor. This is going to be the 6th Marines' primary beachhead, so we need to secure this facility quickly. The PLA is going to throw everything they have at us to keep us from seizing this critical port. Knowing that, we've devised a plan that I believe will work."

He pulled up some maps on the video monitor. "McKnight's Never Company is going to air-assault in and secure Kuk Po Lo Wai Park for 1/10 Marines, who'll be arriving via LCACs. We're getting the entire battalion of artillery to come along with us. That gives us thirty 155mm howitzers for fire support."

Several officers let out low whistles, and others nodded in approval.

Long turned to look at the man who'd be in charge of protecting this critical brigade-level asset. "Captain McKnight, it's going to be imperative that Never Company holds the surrounding hills and approaches. The entire brigade is going to be depending on that fire support. I can't stress enough how important holding your positions will be," Lieutenant Colonel Long asserted.

McKnight nodded, adding, "You can count on us, Sir. No one's getting past us." McKnight was a Marine reservist who had joined Long's command four months ago after 4th Battalion had officially formed. In the civilian world, he was a high school wrestling coach in the fall and a track and field coach in the spring. He was tough as nails and had quickly earned the respect of his men.

Colonel Long relaxed a bit at McKnight's confidence and turned next to Captain Hammermill. "Oscar Company has the critical task of securing the beach near Boluoshan. It places you opposite the port we need to secure. Come hell or high water, you have to lock down those facilities as quickly as possible. Eliminate any threats and then push the perimeter out. The Navy's going to bring in a Ro-Ro ship that'll start offloading our LAVs and tanks."

Hammermill responded, "You've got it, Sir."

They spent the next two hours going over every element of the plan in detail, asking questions and making sure everyone knew what was required of them. Within twenty-four hours of landing, they'd be replaced by their sister battalion, 3/6 Marines. Then they'd head inland to work on securing the next set of critical ports around Chik Wan in the Shenzhen Bay area. This would completely isolate Hong Kong from the mainland and make it much easier to secure. It would also give them the necessary port facilities to quickly offload the rest of the division's equipment and get them in the fight faster.

****

The V-22 Osprey hugged the water as it approached the dark landmass. Every now and then, the pilot would jink to the right and then veer back to the left, just in case an enemy antiaircraft gun was lying in wait for them. In seconds, they were over Grass Island. They made their way toward Plover Cove Country Park and their final objective. Looking off in the distance, the pilots spotted tracer fire starting to lift off from Tong Yan Chung, where the port was.

The pilots deftly kept the Osprey just above the water and then the treetops, doing their best to keep themselves from becoming visible to the enormous amount of antiaircraft fire that had started to saturate the early-morning sky. Shortly after making landfall, the first several Ospreys flared their noses up and settled their giant tiltrotor aircraft down on mainland China. In seconds, thirty-two Marines rushed off. The dust and grass of the empty field before them would soon be turned into a massive artillery firebase.

Two other Ospreys landed their human cargo a kilometer further west, near the small village of Kai Kuk Shue Ha, while two more Ospreys dropped another platoon of Marines to the southwest, at a village called Tin Sam. Both of these platoons were to act as a blocking force and a tripwire in case PLA forces tried to head toward the soon-to-be-established Marine artillery base.

With several hundred Marines dropped off, the group of seven Ospreys turned back to the *Portland*, where they would begin the task of picking up the next company of Marines to ferry to the mainland.

******

While the Marines were air assaulting in hundreds of grunts to secure their objectives, the Navy had sent in six of their littoral combat ships; three of their smaller, swifter Cyclone fast-attack patrol boats escorted the eight LCACs that were bringing sixteen of the thirty howitzers ashore. Several other Cyclones raced in to the port facility and other key objectives to drop off several platoons' worth of Navy SEALS.

Boom, boom, BAM!

Captain McKnight looked off at the port facility a kilometer away and saw several large explosions billowing up into the night sky. He briefly caught the silhouette of one of the Navy's patrol boats as its chain gun raked an enemy position with hundreds of bullets.

"Give `em hell, boys," he muttered under his breath. Then he returned his attention to the task as hand.

"I want those trees down, now!" he roared. "We don't have much time left to get this area cleared out!" The half dozen Marines unraveling det cord around several trees dutifully sped up their process.

Once the howitzers showed up, they would gobble up nearly all of the cleared flatland in the area. His Marines needed to make sure they had a couple of working LZs set up to allow for more reinforcements to arrive and ammunition to continue to be flown in.

Twenty minutes later, McKnight heard the unmistakable noise of the LCACs racing in the water as they headed toward the beach. Captain McKnight hoped they would see the series of infrared lights his Marines had set up, directing the LCACs where to land. In minutes, the first monstrous hovercraft appeared out of the darkness and drove right up on the beach, continuing until it lurched forward in a stop at the signal of a Marine with a pair of handheld infrared signaling lights. Once the hovercraft came to a stop, the front ramp dropped. The first set of heavy trucks roared to life, rolling down the ramp while towing one of the M777 155mm lightweight howitzers behind it.

One by one, the other seven LCACs rolled in and started the process of getting the guns and their crews ashore. As the hovercraft were emptied, they started their engines back up and proceeded to head back to sea, where the sailors offshore would be anxiously waiting to send their next load in. While the artillery crews went to work on identifying where they wanted each gun to be placed, the roar of gunfire and explosions happening across the bay grew steadily in intensity. Captain McKnight observed more explosions blasting around the port area. Meanwhile, the Navy's patrol boats and littoral combat ships continued to move up and down the coast providing direct fire support wherever needed.

Twenty minutes after the first set of howitzers were ashore, the first of the sixteen guns started to deliver their first fire mission for the ground forces already heavily engaged across the bay. Minutes after the first howitzer started to fire, three more artillery cannons added their weight as well.

The Marines of 1/10 FA were inundated with fire mission requests. In short order, they had all sixteen guns delivering a sustained one to two rounds a minute for the Marines battling it out on the mainland.

******

As the Osprey circled the area below, Lieutenant Colonel Long spotted the two platoons Captain McKnight had placed as a blocking force to protect the newly established firebase. Despite the short timeframe, they looked well organized in their new positions.

Long turned to look out the other side. His other company had reached the port, and he could see that they were already pushing the perimeter out beyond it. Already, a group of Navy Seabees was hard at work getting the port's heavy equipment ready to start offloading the first Ro-Ro ship, which was already headed their way.

"You ready to head down, Sir, or do you want us to make another pass?" asked the pilot.

"I've seen what I needed to see. You can set us down now. Thanks again for letting me get a bird's-eye view of my guys," he answered.

The Osprey headed back down to the LZ McKnight's Marines had cleared out nearly an hour earlier.

Once on the ground, Lieutenant Colonel Long headed for the tent his headquarters staff had set up. When he walked in, he saw they had the maps up on the tent wall and the radios going. One of his staffers was plotting the location of the various companies and platoons in the city, as well as the enemy units they had either spotted or the UAVs had found. From the looks of things, there were several large PLA formations heading toward them now. Two were headed toward the docks, and the other was headed toward the lone platoon two kilometers away from their current position.

It was clear that platoon was going to need help soon. Turning to his S3, he asked, "When is Romeo Company going to arrive?"

"They're getting ready to leave the *Portland* now," he replied.

"I want them redirected to this point here," Long ordered. "We have a much larger force heading toward us and not enough Marines to defend this position. I also want a battery of those guns to shift fire and start hitting this location."

His S3 walked over to look at the map. Once he saw the number of enemy soldiers heading toward them he nodded. "You're right, Sir. That looks to be close to two battalions' worth of infantry headed their way."

Boom, boom. BAM!

Explosions vibrated the ground beneath them. Several pieces of shrapnel ripped right through one section of the tent, tearing into one of the map boards and hitting a Marine in the arm as he was updating it.

One of the sergeants in the tent began to administer first aid to the wounded Marine. "Corpsman!" he yelled.

Lieutenant Colonel Long raced outside the tent to see what had happened. He immediately spotted two of the artillery guns a couple hundred meters away, turned over on their sides. One of the trucks sitting between the two guns was also on fire, burning in bright orange flames.

His eyes swept toward the bay. One of the Navy's Cyclone patrol boats was on fire. It looked like the captain was trying to steer the endangered ship toward their patch of shore, away from the port.

Someone shouted, "Incoming fighters!" and pointed in the direction of the city across the bay.

The dark silhouettes of fast-moving objects appeared to be headed right for them. A couple of Marines who had been in the tree line ran out into the open field nearby, each raising a long tube to their shoulders. Seconds later, they each fired a Stinger missile at the incoming war planes.

One of the fighters fired a pair of missiles at the Ro-Ro ship tied up to the pier, while a second fighter shot off two more missiles at one of the littoral combat ships in the harbor. Two more planes continued their flight directly toward Long's firebase.

The littoral combat ship engaged the fighters with their RIM 116 rolling airframe missiles and CWIS system, splashing two of the five enemy planes. One of the Stingers hit the third fighter, which ripped apart and spiraled toward the ground with a trail of smoke behind it. The remaining two fighters continued to head for the artillery base Long's men had established.

Seconds later, the planes buzzed over their positions and four objects fell from their wings, tumbling end over end until they slammed into the ground.

Boom, boom, boom, BOOM!

The blast wave and concussion from the explosions hit Long across his entire body, blowing him completely off his feet and sending him tumbling backwards. The blast wave threw him and his soldiers around like the ragdolls of an angry toddler.

A series of secondary explosions rocked the base— some of the artillery propellant had caught fire and exploded. Colonel Long was vaguely aware of his surroundings, but the world was still a bit dim after being tossed about like that. As Long's hearing started to return and his brain slowly turned itself back on, the first thing he heard was the cries for help. Sitting up, he did a quick check of his arms and legs, making sure everything worked.

He looked nearby and saw the tent his headquarters staff had set up was largely gone, torn apart. Marines lay in heaps all around it. Down toward the artillery gun positions, he saw nearly half of the artillery guns had been knocked over or were destroyed. Small fires spread all over the base, along with the remains of the dead.

Long gingerly got up. He looked down and saw his rifle was still attached to his IBA via his single-point sling. Hearing cries from the wounded near his headquarters tent, he made his way over to the remnant to check on his staff. As he approached them, he heard one of the Marines crying, begging for help.

When he found the source of the desperate pleas, he saw Private First Class Luke Grabowski leaned up against several of the destroyed radios. He was using his one good arm and hand to desperately hold his intestines in and keep them from spilling out of a large gash in stomach, just below his body armor. His left arm appeared to be shattered and unusable.

PFC Grabowski looked up at him, tears streaming down his face. "Help me, Sir. My guts are spilling out of me and I can't stop it."

In that moment, Long wanted to turn away, to throw up or do anything other than walk toward the young man. But he knew he needed to help him. He moved quickly to the young man's side. "Hold on, Grabowski. I'm here now. Help will be here soon."

Long helped Grabowski slide down to lie flat on the ground. He grabbed Grabowski's first aid bandage and quickly applied it across the gash across his stomach. The bandage now held the man's innards where they belonged. He placed Grabowski's good hand on top of his abdomen.

"Hold this in place," Captain Long instructed gruffly. Then he grabbed his combat application tourniquet and tied off the crushed and bleeding part of Grabowski's left arm. Long knew he needed to stem the bleeding if the young Marine was to have any chance at surviving.

Turning to look for help, he spotted a group of Marines heading his direction. "I need a corpsman over here *now*!" he shouted.

One of the people in the group ran toward him at a sprint as the others trotted behind. The Navy corpsman immediately went to work on Grabowski. He gave him a shot of morphine and then did his best to get his abdomen wound sealed up.

"We need some medevacs here ASAP!"

"Romeo Company is almost here, Sir. Once they land, we'll load the wounded onto the Ospreys and get them brought back to the *Portland*. Are you OK yourself, Sir?" asked one of McKnight's lieutenants.

"I'm fine, but clearly most of my headquarters staff have been killed," he replied, waving his hand around at the torn and dead bodies. Many of these tattered remains represented Marines he had only known for a few months, most of them new to the Corps, fresh from training.

"I think you should set up with Captain McKnight, Sir. We have a command post over in that tree line," the lieutenant said, pointing in the direction of where he had just come from.

Lieutenant Colonel Long nodded. He knew the lieutenant was right. "Lead the way, Lieutenant."

As the two of them walked toward the CP, several other Marines looked for more survivors. Long glanced down at the beach; the second wave of LCACs was approaching, bringing with them the rest of 1/10's artillery battalion. He sighed. Of the sixteen howitzers that had landed in the first wave, only four of them were still carrying out fire missions. The rest of the guns had either been destroyed or disabled.

When they entered the tree line, Long spotted McKnight on the radio and he waved for him to come over. "Yes, Sir. He's right here," he said to the person on the other end. Then he handed the radio receiver to him.

"It's General Tillman," McKnight explained in response to the quizzical look Long had given him.

Long nodded. "This is Loki Six. Go ahead."

"Loki Six, this is Rogue Six. What's going on over there? I heard you guys got hit by an airstrike. Is your firebase still operational?" asked General Tillman, voice filled with concern.

"Two fighters plastered our position pretty hard," Long explained. "I lost my entire headquarters staff, and twelve of our sixteen howitzers are down. The rest of 1/10 just showed up, so we should have them operational shortly.

I've also got Romeo Company inbound in five mikes to reinforce our position. How copy?"

A minute went by before the radio beeped and the SINCGARS synced up. "Good copy. 3/6 Marines will head to shore in two hours. Can your battalion hold until they arrive, or do I need to push them to arrive sooner?"

"We can hold, Sir, but I need some air cover and gunship support. I have three battalion-sized formations heading toward our positions. Two are entering the northern side of the city heading toward the port, and the third is heading overland up the peninsula toward our firebase. How copy?"

"Good copy on all. I'll see what I can do about the air cover. I'm going to dispatch Attack Helicopter Squadron 167 to hit those targets for you. When 3/6 arrives, you need to do your best to have your battalion disengage and move to your next objective. How copy?"

Long sighed for a second. He could see McKnight shaking his head at him with a grin on his face. "That's a good copy, Sir. We'll be ready. My vehicles start to arrive on the next wave of LCACs. Out."

"He's eager to get us moving to Shenzhen, isn't he?" asked McKnight.

"Semper Gumby, McKnight. That's about all I can say. Speaking of that—when Romeo lands, I'm going to have them reinforce your second and third platoons on our perimeter. I need the rest of your guys to work on getting those new guns showing up ready. See if the gun bunnies need some help getting some of those howitzers turned back over. Maybe a few of them can be salvaged."

Long looked for a spot to sit down. He was still a little rattled from the airstrike that had wiped out his headquarters staff. So far, only two other Marines from his headquarters unit had survived unscathed.

Minutes later, they heard the thumping sound of the Ospreys' helicopter blades as the giant flying machines landed in the clearing they had built. The helicopters landed two at a time, disgorging their human cargo. As the newly arrived Marines ran off the back ramps, medics and others loaded the wounded Marines onto the helicopters to bring them back to the *Portland*, which had a level one trauma center.

As the newly arrived Marines headed toward their positions, Lieutenant Colonel Long walked out to find Captain Nickles, the Romeo Company commander.

Nickles saw Long and trotted over to him while the rest of his men filtered into the tree line. "It looks like you guys took a few hits, Sir," he said when he got closer.

"You could say that," Long said with a snort. "Listen up, Nickles—McKnight's got two platoons that are about to be a speedbump for an element that's at least battalion-sized and heading our direction." He pulled a map out and hastily pointed to it. "I need you to get your men over to this position here and hold the line. We've got some gunship support headed our direction, so use them as you see fit. Once McKnight's and your LAVs and JLTVs arrive, we'll mount up and head over to help you out. We need to push the PLA back to Sha Tau Kok. When 3/6 Marines land, the rest of our battalion will rally on us here, and then we'll take the Sha Tau Kok Road to the San Tin Highway and the Shenzhen interchange. From there, it should be a straight shot to secure the next port."

The two of them talked for a bit longer before Romeo Company took off at a quick trot to get in position. Meanwhile, the LCACs finished offloading the remaining guns of 1/10 FA and headed back to the ships offshore to pick up Long's battalion of LAVs and JLTVs to bring ashore, along with a company of tanks that had been assigned to them. The next few hours would see some of the heaviest fighting of the campaign as the PLA desperately tried to throw the invaders back into the sea before they could establish a foothold.

****

As he rode in the LCM-8 "Mike Boat," First Lieutenant Ian Slater thought he was going to get sick. Several of his soldiers had already puked their guts out, adding to the acrid aroma of diesel fuel, feces, and urine that wafted toward him from the front of the boat.

He found himself wondering how in the hell his company had gotten stuck doing yet another amphibious assault. *"I swear—I thought we had a Marine Corps,"* he thought angrily. Ian had fought in the slaughter that was the Second Korean War, then invaded Indonesia, then India, and now China. He wasn't sure his luck would hold out much longer.

BOOM, BOOM, BAM.

Explosions blared off in the distance, almost like the grand finale of a Fourth of July fireworks show. When their boat entered the Zhujiang River Estuary, Slater saw several small islands on either side of the LCM, and realized they were nearing their target. His battalion had been assigned the job of capturing a host of small islands throughout the

Zhujiang River Estuary and the mouth of the Shenzhen Harbor.

In front of them, two Navy littoral combat ships and several Cyclone patrol boats led the way. A couple of destroyers had even moved into the waterways with them. Looking behind them, Ian saw at least twenty of these Mike Boats following them in.

While their boat got closer to one of the islands, the sound of machine-gun fire and explosions emanating from the nearby cities grew in intensity. The night sky filled with antiaircraft fire. Green and red tracers crisscrossed back and forth across the sky, chasing after high-flying fighters and ground-attack planes and helicopters.

The thumping rotor blades of hundreds of helicopters filled Slater's ears—the battle for the industrial heartland of China was now in full swing. It was spectacular to see such an awesome display of war machines and military power, but also terrifying. He knew that tens of thousands of enemy soldiers were lying in wait to kill him and his fellow soldiers.

"Five minutes!" shouted the boat commander.

Lieutenant Slater turned his gaze forward. The island before them grew in size as they got closer. Shrouded in the pre-twilight darkness, the landmass looked ominous, shadowy and unknown. Seconds later, several starburst

194

rounds from one of the escort destroyers erupted over the top of the island, illuminating it in magnesium brilliance for them to see what lay in wait for them.

When their boat got within a hundred meters of the shore, green tracers started to reach out for their boat. Several of the rounds hit the front hatch, bouncing harmlessly off. Another string of rounds fired from a higher elevation came in at shoulder height, hitting several unlucky soldiers before they even made it to the beach.

The bottom of the boat scraped against the gravelly beach, and the front hatch dropped. Ian's soldiers raced off the boat as quickly as they could up the beach to the waiting arms of enemy machine guns.

Ratatat, ratatat, zip, zap, BOOM.

Green and red tracers strafed back and forth between the two lines of warriors, intermixed with mortar rounds, hand grenades and antipersonnel mines as the two sides fought the desperate battle of life and death.

"Take that bunker out!" shouted one of Slater's squad leaders.

Pop, swoosh...BAM.

One of his soldiers had fired his AT4 rocket, successfully blowing the machine-gun bunker apart. First Squad charged forward while Second and Third Squads laid down covering fire. When First Squad made it to the first line of enemy defenders, his soldiers jumped right into the enemy trench line, foxholes and machine-gun positions, letting out a guttural howl. The fighting quickly devolved into brutal hand-to-hand combat.

As First Lieutenant Slater ran toward the trench line with Fourth Squad, he saw several of his young privates and specialists using their bayonets against the enemy defenders. He witnessed one of his soldiers get shot point-blank. Another was stabbed to death by a PLA soldier. A few of them had thrown their rifles down to use their trench knives in close-quarters combat. This battle was already gruesome.

"Behind you, LT!" shouted one of his soldiers. Slater turned to see a wild, crazy-eyed PLA soldier screaming as he lunged at him with his own knife in hand. Slater twisted his torso just enough to miss the soldier's blade, but not before the soldier plowed into him, knocking his rifle from him. The two of them fell to the ground, and the PLA soldier landed on top of him. Slater grabbed at his own trench knife, pulling it from the strap on his IBA. With as much power and speed as he could muster, he rammed the blade into the side of the Chinese soldier's rib cage, feeling at least one bone crunch.

The soldier let out a guttural scream and tried to pull away from Slater's blade. As the knife ripped itself out of the man's chest, a geyser of blood erupted, spraying Slater's uniform. The enemy soldier staggered backwards and fell.

A loud roar of voices suddenly overtook the other sounds of war, intermixed with many high-pitched whistles. Slater got back to his feet and grabbed his rifle, and as he did, he spotted a swarm of enemy soldiers charging down toward them from further inland. Surveying his immediate surroundings, Slater saw that most of First Squad was either dead or wounded. Half of Fourth Squad was in the same shape.

"That's a lot of enemy soldiers!" yelled Sergeant Starr, Slater's platoon sergeant. The remnants of Second and Third squads jumped into the enemy positions they had just cleared.

"We need some damn fire support! Where's the rest of the company?" shouted Slater.

"Get those heavy weapons unleashed on that mob!" Sergeant Starr yelled to the squad leaders.

"Mitchem!" shouted Slater to his RTO. Seconds later, Specialist Mitchem plopped his body next to Slater, holding the hand receiver to the radio out to him.

Zip, zap, zip, zap, crump, crump.

More bullets flew over their heads. Some hit the sandbags right in front of them. Dropping to a knee, Slater grabbed the radio. "Ronan Six, this is Ronan One-Six. My platoon's secured Objective Alpha. I need help or we're going to be overrun!" he shouted.

BOOM, BOOM!

Slater lifted his head above the lip of the trench and saw several large explosions erupt amongst the enemy soldiers charging toward them. Many of the PLA soldiers were now seeking shelter amongst the shrubs, underbrush and secondary line of defense they had built. Despite that turn of fortune, the rate of enemy fire being directed at his men was tremendous. That kept his troopers' heads down, which would mean that squads of enemy soldiers would soon be bounding forward toward them again.

"Ronan One-Six, this is Ronan Six. Good copy. Hold your positions. Charlie Company is hitting the beach as we speak. They'll move forward to assist. Out!"

Shaking his head, Slater knew the other platoons must be in as much crap as they were. Sneaking a quick look behind him, he saw another wave of Mike Boats landing. *"That must be Charlie Company."*

Looking to his left, Slater shouted to Sergeant Starr, "Have the guys on your side of the line start laying covering fire for Charlie Company as they rush off the beach toward us."

Slater then dashed down to his right, making sure his guys were firing at the enemy. When he found one of his soldiers who'd been shot in the gut, just below his IBA, he stopped briefly to help get a pressure dressing set in place before moving on.

"They're charging!" shouted a young private, who was only maybe five meters from Slater's position.

"I need you to hold this in place, Private," said Slater hastily. "I've got to get back to killing them before they overrun us." The poor kid was bleeding pretty bad, but he just nodded through gritted teeth and unstrapped his Sig Sauer, in case he needed it.

Looking at the enemy charging again, Lieutenant Slater saw what must have been several hundred enemy soldiers rushing toward them. "*Where do they keep coming from?*" he thought with a mixture of awe and fear.

Raising his rifle to his shoulder, he sighted in on one guy and squeezed the trigger. *Pop, pop, pop, pop.* Enemy soldier after enemy soldier dropped as he carefully aimed each shot. A couple of the PLA soldiers got back up and resumed their charge; clearly some of them had been issued body armor. Slater changed his aim and pointed more toward their guts or midsection, where the body armor usually stopped. "*Aim small, miss small,*" he thought, taking a deep breath to calm his nerves as he continued firing. Slater's only goal at this point was to slow the enemy soldiers down until their own reinforcements arrived.

Several American soldiers jumped into the fighting positions Slater and his soldiers were occupying. One of the newly arrived soldiers plopped his M240G down with the bipod setup and swiftly tore into the advancing enemy. In seconds, the Americans had shredded most of the enemy soldiers before they finally broke and ran back, further into the wooded areas of the island.

In short order, the volume of fire directed at Slater and his soldiers tapered off until it nearly ended completely. With the first real break in fighting, Slater ordered his soldiers to help the wounded, getting them stabilized and then bringing them back to the beach area five hundred meters behind them.

Thump, thump, thump, thump.

The mortar platoon finally arrived and started to drop rounds in the tree line where the PLA soldiers had retreated. The soldiers of Charlie Company then advanced past Slater's company toward the tree line to pursue the enemy. Slater stood and surveyed the area. Everywhere he looked, he saw torn and broken bodies. Enemy and friendly soldiers called out for help, pleading for someone to save them, or at least be with them so they wouldn't die alone.

Captain Wilkes ran toward him. "Lieutenant Slater," he shouted, "I need your platoon to help move the wounded back to the beach area and work with the medics to get them loaded on the next set of boats that come in. I'm taking the rest of the company with me to go support Charlie."

Slater nodded.

With that settled, Wilkes shouted out to the other platoons. "Form up on me!" Soon he led the way after their sister company.

Lieutenant Slater turned to look for his platoon sergeant and found him helping one of their wounded soldiers with another medic. He walked over to check on them and saw his RTO, Specialist Mitchem, lying on the ground with his left arm ripped off. The medic was working on getting an IV in him.

"*I hadn't even noticed he wasn't by my side since I last used the radio,*" Slater thought, ashamed of himself for not having looked after his radioman. The kid had done a great job of staying by his side, and here Slater hadn't even known he'd been shot. He'd been so busy with trying to keep his platoon from getting overrun, he hadn't seen him get hit.

Kneeling down next to him, he placed his hand on his shoulder. "Hang in there, Mitchem. It'll be OK. Doc's taking good care of you now. We're going to move you back to the beach and get you back to the ship, OK?"

The young soldier looked at him, pain written all over his face and fear in his eyes, but he managed a nod. "You saved our platoon, Sir. I'm sorry I got shot and couldn't do more to help," he replied with tears streaming down his face.

"No, Mitchem. I should have been there for you," Slater answered, almost choking up himself. He'd lost so many soldiers under his command, but seeing Mitchem lying there like that really got to him in a way the others hadn't, not since his friend Joe had been killed in front of him in that bunker on the Yalu River in Korea.

"We need to get him back to the beach, Sir," the medic instructed. He and Sergeant Starr lifted Mitchem up and carried the young man to the aid station that had been set up.

A string of six Mike Boats pulled up to the beach, dropping their front hatches and allowing the next wave of soldiers to exit. This was Delta Company. A platoon of medical personnel also came ashore, along with a platoon of engineers. The medics rushed forward to the temporary aid station, immediately going to work on the dozens of wounded soldiers. Before any of the newly arrived boats could leave, one of the sergeants ran inside two of them, making sure they knew they needed to wait so they could load up the wounded.

As the four other boats pulled away, dozens of soldiers assisted in carrying nearly forty wounded Americans to the remaining two boats to be brought back to the motherships and a higher-level trauma center. Looking at the gravelly beach, Slater saw a lot of dead Americans still lying where they had shuffled off this mortal coil. Looking inland toward where his platoon had just been fighting, he saw more dead Americans covering the ground, mostly the soldiers of Alpha and Bravo companies, who had borne the brunt of the initial casualties.

Once ashore, the engineers went to work tying det cord to various trees not far from the beach. Their goal was to get a swath of trees cleared so the artillery battalion could start to bring their howitzers ashore. Big Army was determined to turn this little island into an artillery firebase. Being situated in the center of the Zhujiang River Estuary, it was spitting distance from all of the major ports in the area. The howitzers would be able to provide a solid twenty-four-kilometer radius of fire. The eighteen 155mm howitzers of the 1st Battalion, 108th Field Artillery Regiment, would provide one heck of a punch to support the Army and Marines as they continued to move inland.

****

Shenzhen, China
Futian Residential District

Bullets ricocheted off the armored shell of the LAV as Lieutenant Colonel Long's battalion continued to race down Binhe Avenue on their way to the Chiwan Container Terminal and the Shekou Container Wharf. His battalion had been in nonstop combat since they'd hit the mainland nearly twelve hours earlier. The PLA had rushed two brigades of motorized infantry into the city of Shenzhen, which had bogged them down for several hours. A company of battle tanks had finally been offloaded at the first port they'd seized, which had helped them break through the bottleneck they had been stuck in. Now they were rushing through the city, buttoned up in their armored vehicles as they raced to the two remaining ports they had to secure.

"Loki Six, this is Rogue Six. How copy?" asked Lieutenant Colonel Long's regiment commander.

Long depressed the talk button on the handset. "Rogue Six, Loki Six. Send it."

"How close are you to securing objectives Chiwan and Shekou?"

"We've broken through onto Binhe Avenue. Taking heavy small-arms fire as we race through the city. We're two kilometers from both objectives. ETA five mikes until we have a visual," he replied. His commander had been all over his butt for over an hour to secure their objectives. Never mind the fact that they only had three tanks left for heavy armor support.

"Good copy, Loki Six. Keep the pressure on. 3/6 is pushing to your north. The Army secured a new firebase for us. You're going to start using call sign 'Lightning Eight' for future artillery missions. 1/10 has been retasked to support 3/6 further north. Out."

"They changed our artillery support?" asked Long's S3, who was sitting next to him in the command vehicle.

"Yeah, looks that way...an Army 155mm battalion."

"As long as they can deliver steel-on-steel, that's all that matters," the S3 said, seemingly having a change of heart.

"We're approaching Objective Shekou!" shouted the turret gunner.

More rounds pinged off their armored shell. *Crump, crump, crump.* A handful of small explosions shook their vehicle, adding to the chaos that was going on all around them. The turret gunner returned fire at something, hoping to keep the enemy's heads down.

"Romeo Company is entering Objective Shekou," announced the vehicle commander. "Papa Company is continuing on to Objective Chiwan. Which location do you want us to stop at, Sir?"

"Go to Chiwan," Long ordered. "We'll set up our headquarters there."

Lieutenant Colonel Long turned to his S3. "Get on the horn to Sierra Company and tell them they need to head to our location. I want our mortars with us, along with the medical unit."

As they approached the outer part of the port, they saw a couple of buildings near the wharf and headed toward them. When they reached the building, several dozen Marines dismounted from the vehicles and began to clear the surrounding structures.

A few moments passed before Long got out of his command vehicle, and one of the sergeants walked up to him. "We've cleared the buildings, if you want to use them, Sir. They look to be warehouses for something."

"Good job, Sergeant. Yes, let's make this building the battalion HQ and the aid station. See if we can't get some machine guns set up on the roofs to act as lookouts and keep any enemy forces at bay. I want the LAVs to help create a perimeter as well," he directed.

His devil dogs went to work on transforming the terminal into a forward command center. While his Marines carried some of their equipment and radios into their newly acquired building, the rest of Sierra Company started to arrive. The mortar platoon went to work getting their tubes set up, ready to deliver fire missions. The medical section prepared their aid section, and two landing zones were quickly identified and prepped for use by medevacs.

Once they had their new HQ prepped, Long sent word out to regiment that his battalion had secured their objectives and were holding in place. He also let the other companies know they had the aid station up and running, so if they needed to start ferrying some of their wounded over they could.

In the distance, he heard the sound of rotor blades thumping. He stepped outside the new HQ and saw a pair of Cobra attack helicopters fly overhead on their way to support one of his companies. The Cobras were quickly followed by two Ospreys that had spotted them and headed toward their newly established LZ.

Once the helicopters landed, a platoon of fresh Marines trotted off, and a small group of men and women that he figured must be officers headed in Lieutenant Long's direction. Some of the corpsmen and their lone field surgeon rushed a couple of wounded Marines to the helicopters before they could take off.

"No sense in letting a perfectly good ride back to the fleet leave without evacuating our wounded," Long thought with a smile.

Brigadier General Tillman approached him. "Lieutenant Colonel Long, hell of a job securing these ports!" he shouted over the rotor wash and the distant sounds of battle.

Long gestured for them to head into the warehouse, where several of the newly arrived Marines worked on unloading a couple of pelican cases of radios and other gear they had brought with them. Once they were inside the building, Long turned to his mentor.

"Sir, we're still securing the area," he explained, concern in his voice. "My guys only got here thirty minutes ago. It's not safe to have you this far forward." Long had really taken a liking to General Tillman since he'd promoted him to captain. Working on his staff for five months prior to taking command of 4/6 Marines had taught him a lot about the man as a commander and a leader, and he respected him greatly.

Waving off the concern, Tillman replied, "Nonsense. I need to see what's going on up here at the front. Besides, I've brought another platoon of Marines with me. Once I get a sense of where the front is, I'm going to order 8th Marine Regiment in. I still have them sitting offshore, begging to be unleashed." He grinned. "Bring me up to speed, Long."

They walked over to a map board one of the sergeants had just set up. Perusing the map briefly, Long reviewed the locations of his Marines as well as the designations that showed which of his groups were currently engaged and which weren't seeing any action. "Right now, most of the heavy fighting is happening over in Sector Five, two kilometers north of where we are." While he spoke, they overheard several thumping noises. The mortar platoon must have started a fire mission.

General Tillman in approval. "OK, then that's where I'm going to unleash the 8th Marines. We've got to do our best to push the PLA out of the center of the city and secure a wide perimeter. I've got 2nd Tank Battalion on two Ro-Ro ships, navigating their way to the port right now. We need to get those tanks and other armored vehicles and equipment unloaded."

"We also need ammunition *bad*, Sir," Long insisted. "We're almost black on all types of ammo right now. We got one resupply before we fought our way through the city, but we burned through a lot of it securing these ports."

"Copy that. We'll start work on that now," Tillman replied. He turned to one of his officers, who swiftly walked over to the bank of radios one of the sergeants had just finished setting up.

The remainder of the day was a complete slugfest throughout the city once the 8th Marines and the 2nd Tank Battalion got ashore. The Chinese had moved several brigades of PLA militia forces into the city to try and slow the Marines' efforts to secure the city. During the second and third day of the invasion, the fighting largely devolved into house-to-house, block-by-block combat. Large swaths of the city were torn apart by the conflict. Millions of residents fled to the countryside, desperate to get away from the warring factions.

Chapter 12

Where's My Internet?

Fort Meade, Maryland
National Security Agency

"They're nearly done, Kate," Tyler Walden said as they observed the Chinese blotting the last few satellites from orbit. What satellites they couldn't destroy with their ground-based lasers, they'd used missile interceptors on. In the span of twelve hours, they had destroyed all but a handful of satellites.

Katelyn Mackie snorted. "I'm surprised they've waited this long," she retorted. "Our source said *soon*, and here we are nearly three months later, and they're just now finally doing it." She shook her head. It was hard to explain, but she was almost angry that the Chinese had waited until today to start taking out the world's satellite infrastructure, especially given their plan.

Mackie turned to look at one of the other analysts. "Are we up and running on their systems yet?" she asked.

"We sure are, Ms. Mackie. We're seeing everything they're transmitting, just like we thought we would."

A devilish smile spread across her face. "Now the tide of the war will swing in our direction," she said confidently.

Tyler was almost giddy with excitement at what they were seeing. His team had spent many weeks working on the code that would allow them to mirror the PLA's entire message traffic. "It's really working, Kate. We're really doing it."

"Let's just hope the people upstairs are able to capitalize on the treasure trove of information we're providing them," she said. "I heard they hired two hundred new linguists over the last six months in preparation for this moment."

The two architects of the Allies' modern-day Ultra system couldn't have been happier with their work than they were at that moment, seeing it fully operational for the first time. Soon, a continuous flow of intelligence would be making its way to the ground forces currently fighting inside China. They firmly believed this was the single strategy that would end the war much sooner than it would otherwise.

****

Washington, D.C.
White House

It was nearly 2000 hours when the President walked into the PEOC with his Chief of Staff, Josh Morgan, at his side. The various military leaders and advisors stood when the President entered.

"OK, gentlemen bring me up to speed," he said dejectedly as he took his seat. "Have the Chinese finished taking the world's satellites out?" he asked. He signaled for the others to take their seats as well.

"It would appear so," answered the Air Force general who had been monitoring the event with NORAD and the NSA. "The last handful of them will probably be destroyed when the PLA sends another wave of interceptors after them on their next pass over Asia."

The President turned to look at Katelyn Mackie. "It's official, then—the Chinese have moved everything over to their new UAV communication program?" he asked.

She nodded. "Yes, Mr. President. As soon as the switch happened, we got a flood of data transmitted to us. It's only been a few hours, but in that timeframe, we've been able to identify every location where the PLA have their nuclear missiles, mobile launchers and bombs stored. We're also starting to get livestreaming radio traffic coming in from the front lines: PLA units requesting reinforcements, new units being ordered forward, planned artillery or air strikes, etcetera. We've already been able to send multiple warnings to the ground forces of pending PLA assaults. In one case, they were able to shift enough air assets to the area that they completely destroyed the attacking units before they were able to get their offense underway. This is the game changer we needed, Mr. President." She spoke in a confident and optimistic voice.

The President relaxed a bit, and while his frown might not have turned into a smile, at least his expression was now neutral.

The generals and others at the table all seemed to breathe a collective sigh of relief that the program was actually working. There had been some concern for a time that the PLA had decided *not* to destroy the world's satellite infrastructure, which would have eliminated this new advantage of mirroring their communications network. Now that the Allies could see exactly what the PLA commanders were saying, where they were hiding their remaining aircraft, cruise missiles, ammunition or fuel stores and nuclear weapons, the Allies' ability to accurately hit these targets could very feasibly end the war in months as opposed to years.

The President's expression soured again as his mind turned to a different topic. "Speaking of our offensive—how are things shaping up in Guangdong Province? From what I'm seeing on the news, it looks like a bloody massacre on all sides."

Admiral Meyers nodded to Jim Castle to take this question. He cleared his throat. "Mr. President, we've landed a little over 90,000 Marines in the last forty-eight hours. The Army has another 22,000 soldiers on the ground as well. Our Australian Allies have landed one brigade along with a battalion of soldiers from New Zealand. It *has* been a bloody forty-eight hours, Mr. President, but our Marines have pushed the PLA out of Shenzhen, allowing us to capture the ports and the surrounding infrastructure intact.

"The ANZAC forces landing on Hong Kong should have the entire territory secured within the next twenty-four hours. They've captured the ports and the airport, and we're already putting them to good use. The Army for their part has captured the city of Macau and the surrounding area. We also ordered a single Army battalion to capture a small island in the center of the Zhujiang River Estuary. The Army's victory at Dongwancun Island has given us a secured place from which to launch both conventional artillery and rocket artillery support for the Marine forces in Shenzhen, the

ANZACs in Hong Kong, and the Army on Macau. It was actually a brilliant idea to capture that island—the PLA can't attack the artillery base with ground troops, so the base is pretty well protected," Castle concluded.

President Foss grunted. "Send my regards to that Army battalion," he said. "Make sure they get some sort of unit and individual awards for its capture. They're clearly saving a lot of lives by being there. What have our casualties been like, and how many more soldiers and Marines are we going to send in?" he inquired.

Admiral Meyers nodded, then glanced down at his notes before responding. "Starting with the US casualties, Sir, as of a couple of hours ago, we had 3,900 killed and another 5,000 injured. Some of those injured will be able to return to combat once they've been patched up. The ANZACs sustained 309 dead and another 1,800 injured. Right now, we have no way of estimating the PLA losses other than to say they have to be high. We've been fighting a lot of PLA militia forces, so those soldiers are not nearly as well-equipped or trained as their PLA counterparts."

The chairman flipped his notepad over and glanced at some numbers again. "Over the next three days, the Marines will be offloading another 90,000 additional men and their heavy equipment, tanks and added armored personnel carriers. The Army should have the Zhuhai International Container Terminal captured by tomorrow. It's roughly ten kilometers west of Macau and will give us a large port/cargo terminal on the western side of Guangdong Province. Once it's captured, the newly reactivated 2nd Armored Division or 'Hell on Wheels,' is going to be offloaded along with the 36th Infantry Division, which is a Texas National Guard division.

"The 38th Infantry Division from the Indiana National Guard will form up to create Army Group Three. They will move inland, skirting the major cities as they look to circle around to the western outskirts of Foshan. The Marines who'll form into Army Groups One and Two will take the more direct approach to Guangzhou and the surrounding cities and industrial centers. It's going to be a bloody campaign, Mr. President, with a lot of casualties. There's no way around that, but with real-time intelligence on the enemy's movements, we should prevail and gut the PLA's industrial heartland."

The President shook his head at the thought of how many young men and women were going to die in this brutal war. When he looked up, he turned to the Chief of the Air Force. "What about our bombers? What do we have left that can go after the PLA's munition, fuel, or nuclear capabilities?"

The general leaned forward. "We lost a lot of B-1 and B-2 bombers the past six months. Right now, we have just six B-2s operational with another four still either down for maintenance or being repaired from earlier battle damage. Northrop is still at least two years away from fielding the new B-21 'Raider' bombers, though we've been putting an enormous amount of pressure on them to try and get them operational within the next six months. We've been waiving literally hundreds of tests to try and get them into production. Right now, they have two prototypes that can fly and can carry bombs. They've been running through a lot of safety trials with those aircraft, but I don't believe they're ready for combat.

"As to the B-1s, we're down to twenty-nine of them, Sir. Our bomber force has taken a serious hit during these last few years of war. However, with the information we're getting from the NSA now, we can devise flight paths and bombing missions that avoid the heaviest pockets of enemy air defenses, and hit targets that we know will have an immediate impact on the war, as opposed to us hitting targets and hoping they will have the intended impact we want. There is no mistaking it, Mr. President—this information the

NSA is starting to provide us is going to make the limited bomber fleet we have a thousand times more effective than if we hadn't sustained any bomber losses at all."

The President nodded, then put his fingers together in the shape of a steeple. "I have two follow-up questions, General. One, what are our plans to hit the PLA's nuclear arsenal if they plan on using it? And two, if Northrop has two B-21 prototypes, why can't we try and use one of them in combat to test any potential problems out before it goes into full production?"

The Air Force general looked nervously toward Admiral Meyers and Jim Castle, as if asking for help. Castle nodded and then replied. "Sir, if I may—with regard to your last question, about the bomber—I'll inquire with Northrop to see if that's a possibility. We need to make sure it's actually ready to fly into a contested air space. It's an incredibly expensive aircraft to lose if it's not ready for combat, plus we wouldn't want to give the PLA an inside look at the bomber.

"As to your first question, regarding the PLA's nuclear weapons, right now, we're identifying where they all are. As we get those locations locked down, we'll come up with a plan for how to deal with them. I suspect it's going to involve us using a lot of Special Forces to carry out deep raids behind enemy lines and a series of precision airstrikes by our bombers. What we have to make sure of beyond a doubt is not only exactly where they are, but how many they have. If we attack their nukes and we miss any, they may go ahead and launch whatever they have left. We're still at least four months away from having another two hundred missile interceptors operationally ready, and as you'll recall, we spent most of our interceptors at the start of this war. Until they're replenished, I'm reluctant to recommend an attack at this time and risk a retaliatory attack that we're not prepared to defend against."

The President's brow furrowed, and then he ran his fingers through his hair. "All right, I can see the value in waiting on going after their nuclear capability, but we need to be ready to do so if we even catch a whiff that they may use them. With the walls continuing to close in, you can bet they're going to seriously consider it. As to the B-21, do what you can to get one of them into the fight. Have it carry out strikes in support of our ground forces or something, where it doesn't look like it may be in grave danger until we're more certain of its capabilities. We have a war to win and we need these aircraft operational ASAP, not two years from now when the war will be over. If Northrop can't meet the production deadline, then threaten to have another company take over the project. I want these bombers yesterday!" He smacked the table in frustration. Then he paused for a second and sighed. "By the time this war is over, we're going to need a lot of B-21s to replenish our bomber force. But first we need to win this war."

"Yes, Sir," Castle responded.

Foss took a swig of water. "OK, changing subjects— what's going on with our second landing that's supposed to capture Shanghai? Are we nearly ready to start?"

Admiral Meyers took this one. "We're still a month out, but, yes, we're nearly ready. Once the brunt of our forces is ashore in Guangdong Province, we'll shift our sealift capability back to Taiwan to begin preparation for the next amphibious assault."

The other service commanders nodded.

Josh Morgan, the President's Chief of Staff, asked, "What Allied forces are participating in this assault?"

"This assault will largely consist of our European forces that have relocated to the Pacific," Admiral Meyers explained. "The British will have several divisions involved, along with the French, Germans, Polish and other Allies. The Japanese will also have a couple of divisions participating, and for the first time since the Global Defense Force was formed, we'll have a brigade of soldiers from Brazil, one from Colombia and three brigades from the Israelis. The Israeli 35th Paratroopers Brigade will participate in the initial airborne attack, the 188th Armored Brigade will come ashore with our armored forces, and the 89th Commando Brigade—their Special Forces brigade—will largely augment our own Special Forces teams already fighting in various areas in China. In all likelihood, we'll probably have the Israelis focus heavily on being ready to go after the PLA's nuclear capability if that becomes necessary."

President Foss asked, "Have tensions with Iran receded enough that the Israelis feel they can deploy a large part of their army to fight with us in Asia?"

"They have, Mr. President," answered SecDef Castle. "The Saudis, Jordanians, Egyptians, Kuwaitis, and the rest of the Gulf States have pretty much told the Iranians that if they try to stir any trouble up within Iraq and Syria or attempt to attack Israel, then the Arab Alliance would go to war with Iran. For the time being, they've backed off their threats of war and have largely gone silent. I believe they're hoping to avoid incurring the ire of the Global Defense Force."

Several people snickered.

"OK, fair enough," said the President. "As long as they know that once these forces are committed, they're committed until we defeat the PLA. We can't evac their troops back to Israel for some national emergency."

Castle nodded.

The President stood. "I think we should break for the moment," he announced. "I've got a ton of domestic issues that are going to need to be dealt with now that the world's satellite infrastructure has been decimated." He paused. "I'm going to go ahead and cancel tomorrow's update and push our next war update to three days from now. Please continue with the plans we have in place. If anything major changes, then of course loop me in, but otherwise, run things through Tom and Josh for the time being."

The others in the room stood out of respect as the President left, and then they got to work issuing a few remaining orders and tasks before the night shift took over to keep things running.

Chapter 13
Why Isn't Google Working?

London, England

10 Downing Street

Water glasses were either half-empty, or mostly-empty within the first thirty minutes of the cabinet meeting. The black tablecloth had already shifted a few times as various members moved their notepads around in front of them. As was their usual Thursday custom, each side of the table was taking their customary few minutes to rant or brief the Prime Minister.

Prime Minister Rosie Hoyle continued to sit patiently in her chair. The clock indicated they were now forty-five minutes into their weekly meeting. Noah Grayling, the Secretary of State for Transportation, was railing against the Americans for not sharing in advance what the Chinese were planning to do to the global satellite infrastructure.

When MP Grayling stopped long enough to catch his breath, Greg Hancock, the Secretary of State for Business, Energy and Industrial Strategy, jumped in. "This is ludicrous!" he exclaimed. "The Americans have once again blindsided us and the rest of Europe by not telling us in advance what was going to happen. Now the world's entire satellite infrastructure has been destroyed without so much as a warning. Had they at least informed us, we could have taken steps to prepare the economy and the people for what was about to happen. The loss of our satellites is wreaking havoc on an already-fragile economy. My daughter asked me last night why Google wasn't working…my own daughter! You need to do something about this, Prime Minister!"

Raising her hands, PM Hoyle signaled for them to calm down and allow her to speak. It took a couple of minutes for the raucous group to silence themselves. "I spoke with President Foss three hours ago about this very issue. He informed me that at the time they discovered this nefarious plot, Prime Minister Chattem was the current PM. As such, they didn't feel that they should share this information with him out of fear that he would leak it to the Russians or the Chinese."

MP Damien Mundell, the Home Secretary, asserted, "Then why did President Foss not make us aware of this once PM Chattem had been removed from office? It doesn't seem right that the Americans should have withheld something so vitally important to us. This goes against the 'special relationship' the UK and America are supposed to have had."

They weren't alone in their sentiments. The mood on the street with the average British citizen was even more vitriolic toward the Chinese for what they had done and the Americans for not warning Britain in advance of what might be headed toward them.

PM Hoyle sighed audibly, like she did when her young daughter or son wanted something really expensive and she had already said no' "Listen, *Chattem* hurt our 'special relationship' with the Americans deeply— apparently more deeply than we had initially thought. President Gates, and his successor, Foss, lost trust and faith with Britain. For years leading up to the war, they've seen nothing from us but anti-American, anti-Gates protests; then when the war broke out, PM Edwards's initial lack of support to NATO, and then Chattem's outright betrayal, put our nation in a bad light with the Americans. They don't trust us. Even now, if you look outside the security cordon, what do you see? Endless protests to end the war, and anti-American sentiment. We haven't exactly been a champion of American support, despite the horrific losses they've sustained. Let's not forget, the Americans already lost over a million civilians when the cities of Oakland and San

Francisco were nuked at the beginning of the Korean War, and over a hundred thousand American soldiers have been killed fighting in Europe for a third time in less than a hundred years.

"We have a lot of reputational repair to do with our American brothers before I believe they will trust us with their innermost secrets again." She paused for a second before adding, "If it makes you feel any better, they didn't warn any of the other European allies either. Putting this aside, let's discuss what we're doing to make sure the loss of our satellites doesn't have a long-term negative side effect on the economy or the country."

Home Secretary Damien Mundell responded, "I have a video telecom with my counterpart in the US. After reviewing the road ahead, it looks like she is going to discuss with my department what the US is currently doing to mitigate the loss of the satellite infrastructure. Apparently, they had been working with Google, SpaceX, Facebook, Amazon and a few other technology giants well in advance and have come up with some sort of plan they feel will work around this newly created problem. I'll have more to brief to you all on this next Thursday."

Several attendees nodded in approval.

MP Greg Hancock interjected, "My department has been working diligently with BT and Deutsche Telekom to get our communications and internet services back up and running. While our local telephone services have thus far been unaffected, our ability to make overseas calls has been seriously degraded. We've spoken with our American colleagues, and for the time being, all overseas calls, international time syncing, and the internet are going to be rerouted though the underseas cables.

"The American Department of Homeland Security has established an atomic clock, located at their Massachusetts Institute for Technology in Boston. It's the central focal point for their internet activity, and also their connectivity to the rest of Europe and the world. This atomic clock is piped into the internet exchange, ensuring that all connections from the outside world to the American internet are time-synced through them. We're establishing our own atomic clock syncing in Newquay, on the west coast of the country, where our underwater sea cables connect with the ones in America. The French and Germans are likewise setting up the same system where our cables connect with them, and their cables connect with the Americans. It's going to take a few days to get everything sorted, but once we have this set up, it's going to solve a lot of the latency problems and issues we've been having with the internet," he concluded.

"Greg, can you take a moment to elaborate on why this time clocking is so important?" asked PM Hoyle for the benefit of the others in the room.

Sighing at having to explain something technical to a nontechnical crowd, he nodded and proceeded to explain the issue. "The loss of the global GPS satellites immediately affected the world's economy in many different ways. First, GPS satellites essentially act as highly accurate and synchronized atomic clocks in space, transmitting a uniform time signal to earth. Our receivers on the ground, like your car or smartphone, pick up these time signals from three or more satellites and then compare that time. That allows the device on earth to know exactly where it is. The reason why that's so important is because we live in an era of just-in-time delivery of nearly everything."

Seeing some of the MPs were not totally tracking what he was saying, MP Hancock tried to elaborate. "When your wife or husband goes down to the grocery store to buy some groceries, those items are scanned at the checkout counter. That item is deducted from the number of items the store currently has in stock. When that item hits a certain level of inventory, the store's inventory system will generate a request to restock that item from the grocery store's warehouse. The warehouse will then dispatch a delivery truck the following day with the requested items to restock the store. Likewise, when the warehouse runs low on something, it sends a restocking request to its food producers, and so on. When the GPS satellites go down, then the computer systems won't be able to automatically route the delivery trucks to restock the grocery stores. The warehouses and grocery stores will have to fall back on manual systems to do this. This will cause delays in deliveries for the entire supply chain. This is a serious problem because most grocery stores, pharmacies, and other stores currently typically only hold seventy-two hours' worth of grocery products. This is largely done because of limited storage space at a grocery store, and to limit the amount of food waste that would happen if a store overstocked an item and it didn't sell."

Hoyle could see that everyone was starting to grasp the seriousness of the situation. Hancock continued, "For better or worse, our infrastructure is held together by time. Time stamps on financial transactions are the very protocols that hold the internet together. When packets of data are transmitted between computers and the internet nodes get out of sync, the entire system starts to break down. That's why the Americans immediately began to run all of their external communication cables through their ground-based atomic clocks. This latency issue from being out of sync may cause considerable problems in nearly every aspect of our economy, which is why it's critical that we get it under control."

The rest of the meeting was spent on figuring out what needed to be done to get the country stabilized and ready to deal with the new reality of no satellites, at least until the end of the war.

****

Berlin, Germany
German Chancellery

Chancellor Schneider read over a report from Federal Minister of Transport and Digital Infrastructure Jens Scheuer on how they were going to fix the current internet and communications problem the country had been experiencing the past forty-eight hours since the Chinese began to systematically destroy the world's satellite infrastructure. As she read, she silently nodded in agreement. The others in the room stared silently at her, waiting to see what she would say next.

She finally looked up at Minister Scheuer and smiled. "This is good," she responded. "More than good—this is excellent. You said the Americans sent this to you earlier today?" she asked.

Minister Jens Scheuer nodded. "Yes," he replied. "It was the first thing in my inbox. My office has been working with Deutsche Telekom since this morning, and already we've been able to mitigate the latency issues we've been having with our internet. Once we have everything running through our own atomic clock and synced up with the Americans, our internet should be functioning more or less as it was before. We'll still experience some bandwidth issues, but this will resolve a lot with regard to searches and queries."

Minister of Economics Peter Maas interjected, "This will solve part of our problem, but the other issue we have is with our logistics and supply chains. Most organizations have no way of being able to track where their orders are or if they have been delivered. These are serious issues that aren't going to be quickly solved, even once our internet has been properly time-synced with the Americans and the rest of our EU and Allied partners." He looked thoroughly exhausted and haggard.

"These are issues that we will continue to work through, Minister Maas," Chancellor Schneider assured. "We're only a few days into this newly created crisis. The Americans have given us a series of plans and solutions to put into place. I suggest we move forward with them and give them a chance to work. It's not as if we have much of a choice; the Chinese, who are losing this war, have decided to cause as much chaos and disruption to the rest of the world as possible. We now have to adapt to that change. We can do this. We're Germans...we *will* adapt." She spoke with energy and defiance in her voice.

Schneider turned to her Minister of Defense. "Are our forces in Asia ready to do their part?" she asked.

Ursula Klöckner smiled. "Yes," she answered confidently. "We have nearly 30,000 soldiers positioned in Taiwan for the next major operation, the capture of Shanghai. We have another convoy of soldiers and equipment arriving over the next two weeks, and it'll add an additional 15,000 soldiers to our contingent. The Americans have not asked for any additional German forces to be sent to Asia beyond what we've already committed. However, they have requested that we keep roughly 90,000 soldiers on permanent occupation duty in Russia for the next five years. At the five-year mark, another drawdown in occupation forces will take place, and at that point, we'll learn how many soldiers the Alliance will release back to Germany."

Chancellor Schneider shook her head in disgust. There had been some question as to how many soldiers Germany would keep in Russia for the occupation. Schneider's government had campaigned hard not to have to keep a substantial force in Russia. Having to support and sustain a large force would be both costly and difficult to maintain when they returned their economy back to its peacetime status. She was not at all happy about keeping that many of her soldiers on duty.

"I'd rather send more forces to Asia and know they will come home at the end of the war than to have to maintain a substantial occupation force," she huffed. "Did General Cotton provide an explanation for why he wants Germany to bear the brunt of the occupation duty?"

"You mean as opposed to the Americans?" retorted the Defense Minister sharply.

"That's not what I meant."

"No but it's what you and the others were thinking. I spoke with General Cotton, and he told me that US is most likely going to have to maintain a larger occupation force in China. As such, he wants to focus most of the occupation duties in Europe, to be supported by Germany, France, and Poland as the main contributors."

Schneider's scowl loosened slightly. "What area of the occupation will Germany be responsible for?" she asked.

"Germany has been given responsibility for the territories just east of Moscow through to the center of the country, with a specific emphasis on improving the Russian rail and road infrastructure. I believe the overarching plan is to enable Russia to exploit more of its natural resources and to have a more diverse economy, less focused on oil and natural gas. In either case, it's an enormous engineering task that's quite suited to our strengths as Germans. The main drawback I see is that it's a tremendous amount of territory to cover, and a lot of people who will be in need of help."

"And what of the French and the rest of the alliance?" inquired Chancellor Schneider.

"France will be largely responsible for the Baltics all the way to the White Sea. Essentially most of western and northern Russia. They will be augmented by the Dutch. The Americans, for their part, are going to handle Moscow and most of central Russia and into Ukraine and Belarus. They will also be maintaining an occupation force of roughly 110,000 soldiers. Nearly all of their other forces have been sent to the Russian Far East or to Asia," Klöckner explained.

"You left out the British. Where are they in all of this?"

Klöckner snorted. "The British have been excluded from the Russian Provisional Authority at the request of the Americans and the Russian government. Apparently, neither side trusts the British after the whole Chattem debacle. Right now, the British are relocating their military force to fight in Asia. They will likely participate in a similar occupation program in Asia, but their influence in postwar Europe has essentially been cut off at the knees."

Some of the others in the room snickered at the situation the UK had found itself in.

"They are going to have to mend a lot of fences," thought Chancellor Schneider. *"Some fences cannot be fixed overnight."*

Chapter 14
Domestic Affairs

Tampa, Florida
James A. Haley VA Hospital

Jillian Limpkey was exhausted as she silently slipped into a chair at one of the tables against the wall of the cafeteria. All she wanted to do was drink her cup of java and eat a banana. It had been a long and trying twelve-hour shift and she felt emotionally drained. Another wave of wounded soldiers from overseas had arrived at the start of her shift, and it had been hectic ever since. Trying to get the four hundred new arrivals in-processed and settled into their new surroundings and their families notified of where their loved ones were located was a daunting task. Yet it had to be done. The military hospitals were filled beyond their limits, the VA had to step in and help augment them as best they could. Even the VA system was starting to be overwhelmed, though. Some veterans were having to be given "Choice Cards" to see outside providers because of how maxed out the system was.

As Jillian sipped on her coffee and finally managed to eat a bite of food, she saw one of the doctors pay for his coffee. The two locked eyes for a moment. The physician smiled warmly at her and slowly walked in her direction. He stopped just in front of her chair.

"May I join you?" he asked.

She liked Dr. Stephen Payne. He was in his early forties, single, and attractive. He had a great bedside manner, too. His specialty was spinal injuries, which sadly made him in high demand with this war. Of course, the James Haley facility also had a spinal cord injury center and a new high-rise bed tower, giving the hospital a lot more bed space and specialty facilities to handle this type of care.

"Sure, Dr. Payne," Jillian replied with a warm and inviting smile.

Jillian was one of the many nurses that worked with Dr. Payne. She'd been a nurse for six years now, four of them at the VA. She loved working for the VA; although she'd never had a personal desire to serve in the military, her job still gave her the opportunity to serve those who'd made that selfless decision. The last two years, however, had been incredibly difficult. Seeing all these young men and women return home from the front lines so injured had taken a toll on her. In her mind, so many of them were kids—not even old enough to buy alcohol, but they were old enough to be drafted and have an arm or a leg blown off for the sake of their country.

Sensing Jillian was having a tough day, Dr. Payne reached his hand across the table and gently squeezed hers. "It'll be OK, Jillian. You did a good job today. I see you out there, reaching out to the families, getting people into their rooms. It's obvious you give your patients a lot of care and attention."

Jillian almost burst out in tears at that moment. While trying to maintain her composure, she managed to choke out, "I just don't know if I can keep doing it. These guys are so torn up. I checked in one airman—in addition to becoming paralyzed below L2, she lost her left arm in the blast that sent her here. Can you imagine the struggle of living life with only one functional limb? And a few patients recently only made it to us after they'd graduated from the burn unit. I can just picture how many cruel people would shun someone in a wheelchair with scars on their face and hands." She buried her face into her hands, sobbing uncontrollably.

Dr. Payne got up and moved his chair to be next to her. He wrapped his arm around her. She buried her face into his shoulder, and he just let her release all the pent-up emotions she'd been burying.

After a moment, she seemed to be catching her breath, and Dr. Payne said, "It'll be OK, Jillian. That's why they have us. We'll do the best we can to patch them up and let them know that while life may be more difficult for them, it can still be rewarding, and filled with love and appreciation."

Through tear-filled eyes, she looked up at him. "I hope you're right. I really do."

The two of them sat there in the cafeteria for a little while longer before Jillian headed home to try and get some sleep before she would start it all over again the following day.

****

Lima, Ohio
Beer Barrel Pizza & Grill

"Everyone, raise your glasses!" shouted Sheriff David Grant as he lifted his beer mug high. "It's been almost a year since Deputy Eric Clark and Cindy Morrison were killed by those Russian bastards. Tomorrow, my own son ships out to Asia with the Army to go fight the Chinese." He paused as he looked at his son, placing his hand on his shoulder. "Tomorrow, you leave to go get some payback for

240

what all these people have done to our country, our state, and our community here in Ohio. I couldn't be prouder of you than I am right now, Son." He started to get a little emotional, and as he choked back tears, he pulled his son in tight and gave him a bear hug.

The rest of people in the restaurant erupted in cheers and applause. They all clinked their beer glasses together.

"Congratulations!" several of them shouted.

Several of them came by to give him a pat on the back and wish the young man well on his upcoming journey. Sheriff Grant's son had the backing of the entire town, and he knew it.

The community of Lima, Ohio, had really come together after the vicious attack on the General Dynamics Land Factory the year before. The tragedy had struck a chord with everyone there, and no one had been left unaffected; over five hundred people had been killed, and it had taken more than two days to put out the fires from the refinery. Despite all that had happened, everyone had rallied together to support each other in their time of need. They'd even managed to get the plant operational again, and it was successfully churning out main battle tanks off the assembly line just three weeks after the fateful day.

Chapter 15

Deception

Taiwan International Airport

Camp Victory Base Complex

General John Bennet rubbed his temples; he felt another migraine coming on. A jackhammer seemed to be pounding away inside his skull, and each sound seemed amplified, bone-jarring, even. The light overhead burned its way into his head and his vision blurred. He knew he had been pushing his body too much, that he needed to take a break, but men were dying every second of the war.

"If they have to push through their infirmities, then, by God, so will I," he thought. *"They're counting on me."*

Major General Tony Hyrczyk walked into the general's office, a Rip It energy drink in one hand, and a couple of pills for the general in the other. Placing the medication and energy drink on the desk next to Bennet, he whispered, "I could tell you're having another one of those migraines, so I brought you the usual cocktail."

Bennet looked up at his friend, smiled weakly and nodded. Without hesitation, he grabbed the pills, tossing them down his throat as he popped the top of the energy drink and proceeded to wash them down. Within moments of the sudden rush of caffeine and sugar to his system, his headache had already subsided enough for him to continue on.

"So, what's the word? Has the PLA taken the bait yet?" Bennet inquired.

"Hook, line, and sinker. It's working just as you predicted it would," Hyrczyk replied with a broad smile on his face.

Bennet stood. "I knew this plan would work," he said, almost managing a smile of his own. "OK, let's go tell the others of the change in plans. It's time we got the rest of the team up to speed on our little ruse."

The two of them left his office and headed down the hall to the operations room, where he found the rest of the Allied generals and military commanders already waiting for him.

General Bennet saw the apprehensive looks on the faces of the military commanders who stood around the briefing table, and he knew exactly why they all looked as they did. Everyone had grown impatient with keeping all their forces in a holding pattern off the Korean coast. He'd already heard someone mutter something about the airborne divisions being held in Taiwan too long.

Lieutenant General Sir Simon Carter of the British contingent was the first to voice his opinion. "General Bennet, I have some serious concerns about launching this invasion. Our forces have been marshaled too close to Qingdao for too long. My own intelligence and reconnaissance groups believe the PLA is more than alert to our plans of invading and securing the ports there. Are we still going to go through with it?" he asked.

"If everyone will please take their seats, we'll provide you all with an update on Operation Olympus," Major General Hyrczyk announced.

The generals and admirals dutifully sat down. General Bennet looked at the men and women before him: generals and admirals from Germany, France, Japan, Australia, Poland and Israel. These military leaders represented more than three hundred and forty thousand Allied soldiers, sailors, Marines and airmen that would embark upon the what everyone hoped would be the final major campaign to end the war.

"The invasion of Qingdao...has been an elaborate ruse," Bennet explained. He waited calmly for the reactions before him. Some were clearly shocked; others appeared angry. A few shook their heads. A couple of them let out a soft snicker, seeming to understand that something else, something bigger, was about to happen.

General Bennet held up his hand. "Before any of you launch your complaints or hurl questions at me, let me explain to you what has taken place. Since the start of the year, we've been building a deception campaign to trick the PLA into believing we were going to launch a massive ground invasion at Qingdao. It's the most logical location for us to invade from the sea as it has several deepwater port facilities and it would give our forces a straight shot at Beijing. Couple that with our offensive operations in northern China, and we've been able to make the PLA believe our entire offensive was going to focus on capturing their capital.

"When we invaded Guangdong Province, we kept the other Allies out of that invasion because we wanted to continue the deception that we were still planning on invading Qingdao. That invasion of Guangdong Province has also forced the PLA to send multiple divisions away from Shanghai to stop us from ripping the industrial heartland of southern China apart. Which is perfect, because our real objective is to capture Shanghai and the surrounding area."

Someone let out a low whistle. General Hyrczyk brought up the real invasion plans on the computer monitors.

Lieutenant General Alfred Guderian, Commander of the German Expeditionary Forces, spoke up. "The Chinese Air Force recently deployed their new advanced unmanned fighter drone. Wasn't the reason that you Americans attacked Guangdong Province so that you could go after the facilities producing these fighters?" he asked with a quizzical look on his face.

"That is partially correct," Bennet answered. "The GDP of Guangdong Province is roughly $1.42 trillion US dollars, which means the province contributes approximately 12% of the country's gross domestic product. However, in terms of military production, the province is responsible for more than 70% of their entire aerospace industry. When Shenyang was destroyed during the first day of the Korean War, the majority of the PLA's aerospace industry was wiped out, so they expanded the aerospace footprint in Guangdong Province, which is why so much of the industry is concentrated there now.

"So, yes—we did target the province because of their new UAV fighter. However, our attack there was not limited to disrupting that one specific war fighting element. In addition to the increase in aerospace production, a disproportionate amount of the Chinese small-arms munitions is produced in the Guangdong region. The Pentagon planners believed that if we could target key sectors of their military industrial sector, we could begin to create a massive shortage in their war production and potentially end the war sooner," Bennet explained.

"This makes logical sense, but why shift our focus away from Beijing to focus on Shanghai?" quizzed Brigadier General Sami Barak, the lone Israeli general commanding the Israeli contingent.

General Bennet leaned forward in his chair and made eye contact with General Barak. "Money," he answered. "Our attack in Guangdong is going to rip their manufacturing heart out, and Shanghai is going to rip their bank away. Without a military manufacturing base to produce the weapons of war, and without a financial sector to support the war, the PLA will have to agree to our terms of surrender."

Suddenly it all made sense to the generals at the table. The Allies didn't need to capture Beijing or even large swaths of China. They only needed to take away their ability to make money and produce the weapons needed to wage war. With those two components gone, the PLA would implode in on itself.

"In two weeks, gentlemen, we'll launch Operation Olympus and end this bloody war," Bennet said. He signaled for the new orders to be handed out.

Chapter 16

Operation Olympus

Shanghai, China

Pudong International Airport

"Take that machine gun out *now!*" shouted Sergeant First Class Conrad Price. One of his squad leaders leveled his M240G at the PLA soldiers and let loose a long burst of automatic fire as he stitched up the location they were hiding behind.

Zip, zap, zip, zap. Crack...BOOM.

Gunfire and explosions were still ravaging parts of the Pudong Airport perimeter, and the Ranger companies struggled to secure the area.

"Sergeant Price, we need to get this perimeter pushed out to Airport Avenue Road!" yelled Captain Martinez. "The 82nd is starting to arrive, which means the heavy transports are hot on their heels. Get that parking garage secured!" He waved to the dozens upon dozens of parachutes opening up in long lines across the runways of the major airport.

Turning to his soldiers, Price yelled, "Second Squad, let's move! Third Squad, lay covering fire!"

Lifting his own rifle to his shoulder, Price took aim at a three-story parking garage maybe 200 meters away and fired off several shots at the PLA soldiers firing at them.

Pop, pop, pop.

Green tracers suddenly flew right at him. He sprinted the ten-meter distance to jump behind an airport utility truck.

Crunch, crack, ding, ding.

Bullets slapped into the metal frame of the vehicle. Price did his best to stay hidden until the gunner moved on to another target. Looking back briefly, he saw strings of green tracers flying out toward the paratroopers who were now covering the horizon in parachutes.

Shifting on his back leg, Price popped his head above the back of the utility truck long enough to see the PLA machine gunner fire another string of rounds at a couple of his other soldiers who were bounding forward from vehicle to vehicle as they steadily got closer. Seeing that the gunner was occupied, Price took this moment to run the forty meters of open ground in front of him to a drainage ditch in front of a side road that led to the parking garage.

Several of his soldiers followed him forward, running with all their gear on like they were trying out for the US Olympic team.

"Ten more meters and we're there," he thought. A giant green light flew right for his head.

Snap, snap, snap.

Price nearly tumbled end over end as his body did some sort of acrobatic diving, twisting move into the drainage ditch in a herculean effort to avoid the bullets whipping past his skull. He could feel the heat of the bullets, the air pressure changes with each metal object flying past him. That he didn't get completely torn apart by them was a complete miracle.

As he struggled to right his body in the ditch, dirt and grass rained down on him and the three soldiers that had made it into the ditch with him. Looking back, he saw one of his soldiers lying on his back, both of his hands pressed tightly against his throat as his legs thrashed around, blood squirting through his fingers with each pulse. In seconds, the soldier stopped moving and his body went limp. Another soldier lay on the grass a few feet away, facedown and clearly dead; blood pooled all around him.

"We're too exposed out here. We have to get to the base of the parking garage," Price thought.

Enemy tracer fire shifted from their position to one of his other squads, allowing Price and his two other soldiers to poke their heads above the ditch to see in front of them.

"I think I can hit that position with my 203, Sergeant!" yelled one of the specialists with him. Price glanced down and saw the M203 grenade launcher the soldier had attached to the bottom of his M4.

Price nodded to the soldier. He and the other sergeant with them fired at the PLA soldiers on the third floor of the garage.

Thump...boom.

Thump...BOOM!

"Now! Let's go, go, go!" yelled Price. He launched himself forward out of the ditch to cross the last thirty meters to the base of the parking garage.

It took them less than a minute to race across the open ground, and they found themselves outside the reach of the enemy soldiers above them. As Price scanned the field behind them, he saw Third Squad was still at their starting location, continuing to lay down covering fire on the enemy positions. One of the fire teams from Second Squad was nearly to them, while First Squad was pinned down halfway between them and the parking garage.

"We need to make our way up the garage and clear it out," Price said to the two soldiers still with him. They both nodded and the three of them entered the multistory parking garage.

Steadily, they made their way to the stairwell in the south corner of the garage. As they cleared the stairwell, they systematically moved their way up from the ground floor to the second floor. Pausing for a second at the second-floor door, Price could still hear shooting, but it didn't sound like it was originating from that floor.

They continued up to the third floor. While one Ranger aimed his rifle ahead to the landing, his two buddies moved forward; then the next guy would keep his rifle aimed at the next level while they repeated the process, methodically clearing the stairwell until they reached the top platform and the final door.

Price dropped his magazine and examined it. "Eight rounds left," he said to himself. He placed the magazine in his drop bag and grabbed a fresh thirty-round mag, slapping it in place.

His other two soldiers took the cue and did the same thing. Then Price reached down and slowly turned the door handle, almost holding his breath as he did it. The other soldiers had expressions on their faces that registered both fear and adrenaline-fueled anger. None of them were sure what was waiting for them on the opposite side of the door.

As he pulled slowly on the doorknob, Price saw a string of cars parked against the outer and inner walls of the parking garage. Toward the far side of the garage, he saw a smoking ruin of a car and a couple of dead bodies.

"That's what our grenade launcher just hit," realized Sergeant Price.

Suddenly, they heard the *ratatat* of a heavy machine gun opening fire, along with several voices shouting in Chinese. A couple of AK-74s joined the chorus of death blasting out to the rest of their platoon mates. Price reached down and grabbed a hand grenade off his IBA and signaled for the others to do so as well. The three of them each now had a grenade in one hand and their rifles in the other. On the count of three, he was going to pull the door all the way open and they would toss their grenades at the remaining PLA soldiers, wait for them to go off, and then charge toward them and finish them off.

"One…two…three…"

Boom, boom, BOOM!

"Now!" Price shouted as he raised his rifle to his shoulder, advancing toward the enemy. He pulled the trigger in single-shot mode, one shot after another. One of the stunned Chinese soldiers who had fallen over from the blast reached for his sidearm just as Price rounded the corner on him, leveling his rifle and pulling the trigger three times— two shots to the chest, and one to the head. Seeing that these

PLA soldiers were wearing body armor, it was a good thing he had gone for the headshot.

"Clear!" yelled the specialist who had the grenade launcher.

"Clear!" yelled his other sergeant right before he fired a single shot. "OK, clear now," he clarified as he walked around a shot-up Mercedes-Benz.

"All clear," echoed Price as he pulled a purple smoke grenade from his IBA. He pulled the pin and tossed it further down the row of cars away from them. He wanted to signal the rest of the platoon that they had taken out the enemy position, so they wouldn't accidentally shoot them.

A crackle came over the radio, intermixed with static. "Price, is that your smoke?" called Captain Martinez.

"What color do you see?" he quickly replied. They kicked away the weapons from bodies of the dead enemy soldiers.

"Purple."

"That's us. It's all clear," Price answered. "Send the rest of the platoon over. We can set up our machine guns on the opposite side as we continue to push the perimeter out. We should use this structure as a stronghold, just like the PLA did to us."

A few minutes later, the other squads of their platoon began to filter into the garage. One of the squads set up on the ground floor, pushing some of the cars to block the various entrances to the garage, acting as barricades. A different squad set up a machine-gun position in each of the corners of the west side of the garage as well as one facing the north side. The next squad did the same on the third floor while their lone sniper team found a way up to the roof to set up their perch.

With their position firmly established, the other platoons of their company advanced past them to their right and left flanks, securing the final perimeter positions. They'd stay put now until the 82nd Airborne bubbas got themselves organized and relieved them. Once that happened, they'd head back to the center of the airport and await their next assignment.

****

40 Kilometers South of Pudong Airport
Yangshan Free Trade Harbor

The C-130 cargo plane had finally lined up for the approach to the drop zone, and as far as Staff Sergeant Moshe Dayan was concerned, it was not a moment too soon.

His butt was starting to go numb with all of his gear on, and his parachute rigging was cutting into the circulation of his legs, crotch and hips. They'd been in the cargo plane now for two and a half hours as they droned on toward the Chinese coast to participate in what would probably be hailed as the largest airborne invasion in human history, or at least since World War II.

Paratroopers from America, Britain, France, Italy, Germany, Poland, Japan and Israel were going to carry out a series of jumps around the Shanghai area, capturing several airports, key bridges and ports as the Allies sought to end the largest war in history. As an Israeli paratrooper, it felt incredibly strange to be partnered up with so many Allied nations to parachute into China; Israel had never participated in any sort of large-scale military action this far from their own country. It was also a stark contrast from the inordinate number of training scenarios and exercises the Israeli Defense Force had put them through during his six years of service thus far.

"Ten minutes!" shouted the jumpmaster from the back of the plane, breaking Sergeant Dayan's momentary reflection.

Standing up along with the others, he attached his chute to the static line hanging above him, just as he had done in countless other jumps. He then proceeded to go through the various checks and processes that all paratroopers go through as they prepare to jump. He felt the tugging and pulling of the soldier behind him, checking his rig and chute as he did the same for the guy in front of him. The process helped to take your mind off what was about to happen as you became focused on the multistep checklist of preparing to jump.

As they neared their drop zone, the side doors to the cargo plane opened, letting a rush of air into the cavernous cargo plane. The cool summer air felt good as it circulated around Dayan, drying the sweat on his face, neck, and arms. It was still somewhat dark outside, although the predawn twilight was starting to break through the darkness, heralding the day of days as their commander had told them today would be.

It was a proud day for Israel and its military, and it was an even prouder moment for the 35th Paratrooper Brigade as they had been given a very important task. They were to secure the primary road and rail bridge that connected the mainland with the enormous container port several kilometers off shore. The deepwater port and facilities would be critical to the Allies' ability to offload the thousands of main battle tanks and other armored vehicles that would be needed to capture the Shanghai region. More than 800,000 Allied soldiers would be participating in this operation.

"Get ready!" shouted the jumpmaster. The red jump light next to the door suddenly turned on.

Dayan looked at the other soldiers with him—excitement and apprehension written on their faces. They probably all felt a bit like him, psyched up and ready, but also nervous about what was waiting for them when they landed. The intelligence briefing they'd been given said there was a PLA motorized infantry battalion stationed roughly ten kilometers away from their drop zone. Other than the lone battalion of enemy soldiers, they had been told that they might encounter local police but should not meet any serious enemy resistance right away. The nearest major PLA unit was an armor brigade, fifty kilometers to their west. That unit would be stuck trying to decide if they should go after the Americans who would be capturing the Shanghai International Airport or the paratroopers looking to capture the port facilities.

With the cool morning air swirling around inside the cargo hold of the plane, the jumpmaster next to the door shouted, "Go, go, go!" as soon as the jump light turned green. Dayan made his way forward.

Soon he was out the door, the wind swirling all around him. He felt the sudden jolt of his ripcord pulling his parachute out of its pack, the wind and gravity doing the rest of the job of expanding his chute. Looking down at the ground, Dayan saw he was quickly approaching what appeared to be an empty grass field not far from the water. Then he spotted the bridge his unit was charged with securing.

The ground rushed toward him. He quickly bent his knees slightly and prepared to tuck and roll. Before he knew it, his body was reacting just as it had been trained to do. Once on the ground, he quickly detached his parachute and rolled it up. His eyes scanned the area for any immediate threats. Others in his platoon were doing the same and like him, they didn't seem to have spotted any signs of danger. Once they'd rolled up their chutes, they quickly collected them and then ran to a central point where they all dumped them together, so they wouldn't be in the way of their fellow sky soldiers that would arrive in the follow-on waves.

With his parachute taken care of, Sergeant Dayan called out to his squad of soldiers, "Secure the remaining gear and weapons and rally on me!"

Once they had formed up, he explained, "We're going to head out on foot to a road junction three kilometers west of the drop zone and set up a roadblock. Our orders are to prevent any vehicular traffic from heading in the direction of the drop zone and the port facilities nearby."

His men grunted and did as they were told. Five minutes later, the 48 soldiers of Second Platoon had formed up with their captain in a loose formation and had set out with two single-file columns on either side of the road as they made their way to their objective.

Walking along the road felt surreal. Sergeant Dayan looked to his left and right at the rows of apartment buildings, many of them fifteen to twenty floors in height; there were thousands of people represented by those buildings, and yet no one was out walking around the streets at all. It was like a ghost town. As they continued to march through the area at a fairly brisk pace, he did spot some people peering out their windows, looking down at the sight of his paratroopers walking through their neighborhood. It was almost like they were on some sort of movie set.

As they continued their forward progress, Dayan thought to himself that the faces looking down at them from their homes were the faces of Chinese citizens who, up to that point, had not seen the realities of war apart from the occasional bombing or cruise missile attack.

It took the paratroopers thirty-five minutes to reach their objective. Once they did, they realized this thoroughfare was going to be a lot tougher to defend than they had thought. The road junction was six lanes wide, three lanes going in either direction with on and off ramps on either side. The sun at this point was now cresting above the horizon, and the morning traffic, while still light, was starting to increase. At first, people didn't know what to make of the Anglo-looking soldiers with strange uniforms and oddly-shaped helmets. Most people had never before seen a mitznefet, which looked like a cross between a night cap and a chef's hat.

The Israeli soldiers flagged down the drivers, motioning for them to head toward the exits. One truck driver decided he didn't want to get off the highway. Despite the soldiers waving their weapons in the air, he gunned the engine toward them.

"Shoot his engine out!" shouted Staff Sergeant Dayan to his light machine gunner.

The young soldier leveled the weapon at the truck and fired a short burst of rounds into the engine block of the truck, which instantly veered off course and slammed into the center divider of the highway with a screech. At that point, several other drivers slammed on their brakes as they realized these strange-looking soldiers were not Chinese and weren't going to let them pass. Once the vehicles came to a halt, the paratroopers moved forward with their weapons leveled at the drivers, yelling at them, "Get out of the vehicle!"

While nearly none of the Israeli soldiers could speak Chinese, having their weapons leveled at the drivers was a pretty universal symbol the Chinese people seemed to understand without a problem. The drivers exited their cars with their hands held high as the Israeli soldiers herded them off to the side of the road. Several of the soldiers jumped into the cars and positioned the vehicles to act as a better barricade. Other soldiers used road flares and their weapons to signal and guide motorists off the highway. Then they set up a spot for another squad to direct traffic back in the direction it had come from, down the frontage road.

It took them nearly a half hour to get the roadblock up and running and to finish creating a path for the vehicles to turn around. With the roadblock operational, the platoon went to work on improving their defensive positions in case they needed to repel an attack.

****

Yangshan Shenshu Island

The Merlin gently lifted off from the deck of the HMS *Albion*, like the pilot had just laid his son or daughter down in the crib and was quietly slipping out of the nursery to finish that glass of red wine in the family room. Then the helicopter shifted to the right. It continued to gain altitude and speed, forming up with the dozens upon dozens of other choppers as fighter planes flew overhead.

The Royal Marines of 3 Commando Brigade held on to the troop straps dangling from the roof, shifting side to side with the momentum of the helicopter. Forty-five men hunkered down in their kits and body armor with extra magazines and hand grenades strapped to various spots on their vest. They were ready for war. The Marines were primed for this heliborne assault after having missed out on most of the major ground combat action in Europe. This would be their brigade's time to shine as they moved in to rapidly secure one of the largest deepwater island ports in the world.

When the Merlin banked to the left and headed toward their target, Sergeant Neil Evans could not believe the sight below them. It was both awe-inspiring and terrifying to think of the sheer military power that was floating in the hundreds of warships, transports and container ships below. It was like those images of the Normandy landing he had seen on the telly as a child.

"This is it, lads, our time to go kill us some Chinamen!" Evans bellowed in his best Marine voice to be heard over the noise of the engine and the swirling of the air inside the cabin.

The Marines around him with faces painted in multicam just grinned and snickered. A few howled like wild animals, waiting to be released from their leash. They'd been pent up on a ship and then in various holding stations for far too long. They wanted to be turned loose on the enemy.

With the sight of the fleet below them gone, they found themselves alone, the lead helicopter of this massive aerial assault. Looking out in the distance through the cockpit between the pilot and copilot, Evans could see the first glimpse of land just as the pilot dipped the nose of their airborne chariot down to the water. Evans grabbed for something to stabilize himself as the helicopter dropped altitude like a rock, picking up speed as it went. The sight of the water below them raced up quickly, filling the window of the cockpit before the pilot deftly pulled hard on the stick, leveling them out near the wave tops. The whitecaps and the choppiness of the water racing just meters below them were evidence of why they were doing a heliborne assault instead of an amphibious landing.

The copilot sensed Evans hovering nearby and turned. "Five minutes out, Sergeant. Be ready to get the hell off our bird, because we aren't sticking around long." He had a serious look in his eyes—he meant every word of it.

Evans turned back to his Marines and walked down the center aisle, pushing and shoving his way toward the rear ramp. He yelled out, "We are five minutes away! Be ready!"

Having positioned himself near the ramp, he saw small fishing boats whip past them at a dizzying speed as the tail gunner swiveled his heavy weapon toward each boat, ready to return fire should it be necessary. A few breaths later, they were over land. Below them were hundreds of cargo containers waiting in large yards to be loaded onto ships to be sent abroad, and railcars prepared to be brought to the mainland.

The Merlin flared up hard, dropping the ramp to just meters above the ground as the pilot pulled the nose up to bleed off their high-speed run to the island. Just fractions of a second later, the helicopter thudded on the ground, tall grass swirling all around them from the rotor wash as the crew chief screamed at them, "Get off!"

"Follow me, boys!" shouted Evans. He charged off the ramp, ready to conquer China on his own.

Racing off the ramp of the helicopter, Evans moved maybe fifteen meters away from the helicopters before he suddenly realized there were strings of green tracers zipping right past him and all around him. His body instinctively hit the dirt.

A loud scream pierced the air as one of the Marines screamed for a corpsman. Another Marine yelled out that he'd been hit as well.

Ratatat, ratatat, ratatat, pop, pop, pop.

His Marines returned fire at the enemy that now had them well-bracketed. Looking behind him, Sergeant Evans saw the Merlin they had just left do its best to lift off and gain altitude. It turned back toward the sea from which they had come. One of the door gunners fired a long burst of machine-gun fire at the enemy, his red tracers looking like a laser show as they reached out to hit the PLA soldiers who were doing their best to shoot them down from the sky.

"They've got machine guns set up on that bluff and in those buildings over there!" shouted one of the corporals. Evans looked to see what the young man was pointing at.

Bbbzzzzzz. One of the Apache gunships' 30mm chain gun tore into the enemy machine-gun bunker on the top of the bluff. As the attack helicopter flew over them, its machine gun still spitting death, Sergeant Evans and his Marines were blanketed with the red-hot spent shell casings. A second Apache fired a series of rockets right into the multistory buildings adjacent to the field where they had just landed, silencing a couple of the gun positions.

Several of the remaining enemy machine-gun positions then turned their attention to the attack helicopters, giving Evans's Marines a chance to advance. While they ran to attack the enemy positions, a missile streaked out of one of the building's windows, slamming into one of the Apaches before its defensive systems had time to react. As soon the flames ignited the chopper's fuel bladder, the entire helicopter burst into one spectacular orange firework.

Evans and his men reorganized and continued to return fire at the numerous enemy positions that threatened them. While he aimed and made several well-placed shots, Sergeant Evans overheard a helicopter's blades nearing him. He paused for a moment and saw that the Apache that had flown over them had circled back around. He caught sight of it just in time to watch the chopper unload a series of rockets right into the building.

The Apache continued along its flight path, over the carnage it had just unleashed. Two missiles suddenly flew toward it, launched from the remaining buildings. The chopper spat out flares and chaff canisters, while the pilot deftly banked the helicopter hard to one side. The first missile went right for the countermeasures, exploding harmlessly. The pilot banked hard. The second missile was a few seconds behind and seemed to recognize the change in direction, altitude, and speed made by the pilot; its trajectory adjusted accordingly. It met its mark and slammed into the tail rotor of the Apache, blowing it cleanly off.

The pilot fought hard as the helicopter almost slid in the air. He quickly lost control and altitude, and the chopper slammed into the side of the bluff, a hundred meters in front of Evans's men.

When Evans didn't see any flame or visible smoke billowing from the downed helicopter, he yelled out to his Marines, "Follow me!" and they ran to go check on the crew.

Bullets continued to zip and snap all around him as he ran forward, his eyes searching for a target he could take his frustrations out on. His men were roughly 300 meters from the perimeter of the housing area near the port, where most of the enemy fire was coming from. The bluff ahead of them was still smoldering from the attention the Apaches had given it, and for the time being, it was not a threat.

Sergeant Evans looked back. The other platoons were already bounding forward, attacking the condo complex. "*God speed*," he thought. He continued his dash forward.

In minutes, half of Evans's men had secured the crash site and were pulling the pilot and his gunner out of the helicopter. When that task was completed, the rest of his men maneuvered to get in closer to the condo complex where the enemy was still firing away at the charging Marines.

Evans turned to his radioman. "Try and raise the fleet," he ordered. "I want to see if we can't get some air support out here to help flatten those buildings."

The field the Navy had dropped them off in was a superb piece of real estate to offload a few hundred Marines, but it was also wide open, with little in the way of cover for them to hide behind once the PLA had made themselves known.

While he waited for additional support to arrive, Sergeant Evans lifted his SA80 to his shoulder and fired several shots at one of the windows where a machine gun was shooting from. He watched as the PLA gunner shifted his fire from one group of Marines to another cluster that was charging forward. Evans saw three of the four Marines get cut to pieces by the enemy machine gunner, tracer rounds ripping through their bodies, impacting the ground around and behind them as they fell to the dirt. The fourth Marine made it to the boulder they had been running toward unscathed.

Aiming again at the window, Evans calmed his breathing and squeezed the trigger methodically, placing round after round into the window. After his third shot, the machine gun stopped firing, at least for a few moments. More Marines rushed forward during the reprieve. They sprinted across the ground quickly, unsure if that same machine gun would start to spit more death in their direction.

In the distance, Evans heard the thumping sound of more helicopters. He turned and saw the second wave of choppers coming in to drop off the next batch of Royal Marines. Several attack helicopters sped ahead of them, flying straight for the condo complex. Not waiting to be shot at, the two attack helicopters unleashed their antitank missiles and their rocket pods on the remaining structures. Explosions pockmarked the buildings, blowing out windows and throwing shrapnel from the façades swirling at lightning speeds toward the ground.

Once the debris stopped its violent trajectory downward, the first batch of Marines Evans had landed with rushed forward, into the rubble. They swept for what remained of the enemy soldiers; it didn't take them long to clear the position.

Seeing that his squad of Marines was closest to the bluff where the helicopter had been downed, Evans led his group to the top to make sure no PLA soldiers were playing possum there. When they got to the crest, they saw nearly a dozen PLA soldiers shot to pieces, bodies torn, limbs separated from their owners. Next to their eviscerated remains were two heavy machine guns and a couple of light machine guns.

"Clearly, the PLA had planned on making this a hornet's nest to attack us," Sergeant Evans said, speaking mostly to himself. "It's a good thing those Apache gunships came through here, or they would have caused a lot of casualties for us from up here."

Looking down at the gunship below him and the medic tending to the two pilots, Evans felt mighty glad they'd survived. He determined he'd like to buy them a pint one day for all the Marines they'd invariably saved.

The immediate threat neutralized, Sergeant Evans looked around the island and realized for the first time what an amazing view he and his men had there of the island and the port. A few columns of black smoke were rising from the location of the battle, but otherwise, it looked like the island was peaceful.

Evans nodded to himself; his Marines had survived yet another battle and accomplished their goal. Now would come the fun part, making sure the road and rail bridges connecting the island with the mainland weren't wired with explosives or sabotaged. The Navy would be sailing in their ships to start offloading their armored chariots soon enough.

Chapter 17
Operation Gladiator

180 Kilometers West of Yangshan Harbor
Suzhou Guangfu Airport

Brigadier General Sir Nick McCoil had an uneasy feeling in his gut about this mission. On paper it looked superb—a large airfield that jutted out on a small peninsula, easily defendable and ripe for the taking. Suzhou Guangfu Airport was a PLA Air Force base several kilometers west of the city of Suzhou and a kilometer away from Taihu Lake. It had very few approachable angles from the nearby city, and it also boasted a small, higher-elevated ridgeline to the east and north of the airfield, adding to the defensible terrain nearby. However, what General McCoil disliked about this mission was how deep behind enemy lines it would place them.

The plan called for them to capture the base and ready it for Allied use. His airborne force would be required to hold the base and the surrounding territory until the rest of the British and French forces were offloaded at the Yangshan port, 180 kilometers away. Once the tanks and other armored vehicles were ashore, they'd be able to cross the distance in three or four hours and link up with them. At most, his brigade was being asked to hold the position for seventy-two hours.

To augment his brigade, a regiment of French Foreign Legionnaires would be joining them. He hoped having 1,200 zealot-like warriors in addition to his own brigade would bring them luck. The trick to making this jump work was logistics. The Air Force and Navy had to clear a path through the PLA's surface-to-air missile network. Once that had been achieved, eighty-four British and French Transall C-160 and A400M Atlas transport planes would fly in at varying intervals and begin to offload his brigade and the Legionnaires.

The first units to land would be his pathfinder platoon, a company from the 1st Royal Gurkhas Regiment, or 1RGR, along with most of 2 PARA. While this main force was dropping on the enemy airbase, the regiment of Legionnaires would land at Shangshengcun, three kilometers southeast of the airbase, to set up a blocking position along the main highway at Xiangshanzui. That would effectively isolate the entire southeastern half of the little peninsula the airfield sat on. His company of Gurkhas would advance to the top of the ridgeline at Jiaoli and begin to prepare it for when the rest of 1 RGR arrived in the second wave. The Gurkha battalion would have a several-kilometer vantage point of the surrounding area, giving his brigade plenty of time to spot any enemy formations heading toward them. It would also be one of the first locations the PLA would have to secure if they wanted to recapture the air base.

The second wave of aircraft would be much larger and arrive ninety minutes after the first. This wave would bring with them rest of 3 PARA and the three batteries of 7 Para RHA, giving his brigade eighteen 105mm howitzers for fire support. Three hours after the second wave was scheduled to land, the third wave would bring in the remainder of the brigade along with several air drops of ammunition. Two hours after that, a string of ten American C-17 Globemasters would complete the sortie by drag-dropping ten fully loaded Panhard ERC armored cars on the runway. These French-made 6x6 vehicles packed 90mm main guns, which would act as their light armor support until the main British Army showed up. If the air lanes were still clear, then eighteen hours later, his air taxis would return to offload additional munitions, retrieve his wounded and offload twenty Jackal 4x4 vehicles.

This was by far the riskiest jump any British or French forces had made in the war, and perhaps in their history. The head of British forces in Asia had convinced

General Bennet that the mission not only was possible to achieve but would give the Allies a much-needed air and artillery base deep behind enemy lines, with natural barriers for defense. With the sales pitch already made and approved many months ago, it was now incumbent upon General McCoil to execute the plan. Operation Gladiator was a go.

****

Corporal Jordan Wright had joined the Army at the outbreak of war with Russia. Never in a million years could he have imagined that nearly two years later, he would be jumping out of an airplane, invading the People's Republic of China. After all the political hoopla going on back home, he and his mates were just glad to be soldiering again and doing what they did best, fight.

The men around him had their faces painted for war and were ready to get the show on the road. Wright was eager too, even if hours of sitting in the back of the A400M Atlas was making his backside hurt like never before.

"Everyone up! It's time to get ready," shouted Lieutenant Lou Shay. The platoon sergeant stood next to him and though he didn't say anything, his look implied that the guys better get a move on fast.

The paratroopers grumbled a little at being roused from their slumber, but at the same time, they were also excited to finally be doing something, anything that would get the blood flowing again to their lower extremities.

Once they started moving, Lieutenant Shay announced, "We're twenty minutes out! Run through your equipment checks and make sure you're ready."

Even though the battalion had seen plenty of combat in Ukraine and Russia already, for many of them, this would be their first combat jump. Corporal Wright looked at the green members with a sort of kind pity; the first one was always a bit unnerving. Here they were flying in the back of a cargo plane, hundreds of kilometers behind enemy lines, hoping the American Air Force and Navy planes had successfully suppressed or destroyed the enemy's surface-to-air missile systems...and they all knew that SAMs had already cost the Allies dearly in Russia.

Five minutes away from the drop zone, an urgent voice from the front of the plane called out for the lieutenant. He trotted quickly past Corporal Wright, muttering something under his breath as he made his way to the front. Wright watched as the lieutenant poked his head into the cabin. He couldn't hear what the pilot was exclaiming, but clearly, he was worked up about something. Shay turned to look back at his men, his face as white as a ghost.

"*Oh, this isn't good,*" Wright realized.

The lieutenant walked back and faced his platoon. "Quiet down, men!" he shouted. "I have some news to report. The pilots just told me our fighter plane escorts are engaging some enemy fighters in the nearby area. They also told me the aircraft carrying the pathfinder platoon came under heavy enemy ground fire on their drop near the airbase."

A loud murmur started, and Lieutenant Shay quickly raised his hands in a gesture to try and get everyone to calm down. When they didn't quiet themselves, he shouted, "Shut up! I'm not done talking yet!

"The pilot said one of the German planes escorting us is currently trying to silence the enemy antiaircraft guns at the airfield. Regardless of whether the Germans are successful or not, we are still jumping! We're 2 PARA! Ready for anything!" Shay shouted the unit's motto to try to rile up their spirits.

"*He knows we're jumping into a storm and there's nothing he can do about it,*" Wright realized. At least they could try to make the best of it.

As the lieutenant made his way back to his position near the rear door and his platoon sergeant, Corporal Wright grabbed his arm gently and leaned in. "Damn good speech, Sir. Thank you for giving us the heads-up."

Shay paused for a second, searching Wright's expression. "Thanks, Corporal. I'm counting on you and your squad," he replied. He patted him on the shoulder and then continued down the line of men that made up his platoon.

Turning to the man next to him, Wright said, "Shay's a fine officer, Flowers."

Private Nigel Flowers shrugged. "If you say so, Corporal."

"You know his family's rich—and I don't mean well off, I mean like filthy rich, right? Like billionaire rich. He put all of that aside and joined the Army when the war started with Russia. He's kind of like me. I was a program manager at Google. I was pulling down £160,000 a year before I joined 2 PARA. Of course, my wife nearly divorced me, but now she thinks I look sexy as hell in my uniform with my beret," Wright added with a wry grin.

Flowers stopped fiddling with part of his gear to look at Wright. "You mean to tell me our lieutenant is rich beyond belief and he put all of that aside to join the 2 PARA? And you gave up a job at Google making more than I've made in my entire life up to this point to join the military? You two are both crazy. Me...I got drafted."

Corporal Wright had taken a liking to Private Flowers. He reminded him of his little brother who had died his senior year of secondary school from cancer. Ever since Wright had been promoted to corporal, he had kept Flowers near him, under his wing so to speak, and the two had been inseparable ever since.

"Hey, Nigel, I didn't quit Google, I just took a military leave of absence," Wright said with a smirk. "And like I said before, when this war is over and we all get out of the Army, I'll get you a gig working on my team at Google. You keep sticking with me, Nigel, and I'll look out for you."

Nigel smiled and shook his head. "You're a class act, Wright. I'm sure glad you left Google to be a part of this; I never would have met you otherwise. I told my mum all about you and how you've been looking out for me—she thinks it right nice of you."

Before either of them could say anything more, the plane banked hard to the right, nearly throwing them all off their feet. While they were trying to catch their balance, a loud explosion overwhelmed their senses, causing them to instinctively guard their ears. Then the plane jostled in the air, like they had hit some bad turbulence. With their hands occupied, several soldiers actually fell over; they scrambled to quickly right themselves.

"Stand by to jump!" shouted the lieutenant. One of the crew chiefs pulled the side door to the aircraft open.

Wright caught the first glimpse of what was happening outside. Strings of green tracers appeared to be flying in all directions, intermixed with small little puffs of black smoke.

Plunk, plunk, crack, crack.

Without warning, several new holes appeared on the walls of the aircraft. One of the men in Second Squad dropped to the floor limp, while another soldier grabbed at his leg and screamed in excruciating pain. Then the crew chief grabbed the lieutenant's arm and yelled, "Get your men off the plane!"

The lieutenant nodded, but he was obviously worried about his two guys who had just been hit. The jump lights turned green. Without further prodding, the jumpmasters next to the door yelled at the soldiers who had lined up. One by one, the soldiers moved quickly down the line toward the exit. When Corporal Wright made it to the door, he paused for less than a second before launching himself off the aircraft.

Gravity took over. The wind buffeted his face and body, caressing it like a long-lost lover. His chute opened and jerked him hard as it fought against gravity's inviting pull, slowing his descent in seconds. He looked down at his feet dangling in the air. His ruck was still attached to his drop cord, where it should be. He began to take in his surroundings. At the top of the ridge he and the other Gurkhas were supposed to capture, he spotted the radar station. Nearby, there were at least five Type 85 twin-barrel 23mm antiaircraft guns, firing away at the planes delivering the paratroopers as well as the men dangling from their chutes.

Green tracers from the enemy guns continued to crisscross the morning sky as more and more parachutes opened all around him. It was now a matter of getting enough soldiers on the ground so they could neutralize the threats for the follow-on waves.

He also spotted what appeared to be a four-engine plane, maybe a C-130 cargo plane, that had crashed a couple of kilometers away from the airfield. The thick black smoke added to the surreal scene below him. Closer to the airfield, he spotted several buildings on fire, smoke billowing out of them. On the parking ramp, a few destroyed aircraft were scattered about, and what appeared to be a Eurofighter was burning near the end of the runway.

"That German fighter was probably trying to take some of these antiaircraft guns out," Wright thought, sad that they hadn't succeeded in eliminating more of the incoming threats.

Corporal Wright looked ahead where the wind was leading him, to an empty field at the southwestern side of the runway. An orange X had been painted there, and a red smoke signal puffed away.

"At least the landing site hasn't been destroyed," Wright mused.

Pulling on the navigation cords of his chute, he angled his chute in that general direction. He suspected the rest of his platoon was doing the same.

To his right and on the opposite end of the runway was another orange X with a purple smoke signal, indicating another safe landing place for those who were closer to that location. Half a kilometer to the east, nestled between two housing complex areas, was another large field also marked by an orange X and a yellow smoke grenade. Clusters of paratroopers circled toward each of the three drop zones the pathfinders had established.

"There were supposed to be two more drop zones," Corporal Wright thought. Things were really not going according to plan so far.

Once Wright was closer to the ground, he could make out dozens of small figures running toward the DZ from the main buildings of the airfield that hadn't been destroyed. As he squinted, he saw that some of those figures were pointing weapons at him. The muzzles of those guns began to blink rapidly.

Zip, zap, zip, zap.

Bullets whizzed past his head and all around him. Wright did the best he could to get himself on the ground as quickly as he could. Frantically looking around for help, he spotted a couple of pathfinders shooting at the attackers, doing their best to provide some covering fire for their brethren.

With the ground approaching fast, Wright bent his knees slightly as he prepared for his landing. In seconds he was on the ground, tucking and rolling to his side. Once his momentum had stopped, he quickly unsnapped his chute and rifle case, pulling his SA80 out and slapping a fresh thirty-round magazine in place. With bullets still whipping through the air, Wright quickly found the source. Bringing his rifle to bear, he aimed at the PLA soldier shooting at his comrades. Without another thought, he squeezed the trigger, hitting the enemy soldier squarely in the chest, dropping him where he stood.

His eyes quickly scanned for more targets. The rest of his squad continued to land around him—he needed to buy his guys more time to get on the ground and organized. Running toward what he assumed was one of the pathfinders, he shouted, "Where's the enemy fire coming from?"

The young private turned to look at him with a bewildered look on his face. "I have no idea, Corporal. I must have hit at least four of the buggers, but more and more keep showing up. I can't find anyone else in my squad after I got the smoke grenade going."

Corporal Wright decided it was time to take charge of the situation. He looked back to see who else was ready to move and spotted Private Flowers.

"This way!" he shouted to his friend while waving his arms. Others in his squad heard his voice and ran toward him as well. With nearly a dozen men with him, Corporal Wright turned to the pathfinder.

"Round up our rucks and get them piled up near that cluster of trees over there," he ordered. "We'll take over from here."

The pathfinder nodded, obviously relieved that someone more senior had assumed control, and went about collecting the paratroopers' rucks while they sought out the enemy.

"Let's go!" ordered Wright. His little gang of soldiers moved forward, hunting for targets to kill.

The motley gang made it to the edge of the drop zone and nearly ran into a group of maybe twenty PLA soldiers, less than thirty meters from them. The two groups of soldiers brought their weapons to bear on each other as they each dove for cover.

"Frag out!" shouted Flowers as he threw one of the small cylindrical devices toward a cluster of PLA soldiers near the perimeter fence.

BAM!

Pop, pop, pop, crack, ratatat, ratatat.

Corporal Wright sighted in on two enemy soldiers who were attempting to set up a machine gun. He squeezed the trigger multiple times, sending round after round at them until he saw them both stop moving. Looking to his right, he saw one of his soldiers clutch at his neck, blood squirting out between his fingers as he tried to stop the bleeding.

Crump, crump, crump.

Multiple Chinese and British grenades sailed back and forth between each side.

"Charge!" yelled a voice that sounded familiar to Wright.

He didn't hesitate in the least once the order had been given, jumping up from his covered position screaming like a banshee. Running forward, he saw the terrified look on the faces of three PLA soldiers as he continued to scream, racing right at them. At this point he was practically firing from the hip as he emptied the remainder of his magazine on the three of them. Without thinking, he jumped right into their positions and reached for his Sig Sauer P226 with his right hand. He turned to his left and fired three quick shots at a PLA soldier who was trying to shoot at one of his comrades.

With the immediate threats neutralized, he placed his Sig back in his holster and replaced the empty magazine on his SA80 with a fresh one. "*Damn, that was close,*" he thought, and he vowed never to let himself run out of ammo again.

"Everyone on me!" shouted Lieutenant Shay.

Pointing to the ridge with the radar tower on it and those 23mm antiaircraft guns, the lieutenant said, "We have to take those guns out or more planes are going to get shot down. We're going to collect our rucks, and then we're going to double-time it around the airfield to get at that ridge. I'm not sure if the Gurkhas made it or not, but we can't leave those guns untouched."

With the orders given, the platoon set about rounding up their rucks from the drop zone and proceeded to head off to capture the radar station.

****

Brigadier Sir Nick McCoil couldn't believe how terribly this airborne assault had started. Not only had the Spectre gunship the Americans had sent to provide them ground support on the airfield been shot down, but two additional German Eurofighters had also been destroyed while trying to fill in for the gunship. Then a swarm of those new PLA fighter drones had jumped their air cover and had succeeded in shooting down five of his transport planes before they'd had a chance to offload their paratroopers. He'd lost an entire company of French Foreign Legion troops, a company of Gurkhas and three platoons from 2nd Battalion, 2 PARA. To add further insult to injury, he'd somehow managed to severely sprain his left ankle on his landing, making it nearly impossible to walk.

"Twenty-six years as a paratrooper and the only time I get injured is during the most important combat jump of my career," he mourned.

As he propped himself up against the side of a tree, Brigadier McCoil grabbed the radio handset his radioman held out for him.

"It's connected to the strike group commander," the soldier replied. The young sergeant turned to look for his pad of paper to write down anything important. A captain and major also knelt down near them as a couple of other soldiers secured the perimeter around them.

"Major, I want that damn airfield captured now! We have to get out of this drop zone," McCoil barked at one of his operations officers.

Then he directed his wrath toward the admiral on the other end of the radio receiver. "This is Gladiator Actual. Where the hell is my damn air cover? I've lost five transports—that's nearly seven hundred paratroopers! I'd better get some more air support, or my next call is to General Bennet himself!" he shouted into the receiver, the sounds of machine gunfire and explosions still going off in the background.

****

After holding the receiver to her ear for a minute and not hearing anything, Admiral Cord was about to hand it back to one of the communications officers when a distinctly British accent shouted into her ear. The sounds of explosions, men shouting and machine-gun fire in the background made it feel like she was right there in the thick of the action. She had to hold the receiver an inch away from her ear as the British brigadier ripped her a new one over the lack of air support.

She shot a quizzical glance to the *Ford*'s air boss and captain. Then, placing her hand over the receiver, she whispered, "What the hell is he talking about?"

The air boss leaned in, grimacing. "He's talking about Kestrel flight being ambushed. We lost six Super Hornets in the dogfight. He lost nearly half of his first wave of paratroopers."

Captain Fleece just shook her head. She was still in shock that they'd lost that many Hornets after the Air Force had done such a good job of clearing out the SAM sites.

"Gladiator Actual, this is Task Force 92 Actual. I've just been brought up to speed on your current situation. I'm directing all available fleet assets to assist you. Please have your forward air controller coordinate with my CAG on specific strike packages you need, and where you need them.

I will also ensure your second wave of transports has more protection this time. Out," she said. She handed the handset over to the Commander, Air Group to work out the finer details with the good general. She wasn't about to listen to him chew her out one more time.

She went to find the task force's operation officer. When she did, she stared daggers at Captain Zach Grady as she motioned for him to come to her. As Grady approached, she leaned in close and turned her body away from the others, speaking in a low voice. "I just got my head torn off by the British airborne commander for Operation Gladiator. He says nearly half of his first wave of transports were shot down before they reached the airfield and none of the antiaircraft guns at the base were destroyed. Want to fill me in on what the hell happened, Captain?" There was a sternness in her voice that she seldom used, but she was certain if she didn't get to the bottom of what had gone wrong and fix it, Admiral Richardson or Admiral Lomas would have her head on a platter.

Turning a bit red at being talked down to by a female admiral, Captain Grady tried to reply in the usual macho dismissive manner he tended to use when speaking to a female officer. "Stuff happens, Admiral. We nearly lost an entire squadron of Super Hornets flying escort for them.

They're lucky they even made it to the drop zone, what with the number of enemy fighters the PLA jumped our guys with. The Chinese ambushed us with sixty of those new drone fighter planes. We've never fought them before and had no idea what their real capabilities were." He shrugged his shoulders nonchalantly.

Admiral Cord wanted to slap him for his smugness but knew she couldn't. "Not good enough, Captain," she exclaimed. "Try explaining that to me again, without the sarcasm. While you're complaining that we nearly lost half a squadron of Hornets, *you* just lost seven hundred paratroopers *we* were charged with protecting. Do you know how that's going to look to the brass above me? You'd be wise to remember crap rolls downhill until it goes splat on someone." She took an open right hand and smacked her left fist, so as to emphasize that he would ultimately be the one in the hot seat.

His demeanor changed a bit. "*Good*," Admiral Cord thought. Maybe he did realize that the naval air support planning for this operation was ultimately his responsibility.

"My apologies, Admiral," Captain Grady said. "Let me start over. The Air Force went in ahead of us and cleared out the SAMs. They did a good job, although they lost a couple of F-16s in the process. We sent in two squadrons of

Hornets, one ahead of the transports to go with the AC-130 Spectre gunship. The gunship was supposed to silence the enemy antiaircraft guns and the radar station on the ridgeline around the airfield. Unfortunately, the gunship was shot down before it reached the airfield. When this happened, we redirected two German Eurofighters who hadn't dropped their ordnance yet to go in and do the job. That's when the PLA Air Force jumped our guys with those new fighter drones.

"As I said earlier, we had never fought or even seen them before, so we had no idea how effective they were in combat or how to really engage them. From what I've been able to gather from talking with one of the flight leaders that fought them, they came in two waves. One from high-altitude and one on the deck. The one that came in from high altitude drew all the attention from our fighters. The one that came in from the deck was able to slip past the first wave of fighters and sliced into our second group of fighters, which was escorting the transports. By the time our guys fought them off, half the transports had been shot up," he explained. Then he proceeded to tell her of his revised plan for escorting the second wave of transports, which were just crossing into Chinese airspace.

Admiral Cord listened while he spoke without interrupting. "All I can say, Captain Grady, is that your group had better redeem itself with this second wave of transports, or there's going to be hell to pay. You get me?" Her voice was still full of heat.

He nodded and went back to his section, barking orders to his own little fiefdom.

****

Brigadier McCoil handed the receiver over to his lone American naval special warfare guy who would act as the liaison for his air support. "I think I got their attention for you, Lieutenant. It's now your show. Get me air cover over this place, and start taking out some of these anti-aircraft guns. Our second wave of transports arrive in exactly eighty-two minutes."

A young captain ran up to their position. "Brigadier?" he asked, out of breath. "Sir, we've secured the remaining buildings at the airfield. We can move your headquarters over there now. Also, Baker Coy from 2nd Battalion is moving to assault the radar station and those AA guns on it," he reported. As soon as he finished speaking, he took a swig of water to help catch his breath.

McCoil nodded. "Good job, Captain. Now help me up and give me a hand making my way over there," he replied, holding his hand up to the captain.

The young officer looked down at the brigadier, and it was as if he realized for the first time that the general had his foot all wrapped up in a compression bandage.

"Ah, yes, now you see why I've been propped up against this tree trunk instead of leading the charge myself," Brigadier McCoil said with a chuckle.

The captain pulled him off the ground and placed his arm around his shoulder. Together, they hobbled and walked the half a kilometer to the building that would function as his headquarters. Dozens of other soldiers were working to get communication antennas set up, along with computers, map boards and everything else he needed to run the brigade. Another group of soldiers worked on getting security established around the buildings they were going to occupy and making sure the airfield was being properly cordoned off from potential enemy soldiers as well as curious civilians.

McCoil looked around. The soldiers around him were clearly doubling their efforts to make up for their lack of personnel. With half of their first wave of airborne units killed before they even made it to the ground, they were functioning with a skeleton crew as they worked to get the place ready to receive the main body of the brigade.

****

Lieutenant Shay ducked behind a tree just as several bullets slapped into the trunk. "Someone take that gunner out already!" he shouted to his platoon mates.

Private Flowers heard the order and immediately took action. His SA80 had a grenade launcher attached to it; he was one of the few guys in the platoon with this setup. He popped out from behind the tree he'd been hiding behind and swiftly fired his 40mm grenade at the enemy machine-gun position.

Thump...BAM.

"Now!" shouted Corporal Wright. He and three other soldiers opened fire on the enemy position while another group of four soldiers leapt from their covered positions to charge. Continuing to fire at the enemy, the advancing fireteam of soldiers got to within twenty meters of the enemy line when they dove for cover. Another group of PLA soldiers further up the ridge had just arrived and were doing their best to provide their comrades with covering fire.

"Grenades! Hit them with grenades!" shouted Lieutenant Shay. He ran past Corporal Wright, charging up the hill to the fireteam that was lobbing grenades at the enemy soldiers.

Zip, crack, zip, crack, crump, crump, crump.

Explosions burst everywhere as both sides lobbed grenades at each other. Wright's fire team continued to bang away at the enemy soldiers with their FN Minimi Para light machine gun.

Ratatat, ratatat, ratatat.

"Alpha team, covering fire!" shouted Wright. He signaled for his bravo team to move forward.

Zip, crack, zip, crack.

Bullets snapped past their heads, hitting branches, bushes and everything around them as they rushed forward.

"Oomph," one of the soldiers muttered—he was spun sideways when a couple of rounds slammed into his body armor. Falling to the ground, the soldier yelped, "I'm hit, Corporal!"

Wright stopped charging. He dropped down next to the wounded man, quickly assessing him. "It looks like it hit your armor—did it go through the plate?" he asked.

The young man looked panicked. He used his hands to feel around and then shook his head. "I don't think so," he answered.

Corporal Wright didn't blame the young kid—even through the plates, a gunshot could break ribs or cause some serious bruising. "Listen, Private, I'm going to leave you here while you catch your breath and recover. I need you to keep shooting at the enemy. We still need your help. Do you think you can do that for me?" Wright asked, concern in his eyes and voice.

The young private nodded and gave a thumbs-up. "You can count on me, Corporal. Just give me a few minutes and I'll catch up to you guys."

Wright nodded and then raced to catch up to Bravo Team. When they made it online with Alpha, they switched turns, providing covering fire while Alpha bounded forward, this time into the enemy defensive works. Once Alpha Team was inside the enemy trench and foxholes, Bravo Team rushed forward to join them.

It took them another ten minutes to finish clearing the enemy out of the radar station and the enemy antiaircraft guns, but their platoon had secured an objective that had been assigned to an entire company of Gurkhas. That was no small feat for the men of 2nd Battalion, Baker Coy.

****

Brigadier McCoil hobbled over to the window of the building his headquarters staff had taken over and watched as row after row of paratroopers continued to descend in and around the airfield. More and more of his force was finally arriving and starting to get formed up, which was reassuring considering how the operation had started. He spotted several large packages being dropped directly on the runways. It appeared the Americans were dropping off his Jackal 4x4 vehicles ahead of schedule, which was fine by him.

"Brigadier," called out a new voice. Colonel Jacques Vidal of the French 2nd Foreign Parachute Regiment had just walked into the building. The Legionnaire quickly walked up to him rendering a quick salute. "Brigadier, I'm proud to report the remainder of my force has officially landed and we've secured the road junction at Xiangshanzui and the surrounding area. My men are working on turning the area into a veritable fortress as we speak," he proclaimed proudly.

General McCoil smiled for the first time in hours; he couldn't be happier to hear this news. He'd been extremely concerned when the company of Legionnaires had been shot down early on and unable to secure the site earlier. If any PLA tanks or other armored vehicles were going to attack his position it'd most likely come from the highway interchange at Xiangshanzui or Huqiu to his north, at least until the Gurkhas arrived and moved to the area.

"Glad to hear it, Colonel," said McCoil. "When the ERC armored cars arrive, I'll send half of them to your command. It's imperative that your men hold that junction. Make sure your men have plenty of antitank rockets and missiles ready to deal with the PLA when they do start to show up. My guess is we'll start to see some heavy PLA resistance before the day's out and certainly by tomorrow."

Colonel Vidal nodded. "I believe you're right, Brigadier. I had my men jump with twice as many antitank weapons as they normally do. We'll be ready for the PLA, and when the ERCs show up, it'll only strengthen our position," he said confidently. "If I may, when will our artillery support be available?" he inquired.

McCoil turned to look for one of his operations officers. "Major, when will 7 RHA be operational?" he asked.

The major walked over to them, explaining, "They just landed. It's going to be at least an hour to get them unpacked and moved to their firing locations. If the guns are needed right now, they probably could be made ready, but

I'd like to get them moved to their firing location and out of the way for future drops."

"That's fine, Brigadier," the French colonel responded. "I don't believe we'll need their support within the next hour. I just wanted to make sure they'll be operational by evening, in case the enemy does start to show up." With that, the two officers shook hands, exchanged a few more directions and then parted ways. The French had a critically important area to secure, and McCoil didn't want to keep the colonel stuck here with him any longer than he needed to.

"Now, if only my Gurkhas could get organized and ready," he thought.

A few minutes later, Lieutenant Colonel Ganju Lama walked into the building. As soon as he spotted Brigadier McCoil, he headed over to him. "Sorry for my tardiness, Sir. It appears a few Chinese soldiers wanted to greet my arrival," he said with a half-smile. "My men are now on the ground and getting formed up as we speak. Is there any change to my orders or am I still to proceed to Jiangsu National Forest Park?" he inquired.

"It's good to see you, Colonel," said McCoil as he held out his hand to shake Lama's. "My condolences on your company of men that didn't make it. It was a terrible tragedy, what happened with our air support." He paused as if giving a moment of silence for the departed. "As to your original orders, I want you to continue with the original plan. Your battalion must hold that position at all costs, even though the PLA is going to throw everything they have at you to get at this airbase. You'll have artillery support and as much help as I can give you from here, but we've got to keep our claim on that position. When the rest of 3 PARA arrives, I'm going to send another company of soldiers over to help you as well. Do you have any further questions on your orders, Colonel?"

"No, Sir," Lieutenant Lama answered. "We'll get that place turned into a real nice fortress. You can count on that." A wicked grin spread on his face.

With his orders in hand, the Gurkha commander turned and left the building to go form up with his men. They had a couple kilometer road march to get to their position and they needed to get set up and ready to defend the area as quickly as possible. Nobody knew when the PLA forces in the area would get organized enough to launch an attack, so it was a race against time.

****

Victory Base Complex, Taiwan
General Bennet's Headquarters

Like an expectant father in a hospital, General John Bennet paced back and forth in the operations center as he waited for confirmation that the second wave of his joint British and French airborne force had made it to their drop point. He had been livid when he'd found out the Navy, who was supposed to provide fighter escorts for them, had lost half of the transports they were charged with protecting during the first wave. It had nearly cost them the entire operation.

He had placed a three-way call to Admiral Lomas and Admiral Richardson and thoroughly dressed them down over the loss of 700 paratroopers and those critically important transports. He replayed the conversation in his mind.

"It's not just that we lost those soldiers, which would be horrible enough—we needed those transports to keep ferrying men and supplies behind enemy lines," he'd explained. "Let me clear this up for you. In no uncertain terms, if another loss like this occurs during the airborne operation, I will relieve you both on the spot."

They had assured him that this wouldn't happen again. Admiral Richardson said he'd ordered two additional carrier airwings to beef up air cover for the remaining transports and told him he'd ensure the ground commander had at least one full air wing available for air support until they were relieved by the ground forces from the ports. Still, General Bennet was worried. He continued pacing.

Finally, Bennet went to find his J3, and spotted him standing next to a bank of radios and computers. When he finished making his way over to them, he simply asked, "Did they make it?"

His J3 looked up and nodded, a smile spreading across his face. "Yes, Sir! We just spoke to the pilot of the last transport. They all made it and the paratroopers are on the ground. They're turning back to base now."

Several soldiers exchanged high fives at that news. General Bennet allowed himself to relax a bit, although the wait wasn't totally over. This operation had been a huge gamble, and it wasn't totally in the bag just yet. They still had to get a third wave of transports in to finish off the PLA forces, and then another wave to land their extra ammunition, water, medical supplies and everything else the 9,000-man force would need to hold their ground for the next ninety-six hours.

"Excellent work," Bennet allowed himself to say. "I'm glad to see my talk with the Navy had the desired effect. Now to the ports—how are operations going there?"

His J3 signaled for Bennet to follow him over to the map board he had set up on the wall. "The Royal Marines have secured the entire island and port facilities of Yangshan with few casualties. I think we caught the PLA by surprise when we landed forces there because they had a very small garrison of soldiers for what is truly a prize target. With the entire port facility in our control, the Navy's gone ahead and pushed the security perimeter out and brought in the roll-on, roll-off ships and heavy transports.

"The King's Royal Hussars of the 12th Armored Infantry Brigade are being offloaded now. That'll give us three squadrons of Challenger tanks in a couple of hours. The rest of the 12th Brigade should be offloaded by midnight." He held up a hand. "As soon as an intact unit is offloaded and paired up with their crews, they're moving off the island and linking up with the Israeli forces holding the other end of the bridge. The 12th's main objective is to hold the bridgehead with the Israelis until the rest of our ground forces can get offloaded."

General Bennet smiled at the preemptive answering of his question. "How are things going at the Shanghai Pudong Airport? I heard the fighting there had turned fierce."

"The Rangers captured the airport without much of a problem," the J3 explained. "There was some resistance from a local military unit that was a few blocks away, but nothing the Rangers couldn't neutralize. The entire 82nd Airborne Division has finally arrived. We had to use a lot of commercial airliners to get them all in, but we did it. Fortunately, we didn't have any enemy fighter planes try to interdict our effort either."

Pausing for a second to look at the map, Bennet saw where the paratroopers had expanded the perimeter, and the locations of the enemy units they had spotted up to this point. From his perspective, it looked like a battalion of PLA tanks were slowly snaking their way through the city of Shanghai heading right for the paratroopers.

His eyes studied the map a moment more before he said, "My concern is this large enemy force that's headed to the airport—it looks like at least two full battalions of PLA infantry and God only knows how many militia forces are moving in that direction. There's a major battle brewing, less than a few hours from starting. Do we have enough forces on the ground to handle it? What sort of armor support do we have to help them?"

"All three artillery regiments have been offloaded at the airport, along with the division's attack helicopter squadrons; the division packs more than enough punching power to hold the airport against a substantially larger force than what is bearing down on them, Sir," he answered confidently. "By this time tomorrow, we'll have two full divisions of armor on the ground, along with three divisions of infantry. In three days, we'll have five armored divisions and three more infantry divisions. Unless the PLA somehow mobilizes the population of Shanghai to take up arms against us, they just don't have enough forces in the region that can push us out. By the time any substantive forces do arrive, we'll have landed over 200,000 soldiers and it'll be a moot point. They won't dislodge us."

General Bennet thought for a moment about what his operations staff had concluded and felt a bit more at ease about the situation. Things were certainly still fluid, and a lot could change, but they had the momentum on their side right now, and they'd achieved complete and utter surprise with their attack on Shanghai.

"The question now is, will the Marines further south capture the critical province of Guangdong and hold it?" he wondered. So far, the fighting had been absolutely brutal there, with the PLA resorting more and more to using poorly trained and equipped militia forces to overrun the Marines. In some cases, that strategy had worked, which only further

spurred on their use by the PLA. With casualties mounting, it was becoming a grave concern for the President and the Joint Chiefs back home as to whether or not that offensive should continue.

If they held the ground they'd captured up to this point, it'd put them just shy of taking over the manufacturing centers they had originally invaded the province to destroy in the first place. In Bennet's opinion, at this point, they were pot-committed and needed to see it through to the end. Another 80,000 Marines would be filtering into the province over the next couple of days—he hoped that would be enough forces to capture their objectives within the next week. Once Guangdong Province and Shanghai were firmly in the Allies' control, then the United States would finally reach out to the Chinese government and offer terms of surrender.

"*Just a few more weeks and this bloody war will be over,*" Bennet hoped.

****

Fengxian, China, Eight Kilometers West of the Allied Beachhead

Taking advantage of the lull in the fighting, Staff Sergeant Moshe Dayan savagely devoured his Israeli version of an MRE. He was famished—he definitely hadn't eaten much in the last twenty-four hours.

In between scarfing down bites of food, Dayan and his platoon mates also reloaded empty magazines for their rifles. A couple of the privates had returned ten minutes ago with several crates of rifle ammo and more grenades. They had been running low on ammo after the last enemy charge an hour ago.

One of the young corporals paused eating and looked up at Dayan for a second with a quizzical look on his face. "Sergeant Dayan, how can the enemy keep charging our positions like they are? I mean, how do they not break when they see so many of their fellow soldiers getting cut down like that?" he asked.

The other soldiers in his platoon stopped what they were doing and looked at Dayan, waiting to see what he would say. Even the captain nearby had stopped reloading his magazines to listen to his response.

Taking a deep breath and letting it out, Sergeant Dayan looked back at the corporal who had asked the question, and then to the rest of the soldiers in the room. "They fight like this because we're invading their homeland.

It's no different than us. If someone attacked our homeland, we'd fight just as hard and just as viciously.

"The difference between the PLA soldiers we're fighting and the Allied force we're a part of is we didn't start this war. We didn't invade dozens of countries seeking conquest. We fight not as conquerors, but as liberators— liberators of a repressive communist regime that would seek to impose its version of government on the rest of the world.

"We've all seen the social media campaign of 'social credits' and how we can use technology to censor 'hate speech' and political dissent. It's all a lie to sell us on a form of government and system that would steal our freedom, our ability to politically disagree with each other, all in the name of conformity. No, I won't let my children grow up in a world or country that won't respect other people's views and opinions. I may not agree with you or even like you, but I'll always value your right to your opinion, and I will fight and die to make sure you and your family will always be free to express that opinion without government persecution."

When Staff Sergeant Moshe Dayan finished his little impromptu speech, a man walked in from behind them and clapped, and so did two other people. When the platoon turned around to find the source of the applause, they all jumped to their feet. Sergeant Dayan stood ramrod straight.

"General Barak, we had no idea you were visiting the front," he said. "My apologies if I spoke out of turn."

Brigadier General Sami Barak just smiled, beaming with pride as he walked up to Staff Sergeant Dayan. He placed both hands on his shoulders, looking the man in the eye. "I couldn't be prouder to command such men as you, Staff Sergeant. Your wisdom and courage are why Israel as a country has a bright and long history ahead of it."

The general then turned to face the rest of the paratroopers as he kept one hand on Dayan's shoulder. "Men, I know the last twenty-four hours have been hard on you, and the last twelve hours have been horrific since the PLA started sending in human wave assaults against us…I'm not going to lie to you and tell you it's going to get easier. It's not. The enemy is in its final death throes, and as such, they are desperate."

The general then moved over to a chair and took a seat, signaling for everyone else to do likewise. When the rustling ceased, he resumed speaking. "The most recent intelligence passed to us by the Americans says the Chinese have mobilized a massive militia force several kilometers away. That force is going to move and attack our positions in the next hour, along with a battalion of T-99 tanks and two battalions of motorized regular army infantry. This is it—the big attack that they think will break through our positions and drive us back to the ports.

"What I can tell you is that even as we speak, Allied warplanes are on their way to bomb the hell out of them before they even get to us. However, when they do arrive, they're going to come at us with a fervor like nothing we've seen before. The PLA has been spreading lies to their people, telling them that the Allies are systematically killing their women and children in the occupied parts of the cities. Even though nothing could be further from the truth, this deception is motivating tens of thousands of people to grab a rifle, shovel, or knife to come at us and try to kill us.

"An hour ago, the British 12th Armored Infantry Brigade began to move to our position. Even now, their tanks and infantry fighting vehicles are filtering into the city and our lines to help us hold our positions. When the enemy does attack, they will help us beat back their advances. Once the PLA has spent themselves on our lines, we will go on the offensive. General Bennet has given our brigade and the British 12th the task of fighting our way to a captured Chinese airfield 180 kilometers inland. Right now, a 9,000 man British and French airborne force is holding ground there. They are surrounded and deep behind enemy lines…we *will* break through the enemy positions here and relieve them.

"Once we've broken through the enemy lines here, the British 20th Armored Infantry Brigade will link up with us, along with the German 21st Panzer Brigade. To support our efforts, the American 42nd Infantry Division will secure the ground behind us and act as a reserve force in case we need them." The general paused for a second, letting the information sink in. It was unusual for the general to share this level of detail with a platoon of grunts, but Sergeant Dayan reasoned that seeing the big picture would help them all to fight harder.

"You guys can do this," General Barak continued. "You've got one of the best company commanders in the brigade and probably the smartest, toughest staff sergeant in the airborne to lead you. I'm counting on you all, and so is our country and the rest of the world. Now, if you'll excuse me, I need to get moving. It was a pleasure being able to talk with you all." He stood, as did all the other soldiers out of respect. Then the general's two escorts led him to the door that would take him down the stairs and out of their building.

The soldiers stood there, momentarily frozen, a bit in shock that their commanding general would stop by and have such an open and frank discussion with them.

Finally, Staff Sergeant Dayan spoke up. "OK, enough lollygagging," he announced. "We have work to do. Finish eating and getting your ammo sorted. I want these window positions ready for the next assault. Get those extra Claymores set up in front of those barricades we have downstairs, and make sure first platoon has enough hand grenades. It's our job up here to make sure those guys down there don't get overrun. Understood?"

His gruff orders sent the platoon back into their battle rhythm. Nearly an hour went by as the soldiers listened to outgoing artillery and mortar fire head toward the enemy. The constant sound of explosions and dull thudding became intermixed with the sounds of helicopters and warplanes flying overhead. It was very difficult to attack an enemy army inside a city. Many of the Chinese soldiers simply moved into the buildings or moved along the edges of them, making it very hard to spot them, and even harder for artillery fire to hit them. Most of the artillery ended up slamming into the roofs or sides of apartment buildings. While the projectiles certainly caused a lot of damage, they were also indiscriminate in who they killed; more often than not, the artillery also led to a lot of civilians being killed or injured.

"Here they come!" shouted a voice over the radio. Dayan's men had a couple of snipers placed on the upper floors of the office building they were in; it was their job to find the officers or men who appeared to be the leaders of the army or militia forces and take them out.

Staff Sergeant Dayan walked over to the window and leaned up against the side of the wall. He peered out, spotting the lines of enemy soldiers moving along the edges of the building two or three blocks away. Traveling in the center of the road, was something of grave concern—a T-99 battle tank was steadily making its way toward their barricade. The metal tracks creaked and cracked against the road. The deep rumbling of its diesel engine was the unmistakable roar of a main battle tank. Suddenly, the tank stopped, swiveled its turret to face the barricade and fired.

Boom. Bang!

The explosion blew apart a car the Israelis had parked in the center of the road. Then the turret turned slightly and fired again.

BOOM, BANG!

The next vehicle in the barricade was obliterated, sending flame and shrapnel in all directions.

"Someone take that tank out before he blows our entire defense apart!" shouted their captain into the radio.

Pop...swoosh...BANG.

A missile flew out of the fifth-floor window above them, streaking like man-made lightning toward the T-99. It slammed into the roof of the turret, the thinnest part of the tank's armor, and the shape charge blew its deadly contents directly into the crew compartment. The internal ammunition cooked off, and in fractions of a second, the turret of the tank blasted toward the sky.

Then several loud whistles sounded, which sent a shiver down the spines of every soldier defending the line. A mighty roar of hundreds, maybe even thousands of people could be heard as the street in front of them filled with people, all screaming at the top of their lungs as they charged, fire and hatred burning in their eyes as they sought to close the distance.

Ratatat, ratatat.

The light and heavy machine guns of the Israeli positions opened up on the crowd, cutting down the first several ranks of attackers like a scythe. Yet for every soldier that fell to the ground, another took their place as they continued to charge forward.

Sergeant Dayan looked down the sight of his rifle and continued to pull the trigger time and time again at the mass of humanity that was charging toward them. In less than a couple of minutes, the enemy had made it to the remains of the vehicle barricade, which was now burning. When they reached that position, the soldiers of First and Third Platoon who were on the ground level detonated their Claymores.

When the mines went off, it was as if some giant invisible hand just flattened the first four or five rows of enemy soldiers. In that brief second, the mob halted their advance, but then more whistles could be heard, and they resumed their charge. More enemy soldiers from further behind them surged forward.

"My God, how can they keep coming like this?" thought Sergeant Dayan. Truthfully, the way the Chinese kept attacking in the face of all of certain death was impressive to him, despite the speech he'd given not too many minutes ago.

"Keep shooting, men!" he shouted. "We have to keep them from overrunning our guys on the ground floor!" Looking down the line to check on his guys, he saw the ground was becoming completely covered in empty shell casings from their rifles.

One by one though, his guys were starting to get hit. The façade of the front of their building was becoming riddled with bullets. It was statistically only a matter of time until some of the incoming enemy rounds found the soft flesh of his men and either killed or wounded them. When one of his soldiers hit the ground, a medic would run up to him, grab him by the back handle of his body armor and pull him away from the wall, deeper into the building, so he could begin providing first aid.

Just when Sergeant Dayan didn't think they were going to be able to hold the line, a British Challenger tank fired a canister round into the mob, cutting a huge swath of the Chinese soldiers down. Then a company worth of British soldiers ran forward and shored up the Israeli lines, and more British armored vehicles joined the fray.

In less than a minute, the enemy attack fell apart and began to retreat. At the sight of the enemy falling back, the British troops that had just arrived charged forward, quickly followed by their armored vehicles. As Dayan watched them charge after the enemy, he felt nauseated; the tanks were literally running over both the dead and the dying that carpeted the street below.

Staff Sergeant Dayan slumped to the floor and placed his face into his hands. He began crying uncontrollably, and he didn't even know why. Perhaps he just felt overwhelmed by all the emotions of what he had just gone through, or perhaps the gruesome sound of the bones crunching under the advancing tanks had been a burden too heavy to bear. In either case, he wasn't the only soldier to break down in that moment.

****

Beijing, China
PLA Command Bunker

President Xi was practically beside himself as he listened intently to General Wei Liu, the overall PLA military commander, explain how their most recent attacks against the Allied invasion force in Shanghai had just failed. Somehow, three divisions of regular army forces and five divisions of militia had been badly mauled by enemy air and artillery attacks before they'd even made it to the front lines.

"Sir, it was as if the Allies somehow knew exactly where we were forming up and when we would be moving in order to make these attacks," General Wei concluded, forlorn.

It was a theme. Somehow, over the past month and a half, the Allies had managed to anticipate every move, every attack, in advance. President Xi was beginning to suspect they had a mole somewhere inside the government that was feeding them information.

General Xu Ding then took his turn regaling them with tales about the success of the Air Force's new UAV fighter drone program. Xi did have to give the man credit; the new UAV fighter drones were actually performing pretty well.

"It's too bad we don't have enough of them to really make a difference in this war," he thought. Xi's mind went back to what was happening in Guangdong Province. The bulk of China's aerospace industry had been relocated there after the nuclear attack on Shenyang. It seemed odd that the Americans would launch such a massive invasion in southern China unless they somehow knew of the importance of Guangzhou and Dongguan to their production of these new drone fighters and their aerospace program.

The Minister of Defense, General Kuang Li Jun, leaned forward as he glared at General Wei. "General, you have failed us and your country. Your services are no longer needed," he stated. Then he waved his hand, signaling several soldiers standing near the exit to apprehend him.

General Wei's eyes grew wide as saucers as he attempted to protest his dismissal. "Mr. President, please! You can't allow this to happen!" he exclaimed loudly. The guards rushed forward, grabbing him by his arms, pulling him out of the room.

Shaking his head in disgust, President Xi stood as he signaled for the others to stay seated. "We have meticulously planned this war, collaborating on it with the Russians and many other allies. We should have won this war nearly a year ago. Instead, we find ourselves the last nation standing, our homeland invaded. What I want to know is how are we going to repel these invaders? Can we still defeat them?"

The remaining generals and admirals in the room all squirmed a bit in their chairs, not knowing what to say. They certainly did not want to be the next person dragged out of the room. They all knew what was going to happen to General Wei and none of them wanted to suffer the same fate.

Seeing that no one had the guts to look him in the eye, or even attempt to answer his immediate question, Xi sat down and then reached under the table and depressed a small button. "Since it appears none of you have any ideas on how to defeat the enemy or reclaim victory, it would seem I need to find new generals who do," he said to the sudden shock and horror of the remaining generals. The side doors opened and a group of security personnel, the President's personal bodyguards, walked in and moved to detain each of them.

A short scuffle broke out as some of them pleaded with President Xi to save them. "Please, give me one more chance!" shouted one. "I'm the only one with an idea of how to defeat the Americans!" cried another.

Xi just shook his head and waved them off with a flick of his wrist. Once the generals were removed from the room, he heard several shots fired as they were dispensed with in the hallway. It was a rule of his not to allow any chances for insufficient leadership to call to their commands for help.

"Liquidate them and replace them before anyone can raise a fuss about it," he told himself, rubbing his temples in frustration.

"That went about as well as could be expected," Chairman Zhang said. He took a sip of his tea, the entire scene having no effect on him. The Minister of Defense nodded in agreement.

"It needed to be done many months ago, but this recent setback has given me the latitude I needed to do it and still maintain the confidence of the military," asserted President Xi. He paused. "Bring in General Yang Yin," he ordered.

Zhang nodded and got up to head down the hall to a room where the general was waiting patiently. As the chairman left the room, Xi nodded toward one of his bodyguards, who proceeded to screw a silencer onto his pistol and quickly followed after Zhang.

The Minister of Defense tried to keep his face as neutral as possible. It was obvious that Xi was purging the PLA leadership right now, and he was hoping that he was not next on the list.

When General Yang Yin walked into the room, Chairman Zhang was noticeably absent as the security guard closed the door behind him. He noted the empty seats and read the name placards before him before looking to the center of the table at the supreme leader.

President Xi motioned for him to take a seat opposite him, next to the Minister of Defense, who was looking a little pale.

As Yang sat down, Xi began to speak. "General Yang, I've called you here because our country is in grave danger, and none of my military leaders will give me an honest answer or provide a valid plan for how we're going to defeat the enemy. You have served the people well in the war thus far. Your battlefield defeats are not yours alone. You were defeated because the generals above you gave you an impossible task to accomplish and did not heed your warnings or your pleas for support."

Yang nodded cautiously.

"I've read your many requests for reinforcements, changes to battle plans and suggestions for how to turn the war around," Xi continued. "Each of them fell on deaf ears, but not mine. I've heard your pleas for help, and your ideas for how to turn the war around. What I need from you now is to take charge of the military and lead us to victory. Can you do that?" President Xi asked. He leaned forward, staring into the eyes of the one general who had given China its only victories in this war.

In that moment, General Yang seemed to understand exactly why these chairs were empty. He took a deep breath in and slowly let it out as he sat up a bit straighter. Doing his best to keep his face stoic, he said, "I need to know what the status of the country's military force is if I'm to make an accurate assessment of whether the war can be turned around. As you know, I have been focused on fighting the Americans in the south of China, where my command is. I'm not fully aware of what the Allies are doing in the north or in Shanghai."

Xi smiled at the bluntness. *"Finally, a general who isn't afraid to speak his mind, even if it might get him killed."*

Xi depressed an intercom button and instructed several PLA colonels to come in and provide General Yang with an update on the war. The Minister of Defense also brought him up to speed on their military production capability and ability to support and sustain the war.

For the next three hours, the colonels presented Yang and Xi with an update on each sector the Allies were attacking from. The last brief was on the country's economy, its financial health, and then the overall morale of the people. It was a lot of information to take in.

Xi had no intention of losing power. If he had to make a peace deal with the Allies, then the only one he'd accept was one that left him still in control. He hoped General Yang could accomplish that task.

****

After the colonels left the room, General Yang sat silently looking over the materials they'd left behind. First, he looked at some of the maps and initial statements of what was happening in the north, then he focused in on Shanghai, and then his own theater, the south. What astounded him the most was how effective the Allies had been at deceiving them with their invasion of Shanghai—the PLA leadership had been caught completely flatfooted by the invasion.

The other thing that confounded him was what the American Army group was doing in the western part of

China. It appeared a large American Army group had invaded through Mongolia last fall and that, when spring had come, they'd entered Inner Mongolia. Even now, they were driving nearly unopposed on Beijing from the west. The Allies had truly encircled China and were slowly chopping her up into smaller, more manageable chunks.

Looking up at Xi, Yang asked, "You know how you eat an elephant, Sir?"

Snickering at the question, Xi replied, "One bite at a time."

"Exactly," Yang responded. "In this case, the Allies knew they couldn't defeat us by attacking from one front, so they've opted to attack us from multiple directions. They also knew they needed to destroy our Air Force and our ability to protect the skies and our ground forces. The army that rules the skies tends to win."

President Xi nodded, but he didn't look very pleased. "You're not telling me anything I don't already know," he quipped. "Why do you believe the Allies invaded Shanghai and Guangdong Province? It would have made more sense for the Allies to marshal all their forces in the north and sweep down across the country from a land border they had already secured. Why did they deviate from that conventional wisdom?"

Leaning back in his chair, Yang knew exactly what Xi was after and why none of the generals before him were still alive. Holding his chin out a bit, Yang replied, "If you will indulge me, Mr. President, I'll attempt to explain why the Americans have done what they've done and why the other generals failed to see it."

Xi nodded for him to continue. He also signaled for an aide to bring them more fresh tea and some food as well. General Yang was grateful for that—it was likely they'd be there most of the evening, talking.

"As you already know, Mr. President, I grew up in America," Yang began. "I was educated in their schools and I even went to the prestigious American military academy, the Citadel, in the state of South Carolina. While studying to become an American military officer, I was extensively taught American military history and how their generals think. As a cadet, I was taught what every officer in the military is taught, how to lead soldiers and to accomplish the mission, to think outside the box and bend the rules when necessary. I was also able to attend the prestigious advanced infantry school's Ranger program my senior year."

President Xi nodded, but it was clear his patience was wearing thin.

"I tell you this because I've been trained to think like an American officer. Many of the American colonels and lower-level generals we're fighting now are some of my classmates from twenty years ago. The reason the Americans are attacking us from Inner Mongolia, northern China, and the Korean Peninsula is simple: they wanted our focus and attention to be on northern China. They wanted my predecessors to move all our forces toward the north, and to that end, they were very successful."

Xi leaned in at this point and interrupted him. "Are you saying the Americans wanted us to believe these three fronts they've been attacking us from in the north for what, eighteen months, were a ruse? A well-groomed trap?" he asked incredulously.

Yang leaned forward as he replied, "Yes, that's exactly what I'm saying."

"Explain," Xi said, voice tense.

"When the Americans launched their massive offensive in the north, General Wei Liu moved nearly all of our reserve forces there and to the west to deal with them. While this move has largely stalled the Allied offensive, it has also left us with very few reserve forces to deploy anywhere else. Let's also look at the air side of things. The American stealth bombers, or what's left of them, have focused nearly all their attacks not on going after our command-and-control headquarters, communications nodes, or even our Air Force or military units—they've focused their attacks on key railheads, bridges and tunnels linking northern, central and southern China together."

He pulled out a series of rail maps the briefers had left behind and showed Xi what he was talking about. "Once we had committed our forces to the north and stopped their offense, the Americans invaded Guangdong Province."

Xi obviously became annoyed with the history lesson and slapped his hand on the table "I know this! Tell me why!" he demanded angrily.

"To go after our manufacturing base and our finances. If we can't produce the tools of war—the drone fighter planes, infantry fighting vehicles, small-arms munitions—then we can't fight. By attacking Guangdong Province, they're hoping to capture more than forty percent of our military manufacturing base."

"Then why did they also invade Shanghai?"

"Because Shanghai accounts for more than thirty percent of our tax base. With the Shanghai region and Guangdong Province in their control, the Allies will occupy more than fifty percent of our military manufacturing base and more than sixty percent of our tax base. They're going to starve us financially and cripple our manufacturing ability to sustain the war." Yang concluded his explanation of the Allies' strategy as he saw it.

President Xi had this look on his face as if a literal lightbulb had just illuminated in his head. "Is the war lost?" he asked.

"Th*at's an incredibly loaded question*," thought Yang. He looked at the empty chairs before him and considered carefully whether he should tell the truth as he saw it or lie and try his best to prolong the war as long as possible.

Xi must have seen his perplexed look. "General, please give me your honest opinion. I'm not going to have you shot for telling me what I don't want to hear. Unless we acknowledge the obvious, we can't hope to find a solution."

Yang nodded and let out a deep sigh. "Mr. President, the war is lost. We can't reverse the damage that has been done. At this point, it's more about managing the loss. The Americans have a presidential election coming up. For the next twelve months, their political parties will be fighting amongst themselves to win or retain control of the government. As I see it, we have two options: we can either try for a peace deal with the current administration, or we can try and prolong the war and hope the opposition party

331

wins control of the government and we can achieve a better peace deal."

General Yang's heart raced as he waited for Xi's reaction. When he wasn't immediately executed, he slowly began to try and breathe again. President Xi didn't say anything for a few moments. Yang could tell that the wheels were turning inside his head as he weighed his options. The general wondered what his decision would be as the leader of the country. If they tried to prolong the war, it would mean more of China would fall to the Allies, and if that happened, it would be harder for him to negotiate an acceptable peace deal. Then again, if he threatened to wage an endless guerrilla war if they didn't accept his proposal, he might be able to gain a better deal.

Finally, Xi spoke. "What about our nuclear weapons? What if we used them on our own soil to destroy the Allied armies? Could that be enough to turn the tide?"

Yang paused briefly. "That's a tricky question, Mr. President. The Americans know where our nuclear missile silos are, so using them is out of the question. They would move to destroy them all as soon as they thought we might use them. If we used our mobile launchers, I believe we could catch them by surprise, but personally, I'd recommend against using nuclear weapons. Once we do, you can bet the

Americans will use them on us. We saw what they did to North Korea and to Shenyang." General Yang hoped the President would not pursue that path.

Xi slumped back in his seat, the wind taken out of his sails. He had finally heard the sobering truth...Yang wondered what he would choose to do with that information.

Chapter 18

A Desperate Push

Radar Station Ridgeline

Sitting in the bottom of his fighting position, Corporal Jordan Wright looked at the sky above them, marveling at the beauty of the stars on full display. As he watched some of the glowing specks twinkle in the night sky, Wright thought these were some of the best times to be in the Royal Army, away from the hustle and bustling of London and his never-ending work at Google. He'd been telling himself that he was going to buy a place in the country one day, but thus far, he'd never gotten around to it.

"Maybe I'll sell a ton of my Google stock and just do it when I get back from this war," he considered. Then he almost laughed aloud at the thought of trying to convince his lovely wife to live in a small village in the countryside, several hours from London. She was quite the London socialite, what with her yoga class she taught in the evenings and her work at an art gallery. She loved the high energy and fast-paced life of the city. Really, that was one of the things that had attracted him to her—she was a ball of constant energy, full of life and passion.

Looking to his left, Corporal Wright saw that Private Nigel Flowers was still asleep. He'd let the kid sleep a bit more; they still had another twenty minutes until "stand-to." They were nearing the scariest moments of the day now though; for some reason, the Chinese liked to use the time when the sun had just started to break through the evening darkness to launch their first attacks of the day.

Wright heard a rustling behind him. He craned his head to the left, looking for its source. He gripped his rifle a little tighter and stood to see who or what was making the noise.

When he spotted Lieutenant Lou Shay creeping up to his position with a couple of other soldiers in tow, he let out the breath he had been holding. "Good morning, Lieutenant," he whispered as good-naturedly as he could manage. He waved to the other visitors to welcome them to the trench. The new arrivals woke Private Flowers up, but he seemed glad to see a few more people joining them in their part of the trench.

Once B Coy had secured the ridgeline containing the radar station and enemy antiaircraft guns on it, their captain had ordered them to build a series of fortifications at a couple of strategic points facing the city below them. When the PLA had failed to attack right away, the paratroopers had taken full advantage of the time to dig themselves in deep. They were also able to get some help from their engineering unit, which had finally arrived in the fourth wave of transports. In the short two days they'd been left alone to work, they'd managed to cover most of the ridge with trenches that were two and a half meters deep, as well as construct bunkers for their machine guns. They'd even managed to string up rows of concertina wire roughly a hundred meters in front of their positions.

Lieutenant Shay introduced the newcomers. "Corporal Wright, this is Lance Corporal Benjamin White from A Coy, 6th Battalion, Royal Australian Regiment. Corporal White here has five privates with him to help keep their FN MAG 58 machine gun up and running. You know this quadrant better than I do—tell them where they need to have the gun set up and what their fields of fire should be." He paused for a second to look at his watch. "Stand-to is in ten minutes. Get these guys ready. The captain told me we should expect a large attack within the next hour, so we need to be prepared."

Corporal Wright shook the Australian's hand, and then Lieutenant Shay didn't wait any longer; he moved past him and headed further down the line to speak to the next group of soldiers.

The six Australians stood there for a moment, staring at the eight British soldiers they'd just been dumped on. Lance Corporal White was the first to speak. "So, where do you want us to get this pig set up?" he asked, gesturing to the private carrying the large machine gun.

"Let's set you guys out over here," Wright replied, pointing to a small outcropping of their trench. He had been using that as his firing position, but it would make more sense to place the machine gun there. It had a better arc of fire and could cover more of the approaches. "How much ammo did you guys bring for that thing?" he asked.

"Ten belts. You think we'll need more?" one of the privates asked nervously.

Wright chuckled. "Yeah, we're going to need a lot more than that. Look, one of you guys get the extra barrel set up on its bipod on the ground near the wall; that way, when you need to swap out barrels, it'll be quick and easy. I need two of you privates to crawl back to wherever you came from and grab more ammo. Bring at least another ten belts of ammo. I hope like hell we won't need it, but I'd rather have it here than start to run low during a battle and have to send one of you guys to go grab more then."

With his initial orders given, the two privates headed off to go grab more ammunition while the four of them remained at the trench, awaiting stand-to and what the dawn would bring.

******

As the sun slowly crept its way up in the sky, the last remnants of the darkness evaporated to reveal a city in turmoil below them. Dozens upon dozens of buildings, roads and bridges had been destroyed by airstrikes and artillery from two days prior. Most of the fires were out at this point, only leaving behind the charred remains of what used to be a thriving city.

"What the hell is that?" asked one of the Australians as he pointed to a group of shadows.

"*Oh crap, here they come,*" Wright thought to himself. The ground below them started to move.

"Get ready, lads, it looks like the Chinese are finally going to pay us a visit this morning," he replied.

The young man turned and looked at him as if to say, "You can't be serious?" Then they heard the first rounds of incoming rocket and artillery fire.

"Everybody down!" yelled Wright. He grabbed Private Flowers's arm and pulled him down to sit at the bottom of the trench with him.

The high-pitched shrieks of Katyusha rockets filled the sky just before the loud, bone-jarring roar of explosions.

Boom, boom, boom. BOOM!

The world around the paratroopers was disintegrating. Dirt, tree branches, pieces of sandbags, and everything else above the lip of their trench was being torn apart by the pieces of hot shrapnel whipsawing back and forth across the air above them.

The bombing itself lasted for only a few moments, but it had severely shaken their confidence. Then the new silence was broken by dozens of whistles and an enormously loud guttural yell that sounded like thousands of individuals screaming together.

"Up! Everyone up!" yelled Corporal Wright to the fourteen soldiers he was in charge of.

Lifting himself above the lip of the trench, he glanced down toward the burned-out city and saw a massive wave of humanity charging up toward them. They were roughly 300 meters away and closing the distance fast. Several of the machine-gun bunkers on either side of them opened fire, sending lines of red tracers into the crowds of advancing enemy soldiers.

"Get that gun going. Sweep it back and forth across them!" Wright bellowed. Meanwhile, Private Flowers used his grenade launcher to lob 40mm HE rounds into the enemy formations.

With two of the Australian soldiers manning the MAG 58, the other soldiers fired away at the attackers with their Steyr EF88 rifles. Wright brought his SA80 to his shoulder, looking down the sights at the wave of enemy soldiers rushing toward him.

Pop, pop, pop, pop, pop.

He kept pulling the trigger over and over again, watching one soldier after another drop to the ground only to be trampled on by the person behind them as they charged forward to take their place. The machine guns interlaced along the trench tore into the enemy ranks, hitting an enemy soldier with nearly every pull of the trigger. They burned through ammunition at a prodigious rate.

Thump, thump, thump.

The heavy weapons platoon a few hundred meters behind them started to fire their 60mm and 81mm mortars on the enemy. This was quickly being intermixed with 105mm artillery rounds from their artillery unit near the airport. As each mortar or artillery round landed among the charging horde, a small swath of them would simply be blown apart. Yet somehow, like waves of the ocean relentlessly pounds the beach, the enemy soldiers just kept charging.

Dozens and then hundreds of enemy bullets slapped into the sandbags in front of them and the tree branches that still dotted the side of the ridge. The terror building up inside of each of the soldiers became almost overwhelming. The ground in front of them was alive with men and women, angrily charging them with AK-74s.

Suddenly, one of the Australian soldiers screamed as he reached for his face. A bullet hit him in the jaw, destroying most of his mouth. He slumped to the ground, writhing in pain and pleading for help. One of the medics further down the trench heard his cries and came running over. When he saw the mess of the poor man's jaw, he immediately applied a dressing on it to try and hold everything together. Once the bleeding was stemmed, he quickly pulled out a syringe of morphine and administered it.

With his immediate task at hand complete, the medic grabbed the soldier's hand. "Hey, man, I wish I could do more right now, but I need you to head to the aid station further behind our lines. Do you know where it is?" he asked.

The soldier nodded.

"Good. I have to stay here with the rest of the soldiers in the trench. Lord knows you aren't going to be my last patient today."

The young soldier's eyes welled with tears from the pain, but he nodded and headed off in search of the aid station.

Corporal Wright tried to return to the task at hand. Just beyond their own positions, he could see the national forest preserve the Gurkhas and a couple of their sister units were dug into. They appeared to be getting overrun. A lot of friendly artillery fire started landing really close to where he knew the edge of their lines were.

"I hope my mates in those units will be OK," he thought.

Corporal Wright heard the sound of a jet and turned to look up just in time to see a German Eurofighter swoop in, releasing four objects from under its wings. They tumbled from the sky until they impacted near the middle of the swarm of enemy soldiers, maybe four hundred meters away. Within milliseconds, the jellied mixture of the bombs sprayed outward in a pattern that stretched nearly fifty meters wide before something inside the bomb ignited the sticky mixture. In the flash of an eye, everything that jellied mixture had touched—fabric, skin, metal and trees—erupted in red and orange flames.

Wright continued to fire away at the still-charging enemy soldiers, but the scene before him was overwhelming and gut-wrenching. Several hundred PLA soldiers were enveloped in flames, screaming wildly; some of them dropped to the ground, rolling around in a vain attempt to put the flames out, while others ran around flailing their arms in the air, screaming until they simply collapsed. It was the most horrifying thing Wright had ever seen.

He turned to look for Private Flowers and saw him doubled over in the trench, puking his guts out. The young Australian soldier manning the MAG 58 had tears running down his face as he screamed at the charging enemy, killing as many of them as he possible could.

"Flowers! Snap out of it and start shooting, or we're all going to *die*!" Corporal Wright screamed.

Private Flowers looked up at him with anger in his eyes. Like Rocky Balboa getting up after a punch to the face, the young private wiped his mouth and turned back to shooting at the enemy.

Wright then moved over to the MAG 58 gunner, placing his hand on his shoulder. "I need you to take a break and start lobbing grenades at them," he yelled. "Can you do that for me? I'll take the gun."

The young man, who still had tears streaming down his face, just nodded and handed the gun over.

While the others around him continued to shoot, Wright pulled the gun from the trench line and dropped it down to the floor of the trench, so it sat on its bipod. He hit the quick-release on the barrel, which was now glowing hot, and disconnected it. Then he moved over to the second barrel and mated the two pieces. Once it was locked in place, he returned to the trench line. One of the privates handed him a fresh belt of ammo and proceeded to connect another one to it so he could just focus on shooting while the assistant gunner made sure he had bullets to shoot.

Corporal Wright tucked the butt of the weapon into his shoulder and sighted down on a tranche of enemy soldiers that had just reached their concertina wire at the one-hundred-meter mark. He pulled the trigger, giving three-to-five-second bursts into each section of enemy soldiers before moving further down the line. He didn't even have to aim; there were just so many enemy soldiers charging them, all he had to do was point in their vicinity and pull the trigger and he'd hit huge swaths of them.

Then the grenades came into play. The British and Australian soldiers lobbed them as fast as they could at the enemy, and likewise, many of the Chinese soldiers started throwing them at their trench as well.

Bang, boom, pop, BOOM!

Corporal Wright realized with agony that the PLA bullets were also starting to get a lot more accurate. One of the British soldiers in his squad took a bullet to the forehead and collapsed, dead in the trench. Another soldier clutched at his right shoulder when he took a hit, and then the Australian soldier helping to keep his machine gun fed with ammo took a bullet to the left arm. In a matter of seconds, most of the Australian and British soldiers around him had been hit in one form or another.

The enemy just kept coming. The Chinese soldiers eventually succeeded in cutting several breaks into the wire, and the horde of humanity pushed its way through the gaps. Wright turned his barrel on the mass of bodies that was now less than fifty meters from him and quickly gaining ground; he let loose a nearly ten-second string of bullets into their ranks. Twenty or thirty enemy soldiers fell, only to be quickly replaced by the next cluster following up behind them. With virtually nowhere to go, and nothing more he could do, Wright stopped shooting the machine gun just long enough to grab the detonators for the Claymore antipersonnel mines the Americans had given them.

He pushed the buttons to systematically detonate them all, one by one. Each explosion ripped huge ribbons of enemy soldiers apart. Finally, when Corporal Wright didn't think he could take it any longer, he heard a bugle sound.

The enemy soldiers that had gotten so close to them began to fall back. In minutes, the nearly constant roar of gunfire subsided to just the occasional single shot, and the agonizing cries of the wounded and dying became the pervasive noise around him.

When Corporal Wright realized that his death was not imminent, he turned to look for Private Flowers and found his friend slumped down in the trench. He left the machine gun and moved quickly to his side. "Flowers, you OK, buddy?" he asked. "We made it. The enemy is retreating."

Flowers didn't immediately respond. Wright turned his shoulder to reveal the extent of his friend's wounds. Blood soaked through several parts of his right arm and chest area. He was pale and clammy, but the private managed a groan. "I thought we were done for, Corporal," he said. Suddenly, he had a fire in his eyes, like he was ready to be propped up against the trench with his rifle again. "What now?" he asked.

"Now we get you some help, Nigel," said Wright, fighting back his emotions. "This is your ticket home, back to the real world, away from all this craziness. I just need you to hang in there, OK, Nigel?" he asked. He scanned his surroundings for a medic.

Wright spotted one of the medics closing the eyes of one soldier, clearly a person he couldn't save. He ran toward him as he waved his arms to flag him down. Within moments, the medic was helping him carry Private Flowers back to the rear of their lines where the aid station was.

With his friend taken care of, Corporal Wright looked around his stretch of the lines. He only found six able-bodied soldiers: five British, one Australian. All the other soldiers around them were either dead or wounded and being treated by the medics.

****

Suzhou Guangfu Airport

Brigadier Sir Nick McCoil wasn't sure how much longer his force was going to hold out. The PLA had been throwing everything they had at his airborne brigade and then some. His brigade was supposed to be relieved by the main ground force coming in from the port, but they had been held up by heavy fighting in several of the cities along the way. It was looking more and more likely that they might be on their own for at least another day, and he wasn't sure his command would be able to make it—they were running extremely low on ammunition and had already sustained more than fifty percent casualties.

One of the communications officers walked up to him. "Sir, I have General Bennet on the radio for you."

Brigadier McCoil looked at the haggard faces of the men around him and the streams of wounded soldiers being brought to the brigade medical tents just outside his headquarters, and he knew he had to get some help from Bennet or they were done for.

He nodded at the communications officer and followed him back to the radio. He picked up the handset. "This is Gladiator Actual. How copy?"

"Good copy. Gladiator Actual, this is Eagle Actual. How long can you hold your current position?"

"If the commanding general is asking you how long you can hold out, it's not good," McCoil thought. He immediately wondered how long his help would be delayed.

"I've taken some major casualties. We're down to fifty percent strength and I'm starting to run out of ammunition—not sure that we can hold another day without a major resupply and reinforcements," he explained.

There was a short pause before Bennet replied. "Our ground force isn't going to be able to relieve you in twelve hours," he said glumly. "I'm not confident they will be able to relieve you for another forty-eight hours. Given your situation, I'm organizing a major resupply to your position and additional air support. Stand by to receive more reinforcements and ammunition in the next several hours. Out."

And like that, their orders were changed. Instead of holding the airfield for three days, it was now looking like six. Meanwhile, half of the PLA had been attacking his forces for nearly two days straight.

"Whoever the general sends, they better be some really damn good soldiers, or this is going to turn into a slaughter," McCoil thought in disgust.

****

Six hours later, true to his word, General Bennet had arranged for a massive increase in air support. His forward air controllers had ground-attack planes and fighter bombers stacked up for near-constant missions. They were hammering the PLA positions wherever they found them. They even had A-10 Thunderbolts patrolling ten kilometers outside his perimeter looking for clusters of enemy troops to engage. The US Air Force had flown in fuel, munitions and maintainers to the airfield so the squadron of A-10s could rebase there to help McCoil and his men.

Then the air bridge of supplies began to arrive. The first to fly in was a string of ten C-130 cargo planes, which soared over the western side of the airfield where most of his artillery batteries were set up. They airdropped pallets of ammunition for his 105mm guns and 81mm mortars.

Then the sky above the airfield filled with hundreds and hundreds of parachutes. Three battalions of soldiers from the 82nd Airborne had arrived to help shore up his positions. With virtually no enemy aircraft or antiaircraft threats near the airfield, General Bennet had also ordered in five C-5 Galaxy heavy lift cargo planes. Once they had landed and taxied off the runway, they offloaded twenty Stryker vehicles, along with 500 additional troops and pallets of ammunition.

Meanwhile, the medical staff quickly worked to get all the wounded loaded for the trip out. Looking out the window, McCoil watched the long line of wounded soldiers—some walking, some being carried on stretchers being loaded into the cavernous beast of an airplane. He felt good about getting them out of there.

Just then, a US Army colonel wearing his camouflage war paint walked in. "Brigadier McCoil?" the tough-looking soldier asked. He had a sharpness in his eyes that only decades of combat could hone.

Of all the Allied officers McCoil had met, this was the first time he'd seen an American senior officer loaded for bear and ready to personally fight if necessary. Looking past the man, he saw hundreds of warriors with full face paint on, gathering up a bunch of gear and loading it into what had to be some sort of American Special Forces vehicles.

Returning his gaze back to the man in front of him, he replied, "Yes, I'm Brigadier McCoil. And you are?"

Smiling at the look of confusion on the British commander's face, he answered, "I'm here to pull your butts out of the mess you appear to be in," he said with a wry grin on his face. Then he added, "I'm Colonel Adrian St. Leo, commander of the 75th Ranger regiment. I was directed by General Bennet himself to get my men in here and assist you in any way possible. I'm also the ground commander for the US Forces that are arriving. Landing right now is the 2nd Battalion, 501st Infantry Regiment. Over the next six hours, the 1st and 2nd Battalions, 504th Infantry Regiment will start to arrive at staggered times. If you'll show me where you need me to plug some holes in your lines, I'll see to it these battalions relieve your forces."

Now it was McCoil's turn to smile. General Bennet had not only sent him more help, he'd sent him some of the best crack infantry units in the US Army. He suddenly felt a lot better about being able to hold their positions—his airborne force had more than doubled.

"Well, Colonel, you couldn't have come at a better time," said McCoil. "Let's walk over to the map and I'll show you exactly where I need your guys. Did General Bennet or anyone else tell you if additional reinforcements are still coming, or are you guys it?"

"I'm not sure about additional troops, but I do know at least two companies of Abrams battle tanks are on the way, along with another twenty Stryker vehicles and a battalion of 155mm artillery guns. Probably a ton of food, water, and ammunition as well, but I think we're it for troops," Colonel St. Leo explained. "You wouldn't believe how bad the fighting is around the Shanghai Airport or the ports right now. It's a real slaughter, if you ask me." His face showed some of the horrors he had witnessed.

McCoil nodded as he took in the information; it was hard to spend energy worrying about what was happening at the ports and other landing points, but clearly, what was happening there was having an impact on his force being relieved. Since Colonel St. Leo was the first outside person he'd seen in over a week and had just come from headquarters, he pressed for more information.

"What's the hold-up at the port? Why haven't we been relieved yet?" He asked his questions quietly so no one else around them could hear.

St. Leo likewise leaned in and in a similarly hushed tone replied, "The PLA has been throwing massive human wave attacks at us. They'll throw a battalion or two worth of militia forces at us to tie us down or expose our positions, and then a regular Army unit will follow in behind them. I mean, we're killing them by the thousands, but we're also taking a lot of casualties. It's like they've suddenly become suicidal or something—like if they lose this battle, they'll lose the entire war. They're hitting us with everything they've got. Last I heard, the British 3rd Division was supposed to relieve your position, but they've since gotten bogged down in the city of Fengxian. My understanding is the German 10th Panzer Division is skirting along the coastline to swing out behind Fengxian and push their way to our position right now."

McCoil shook his head in disgust. "OK, we'll have to make this work and hold out for a while longer then."

The two discussed where to place the new reinforcements that were arriving and what they wanted to do with the steady stream of armored vehicles being sent to them. Colonel St. Leo and Brigadier McCoil agreed the best use of the Rangers for the time being was to act as their QRF. If a spot opened up in line that looked like it was going to break, or intelligence indicated a large enemy force was heading their way, they'd shift the Rangers and their armored vehicles to meet them. It was the surest way to hold the line without making any one point too weak by shifting units around the battlefield.

Chapter 19
Awakening

Fort Meade, Maryland
National Security Agency

Katelyn Mackie had spent the night in her office, struggling with a problem and what to do about it. The reports streaming in from the frontlines were just appalling. While her Trojan horse program inside the Chinese communication system was undoubtedly saving lives and changing the course of the war, the casualties were horrific. The PLA leadership had to know the war was lost, yet they kept throwing more and more soldiers at the Allied positions. In many cases, her program would identify where an enemy attack was going to take place, and the Allies would use that information to vector in bombers and artillery, slaughtering them before they even got close to the Allied positions.

She shook her head as she read a report about the Allied airborne force at Sangyuanli. The paratroopers had held out against nearly four straight days of human wave assaults. "*The Chinese are offering up untrained soldiers like sacrifices to Incan gods,*" she thought in horror. She knew they had to find a way to put a stop to this.

A knock at the door broke her concentration. Looking up, she saw her friend, Tyler Walden, peering into her office. "You look like crap, Kate. Did you sleep at all?" he inquired, concern written on his face.

Katelyn gave a weak smile. "I laid my head down on my desk around 3 a.m. I think I nodded off for a couple of hours. You want to get some coffee?"

He nodded his head and snickered. "Yeah, pumpkin, let's get you some brain juice. I want to talk with you about something the director approached me about on my way into the office today," he replied.

As she followed him out of her office, she raised an eyebrow. Without saying a word, it was clear she had responded, "Do explain."

Tyler took the cue. "You know Hung Hui-ju, the President of Taiwan, right? Well, the State Department has been working with her for nearly a year on creating dozens of different social media posts, videos, and pleas to the citizens of the People's Republic. The problem has been getting those messages through the 'Great Firewall of China.' Well, that got me to thinking about our program."

Before they'd even reached the hot plate with a fresh pot of coffee on it, she paused and looked up at him with tired eyes. She was concerned about exposing her precious program.

"I can already tell you're against it," he muttered, obviously disappointed that he hadn't even mentioned his idea yet but could tell it was dead on arrival.

She took a deep breath as she poured the java into her mug, adding two creams and no sugar to the caffeinated mixture. "I'm not automatically opposed, I just don't know how we would make it work without giving away our secret."

"I was thinking about that as well," said Tyler. "As long as we don't try to upload anything, we're essentially a ghost in their systems. If we try to tamper with it, we'll give ourselves away, and then they may change the way they're communicating."

Katelyn reluctantly nodded. "Exactly. The program was built to mirror what was going on, not allow us to ghost around inside it, and especially not transmit data. We'd be detected in seconds. If that happened, it would be devastating to our forces on the ground. Have you read some of the reports coming in from the fighting?" she asked as they walked back into her room. She sat down at her desk and rifled through some of the papers in front of her until she found the one about the airborne forces she'd been reading before she fell asleep.

Mackie handed him the report. "Look at this one. It's a British and French airborne force deep behind enemy lines. They were supposed to be relieved by the ground forces within seventy-two hours. It's been *six days* and they still haven't been relieved yet because the ground forces are stuck fighting it out in the cities on the way to the airbase. Apparently, the casualties and fighting have gotten so bad, General Bennet ordered three additional battalions from the 82nd Airborne and a battalion of Army Rangers to try and save them. I mean, look at the casualties—over two thousand killed and twice that many wounded," she said. Tears formed in her eyes.

"The sad part, Tyler, is this is just *one* battle," she continued. "Since we started the Shanghai invasion six days ago, the Allies have sustained over 28,000 killed and 40,000 wounded. In the south at the Hong Kong landings, the Marines have suffered 32,000 killed and another 50,000 wounded. These are just *our* losses; the PLA has suffered over 300,000 killed in the last thirty days. How much longer can this killing go on?" she exclaimed. She started sobbing.

All the late nights, the emotions of so many lives depending on her, were finally taking their toll. Tyler got up and closed her door, so no one else who might just happen to be walking by her office would see her like this. Everyone had a breaking point, and there was no need for more people to be involved in hers. He walked around her desk and knelt down next to her, putting his arm around her shoulders. Then he just let her cry.

When she appeared to be all cried out, he pulled back and looked up at her. "You're the strongest woman I know, Katelyn, but even the most stoic person needs a shoulder to cry on from time to time. This has been tough, Kate. I know the casualties are really high and it's starting to get to you. But know that if you hadn't developed this cyber code and penetrated their communications system, the casualties would probably be ten times higher. You've saved tens of thousands of lives, Kate—just remember that when you get discouraged."

She wiped her face with a tissue and nodded.

Tyler waited for her as she reached for her purse and hurriedly fixed the mascara that had smeared across her cheeks. Then he pushed, "Now, let's figure this out. If we used our program to pump out President Hung's message, how long could we do it for, and how wide could we spread her message? How could we shape it to help end the war? That needs to be our goal now."

Her mind churned.

"I need to look at the code again. I'd like to wargame out the various types of responses we'd get from their cyberwarfare group as well. We need to figure out how long we'd have before they found out what we were doing and shut us down. We also need to figure out, if they shut us down, will they have to shut down the entire communication system or will they find a way to lock us out? I don't want to bring this idea up to the director or the White House without having gone over the viability of it," she replied.

"I was thinking about that very problem, Kate. I'm not sure they can lock us out. Remember, we built that code into the firmware of the UAVs. They'd be forced to go back to the old-fashioned radio systems, but we can easily jam those." Tyler drained the rest of his coffee.

Katelyn rubbed her temples. "If the PLA did that, then their entire country would be open to our broadcasting President Hung's message directly across the AM and FM bands, wouldn't it?" she asked. "I mean, if they wanted to jam the signal, they could, but they'd be jamming their own communications as well, right?" She hoped this was an accurate assessment—radio communications was not her specialty.

A devilish grin spread across Tyler's face. "I like where you're going with this," he responded. "Now, I'm no radio expert myself, but I think we could find a few guys who are. From what I understand, the PLA has a pretty firm grasp on jamming that kind of stuff right now. As long as they're operating their communications system on the UAV platform, the AM/FM radio waves aren't important—they don't need them or use them. But if we take the UAV platform away from them, they'll have to switch back to the older systems."

The two of them talked for a little while before they called the rest of their little cadre of cyber coders and hackers into the conference room. They wanted to start hashing over the scenarios immediately. They also sent a request to the director's office to get them some AM/FM radio specialists ASAP. They needed to talk with some commercial and military radio and TV broadcasting specialists to see how they could capitalize on this plan if they did move forward with it.

****

Taiwan

Yonghe Residence

Office of the President of the Republic of China

Ambassador Max Bryant was growing frustrated with these social media gurus and Hollywood types, constantly trying to make suggestions to President Hung Hui-ju on how to craft a better, more compelling message for the weekly broadcasts she had been creating since recapturing Taiwan. While the messages were helping to lift the spirits of the Taiwanese people, they appeared to be having very little effect on the people living on the mainland. Even in the captured areas of the PRC, where the Allies controlled the airways, most Chinese communists were just not connecting with her. They still viewed her as a puppet of the West and saw the Allies as invaders, not liberators.

Seeing that they still had a few more minutes until the tech gurus arrived, Ambassador Bryant turned to President Hung. "Madam President, if you could produce just one video, give one message to the people on the mainland, what would it be? How would you convince them to either turn on the communist government or demand an end to the bloodshed?" he asked matter-of-factly.

President Hung was a bit taken aback by the question.

"She probably thought she'd already been doing that with these weekly addresses," Ambassador Bryant thought as he waited for her to say something.

"Mr. Ambassador, are you trying to tell me these messages are not working?" she finally managed to say.

Bryant sighed; he knew he needed to be delicate in his response. He didn't want to offend her. He personally knew President Xi of China, but that personal relationship hadn't been enough to keep the US and China from going to war, nor had it been able to put a stop to this madness.

Looking the Taiwanese President in the eye, he replied, "No, Ma'am, they're not."

Her mouth opened slightly with the shock of such a blunt reply.

"I'm not sure what your advisors have been telling you, or what the CIA or military advisors have said, but even in the occupied territories, the average citizens are not warming up to your messages or pleas for peace," Ambassador Bryant explained. "In northern China, nearly two hundred million people live in the occupied territory. Your weekly messages are played across every medium possible, yet the people still view you as a puppet of the West, not the rightful leader of a unified China. That has to change. If we can't convince even these people, who by all accounts are now living in a freer society, then I'm not sure how we're going to get the rest of the country to accept you. They have to believe living under your leadership is better for them and their children than a continued life under the communist dictatorship of President Xi."

President Hung thought about that for a moment, then nodded in acceptance. "Perhaps you're right. Maybe I've been listening to too many suggestions from others. How do you think I should approach this?" she asked.

"I think you need to speak from the heart. Outline a vision for a unified China—one that sees all people prosper and not just the politically connected. Talk economics with them; tell them about how you want to clean up the air pollution across the country, how you want to diversify the country's economy, so all of the jobs aren't concentrated in the major cities. Talk about things you know the communists are not addressing. Talk about how people should be free to express their own opinions without fear of being blackballed by the government, or worship the God of their choosing," he said.

Bryant was tired of the same old drab messages the political advisors kept telling her to focus on. They just weren't working. Something else needed to be tried, and soon. As the Allies gobbled up more of the country, they needed a more effective message than what the political consultants and tech gurus had been coming up with.

President Hung called her secretary to tell him to cancel her meetings for the rest of the day. She wanted to spend a few more hours with Ambassador Bryant and see if they could craft a better message.

****

Washington, D.C.
White House
Presidential Emergency Operations Center

President Foss sat back in the oversized leather chair as he digested the proposed plan from his Senior Cyberwarfare Advisor, Katelyn Mackie. Turning to his Secretary of Defense, he asked, "What are your thoughts on this, Jim? Is this worth the risk?"

Jim Castle sat there, silently pondering that question for a moment before he responded. "My gut says no, but I believe the proposal should be studied a bit more by my staff. I don't want to dismiss it out of hand either, because I can also see the value in moving in this direction. My concern is, what happens when we lose our window into the PLA's communication apparatus? That intelligence data has saved the lives of countless thousands of Allied forces. We may not have been able to establish the foothold in mainland China had it not been for the inside access to their troop deployments, attack plans, and everything else we've been able to see. Hell, if we'd had this access at the outset of the war, we would have already defeated them."

Tom McMillian, the National Security Advisor, chimed in. "It's a huge risk, Mr. President. We've already lost nearly ninety percent of our commercial and military satellites since the PLA turned everything over to their new UAV communications platform. I'd hate to lose the tactical advantage we have right now in hopes of broadcasting a series of messages from President Hung Hui-ju. On the one hand, it may work—she may be able to help foment a popular uprising against the war that ultimately leads to the collapse of the PRC. On the other hand, it may cost us our access to their ongoing war plans and troop movements. We've only had this advantage for roughly six weeks. In that timeframe, we've devastated the Chinese military. I'd almost be more willing to try this in two or three months, once we've further destroyed the PLA with it."

"The casualties are starting to become appalling. We can't ignore that," asserted Admiral Meyers, the Chairman of the Joint Chiefs.

As President Foss looked at Admiral Meyers's face, he noticed new wrinkles and gray hair he hadn't seen the last time they'd met. *"The poor guy has aged ten years in the span of a year from the stress of his position,"* he thought. *"I wonder how much that's happening to me?"*

The President rubbed his eyes with his hands as he tried to figure out what to do. He knew they were winning the war, but at what cost to the country and the world? The global economy was coming to a screeching halt with the loss of most of the world's satellites. Then there was the complete and total cyberwarfare the Chinese were waging against every Allied country. Dozens of Allied nations were having their utility systems, transportation networks, and banking systems hacked. By and large, most of them were holding up pretty well. Cybersecurity had been increased exponentially since the start of the war and a lot of redundancy systems had been established to prevent a complete black out or economic collapse, but that didn't negate the impact these attacks were still having on the general population.

Then there were the casualties. In the last three months, the US alone had sustained over 71,000 killed in action, with nearly three times that number wounded or missing. The country was almost numb at the number of losses they had been sustaining since the start of the summer. The President knew it couldn't go on for much longer. Something had to be done to bring an end to the war, a just victory the country and the Allies could accept.

The President looked back at the men and women at the table. He didn't have a good answer—he didn't feel he could make a good decision with the information he had. Knowing he needed to say something, he finally said, "All right, I want you to begin testing messages from President Hung with the PLA prisoners we've captured and within the occupied territories. If you can show that her social media messages can work, and the intelligence community can't figure out any other means of pumping out these messages to mainland China, then I'll authorize you to go forward with this plan."

With the decision made, the President examined the faces before him. He saw a mixture of hope, dread, and a determination to win, no matter the cost.

Chapter 20

Breaking Point

Jiangsu Dayangshan, National Forest Park

"Grenade!" shouted one of the Rangers. Several of them jumped out of the trench just as it blew up.

Pop, pop, pop.

Sergeant Price fired at the next wave of Chinese militiamen charging them. Bullets zipped and cracked past his head and body as he rolled himself back into the protective cover of the trench.

"*Holy crap, that was close,*" he thought. There was no time to dwell on the danger though; he stood back up to fire at the enemy.

"They just keep coming!" shouted another Ranger as he unslung another belt of ammo for the M240G gunner, who was busy raking the charging enemy soldiers.

"Frag out!" shouted another soldier. Several of them began lobbing grenades at the charging enemy.

Crump, crump, crump.

"Keep shooting!" Price yelled to the men near him.

As the enemy reached thirty meters away from their trench, one of the British Gurkha soldiers detonated one of the Claymore mines.

BOOM!

He reached for the second clicker to set the next one off, but half his face imploded as a couple of enemy bullets found their marks. One of the Rangers pushed the now-dead soldier over so that he could get at the Claymore clickers. Grabbing the three remaining detonators, he started depressing them as quickly as he could.

Boom, boom, boom!

Bands of enemy soldiers were turned to pink mists as hundreds of steel ball bearings exploded in their faces.

The machine gunners continued to fire to the point that their barrels were starting to noticeably change colors from the heat of the constant shooting.

When the smoke cleared from the Claymores, the machine gunners finally relented when it became clear there was no one left to shoot. The few remaining enemy soldiers fell back, shattered and stunned from yet another assault repelled by the Allies. With the enemy fading away, the remaining soldiers in the trench line and bunkers breathed deeply, relieved they had survived. Now came the time to tend to the wounded and get ready for the next Chinese attack.

Turning to look down the trench line, Sergeant Price shouted, "I want new Claymores set up ASAP!"

Price didn't waste any time. Now that the enemy attack had been broken, they had to rush to get ready for the next one. The Gurkha and 3 PARA units they'd come to help were practically broken as combat units; after nearly six days of combat, they had been ground into the dirt by relentless attacks. Even after sending two companies of 82nd Airborne paratroopers to reinforce them, they'd still had to call in a Ranger company to shore up their positions.

Price wasn't sure how much more they could take. They were killing the enemy wholesale, but they just kept coming. Even a well-trained and disciplined soldier would break down at some point if this level of slaughter wasn't stopped.

****

Brigadier McCoil and Colonel St. Leo were looking at the map of the area when the various combat outposts began to report in. The COPs had all successfully held off another multihour human wave attack by the PLA, but at great personal loss. Despite having been on the ground for only about forty-eight hours, the American units were down to sixty-five percent strength. The Ranger battalion was down to fifty-two percent strength—they had seen the worst of the fighting as they were being shuffled from one COP to another, depending on where the enemy was looking like they might break through.

"How much longer do you think we can sustain these kinds of losses?" asked Brigadier McCoil in a hushed voice only St. Leo could hear.

Rubbing the stubble on his face with his right hand, Colonel St. Leo answered, "As long as our airbridge continues to hold and we stay supplied, I suspect we can hold for a while longer. My real concern though, is not the losses we've been sustaining—they're bad, to be sure, but I'm more concerned with how these massive human wave attacks are affecting the troops psychologically. A good soldier never wants a fair fight, he always wants the odds stacked in his favor—but this is pure madness. What these PLA commanders are ordering is mass suicide. They know they can't break through our lines—we have too much artillery and air support. Yet they keep ordering these poorly trained, poorly equipped militia units to their deaths."

Colonel St. Leo had just gotten back from a tour of one of the COPs a few minutes ago. He had seen firsthand what the front lines looked like. The ground in front of the Allied positions was covered in dead, dying, and torn bodies. It was utterly horrific, and the stench of it was only getting worse with each day those dead bodies baked in the August sun.

"We will need more reinforcements if don't get relieved shortly," McCoil added.

As the two officers were conferring with each other on what to do next, one of the staff officers walked up to them. "Sir, I just received a message from one of the Germans. He wants to speak to you," said the young captain.

McCoil gave St. Leo a quizzical look and then made his way over to the table with the radios set up on it. He picked up the handset from the sergeant who held it out for him. Depressing the talk button, he said, "This is Gladiator Actual. To whom am I speaking?"

A second later the radio clicked and there was a short beep as the SINCGAR radio synced. "Gladiator Actual, this is Löwen Actual. My lead element, the 13th Reconnaissance Battalion, is approaching your lines from the southeast. We should arrive near your perimeter within the next half hour. Please advise friendly units in the area of our arrival. How copy?"

Colonel St. Leo gave a look of surprise to the captain and sergeant who'd been manning the radio. Before he could get out a question, the captain grabbed a sheet of paper that had the radio call signs of the Allied unit that was supposed to relieve them. He quickly noted that Löwen was the call sign for Major General Ernst Graf, the German 10th Panzer Division commander.

Brigadier McCoil smiled broadly. After nearly eight days, their relief was finally starting to arrive.

He depressed the talk button again. "Löwen Actual, that's a good copy. We'll relay your arrival to our perimeter units. Please be advised that we have two PLA battalions of motorized infantry on the north side of Suzhou and at least three brigades of PLA militia. Our positions have been under siege by these units. Intelligence also shows at least one battalion of armor heading toward the city from the northwest near Wuxi. How copy?"

If the German unit was still in fighting shape, then maybe they'd be able to hit these enemy formations before they were able to reorganize themselves to attack their positions again. With only eight Abrams battle tanks, McCoil wasn't confident they would have been able to prevent that PLA armor battalion from finally finishing them off.

A few seconds went by before the radio crackled for a second and beeped again, syncing the crypto keys. "That's a good copy. We'll move to engage them once we've lifted your siege. Out."

With that, the enormous weight McCoil and St. Leo had been carrying was lifted. Within an hour, elements of the German division would arrive at their perimeter while the rest of the German tanks moved to rout the rest of the enemy units from his beleaguered COPs.

****

Beijing, China
August First Building
Ministry of National Defense HQ

General Yang Yin sat in the command center, deep underground in the bowels of the August First Building, looking at the most recent reports coming in from the Shanghai sector. None of the news was good. The division commander that had insisted his force would be able to crush the British and French airborne force at Sangyuanli had failed yet again.

"Eight days they had that force encircled, cut off from the world, and they still couldn't wipe the British out,"

Yang thought in disgust. If they lost the war, it wouldn't be because of lack of will; it would be due to the incompetence of military leaders like this one.

Yang was angry at the sheer level of ineptitude of many of the division commanders; generals that largely held their positions prior to the war did not actually have the ability to lead men, but because of their political and family connections, they had found themselves a place here in this very building. If he didn't purge the PLA of these incompetent generals and get new officers—men who knew how to lead and fight—they were doomed.

When he had taken over command of the PLA nearly a week ago, he had brought with him most of his senior staff from his southern command. He wanted officers he knew and trusted. The first few days had largely been spent trying to organize some sort of effort to block the Allies from entrenching themselves in Shanghai region. If the Allies were able to solidify their position, then it was only a matter of time until the Chinese were officially defeated.

The major problem Yang faced right now was that he had very little in the way of armor or mechanized forces in the Shanghai region. Most of those units had been sent to his southern command when the American Marines had landed in the Guangdong Province and to the north, around Beijing, to battle the Allies' multipronged offensive driving on the capital. Even now, hundreds of thousands of civilians were busy building hundreds of miles of tank ditches, trenches and other fighting positions at strategic points as far as a hundred kilometers from Beijing. Like the Russians had done with Moscow at the height of World War II, General Yang planned on turning the capital into a fortress.

What troubled him most was how effective the Allies' strategic bombing had become. Something just wasn't adding up.

Sensing that someone had walked up to him, General Yang looked up from his reports. He smiled when he saw Colonel Su Yu, the commander of the vaunted PLA Unit 61398, the Chinese group responsible for nearly all of the PRC's cyberwarfare and espionage activities. Yang pushed his chair back and he stood up to greet his visitor.

"Thank you for coming on such short notice," he said with a bow. "Please, let's go into my office and talk away from prying eyes and ears," Yang offered. He gestured toward a door nearby.

Colonel Su smiled and followed Yang to his office. Once inside, Yang closed the door and gestured for them to take a seat in the set of chairs that sat on one side of the room with a small coffee table between them.

Once seated, Yang opened the discussion. "Colonel Su, I'm not like my predecessor. I don't want to be told that everything is going well, and we are winning the war. I want the honest truth, no matter how bad it may be. I need to know what's happening in the war, or I'm not going to be able to make appropriate decisions. Will you agree to be honest with me?" Yang asked.

Colonel Su's face registered no emotion at all. Yang couldn't get a read on him.

"He's probably not used to a straight shooter," General Yang realized. Su must be calculating whether or not he would be shot for being honest. He might also be trying to assess whether or not Yang was trustworthy.

Finally, Colonel Su nodded. "I agree, General Yang," he responded. "If we aren't honest and forthright about what's going on with the war, then we can't make the necessary changes to defeat the enemy. What can I do for you?"

Yang smiled. "I need your help in understanding something technical, outside my area of expertise. When President Xi gave the order to bring down the world's satellite infrastructure, it was supposed to have greatly affected the Allies' ability to wage war. This should have nearly crippled the Americans. However, while I can point to significant reductions in the effectiveness of the American military, in many cases, we have seen an increase in the Allies' ability to target critical aspects of our ability to wage war."

Colonel Su interjected, "If I may, General, would you be able to give me a frame of reference to your last statement?"

Yang nodded, not at all angry at the interruption. "Prior to this disruption in the satellites, the Americans occasionally used to get lucky and identify a fuel depot or a battalion moving to an attack point and destroy it, but this was limited. Our destruction of the satellites should have made their ability to preemptively strike even more ineffective. Instead, it's as if they suddenly know where all our troops are moving at all times. They've attacked ammunition storage facilities, critical component production facilities, and all very successfully. Their accuracy has increased exponentially."

Colonel Su nodded. "This does sound problematic. It sounds like someone is either betraying us, or the Allies have found a way to penetrate our communications system. Have you spoken with the Ministry of State Security?"

"I haven't. I believe this problem is technical, not human, which is why I've asked you here," Yang replied. He leaned in closer. "If this were a human problem, Su, then this issue would have also been persistent prior to our switching over to the UAV communications system. However, this degree of enemy accuracy only began after we made that switch. Hence, the only logical explanation is that the problem is technical."

Colonel Su sat back in his chair for a moment. "I think I see what you mean," he said. "I must admit, I was not aware of a possible problem with the UAVs or our communications system. To be honest, when the globe's satellite infrastructure was destroyed, I had thought the threat of cyberwarfare would diminish. Now that I see how wrong that assumption was, I'll need some time to look into this, General Yang."

"Yes, please do, Colonel, and get back to me as soon as possible." He paused for a moment. "Has your office had any problems relocating?" Yang asked. Colonel Su's Unit 61398 had originally been headquartered in the Pudong neighborhood of Shanghai. They'd had to make a hasty withdrawal from the city when it had been invaded.

"No, Sir. We've relocated without incident. None of my hackers were killed or injured in the process. Fortunately, we had moved most of our operations to underground bunkers and further inland, away from

American cruise missiles. My predecessor had failed to take that threat seriously when the war first started, and a lot of very good hackers were killed by this incompetence."

Colonel Su shifted in his seat. "General Yang, if you have nothing further, I'll take my leave and look into this problem. I will contact your office as soon as I have something."

General Yang nodded.

After Su hurried out of the room, Yang sat pondering for a moment. If his gut was right, President Xi would throw a conniption. He couldn't bring this forward until he was really sure of the facts and had hopefully come up with some sort of solution to the problem.

Chapter 21
Decisions

Washington, D.C.
White House

A decision needed to be made, but President Foss wasn't sure if he was about to make the right call. He'd been mulling over whether or not to let the State Department and the DoD's own psychological operations group broadcast a pirate message to the Chinese people throughout the PRC. President Hung Hui-ju from the Republic of China had been working with Ambassador Bryant, along with Secretary of State Philip Landover and the Army's psychological operations folks, to create a series of compelling messages to distribute. This would be followed by pleas to the people of China to either demand peace or overthrow the dictatorial regime that was continuing the slaughter of their sons and daughters.

The President wasn't sure if spreading these messages would be worth giving up the access to the PRC's internal communication system. It wouldn't take the government long to identify how the Allies were broadcasting their message, and then they'd move to shut them down—and when they did, the window the Allies held into the inner workings of the PRC and the PLA troop movements would be gone.

Sitting across from him on the couch and chair, was the Chairman of the Joint Chiefs, the SecDef, the Secretary of State, his National Security Advisor, and Katelyn Mackie, his cyberwarfare czar. They sat patiently, awaiting the President's final decision. Foss sighed and then looked up at the group.

"If we move forward with this initiative...how long will it take the PLA to figure out what we've done to their UAVs? When would we lose access to their network?"

Ms. Mackie took a breath in and out. "We estimate it'll take the PLA maybe a few hours to a day to figure out what has happened to their UAVs. Once they have determined where the problem is, they'll move to ground the UAV fleet, or at least move all their secured communications off it. However, we also believe that will happen soon anyway as they figure out that we've been listening in on them."

"How do we know this message President Hung and Ambassador Bryant have crafted is even going to be effective?" the President asked next, directing that question to Secretary Landover and Tom McMillan.

Secretary Landover jumped at the question. "It'll work, Mr. President," he asserted. "We've tested the speeches on the prisoners of war we're currently holding. In all cases, the average Chinese person who has seen one or all five of these messages has responded positively. In the case of the occupied territories, we've seen many of the people ask how President Xi's government had been able to deceive them for so long. Many of them had no idea how the war had started, or the reality of how the conflict has been going. Many of them said they had been led to believe that it was America and the Allies who had started the war to keep China poor and in its place. As they learned the truth, many of them became angry at having been deceived and misled. In the case of the occupied territories, many of the people have even asked unprompted how they can help or support President Hung's government."

Tom McMillan added, "I wasn't sure this whole idea would work at first, but having seen the results and talked with many Chinese citizens, it does appear that it just may have the intended effect." McMillan had just returned from a trip to China and South Korea, where he had toured the front lines. During his expedition, Secretary Landover had also arranged for him to talk with several groups of Chinese citizens in Changchun, the capital of Jilin Province.

Foss turned his head to look at his military advisors, seeking their input next. "Thoughts?" he asked.

Jim Castle looked at the others sitting across from him before turning his gaze to the President. "Sir, it's my recommendation as your Secretary of Defense that we not move in this direction. I know the evidence that this plan may work looks good. However, I'm not confident that it'll bring about the change we're hoping for and betting on to end the war. Truthfully, I've been skeptical about this idea ever since it was first brought up. I don't want to give up the intelligence advantage we have—that has produced tangible results on the battlefield—for a strategy that we don't know for sure will end the war."

Foss saw the looks of disappointment from Tom McMillan and Secretary Landover at his remark. Castle swept past the reactions and continued, "Mr. President, right now, we are gaining valuable, actionable intelligence on a minute-by-minute basis from this program. Since its inception, we have intercepted or interdicted nearly every enemy air and naval attack on our forces. We have crushed or forced the PLA to cancel or suspend several ground offensives because we were able to take out those unit's fuel depots, munition stores or bombed them outright before they could attack. Had we not had this program up and running when we invaded the Shanghai region or Guangdong Province, then in all likelihood, our forces would have either sustained many times more killed in action or been defeated outright. I can't in good conscience recommend a course of action that would end our ability to obtain this level of intelligence at this juncture in the war."

Admiral Meyers had largely stayed silent during the discussion but stepped in at this point. "Sir, Secretary Castle is right about the importance of this intelligence-gathering program. However, Secretary Landover is also right in that this proposal might be the final nail in the coffin of Xi's regime. Perhaps we give it another month of using the intelligence we're gleaning before we move forward with a course of action that will end the intelligence gravy train we've been feasting upon," he offered.

The President smiled. This gave him an out—not outright picking one way over the other, but still keeping both options on the table.

The President had made his decision. He turned to Katelyn Mackie. "I'm going to give the military a bit more time with your current program before we try the State Department's proposal. Have your team continue to stand by to execute State's proposal should we need to, but for the time being, we're going to stick to the military need."

Katelyn bit her lower lip and nodded. "Yes, Mr. President. We'll continue to stand by."

With the decision made, Secretary Landover and Ms. Mackie proceeded to get up and head for the door. Their part of the meeting was over; it was time for the military leaders to discuss the next steps now that they had a couple more weeks of Project Enigma.

While they were leaving the office, the President signaled to one of the White House stewards to bring in a fresh pot of coffee. An aide also ushered in the chief of staffs for the Army and the Air Force, along with the Chief of Naval Operations.

Once the newcomers took their seats, the President asked, "How are the troop deployments going?"

Admiral Meyers took the question. "In the Guangdong Province in the south, the Marines have offloaded another 110,000 men. That brings their total number up to 380,000 Marines. Most of our ANZAC allies are there as well. Between the Australians and New Zealanders, they have 42,000 soldiers. In the last couple of weeks, the Army's offloaded the rest of their force, roughly two divisions' worth of men. We're trying to keep the southern operation mostly a Marine-led operation while the Army focuses on the Shanghai region and northern China."

The conversation temporarily ended as two of the stewards brought in the tray of fresh coffee the President had requested. Being a bit of a java snob, President Foss insisted on having his favorite coffee served during certain meetings throughout the day—at $79 a pound, the Saint Helena coffee was once a favorite of Napoleon Bonaparte. No one there was complaining about it, to be sure. Once everyone had a cup of the famed coffee the way they liked it and the stewards had left, the meeting continued.

Admiral Meyers took one more big sip of coffee before he placed his cup down on the table between the couches and resumed his explanation. "Now that we have the city of Shanghai and the surrounding area largely secured, we've been able to ferry in vast numbers of soldiers via commercial aircraft and bring in heavy equipment through the dozen or so ports we've captured. In the last nineteen days, we've brought ashore 390,000 soldiers. That number will grow by 90,000 a month until the end of the year. In the north, we have a considerably much larger force. The South Koreans have committed 300,000 soldiers, the Japanese Defense Force has committed 160,000 soldiers, and then we have 670,000 American soldiers along with the 190,000 troops that invaded western China through Mongolia."

The Army Chief of Staff added, "If you give us the order to capture Beijing, I believe we could have it captured by Christmas."

"Is capturing Beijing still essential? Hasn't the capture of Shanghai and Guangzhou negated that necessity?" inquired the President between sips of coffee.

"Yes and no, Mr. President," said Admiral Meyers. "The issue isn't so much the capture of Beijing as it is the destruction of the PLA 20th, 27th, and 38th Armies, which have dug themselves in around the capital. The 54th and 65th Armies are facing our forces now. Our soldiers could bulldoze their way through them in a matter of weeks—the challenge is the 100-kilometer-deep defensive network these other three armies have constructed that encircles the capital region."

Tom McMillan interjected. "What about strategic bombings? Can't we make heavy use of our B-52 bombers to carpet bomb these positions?"

The Air Force general chimed in. "We would certainly do that. However, we have to continue to work at removing the enemy SAM threat and their remaining air force assets. They've concentrated a lot of their remaining fighters to the capital region, along with a lot of their newer SAM systems. While we're inflicting a lot of aerial losses on them, it's going to take some time before that gives us the tactical and strategic advantage we need to fully dominate the skies. Now that we have destroyed a large portion of the aerospace industry in Guangzhou, the PLA Air Force won't be able to replace their losses as quickly or as easily as they have been doing up to this point."

A few of the other generals nodded. President Foss still wasn't sure if the Allies would *ever* be able to fully dominate the skies, considering the sheer number of losses they had sustained in frontline aircraft over the last two years of war.

"I'm not trying to get too far into the weeds here, but how long is it taking us to produce a new fighter plane to be sent to China to replace our own losses?" asked the President.

The Air Force general smiled, not fazed in the least by the question. "Now that we've fully repaired the damage to our manufacturing facility in Dallas-Fort Worth, Lockheed is cranking out sixty-four F-16 Vipers a month. They've just finished training a full third shift of workers and will now be running a full twenty-four-hour, seven-day-a-week production schedule. Starting in October, the plant will be producing 150 Vipers a month. In St. Louis, the Boeing plant is finally running at full capacity, rolling out

118 F/A-18 Super Hornets a month. Even the F-35 plant is now churning out 130 new fighters a month. For the first time since the war started, we're finally starting to produce more aircraft than we're losing."

Jim Castle placed his coffee cup down and leaned in. "When the war first broke out in Europe and we sustained those horrific aircraft losses, President Gates authorized me to begin a massive procurement order for new fighters and other weapons needed to win this war. It has taken us nearly two years to retool our factories, train workers, and get our supply systems up and running. However, I assure you, they are fully up and running now. As the general just elaborated, we've turned the tide. It's only a matter of time now until the Chinese are defeated," he asserted.

Foss held up a hand. "OK, Jim, you've succeeded in reassuring me that we're going to win. My only concern is how long will it take. Everyone here knows our country's past history with wars. For better or worse, the democracies of the West only seem to be able to stomach a war for a short period of time before they demand either victory or an end that they can live with. The next presidential election cycle is going to start in a couple of months, and already my opposition has taken on the mantle of 'a vote for me is a vote to end the war.' And while I want an end to this war as well,

I want an end that will leave the world in a better place than when we started."

The President sighed and then turned to the Air Force general. "What about the B-21 Raider we talked about last month? Is it ready to be tested over China?" he asked.

The general nodded as a smile spread across his face. "Yes, Mr. President. I spoke with the program manager and the test pilots, and they've flown it out to Japan. Tomorrow, it will fly its first combat mission over northern China, attacking a collection of PLA command-and-control bunkers we've identified through Project Enigma. Pending the results of that mission, we'll test it against a much tougher target in Beijing."

The President scratched his chin and a mischievous smile curled up the corners of his lips. "If Project Enigma can identify these command-and-control bunkers, can it also identify where the senior PLA leadership is located? Or even President Xi?" he asked. "If we can locate them, then perhaps we should try and go after them more directly."

"We'll look into it, Mr. President," Admiral Meyers replied as he scribbled something on his notepad.

******

29,000 Feet above Northern China

When Lieutenant Colonel Rob "Pappi" Fortney's B-2 stealth bomber had been shot down over Russia, he'd figured his career in the Air Force was over. After twenty-five years of service, he was certain the brass would put him out to pasture in disgrace after losing a $2 billion warplane just days into the start of World War III. Then, when he'd found out his co-pilot, Major Richard "Ricky" James had been captured, he'd truly felt like a failure.

Within a couple of days of being rescued by NATO soldiers on the Lithuanian border, he had been flown back to the US to be treated for his injuries. While he was recovering at the Army's Walter Reed Hospital in Bethesda, Maryland, a major general in charge of the Air Force's B-21 Raider program had paid him a visit.

"I heard a rumor that you had planned to retire at the end of your service obligation, Fortney," he'd opened. "Any truth to that?"

"Yes, Sir," Pappi had replied cautiously, wondering if he was going to be forced out sooner.

"Well, I'm here to ask you to reconsider," the major general replied. "I'd like you to stay on and be the lead Air Force test pilot for the new stealth bomber program."

Pappi's mouth hung open in surprise.

Unfazed, the general continued, "With twenty-five years of service flying stealth bombers, you've flown combat missions over Serbia during the NATO Kosovo campaign and also carried out numerous missions over Afghanistan and Iraq. Since you no longer have a plane to fly, the Air Force wants to leverage your flight experience with the B-21 as we rapidly move the program forward to meet the new demands of the current war."

"Sir, I appreciate the offer, but honestly, I just want to retire and put the memory of my last bombing run behind me," Pappi responded.

The major general had tried unsuccessfully to convince him to change his mind. However, within the week, the Air Force Chief of Staff had shown up at the hospital. When he'd made his plea for Pappi to reconsider, he'd also offered a promotion to go along with the Silver Star they were awarding him and guaranteed him the first B-21 bomber. It was an offer he couldn't turn down, especially when President Gates also paid him a visit later that same day.

****

"Raider Zero-One, this is Mother Goose. We show five enemy aircraft eighty-two kilometers from your current position at heading two-two-four, 520 knots. Altitude nineteen thousand feet. How copy?" asked the air battle manager on the Boeing E-3 Sentry loitering one hundred and twenty kilometers behind them.

Double D depressed the talk button on her radio. "That's a good copy, Mother Goose. We are twenty mikes to target. Proceeding with mission," she replied.

Major Donna "Double D" Daniels was Pappi's smart, yet brash young copilot who was eager to release their twenty-four GBU-31 2,000-pound laser-guided bombs and get back to the protection of the Allied lines.

Today was the B-21's first combat mission, and her first time flying over enemy territory. They were going to test the bomber's ability to release, guide and hit twenty-four separate targets with its onboard targeting computer. With the loss of the DoD's military satellites, aircraft were having to rely on their own ability to guide their bombs to the target as opposed to leveraging GPS satellites to do it for them.

Not taking her eyes off her instruments or radar screen, she asked, "How are we looking, Boss?"

Pappi pressed a couple of buttons and then looked up at Double D. "We're good. Just finished arming the bombs and double-checking the targets. Everything is set," he replied. Looking at his copilot again, he raised an eyebrow. "You look nervous, Daniels," he added.

"We're flying an experimental bomber over enemy territory with fighters hunting us less than 80 kilometers away. Yeah, I guess you could say I'm nervous."

Pappi snickered. "Oh, come on, Daniels. You were full of piss and vinegar about how we were going to turn the tide of the war with this bomber two weeks ago."

"Yeah, well, that was when we were still back in Nevada at the test facility. I had no idea they were going to send us to China to test my theory a week later," she replied with a bit of embarrassment in her voice.

Turning serious, Pappi added, "It's OK to feel nervous or scared. We all do. Remember, I'm the one who's already been shot down once. Yet here I am, back in a bomber, flying over enemy territory again. Just stick to your training, take deep breaths and remain calm. We're fine. The enemy can't see us, and they have no idea we're here."

Daniels took a deep breath, letting it out slowly as she nodded. The pep talk seemed to help. A few minutes went by as the two of them flew in silence, the sound of the engines and the air flowing past the outer shell of the bomber the only audible noise.

The navigation system popped up with an alert. "One minute to weapons release," she announced.

Pappi reached down and depressed the weapon standby button. In seconds, the doors opened up, exposing the bomb bay and their precious cargo to the world below. He then moved his finger over to the targeting computer, selecting the bombs he wanted to release. Pappi waited until the system indicated they were over the predetermined drop site, and then, in a single fluid motion, he hit the weapons release button. The targeting computer would automatically begin releasing the Raider's bombs.

One by one the bombs fell, heading to their predetermined targets 29,000 feet below them. In roughly sixty seconds, the targeting computer had released all twenty-four bombs. Now it was time for them to watch and wait as their laser designator directly beneath them guided the bombs to their intended targets. Minutes passed by as Pappi and Double D waited for the bombs to hit. After what felt like an eternity, the bombs started to hit their marks. In the span of a single minute, they had hit twenty-four command-and-control bunkers and communication nodes of the PLA's 54th and 65th Armies, to devastating effect.

Chapter 22

End-State

Beijing, China
August First Building
Ministry of National Defense HQ

The fall weather had finally arrived in Beijing. The leaves on the trees had changed colors and a cool breeze was starting to blow in from the north and northwest. Colonel Su looked up at the doors leading into the August First Building; he dreaded going inside. The building had been hit by American stealth bombers three times in the last five days. Each time, the edifice had taken multiple bomb hits, causing significant damage to the structure and the guts of the building. Strangely enough, none of the bombs had managed to penetrate down into the command center deep below.

He knew it was only a matter of time before the Allies got lucky and punched a hole right down into it. *"With my luck, I'll be inside when that happens,"* he thought glumly.

The war had not been going well these past six weeks. With each passing day, it felt more and more like the walls were closing in on them.

As he approached the side door to the building closest to the tunnel entrance, Colonel Su watched as hundreds of workers used their hands, wheelbarrows, and other tools to clear and remove the debris from the inside of the building.

Fortunately, the other side of the massive structure had not been hit yet. When Su neared the entrance, several sentries snapped to attention. One of them then held his hand out, demanding that Colonel Su show his credentials. A couple of other guards nearby kept a wary eye on him until the guard had verified his identity. Then the outer door was opened, and he was ushered inside. He made his way over to a hallway that led to a ramp, at the end of which was the next checkpoint and the armored blast doors that protected the bunker beneath the building.

Every time Colonel Su walked into the underground fortress, he marveled at how high-tech it was. There was a group of rooms divided by half walls with soundproof glass that separated the various departments, and each room had wall-mounted monitors showing whatever that group was working on. The signals intelligence group, radio communications, computer networks, the PLA ground force, the air force, and the UAV groups all had their own rooms. In the nerve center of the bunker though, it was more like an amphitheater. Multiple massive wall monitors displayed various combat front lines, friendly and enemy troop dispositions, and any other information that a high-level decision maker would generally need.

Inside this central room, the rows of seats were filled with various liaison officers from the different commands in those battlefronts, intelligence, communication and logistical groups, along with the air force and other groups needed to manage and wage a war. Colonel Su stood there for a moment looking at everything, taking it all in like a person seeing Times Square for the first time.

Su had marveled at how the PLA leadership could have so much information at its fingertips but still not be able to effectively coordinate and execute this war. However, now that his directorate, Unit 61398, had relocated to a new location outside of Beijing, he was suddenly being included in a lot more of the military decisions and seeing a lot more of the big picture. Unit 61398 had largely been focused on the cyberwarfare aspect of the war. His unit had been incredibly good at waging this aspect of the war, but his unit could not take or hold land. That was the responsibility of the ground forces.

Suddenly, Colonel Su felt like someone was standing right behind him. He turned to see General Yang, the new overall PLA commander.

"Impressive, isn't it?" he inquired.

Su nodded, not sure what to say.

"Prior to being appointed overall general of the PLA, I'd never been in this room," General Yang admitted. "I had no idea the generals running the war had such an operations center with this level of information. My focus had been defeating our enemies in the field, not running a war. I must admit, having this much information at my fingertips makes me question how my predecessors fouled up the war so badly for us." He spoke in a hushed tone that only the two of them could hear.

Colonel Su raised an eyebrow at the comment but didn't say anything further. He didn't know if General Yang was testing him or not. He didn't want to sound defeatist.

"Come with me; let's go to my private office. We need to talk," Yang suggested.

****

As the two of them walked into the modest office, General Yang hoped he wasn't making a mistake by bringing the colonel into his inner circle. However, he didn't have much of a choice—he needed Su and his directorate's capabilities for what he wanted to do next.

Yang gestured for Su to take a seat in a pair of comfortable chairs on the far side of his office. Then he depressed a button on the side of his desk, which turned on a white-noise maker and whited out the glass windows, preventing anyone from seeing or hearing their conversation. Once these formalities were taken care of, he pulled a bottle of American whiskey out of the bottom drawer of his desk, along with a couple of tumblers. Placing the glasses on the desk, he proceeded to pour an ample amount into each and carried them over to the small coffee table next to the chairs.

Colonel Su smiled softly when he saw the dark liquid and nodded his approval. The two of them sat quietly for a moment as they sipped on the rocket fuel, sizing each other up while they let the alcohol take the edge off.

After a few minutes, Yang opened the conversation. "I have a question for you, and I would like an honest answer. I assume your office has been monitoring the social media messages being shown across the occupied territories by President Hung Hui-ju. Am I right?"

Colonel Su lifted his glass and drained the rest of its contents before he answered. "I've seen the messages. My directorate has been tracking them, and we're doing our best to suppress this propaganda from being promulgated on the internet, radio and TV airwaves."

Yang nodded, not allowing his facial expressions to betray his approval or disapproval. Instead, he got up and walked to his desk, retrieving the bottle of whiskey. He poured them both another glass.

"What are your thoughts on their effectiveness? Do they appear to be working?" he probed further.

"It's hard to say. Some of our human intelligence assets in the occupied territories have reported that they are. Many people are disillusioned with the war. Their cities or villages have been bombed, and many of them have family members that either have been killed in the army or are currently serving in the army, and they fear for their safety."

"What else are they saying?"

Colonel Su took another long drink of the whiskey before he added, "Many of them just want the war to end. President Hung is promising better jobs under her economic model. She cites the successes in Taiwan and South Korea as examples of what mainland China could experience if the Xi regime is defeated. Many people dismiss her claims as Western propaganda, but many others are starting to believe her."

Yang asked, "What specifically is causing the people to doubt our government? Is it something we can counter?"

Su shook his head. "No, I don't believe we can counter it, at least not in the occupied zones. We don't have any control there. We can't imprison people for listening to her messages or supporting them like we can in the areas we control. Recently, President Hung has been playing messages of Chinese-Americans who have family ties to those in cities in the occupied zones. More than any others, those messages are having a huge impact on the people."

Yang thought about that for a moment as he took another sip of his whiskey. "That's going to be hard to overcome," he remarked. "There are four hundred million of our citizens now living in the occupied territories. The longer the Allies are able to control them, the harder it'll be for us to keep this message from spreading and permeating the rest of the country."

Colonel Su shifted uncomfortably in his chair. "We're doing everything we can to prevent that, General. The Allies have not found a way through our firewall just yet. There is only so much we can do inside the occupied territories, but we have complete control of our own."

Yang nodded in acceptance. Unlike his predecessors, he knew there was only so much his subordinates could do.

Placing unrealistic expectations on them was just setting them up to fail, or worse, falsify information and results. Creating that type of environment would only place a question mark on everything his subordinates told him, and he needed accurate information.

General Yang changed subjects as he poured Su yet another glass of whiskey. "When we last spoke, you said you were going to look into the possibility that we have a mole or leak somewhere in the command staff or army that was providing the Allies with highly sensitive data. What has your investigation turned up?"

Colonel Su paused and took several sips from his glass before he finally answered. "There *may* be some traitors in our midst; I'm confident we'll probably find a few as we continue to examine the electronic data of the PLA general staff. What we have *already* found is a possible problem in the Y'an communication drones."

Yang suddenly felt a feeling of panic. "*Have the Allies found a way into our communications system?*" he wondered.

He signaled for Su to continue and did his best to hide any emotions.

"I had the engineers reverse-engineer the components of the drone—tear the entire thing apart and examine it for malware or malicious code in the components and the operating system. The OS appears to be fine. None of my coders found a problem or anything out of the ordinary. However, when we scrutinized one of the microprocessors that's responsible for the G5 capability, we came across something unusual—"

General Yang interrupted, "—Is it compromised?"

"We aren't sure. It might be," Su replied.

General Yang tried to remain calm, though he had this growing sense of dread at the possibility that the Allies could even now be listening into the daily communications of the PLA.

"Explain what you mean by 'might be,'" he demanded.

"Prior to the war, we'd purchased this component in large quantities from an American telecom company we had a joint venture with. One of the other intelligence directorates had already stolen many of the chip designs prior to the beginning of the conflict, as we knew this was going to be a critical component in our unmanned aerial vehicle programs. When we went back and dug deeper into the employees at the facility, we discovered one particular engineer who had worked at the American plant for nearly a decade prior to being transferred back to our facility several months before the war started."

Colonel Su continued, "At first, we didn't see anything out of the ordinary, until we discovered the engineer was a bit of a fitness enthusiast. We then learned that he regularly used a Fitbit device. In short order, we were able to hack into the Fitbit application he used on his Apple smartphone, and through our access in the Apple cloud, we were able to track down his geolocations during his time in America. It took many days of digging, but we identified at least five times that he met with at least one person who has a direct connection to the American National Security Agency."

Yang held up a hand before Su could go any further. "How could you possibly know he had met with someone from the NSA just by hacking into his Fitbit?"

Su grunted and a devilish smile spread across his face. "We've been using Fitbit data to track every known American government and military member possible for years. It's rather complicated for me to explain. Suffice it to say, if you're a military member or have a US government security clearance and you use a Fitbit, then chances are, we've been geotracking you for years, and all that data gets timestamped for later use. In this engineer's case, we took his geolocations and overlaid them with known government or military members who have security clearances. Once we made a few matches, then we did a workup on who they were and if they posed a potential problem. In this case, several of them created cause for concern."

Shaking his head in disbelief, General Yang feared the worst. "Tell me what your directorate may have found," he said, not sure he really wanted to hear the answer.

"We looked at the specific projects this engineer worked on and then tore those parts apart, looking for anything. Once we knew where to look, we found it—a simple code buried in the firmware of the processor." He held up a hand to stop Yang from asking another question before he was finished. "We're currently examining exactly what the code does. As of right now, all we know is that it's there and it doesn't belong there. I spoke with several of my people before coming here, and they assure me that we'll know soon enough. Once we do, I'll make sure to relay that information to you."

Leaning forward in his chair, Yang fixed Su in a deadly stare. "When you find out what this code does, I want you to come and brief me *in person*. You're not to talk to anyone else about this but me. If what you're saying is true, then we need to figure out how we can replace this component without the Allies finding out what we're doing or that we have identified their spy. This has to be kept secret. Do you understand?"

Su nodded and assured him he would make sure the circle of people who knew this information stayed small. The two talked for a few more minutes before Yang dismissed him.

After spending a full hour with the man, General Yang judged that Colonel Su was a straight shooter—someone who would tell him what he needed to know, not just what he wanted to hear. He held off on telling Su anything further just yet. Right now, he needed the man focused on figuring out what the Allies had done to their communications drones.

****

The morning sun finally broke through the clouds and smog, revealing the layers of earthen trenches the tens of thousands of civilians and military engineers had been constructing around the city of Tangshan, fifty-six kilometers east of Beijing. The combined Allied army was now less than ninety kilometers from this very position, and God only knew when they would begin their final assault on the capital.

A colonel from the 5th Engineering Regiment guided General Yang and a couple of his advisors toward a series of large machine-gun bunkers and other large-scale structures they had been constructing.

Several cement trucks had pulled up to the wooden frames some of the workers were crowding around. A minute went by as the workers guided the troughs that would allow the cement to pour into the wall molds of the structure. Once the mixture started to flow, other workers began to inset strips of rebar between the mold of the walls to give the cement more strength once it had settled.

Yang stood there quietly for a few minutes, just watching the process, mesmerized by how quickly the engineers and civilian militia units were turning the area into a fortress. For nearly ten kilometers up and down the line, work crews were busy building similar structures in preparation for the Allied advance.

"Once the cement has settled in a couple of days, we'll remove the wooden molds and then begin to cover the structures with several feet of sand and dirt to give them further protection," the engineer explained. "In time, as grass and other undergrowth returns, it'll add to the camouflage of the structure."

"How many machine guns and soldiers can this particular structure hold?" one of Yang's staff members asked.

"This is the largest type of structure that'll be built on the defensive line. It's essentially an anchor point. We've placed a structure like this every three kilometers, so they can provide each other with interlocking fields of fire supported by a series of four small machine-gun bunkers on each side. In this structure, there will be three light machines guns supported by two heavy machine guns. In addition to that, it'll have two antitank guns and one 152mm Howitzer at the center of the structure. We've even gone so far as to design five different firing positions on the side of the bunker, where soldiers can quickly exit the structure to fire off an antitank missile and then quickly duck back inside for cover and grab another missile. Of course, those same soldiers can also swap out the antitank missiles for MANPADs as well.

"Each of these bunkers will have a crew of between 130 and 200 personnel. This area here," he said as he pointed to a large carved-out area of dirt where a few dozen workers were busy setting up more wood molds for cement walls, "will be the bunker or living area where most of the soldiers will ride out any large bombardments, as well as sleep and eat. It'll have enough beds for up to two hundred soldiers and enough food and water to last thirty days."

General Yang was impressed with the structures themselves, but also concerned that such a stronghold could simply be bypassed and avoided. He'd need to make sure the northern approaches were made unusable so the Allies would be forced to funnel their men and tanks through this line.

"Colonel, this is a most impressive fortification your engineers have constructed," he praised. "I do have a couple of questions for you. First, how will you prevent the Allies from dropping a laser-guided bomb directly onto the bunker, rendering it useless? Second, while I like the idea of the 152mm Howitzer in the center of the structure, how will you protect it from the Allies' own artillery or rounds from the enemy tanks?"

The colonel nodded. "To answer your first question, General, as you can see, we're pouring the inner mold of the structure. This inner mold consists of a new type of cement mixture, which we have found to be nearly ten times stronger than the standard cement used in normal construction. We have also placed reinforced steel bars throughout the cement to give it more strength.

"Prior to selecting this process to build these fortifications, we tested them against the likely bombs and artillery fire they would receive from the Allies. We built this exact structure nearly a year ago and hit it with every type of bomb, missile and artillery the Allies have. In each case, it held up. We found that if we placed a specific layer of earth on top of the structures, we could prevent it from being demolished by a standard American bomb. They would need to use one of their specially designed bunker-busting bombs, and frankly, the Americans don't have an unlimited supply of those.

"Also, to prevent enemy artillery from scoring direct hits, we've built a shelf that protrudes several meters over the structure, and this shelf is what the enemy artillery will hit. It'll prevent artillery from being able to fly in at an angle and hit the front of the structure. As for tank rounds, a lucky shot may still get through, but we've minimized the likelihood as much as we could. Each gun room is also closed off from the rest of the structure, so even if one room took a direct hit, the explosion wouldn't ripple through the rest of the fortification."

The colonel obviously took pride in what his unit was constructing. General Yang had to give the man credit—he'd really thought this defensive network out well. If the bunkers held out as well as their tests had shown, then it should give the Allies a real bloody nose when they did eventually come calling. Yang was still concerned about the Allies' Air Force though—he knew from his own military training at the American Citadel that the Americans would hammer these positions with precision strikes.

"Colonel, you and your men have done an exceptional job preparing this position," Yang praised. "Please continue the work you're doing. I fear we don't have much time before these positions will be put to the test. When do you believe they'll be complete?"

"We need another week to finish the cement work of the bunkers. Once that's done, we should have everything else completed a week later. We'll be operational in fourteen days, assuming the weather doesn't give us any serious problems," replied the colonel confidently. The other engineers around him nodded in agreement.

"Very well, please continue, Colonel. Your country is counting on you and your men. I must get going; I have many more positions to inspect today. Thank you for your time." General Yang shook several of the colonel's men's hands, encouraging each of them to do their best before he left.

When the inspection was over, General Yang and three of his most trusted officers headed back to the Harbin Z-9 helicopter that would take them on the rest of their tour. A small contingent of Special Forces soldiers who were his personal bodyguards also got on board, though they sat in the back of the helicopter. Yang and his three compatriots sat in the center of the helicopter, directly behind the two pilots.

As soon as everyone was seated, the helicopter's rotors started whirring. A few minutes later, the chopper was airborne. The pilots deftly turned toward their next destination, the mountainous region to the northeast of Beijing.

With the added noise of the helicopter, Yang and his three officers leaned in closer to talk.

"These positions won't stop the Allies," Colonel Commandant Han Weiguo exclaimed. "Lieutenant General Zhou is going to recommend that we use tactical nuclear weapons." Han had been General Yang's personal assistant and staff officer for three years. Yang had come to trust his honest and blunt assessments over the years.

Major General Cao Xueen, General Yang's deputy, added, "He's right about General Zhou. He's going to insist we use tactical nuclear weapons to stop the Allied advance. Will the President side with him or with you on this matter?"

Yang thought about that for a moment. Since assuming command of the PLA six weeks ago, he had managed to slow the Allies' conquest of China. He had been building trust with the president, but Xi had known General Zhou for many years.

General Yang shook his head. "I'm not 100% sure," he admitted. "Xi is pretty insistent on holding Beijing no matter what the cost to the city or people."

Cao shook his head angrily. "You have to convince him to pursue a peace with the Allies before more of the country is destroyed. Have you seen how many people have been fleeing the cities ahead of the Allied army? There has to be nearly a hundred million people displaced as refugees—*refugees* in our own country!"

The other officers nodded. Yang sighed, not sure what more to say. He'd ask the President about it when they met up again in a few more days. Until then, he was going to do his best to make sure the city was as prepared as possible to repel the all-but-inevitable attack.

Chapter 23
Eerie Calm

Qingyuan, China
Forward Operating Base Spartan

Nine weeks of ground combat had taken its toll on the men of 4th Battalion, 6th Marines. They were tired, beaten up, and ready for a break, and it looked like they had finally caught one. The PLA forces in the area had finally withdrawn into the countryside outside the major cities.

Despite having chased the remnants of the Chinese Army out of the area, Lieutenant Colonel Long's battalion now needed to expand the perimeter outwards and begin the long process of occupation duty and hunting down the remaining enemy units. With his new set of orders, Long set out looking for a suitable location to establish a large Marine base that could support operations within the cities he was now in charge of as well as the frontier countryside his Marines would still need to patrol as they looked to keep the remaining PLA units at bay.

After spending a day examining the area from the air in an Osprey and then following up with several ground inspections, Long finally settled on a large undeveloped plot of land not far from the Beijing River and the bridges that connected each side of the city. With his site picked out, he sent the engineers and two of his companies to work on getting the perimeter established so they could begin building out the guts of the base.

****

Lieutenant Colonel Long had just finished walking the perimeter of his newly established base, and he was satisfied with what he'd seen. The city of Qingyuan, a suburb northwest of Guangzhou, was a pivotal city to hold; Long planned on leveraging the forward operating base's location near the Beijing River as a natural means of preventing any PLA units from thinking they could easily retake the city.

Long was content with what the engineers had been able to build in such a short period of time. They'd brought in miles worth of material to build twelve-foot Hesco barriers, and the engineers had wasted no time in building this perimeter with them. As the wall segments were constructed, many of the enterprising Marines had built improvised bunkers and fighting positions on top of the barriers along with guard towers, spaced out every couple hundred meters. Inside the FOB, his units were busy building up their company areas. There were tents for sleeping in, tents to act as orderly rooms and operations centers, kitchen tents, ammunition lockers, medical tents, vehicle yards, maintenance sections and every other function that would be needed to support the forward operating base.

Captain Stone, Long's weapons company commander, caught up with him. "This is a good location to establish the FOB, Sir," he praised.

"I agree, it's a solid location," said Captain McKnight, the Never Company CO. "I know some of the locals didn't like us setting it up here and all, but it really gives us a solid commanding view of both the city and the bridge across the river. We've got great defensive positions as well."

"It's big enough for what we need without us having to commandeer large swaths of condos or parts of the city," Long responded. His tone was confident without being cocky. "There are a ton of fishery farms in this area…I can't believe how much of the land around the city has been dedicated to industrial fish farms." He shook his head. "I had wanted a location with a bit more standoff room from the city, but that didn't seem possible," he added.

Captain McKnight pointed to a cluster of condo high-rises that would butt up against one perimeter of their wall. "What about those buildings? Are they occupied? If they aren't, maybe we could have the engineers expand the perimeter and include them in the base. I'll bet they could provide us with enough housing for the entire regiment, Sir."

Long looked at the condos. He hadn't given them a lot of thought other than realizing how good of a sniper nest they'd make. Then an idea formed in his head. "Tell you what, Captain—take your men over there and find out how many residents are there. I think I have an idea that might kill a few birds with one stone," he directed. A grin formed on his face.

******

Two days later, his engineers had expanded their perimeter to include the additional buildings. Gobbling up the condos gave his FOB the sudden ability to house ten thousand additional Marines. When Captain McKnight's men had gone through the buildings, they'd discovered that more than ninety percent of the residents had fled the city and not returned. The few hundred residents that remained were biometrically enrolled in the base security system, given an ID card and allowed to stay on the newly built FOB, but only in the area where they currently lived. They were even offered jobs on the base. Many of them jumped eagerly at the opportunity for employment, especially since they would be paid in US dollars and be allowed to eat at the same dining facilities where the Marines did.

With the sudden increase in housing, most of the 6th Marines quickly moved onto the FOB, turning what had been intended to be a small forward base into a major base of operations. Lieutenant Colonel Long suddenly found himself not only the 4th Battalion Commander, but also the FOB commander and mayor of a base that now housed more than 11,000 service members and 6,000 contractors. Whether it was fortunate for him or not, the regiment commander focused his resources and attention on maintaining the peace in the surrounding area and continuing to hunt down the remaining enemy army units still operating in the region, leaving Long to handle the day-to-day affairs of managing the base and his own battalion.

With the brunt of the heavy fighting over, the Marines moved to expand the American perimeter and control of Guangdong Province. The Allies now had nearly 90 million Chinese civilians for whom they were responsible for providing security, food and every other necessity of life. Fortunately, the brass had a well-developed plan for how to manage the occupation of these major cities and specially trained units to come in and help advise and work with the local government officials.

One of the keys to getting the occupation off to a good start was making sure the Allies got the cities' general functions back up and running quickly, including running water, waste management, electricity, hospitals, fire departments, and police services. In addition, they had to make sure a steady food supply was being made available that consisted of both foods produced in their region and imported food.

While the Allied military forces worked to make sure the basic necessities were being provided for, President Hung Hui-ju's Republic of China worked diligently to make sure everyone in the province knew it was her government that was working to provide the people with the food, security, and economic opportunity they needed to try and return their lives back to normal. Her constant pleas for the locals to disavow the Xi regime were still being met with mixed results. Some favored a more open, democratically elected form of government. Many others, however, preferred the autocratic form of government they had always known.

****

32,000 Feet Above Beijing

The night air was cool as it buffeted the B-21 Raider. The slight turbulence was normal as the sleek Batwing-lookalike bomber sliced through a storm cloud. Lightning strikes were visible not very far away, and rain pounded on the windshield of the bomber. Looking at the weather radar, Major Daniels made the decision to take them up a few thousand feet and see if she could get out of this soup.

She pulled back on the flight controls slightly. The bomber rose slowly at first, then with a bit more speed as they steadily moved out of the clouds. A few minutes passed by, and then they completely broke free of the storm. The turbulence dissipated until it eventually left all together leaving them nothing but calm smooth air as they continued on their mission.

Her flight commander, Colonel Rob "Pappi" Fortney, was doing something on the targeting computer and also periodically checking some of their electronic warfare systems to make sure everything was still working correctly. So far, they had not been detected. For all the success they'd had with the B-21 these past four weeks, Major Daniels had to remind herself that this was still very much an experimental plane. After each mission, their flight data was downloaded and sent off to the manufacturer to be examined, and before each new mission, their software was updated or changed based on recommendations by either an engineering group or an electronic warfare group. She would have hated to admit it out loud, but each time the engineers made an update, the bomber flew better, conserved more fuel, and generally handled better.

She glanced to the side and saw that Pappi had a mischievous look on his face.

"What's so funny, old man?" she asked.

"I was just thinking to myself how awesome this new bomber is. When we flew our first mission, we mostly avoided flying inside clouds, and when we did, the flight computer had a hard time keeping the bomber from bouncing around from the turbulence. When we left that system a few minutes ago, it hardly bounced or had trouble at all," he explained. "Plus, I'm not even showing the slightest bit of detection by the ground radars."

"I'll bet that change in radar detection has more to do with the five days our bird spent in the hangar while they put a new coat of that super-secret radar-absorbent paint on," she said with a grin.

"This bomber is so much deadlier than my old one. Don't get me wrong, I liked the B-2—but it wasn't completely invisible to radar. A good radar operator could still spot us periodically. I have it on good authority that when our bombers flew deep-penetration raids over Moscow, their air defense guys would see us fading in and out on their radar scopes," Pappi added.

Major Daniels crinkled her eyebrows. "If they could see you guys coming in and out of focus, how come they couldn't shoot more of you guys down?"

Pappi flashed a sarcastic smile. "Stealth doesn't mean invisible, Double D," he explained. "It just means our cross-section or radar signature is significantly reduced. In the case of our B-2s, the Russians could get a general idea of where we were, but they couldn't develop a good enough picture to generate a targeting lock to engage us with one of their missiles."

Her face became pale. "How did you get shot down then? What happened on that mission, Pappi?"

An awkward moment of silence passed between them before Pappi sighed. "I suppose you deserve to know," he began. "I screwed up our mission. The Russians had the entire place lit up like Christmas with search radars, airborne early-warning aircraft, and fighters. By and large, we had flown in relatively undetected. I mean, they had a few soft hits on us, but nothing that could pin us down. They knew we were in the area, or at least headed to Moscow, but they hadn't locked us up yet.

"I was flying the plane. My copilot, "Ricky," was a combat virgin like you. He'd missed out on the previous combat operations, so he wanted to be the one to deliver the payload. For this first mission, we were sent in on a decapitation strike. The brass wanted to see if we could take Petrov out right at the beginning of the war. When we entered the strike zone, Ricky opened the bomb doors and proceeded to drop our two bunker-busters."

Pappi paused for a moment as he looked out the window at the dark air whipping past their plane. "Once the bombs had been dropped…all I wanted to do was get out of there. We'd been getting painted by targeting radars on and off for nearly an hour. When I felt the weight of the bombs leave the aircraft, I immediately turned us for home before Ricky had had a chance to get the bomb bay doors closed. That left an exposed part of our underbelly open, and as I turned, it provided the dozens of radars searching for us with enough of area for them to gain a solid return on us. In fractions of a second, multiple radars suddenly had a firm lock on us, and before either of us knew it, an SA-21 fired two missiles after us.

"At first we didn't think anything of it. We knew that as soon as the bomb bay was closed off, our stealth ability would be intact once again, and we figured the missile would lose track of us and we'd escape. At first, that's exactly what it looked like would happen. However, we didn't know that the Russians had recently upgraded their guidance systems to use a lot of unique AI technology; that allowed the missiles' warheads to take the known data it had for us and calculate with a degree of certainty where we would be.

"When the missile got to within ten kilometers of our position, a new sensor in the targeting computer took over, which looked at the displacement of air in the area. This obviously led them to the anomaly our aircraft created, and the missile zeroed in on us. Before either of us knew what had happened, it had gotten within range of its proximity sensor, and the warhead detonated."

Pappi paused for a second again, reliving that fateful day. He took a deep breath and continued, "When it hit us, it didn't destroy our bird right away. We had all sorts of damage, but we were still flyable. What really doomed us was when one of the SA-10s further away from Moscow was able to lock onto our damaged bird and fired another missile at us. After that, we both ejected and then tried our best to escape and evade our way back to friendly territory."

Daniels just took it in; she didn't judge him or second-guess him. She could tell he was still struggling internally with what had happened, and she knew he probably blamed himself for getting them shot down. She knew from the stories she'd been told that Ricky had been taken prisoner and later died in a POW camp.

She looked over at Pappi and saw him wipe away a tear. "You did the best you could with a crappy situation, Boss. Don't let anyone else tell you otherwise."

Pappi nodded. "I know," he said glumly. "I've accepted it. I know I made mistakes, and I know some of it was also outside my control. I've made peace with it at this point."

Before they could continue their conversation, one of the instruments on the bomber started to beep. Pappi saw on the navigation screen that they were roughly five minutes from weapons release.

"Looks like we're almost over the target," Pappi announced. "Stay frosty, Double D. I'm showing a massive increase in enemy search radars." Then he went to work getting the Raider's bombs ready to be released.

Their current mission over Beijing was focused on going after the party leadership of the government. They had been given the home addresses of one hundred out of the one hundred and fifty members of the Standing Committee of the National People's Congress. Next to the Central Military Commission or CMC, the Standing Committee was the largest body of senior government officials. Washington was hoping that going after the senior leadership of the country might convince the PLA and the government to surrender so further bloodshed could be avoided.

Pappi double-checked the targeting system, making sure each of the one hundred GBU-38 500-pound laser-guided bombs was ready to go after their individual targets. If everything went according to plan, they'd nail two-thirds of the Standing Committee in a single blow.

A few minutes went by in relative silence as they worked on their own parts of the mission. Then the computer indicated they'd reached the optimal position to release their bombs, ensuring that each of them would have enough altitude and speed to silently glide to their intended targets. Pappi silently hoped each of them would be successful in delivering their intended message to the Chinese government from the American president...*surrender*.

Chapter 24
Crisis Brewing

Beijing, China
August First Building
Ministry of National Defense HQ

President Xi sat at the table while one of General Yang's subordinates provided them with an update on the latest bombing raid on Beijing. Over the past two evenings, the Americans had made a concerted effort to go after the Standing Committee, and the members who had not been killed during the first night of attacks were rightly concerned about their safety.

What gave Xi some serious pause was not that the Americans had gotten lucky and killed eighty-six of them on the first night—an enemy could get lucky with intelligence. What bothered him the most was that despite the PLA relocating the remaining members of the Committee, the Americans had somehow managed to carry out a devastating strike the very next day that had killed *another* forty-eight members. That left a mere sixteen members of the Standing Committee alive, and the only reason they hadn't been killed was because none of them had been in Beijing at the time of the strike. Something was wrong. Xi was hell-bent on figuring out who the mole was inside the military or the government—whoever it was needed to be eliminated.

****

General Yang knew the President wanted to talk about how the Americans had found out where the PLA had moved the Committee members, and he knew the answer. He also knew the President was going to be furious once he was made aware of how thoroughly penetrated the Chinese communications system had been. He had only found out how big the vulnerability was himself the day before, and he'd wanted to wait to brief the President until he had a solution in place to solve the problem. Unfortunately, the Americans' nearly complete decapitation of the PRC's civilian government had moved that timeline up.

When General Yang's deputy finished briefing them on the strike, Yang immediately dismissed everyone in the room and asked for Colonel Su to be brought in. President Xi looked at him with curiosity but also fire in his eyes.

President Xi seemed a bit put off at having some colonel he'd never heard of join the meeting, but he remained silent and gave Yang a chance to explain.

"Mr. President, I wanted to bring Colonel Su in to speak with you about our mole," Yang said, cutting to the chase.

President Xi sat a little straighter. "Go on," he said eagerly.

"Colonel Su is the Director of Unit 61398, one of our cyberwarfare directorates. More specifically, his unit conducts foreign communication penetration activities and defensive activities. I've had him looking into the possibility of a mole within the PLA for a while. Actually, I've had him looking into this since I took over as the overall PLA commander," Yang explained.

Xi leaned in, a devilish smile spreading across his face. "I knew you were a clever man, General. So, you'd thought we had a mole this entire time, and now you've found him?"

Yang allowed a half-smile as he bowed his head slightly. "I merely used deductive reasoning, Mr. President. However, I'm afraid the situation we're about to brief you on is far more severe than we thought possible. It's also not something we can readily fix by simply executing someone."

Now Xi had a look of concern on his face.

"He's probably wondering if there is a coup ready to take him out," Yang realized.

Colonel Su asked, "Do you want me to go into the technical specifics right away, or do you want to provide some background information and then allow me to go over the details?"

"I'll give the President a brief summary of what's happened, and then you follow up," Yang replied. He saw a bit of relief on Su's face at not having to be the main bearer of bad news.

Clearing his throat, Yang explained, "Mr. President, the Americans have done to us what the British did to the Germans during World War II." He held up a hand to forestall the interruption he knew the President was about to make. "If you'll allow me to explain, I'll go over what happened, how it happened, and what Colonel Su and I are doing about it. Because of the sensitive nature of what we're about to tell you, I've asked that no one else be present. Right now, Mr. President, the list of people who know what's happened can be counted on one hand, and I want to keep it that way."

The President nodded. "This had better be good," he grumbled.

Yang took in a deep breath before he began. "In the early part of World War II, the British had captured one of the German Navy's Enigma radio systems and the codebook.

The Germans never found out this happened and so they didn't change their codes or develop a different type of cipher code system. Once the British had the tools to decipher the Germans' communications, they were able to read all of the military's messages for the duration of the war. That has essentially happened to us."

Xi's face turned beet red. He interjected, "How did the Allies do this to us, and how long has this been going on?"

Yang turned to Colonel Su and signaled for him to take over.

Colonel Su stood and walked over to a whiteboard, where he wrote several names down along with a few other pieces of information. He then turned to face the two of them. "Mr. President, in the lead-up to this war, the PLA Air Force had been working on the Y'an communication UAV for several years. We knew in a war with the West, we'd need to disable or eliminate the Allies' satellite communications system because the Western militaries are heavily dependent on this capability."

"Yes, but somehow the Allies have managed to bounce back from that dependency much faster than anyone had anticipated," Xi retorted.

Nodding, Su continued. "We can thank the Russians for that, Mr. President. At the beginning of this conflict, the Russians' DDoS attack on the American GPS and military satellites was successful in disabling their systems for a few months, but once the Allies figured out how to overcome it, that option was off the table for us to use further down the road. Instead, we moved forward with the Y'an UAVs. In producing the UAVs, we acquired tens of thousands of microprocessors from an American company with which our Ministry of Industry had a joint venture. Because of the strict timeline required to get the Y'an into production, we purchased tens of thousands of these microprocessors rather than produce them ourselves.

"One of the engineers—a Chinese citizen, no less—had worked at the company's American plant for five years. During that timeframe, he was recruited by the American National Security Agency. When he came back to China prior to the war, we believe he was activated. Using his position as one of the lead engineers on the communications package of the Y'an, he inserted a piece of malware into the microprocessor. When we then activated the Y'an and moved all of our communications systems over to it, the malicious code was activated. From the day we transitioned our communications to the UAVs, the code mirrored all of our transmissions to each other and sent them to the Americans."

President Xi looked positively ill. "How could this happen?" he yelled. He screamed a stream of curse words, the obscenities flowing out of him like a geyser. When he calmed down a bit, he asked, "So what can be done?"

"We do have a plan to fix this problem, Mr. President," Colonel Su said gently. "Now that we know where the problem is, we're able to begin swapping out these microprocessors for ones that aren't compromised. I've spoken with the Y'an program director, and he informed me that they could begin removing the corrupted processors immediately." He paused and shifted uncomfortably. "Unfortunately, it'll take us several months to fully fix the problem," he admitted.

Turning to look at General Yang, Xi asked, "This is how the Americans were able to kill so many of the Standing Committee members yesterday and the day before, isn't it?"

Yang nodded. "Yes, Mr. President. It's also how the Allies have been able to anticipate every offensive move we've made. It's why our forces are getting pummeled before they even make it to the front lines, and how the Allies have been so successful in finding our fuel or ammunition dumps and storage facilities. They've had complete access to our communication systems for the past fourteen weeks."

"Colonel Su, thank you for your efforts in finding this problem," said President Xi. "I trust that you all will handle the traitor that brought this about. Make sure his family is dealt with as well. Now, if you'd please leave, I have some matters I'd like to discuss with the general alone."

Su bowed and hastily made his exit.

Once he'd left, Xi sat there silently for a few minutes. General Yang hoped he was only trying to figure out what to do next and not contemplating whether or not to execute him.

Finally, Xi sighed. He looked at Yang, defeated and deflated. "The war is lost, isn't it?" he asked.

General Yang nodded cautiously. "Mr. President, I've tried to be honest with my assessment that we will inevitably have to surrender. It has never been a matter of if, but more a matter of when. I've done the best I could to hold Shanghai and Guangdong Province, to no avail. We've lost over 500,000 soldiers in Guangdong Province, and nearly 400,000 more in Shanghai. I have more than two million soldiers and militia men positioned to defend the capital region. However, I just don't have any more men or material to retake Guangdong Province or Shanghai."

General Yang was dejected. He'd done the best he could to turn things around from the colossal failure that his predecessors had left him, but after realizing that the Allies had been seeing every order, every strategy, every attack plan before it was even implemented—he knew his men had never had a chance.

President Xi examined his general's forlorn expression, but he suddenly sat up straighter, as if he'd just had an idea. "General, the situation is grave, I know that. However, now we know why—we've been losing these past fourteen weeks because the enemy knew our plans. I want the solution for this expedited as much as possible. In the meantime, we need to revert to using human carriers for as much of our highly sensitive information as possible. We can also go back to using our secured ground communications— you know, telephones. I know it's not digital data, but it will work for voice communications.

"I will not accept defeat. No. China is still too big and too populous a country for the Allies to defeat or occupy us. I want you to accelerate the arming of the PLA's militia force—we have hundreds of millions of young men and women. Give them weapons and rudimentary training and place them in fortified positions. A soldier doesn't need months of combat training to stand in a trench or foxhole and fire at the enemy when they charge."

Xi let out a breath and shook his head. "I never thought we'd be in this situation. We spent years developing the plans for this war. Everything had been thought out, planned, and carefully calculated." He sighed despairingly. "This war should have been over with by now, Yang. It never should have gone on as long as it has. Everything we wargamed said it would have ended a year ago."

The President paused again, looking at the ceiling for a minute. General Yang waited silently for what he was going to say next.

Xi eventually fixed his gaze on the general again. "General Yang, I know the situation is bleak," he admitted. "You have to stay focused though on figuring out how we can turn things around. You've been trained by the Americans—you understand how they think." He shook his head again. "If you'd been in charge from the beginning, we would have won this war already. I'm supremely sorry that my senior generals failed you and the people of our great nation. I can't undo what they've done; the best I can do now is give you every tool and resource you need to try and win or at least stalemate the Allies. Do you believe you can force the Allies to sue for peace, or at least an armistice? Maybe push the war beyond the American election? If the Americans elect a new President, that person may see reason and agree to an equitable end to the war." Xi's voice was almost pleading at this point. It was obvious that he was desperate for a way to save the war, or at the very least, save his position of power.

General Yang let out an audible sigh. His mind was racing a million miles a minute, trying to figure out what to do next. He scrambled to think of a way to outfox the Allies—or at least force them to the negotiating table. A nugget of an idea came to mind. He calculated the angles before he dared to speak.

"Mr. President, I believe I might be able to buy us some time—time that we desperately need right now while we fix our communications problem."

"I'm all ears, General. What do you propose?"

"The Americans are clearly trying to position President Hung Hui-ju to replace you. What if I made a ceasefire request to the Americans to meet with President Hung and the Allies to discuss an equitable end to the war— one that still saw you retaining control of the PRC?" Yang asked, hoping Xi wouldn't dismiss the idea out of spite. He desperately needed time, and prolonged peace talks could be the answer.

Xi sat there silent for a second, probably trying to decide if Yang was serious or trying to find a way to stab him in the back.

"How much time do you think these talks could buy us?" Xi finally asked.

"At least a week—maybe more, but at least a week. It may not sound like much, but please keep in mind that would be a week of no more strategic bombings by the Americans, a week of us being able to move troops, equipment and other war stocks without being attacked. It would also give us some insight into what the Americans are willing to accept to end the war," Yang explained.

Xi thought about it for a moment. General Yang became more nervous the longer the silence grew.

"OK, General, you have my permission to pursue this with the Americans," Xi finally said hesitantly. "If you do this though, make sure you have everything ready on our end to capitalize on the temporary halt to the Allied offensive and bombings. We need to make use of every moment the Allies are not bombing us. Is that understood?"

Yang nodded, smiling now that he had a viable plan for how to end the war without annihilating his country or the rest of the world.

Chapter 25
When Opportunity Knocks

Washington, D.C.

White House

Presidential Emergency Operation Center (PEOC)

President Wally Foss watched with bated breath as the SpaceX Falcon heavy rocket released its payload module for the final part of its journey. Within seconds of the booster rockets separating from the main body, they began their turn back to Cape Canaveral.

"God, I hope the Air Force is right about the Chinese not being able to shoot down these satellites," he thought. Otherwise, this was going to be a very expensive waste of limited resources.

"The payload module will now move the DS2000 satellites into their geostationary orbit or GEO over North America and Asia," announced the Air Force colonel from the newly created US Space Command.

"You all are sure the Chinese aren't going to be able to shoot these satellites down this time?" inquired the President.

Colonel Ralph Reyes from US Space Command nodded. "Yes, Mr. President," he replied. "We've specifically tasked the B-21 with neutralizing the PLA rocket force's ability to interdict these satellites. A month ago, we launched a series of decoy satellites that drew out the Chinese weapon platforms and the locations they were using to destroy our satellites. Once we identified the systems, the B-21 was dispatched and six launch facilities and ground laser facilities were destroyed. Based on the communiques we intercepted after those attacks, we are confident we've removed the threat to our satellites. We've also moved the DS2000s to a much higher GEO to further mitigate the possibility that we missed a launch facility. These satellites should be safe from future PLA actions, Mr. President."

Several of the other military members nodded. JP from the CIA and Tom McMillan seemed a little less certain, but they held their tongues.

"Explain to me again how these satellites are going to be a big game changer for us," the President said as he rubbed his temples. He reached for his cup of coffee; it was time to try and dispel his most recent stress-induced migraine with added caffeine.

Colonel Reyes smiled. "Essentially, the Mitsubishi DS2000 satellite will be able to provide real-time, high-speed communication connectivity to our military forces. Each of the satellites has one hundred HTS multibeam communication beams, meaning they'll be able to provide coverage to many thousands of square miles of the earth's surface. With three of them in high GEO over Asia and the Pacific, and two of them over North America, we will have effectively restored our military communication to what it was prior to the beginning of the war. In fact, it's probably going to increase our capabilities, as these satellites are significantly better than the ones there're replacing.

"Tonight, we launch the next Falcon heavy rocket from Vandenberg Air Force Base. That rocket will be carrying ten Iridium4 satellites into high GEO, with five more of them being placed over North America and the other five over Europe. While the DS2000 set of satellites is designated purely for military purposes, the Iridium satellites are slated for commercial use. It's not going to completely reestablish our civilian satellite infrastructure, but it's a start."

Admiral Meyers added, "Once we've made certain the PLA isn't able to shoot these satellites down, we'll begin a rapid deployment of new military and commercial satellites. Iridium and Mitsubishi have dozens of satellites ready to go at our launch facilities in California, Texas, Florida, and Virginia."

"What's in the next batch of satellites?" asked Tom McMillan.

Colonel Reyes answered, "A series of weather satellites, communications and GPS satellites. All total, SpaceX will be sending roughly 67 new satellites into orbit over the next ten days. It's going to take some time, Mr. President, but we'll get the world's satellite infrastructure restored within a year. The new satellites are significantly better, more capable, and have a longer shelf life than the ones they're replacing."

The President relaxed a bit. "OK, gentlemen, you've satisfied my questions and alleviated some of my concerns. I suppose we'll know over the next twenty-four hours if our assessment of the PLA's ability to shoot them down was truly accurate. I hope we're right, because these satellites aren't cheap or quick to build. We can't afford to lose them needlessly."

President Foss then turned to Secretaries Castle and Landover. "I suppose since this part of the meeting is over," he announced. "We should discuss the communique you both received."

Colonel Reyes and a few other staffers took their cue and left the PEOC.

Turning to look at his advisors, President Foss asked, "So, what do we know about this General Yang? Is this offer something we should take seriously or rebuff?"

A few of the generals stirred in their seats, not sure what to say. Up to that point, they'd been executing the strategy of complete and utter destruction of the PLA and the communist government, and since the start of Project Enigma, they'd been exceptionally successful at it.

JP tackled the question first, which made sense to Foss; the CIA had developed a deep personality bio and profile of the mystery general. "General Yang is actually not as big of an unknown commodity as we'd first thought, Mr. President. As it turns out, Yang Yin grew up in the United States. His father owned a Chinese company that had a joint venture with a US firm, and Yang's father moved his family to America to run the US side of the company when Yang was ten years old. He attended a prestigious private school, and when he turned eighteen, he was accepted into the Citadel as a foreign student. During his time at the Citadel, he excelled academically and physically. In the summer of his freshman year, he went through Army basic combat training at Fort Benning. Then he completed airborne school the next summer and Ranger school his final year at the Citadel. He was offered a commission in the Army upon graduation, but he turned it down when his father and family transferred back to China.

"His father's company had a lot of contracts and connections within the Chinese defense industry, so he also had a lot of contacts within the PLA. His father used some of those connections and got his son accepted into the PLA as a captain. Yang was taken under the wing of several benefactors who helped to mentor and train him in the ways of the PLA ground forces as he also shared his insight into American military operations. During the next twenty-five years, his military career rose as his benefactors' careers did. When the war started, he had risen to be the commander of the PLA southern theater of operations. His force led the invasion of Vietnam and the rest of Southeast Asia. Later, his forces led the invasion of Taiwan and the Philippines. He is by far their most capable military commander."

Foss leaned forward. "This is good background information, but what does it mean?" he pressed. "Is this a legit offer to talk about ending the war, or is this just a stall tactic to take the pressure off them?"

"That's a tough question to answer, Mr. President," replied Secretary Landover. "It's also hard to turn down a legitimate opportunity to talk face-to-face with the one man currently in charge of the Chinese military. I think our current strategy we've been pushing with President Hung inside the occupied territories has President Xi's regime nervous, and rightly so. Our current polls show President Hung has been making significant ground in both acceptance and approval."

Castle added, "I don't like the idea of pausing our current military operations. We've been hammering the PLA and the civilian government hard. The introduction of the B-21 Raider has been a true game changer in our strategic bombing operations as well. We may only have the one bomber right now, but we've been using it with devastating effectiveness. Especially around the Beijing capital region as we hunt down the military and civilian leadership of the country.

"At the same time, I also know that if we aren't able to come to some sort of terms with them, this war is going to drag on well into the spring or summer of next year. We may take Beijing in the next two or three months, but it's going to be a bloody campaign. Probably more so than Shanghai, which is hard to comprehend. My opinion is that we should take the meeting but limit its duration. General Yang asked for seven days; I propose we counter with forty-eight hours."

"I agree, Mr. President," said Admiral Meyers. "We should take the meeting but reduce the timeframe. The PLA is clearly going to use any reprieve we give them to strengthen their positions, so let's not give them any more time than is absolutely necessary."

The other military chiefs around the table nodded.

Sensing that he had a consensus from his senior advisors and military leaders, the President consented to the meeting and a forty-eight-hour ceasefire. The ball was now in the Chinese court—they could accept the new terms, or until then, business would continue as usual.

****

Fort Meade, Maryland
National Security Agency

Tyler Walden had a concerned look on his face as he read through the data of the Y'an UAV deployment schedules. Over the last week, their office had noticed some gaps developing in the Enigma program. Some sections of the UAVs were suddenly not providing the same level of information they had been. Gaps in coverage were starting to become more pronounced, and that meant only one thing—the PLA was on to them and was correcting the problem.

He turned around in his swivel chair, got up and headed for Kate's office. After knocking on the door frame, he inquired, "You got a minute, Kate? I think we have a problem with Enigma."

Kate paused typing on her keyboard and looked up at him. "A problem? What do you mean?" Her face contorted with an obvious distaste for the words that had just come out of her mouth.

Tyler came all the way into her office, closed the door, and then plopped himself down in the chair in front of her desk. "I've been monitoring the Y'an drones to see how many of them are still operational and to see if there are any major holes or gaps in coverage. As the PLA Air Force's fighter presence and their air defense systems continue to fall apart, more of the Y'ans have been getting shot down by Allied fighters, which is both good and bad for us. Less drones mean a more limited window into their communications.

"The main issue is that over the last four days, we've seen a significant drop in data being transmitted by the UAVs. At first it was just a few dozen, then it became entire cities and parts of a province. I initially thought it was related to the Allies shooting down more of their UAVs; however, when I looked at the number of Y'ans operating in the area, I didn't see a noticeable difference. I just saw that they were no longer transmitting data to us like before."

"So you think they're on to us?" Kate asked.

Tyler nodded. "I do. I think they've figured out what we were doing and are bringing the drones down as fast as they can to swap out the affected component."

"Crap," Kate exclaimed. "If that's the case, then we need to let the White House know. We need to work with State and get President Hung's message pumped out across whatever Y'ans we still have access to before they've completely cut us out of the network."

She immediately reached for her SIPR Tandberg. It rang a few times before Tom McMillan picked up. The image of his office came into view as he got up to close his office door. Turning to look at her and Tyler, he said, "I suppose it's serious if you're calling me on this thing."

She nodded. She filled Tom in on what Tyler had just told her, then concluded, "If you guys still want to hit the PLA with President Hung's social media messages, now's the time. We're probably going to lose our access within a week, maybe two tops."

Tom let out an audible sigh but nodded. "OK," he said stoically. "I'd hoped we'd be able to maintain this edge a little longer, but I guess we'll have to go for it. Let me go brief the President and the Secretary of State. I'll get back with you later." Then he disconnected the call.

Kate turned to Tyler. "Get the team ready to disseminate the video, just like we rehearsed," she ordered. "I have a feeling the PLA is going to cut the cord to the program entirely once this message goes live. Then they'll know for sure we're inside their system."

Chapter 26
Battle for Lingyuan

Yutian, China

The hangar felt cold and damp, but at least there wasn't any wind. "Hurry up and grab your gear!" shouted Staff Sergeant Jose Sanchez, the platoon sergeant. "When the helicopters show up, I want everyone to run out to our bird and get on. No lollygagging!"

Private Liam Miller turned to Corporal Webster. "Have you ever ridden in one of these new helicopters before?" he asked.

Webster shook his head. "No, this'll be a first for me," he admitted.

Specialist Nathan Ryle, who'd overheard their conversation, interjected, "I rode in one once. When I caught a ride back to the unit from the hospital. They're super-fast."

Since getting shot and returning to the unit, Nathan had lost the attitude problem he'd had at the start of their deployment and had finally started to fit in with the platoon. It was like his brush with death had suddenly given him a reason to live, and he found he'd have a better chance of surviving the war if he wasn't such a jerk to the other guys in his unit. Maybe he was also grateful for how they'd helped save his life by risking death to get him to a medevac.

Captain Joel Garcia walked up to the group. "Listen up, guys!" he announced. "The helicopters will be arriving soon. When they do, we're going to pile in. It's about forty minutes to the target. Once on the ground, we're to dig in and hold the area until the main body of the ROK 16th Mechanized Brigade and the 1/8 Cav arrive." As he spoke, he continued to walk back and forth in front of the company, going over their objective for what must have been the tenth time that morning.

The captain paused for a second, surveying the men and women before him as they stood in loose formation, waiting for their ride. "I know I've said this all before," said Garcia. "This is going to be a tough fight, men—but we're going to end this war. Remember your training, listen to your officers and NCOs, and we'll get through this. Golden Dragons, lead the way!" When he shouted the battalion motto, it forced everyone to shout it right back at him.

Once the captain turned to go talk to some of the battalion brass, Staff Sergeant Martinez snorted. "He must be auditioning for his next promotion," he said in a hushed tone. Lieutenant Fallon chuckled at his comment.

The captain was a decent guy. When his company had found a way inside the mountain that formed the Jinzhou-Fuxin Line, the Allies had found their way to break through the PLA fortress. Martinez, Fallon and a handful of other soldiers in their platoon had been awarded Silver Stars for finding the entrance and emerging victorious in the fight that had ensued, but their captain had been awarded the Distinguished Service Cross. Ever since then, he seemed to feel that he was on the verge of being promoted to take over command of the battalion.

However, after that major battle, their brigade had been pulled from the line for a couple of months of R&R and occupation duty while replacement soldiers were filtered in to bring them back to 100% strength. With no major battles or combat losses, promotions within the brigade remained low, and he hadn't gotten his major's oakleaves.

A few minutes later, the soldiers of 2-14 Infantry heard the familiar rhythmic thumping sound of helicopter blades getting closer. Turning their attention to the open hangar doors, they spotted a squadron of the army's newest aviation member, the Bell V-280 Valor. The tiltrotor helicopter flared its nose up slightly and then settled into a soft touchdown on the parking pad a hundred meters in front of the hangar.

"First Platoon, follow me!" shouted one of the lieutenants. This call was quickly followed by similar orders from the rest of the platoon leaders.

Corporal Shane Webster seemed to be geeking out a bit. "This helicopter is so cool looking!" he told whoever could hear him. "It's like something from a sci-fi movie."

The other soldiers chuckled. They were probably thinking the same thing, but they just kept it inside. In short order, they had all strapped themselves into the six-point harnesses. Moments later, the helicopter lifted off and went into its holding pattern, out of the way, so other helicopters could land and load up their human cargo as well. With a battalion-level insertion, the sky was practically a swarm of choppers.

In addition to the V-280s, a squadron of AH-64 Apache gunships were tagging along to help provide any immediate ground support the battalion may need. Ten minutes went by with them circling the airbase, and then the air armada turned as a group and headed for their objective.
****

The flight to their objective was relatively uneventful. They avoided flying over most of the front lines, opting for a flight path that took them over more of the mountainous terrain to the north.

"*If there wasn't a war going on, this would be a beautiful helicopter ride*," thought Corporal Webster. Then he looked back around him and was reminded bluntly that this was not a scenic tour; the soldiers surrounding him were all fully weighed down with the tools of war, ready to unleash the awesome and terrifying military power strapped to their bodies.

"We're approaching the target!" yelled one of the door gunners. From his tone, it was obvious that they weren't sticking around any longer than absolutely necessary.

While they made their approach, the tiltrotor shifted its position to allow the helicopter to hover and land—airplane mode was no longer needed. When the nose of the Valor flared up, it bled off their airspeed immensely, enabling them to make a soft yet quick landing. Once on the ground, the crew chiefs and sergeant yelled at everyone, "Get out and move away from the helicopter!"

It took less than a minute for all the soldiers to get off the choppers and place some distance between themselves and their airborne chariots.

Zip, zip, crack, zip.

Bullets zinged right over their heads. Enemy soldiers nearby did their best to shoot down the helicopters before they could get away.

"Enemy soldiers, six o'clock, three hundred meters!" shouted one of the sergeants.

Ratatat, ratatat, ratatat.

Several of the M240G gunners opened fire on the small band of enemy soldiers.

Corporal Webster ran for cover next to a row of trees.

Snap, snap, crack.

Several bullets hit the tree trunk just as his body slammed against it. A single bullet zipped right past his head, close enough for him to hear the bee-like buzzing sound as it flew past him. He quickly brought his M4 to his shoulder and found the source of the gunfire. Several hundred meters below them was a small dirt trail, and from the looks of it, a squad of Chinese soldiers must have been patrolling there before their helicopters had suddenly showed up out of nowhere.

Taking aim at one of the soldiers, Webster squeezed off several rounds, forcing one of the enemy soldiers to duck behind a tree. In response, one of the PLA soldiers turned the PKM machine gun he was brandishing toward the section of trees Webster and his squad were using for cover. Rounds slapped the trees and brush around them as they ducked.

Before any of Webster's men could return fire, one of the Apache gunships that had been escorting their rides opened up on the dirt trail with several antimaterial rockets. Showers of flame, shrapnel and dirt peppered the area. An eerie calm replaced what had been a chaotic scene seconds before. Everyone held their fire to see if the gunships had killed them all. When no one fired back, one of the officers yelled, "Hurry up and get your positions set up!"

The soldiers moved swiftly, as though they had suddenly awoken from a dream. They had no idea how long it would take for the enemy to find out where they were and send them another welcoming party, and they needed to do their best to prepare.

Five hours went by as Corporal Webster and his fellow soldiers worked on digging their fighting positions. They moved down the ridge a few hundred meters to the dirt trail where they'd first encountered the enemy soldiers. Since the underbrush had already been cleared there, that trail would make an excellent front edge of their lines; they'd have an open area in front of their firing positions while remaining tucked away just inside the tree line.

While many soldiers were tasked with digging three-man fighting positions or four-man machine-gun positions, others unraveled rolls of concertina wire roughly forty meters in front of their new fortifications. Just behind the rolls of razor-tipped wires, some of the other soldiers set up and concealed Claymore anti-personnel mines and other nasty surprises some of the engineers were rigging up. Further out, about a dozen meters in front of the razor wire, a few soldiers strung up trip flares with some Claymores— those would act as an early-warning system of sorts once the sun went down.

Corporal Webster took a break for a moment to stretch and crack his back and smiled at all the bustling activity and layers of defense they were building. They had no idea how long they'd have to hold this position; they might as well do their best to make it as tough on the enemy as possible.

He looked back. Roughly three hundred meters below them was the bottom of the ridge. The trees there opened up to reveal relatively flat farmland and the edges of a small village or city another seven to ten kilometers away. That was where their armored reinforcements would be linking up with them from.

"*I hope we can hold out long enough,*" Webster thought.

****

Staff Sergeant Sanchez was walking the line his platoon was responsible for when he came upon Corporal Webster, Specialist Ryle and Private First Class Miller, all sitting with their feet dangling over the edge of their foxhole and their MREs in their laps.

"You guys look like the Three Stooges—you know that, right? Your fighting position looks like crap," he proclaimed. He proceeded to point out the fact that their foxhole was still only a meter deep, the edges were falling in on it and they had little cover in front of their fighting position.

"We're taking a break, Sarge. Can't you see we're eating?" Ryle retorted.

Sanchez snickered. "Five months ago, you guys hated each other, now you're all jokes and sharing an MRE. Never mind. Get this position ready. I'll give you guys another five minutes to finish your food, then I want to see you guys clean this up. Most of the platoon is already done."

When he'd left, Corporal Webster asked, "You guys think this war is almost over? It's practically November, which means winter is almost here. I really don't want to be sitting in a foxhole when it starts to snow."

"How should I know? I'm just a dumb guy from Compton," replied Ryle in his usual manner.

"You're lucky, Ryle. You didn't spend months on end pulling occupation duty," Private Miller responded. "I'd rather be out here in a foxhole facing off against enemy soldiers than patrolling through one of those Chinese urban jungles." With that, he finished off the last bite of his cheese tortellini and stuffed the empty pouch back into the MRE bag.

"Hey, if you're done, get back to work," gibed Corporal Webster, who was still finishing off the last of the cheese spread on his crackers.

"I wouldn't call getting shot lucky," Ryle shot back, "but the ice cream and pretty nurses were a nice break from looking at your ugly mugs." They all snickered at the joke.

"OK, guys, let's finish off this position," said Corporal Webster. "We've delayed long enough to avoid getting picked for any special duties Sanchez or the lieutenant might have for those overzealous gophers who already finished their positions."

The three of them chuckled at that. They'd learned early on that if you finished your task too quickly, you could find yourself "voluntold" to go work on another task, so they'd learned how to milk a project just long enough not to get in trouble.

Slowly and steadily, the day turned to night as the soldiers of 2-14 Infantry settled into their newly dug fighting positions and waited.

Corporal Webster wondered if they'd be attacked during the night, or if their luck would hold out and the enemy would decide they weren't worth the trouble.

****

"Stay frosty, and get ready for stand-to," Staff Sergeant Sanchez announced. "Several of the LP/OPs radioed in a large concentration of enemy troops headed our way." He quickly moved down the line to the next foxhole to spread the word.

The three of them exchanged nervous glances as they readied their weapons, shifting uncomfortably in their fighting position.

"*Maybe we should have made this thing a little bigger,*" thought Webster as he placed a couple of hand grenades on the ground in front of him, ready in case he needed them.

"You think the sarge could be any more vague with his description of what's out there?" asked Specialist Ryle. He pulled himself up and stood behind the squad's heavy machine gun.

"Maybe the LP/OP spotted a squad or platoon and thought it was larger than it really was. It's dark out," replied Private Miller nervously. He pulled another hundred-round belt for the M240G out of his ruck and began to link it together with the one already fed into Ryle's weapon.

Before any of them could say anything more, what sounded like a freight train zoomed right over their heads, then impacted violently several hundred meters up the ridge.

BOOM! Boom, boom, BOOM!

"Everyone down!" shouted one of the sergeants in a nearby fighting position.

The next five minutes was sheer terror for the infantry soldiers dug in on the side of the ridge. Enemy artillery rained down on them. Trees, parts of trees, rocks, dirt and everything else on the ridge were torn apart and thrown into the air and all around the soldiers. They did their best to ride out the horrendous experience.

Suddenly a shrieking whistle sound pierced their ears, followed by the guttural howl of an untold number of men and women below their positions.

Pop, pop, pop.

Illumination rounds started go off all along the ridge, turning the predawn twilight into full daylight.

"Holy hell, that's a lot of enemy soldiers!" shouted Private Miller. He brought his M4 to his shoulder and fired.

Specialist's Ryle's eyes went wide as saucers when he saw the wave of humanity charging up the ridge at them. He shook himself, then lowered his head down until his cheek was flush with the stock of his M240G. He fired three-to-five-second bursts of automatic fire into the ranks of the charging enemy soldiers, making sure to sweep back and forth across his field of fire.

Lifting his own rifle to his shoulder, Corporal Webster sighted in on one enemy soldier after another as the enemy charged relentlessly up the hill at them.

Pop, pop, pop, zip, crack, zip, crack.

Bullets flew back and forth between the two sides at a dizzying rate of speed, cutting dozens of people down before they even knew what had hit them. At two hundred meters, the enemy soldiers started tripping some of the flares the Americans had set up, which further illuminated them. Then several of the daisy-chained Claymore mines and hand grenades they had boobytrapped began to go off, cutting huge swaths of the enemy apart.

Boom, boom, boom, boom, crump, crump, crump.

Dozens of enemy soldiers were thrown sideways in the air or were blown apart outright as the cacophony of explosions rippled up and down the ridge. More whistles sounded as yet another wave of enemy soldiers charged upward to replace the first wave, which had been utterly decimated by the American Claymores.

"I'm changing barrels. Get more ammo ready!" shouted Ryle. He carefully disconnected the barrel with the specialized glove. It was practically glowing; it had definitely needed to cool. He deftly grabbed the spare barrel and snapped it in place while Private Miller attached a new hundred-round belt to the few remaining bullets left of the belt still loaded in the weapon.

Webster did his best to keep firing at the second wave of enemy soldiers, giving them as much covering fire as he could until they got the machine gun back up and running. Then he heard the most sickening noise of his life—a wet splat.

Private Miller cried out in agony. "I'm hit! Oh God, my arm!" he wailed. His left arm was dangling, barely hanging on by some muscle and tendon. With each heartbeat, blood spurted out on the ground.

Specialist Ryle stopped shooting. He turned his body toward Miller, but Webster shouted, "Don't stop shooting—I'll help him!"

Shock and blood loss took hold of Miller, and he slumped down to the bottom of their foxhole.

"Hang in there, Miller! You're going to be OK," Webster reassured him. "I'm going to get a tourniquet on, and we'll get you back to the medics." He pulled his tourniquet from the medical pouch attached to his IBA and tied off the arm an inch above the wound. With the bleeding stemmed, he stood up and started shouting, "Medic!"

With a half-glazed look and sweat running down his face, Miller looked up at his friend. "I don't want to die, Shane…I'm scared," he managed to mumble.

Wiping a tear from his own eye, Webster leaned in to be heard over the roar of Ryle's machine gun. "You're going to be all right, Liam. I've got the bleeding stopped. I'll help you get back to the aid station when the medic gets here." He looked above the lip of their foxhole, hoping to spot a medic.

Seconds later, one of the platoon's medics came running over and motioned for Webster to help get Miller out of the foxhole. The two of them did their best to carry Miller further back behind their lines to the battalion aid station, where one of the doctors could help patch him up. As they shuffled along, Webster saw the extensive damage from the enemy artillery attack. Then he spotted the aid station; it was inundated with wounded soldiers.

Meanwhile, the roar of battle continued unabated. Before heading back to his foxhole, Webster made a point to grab as much ammo as he could for Ryle and himself, and then he raced back down to their positions. As he got closer to their foxhole, he was horrified to see that the enemy had reached the concertina wire—they were practically on top of their positions at this point.

Jumping back into the foxhole, Webster dumped another four one-hundred-round belts of ammo next to Ryle's gun.

"'Bout time you got back here. For a minute I thought I was on my own," Ryle shouted. He stopped shooting just long enough to reload and to pour one of the canteens of water he had across the barrel in an attempt to cool it off.

"Damn, those guys are getting close," Webster remarked. He took a moment to link another belt of ammo to the one Ryle had just loaded. This would give him at least two hundred rounds.

"Oh crap, they just broke through the wire!" Ryle shouted. Webster saw the enemy soldiers pouring in through a several-meter-wide opening they'd managed to create.

Suddenly, a string of bullets tore into their position, forcing the two of them to duck for cover. A voice somewhere to their right yelled, "Get that machine gun going! We're going to be overrun!"

"Cover me!" Ryle shouted. Then he popped up and tore into the charging enemy.

Webster grabbed one of the Claymore clickers and depressed it. A fraction of a second later, the electrical charge reached the blasting cap and detonated the mine, spraying hundreds of ball bearings at the enemy like a giant shotgun at point-blank range.

Without pausing, Webster picked his rifle up and began to fire.

Pop, pop, pop!

Then his bolt locked to the rear. His magazine was empty. Dropping the empty magazine, he snatched a fresh one from his IBA, slapped it in place and hit the bolt release. With a fresh round in the chamber, Webster aimed right for a cluster of soldiers that were now no more than twenty meters from them.

He paused just long enough to reach down and grab some grenades. Then he started lobbing them at the enemy.

Crump, crump, crump.

Other soldiers also threw grenades in a desperate attempt to cut down the attackers before they overran their positions. Just as Webster thought they weren't going to make it, they heard a thunderous roar in the sky. It sounded like a monstrous ripping noise, like some massive piece of paper or fabric was being torn apart. Then what almost appeared to be the finger of God began to rip through the charging enemy.

A near-constant red line emanating from somewhere above them systematically danced across the ground in front of them, obliterating the enemy soldiers just as they were about to overrun the American positions. What they were witnessing was a mixture of red tracers from the 25mm GAU-12/U Equalizer five-barreled Gatling cannons and smaller explosions from 40mm Bofors cannons. Further behind enemy lines, 105mm Howitzer rounds started to hit, decimating a third wave of enemy soldiers that was about to filter their way.

In seconds, the mass of enemy soldiers that had been moments away from wiping out their unit was turned into a torn and bloody mess of bodies as the entire attack collapsed.

"What the hell was that?" shouted Ryle. He stopped shooting and turned to Webster, a look of horror mixed with thankfulness on his face.

Shaking his head in amazement, Webster replied, "That, my friend, was a miracle."

Then the loud tearing sound and wave of explosions started up again, only this time a little further down the line. It tore into the next enemy position.

"Seriously, what the hell was that? I've never seen something like that," Ryle added. He craned his head around to look up at the sky. Corporal Webster looked up too, but all they could see was a layer of clouds and intermittent red lines slashing through the gray covering.

"That was an Air Force AC-130 Spectre gunship, Ryle, and it just saved our lives."

****

90 Kilometers Northeast of Tangshan, China

Captain Jason Diss and his tankers were physically exhausted. Their brigade had been in almost constant combat for the past four days as the Allies began their final move on the PLA amassing around the Beijing capital region. The 2nd Brigade Combat Team or "Black Jacks" of the 1st Cavalry

Division still had another 130 kilometers to travel to relieve a brigade from the 10th Mountain Brigade that was hunkered down deep behind enemy lines.

Looking behind him, Diss saw the Abrams tanks and Bradley fighting vehicles of his battalion steadily moving along the G1 or Jingha Expressway. They had been making good time ever since they'd finally jumped on this route.

"*Anything is better than snaking through one endless village after another,*" thought Diss. Tanks didn't belong in cities. They needed room to maneuver.

Looking up, Diss saw a pair of Apache gunships several kilometers to his right zoom ahead of them, scouting for possible enemy armor or threats.

"*As long as the flyboys keeps the Chinese Air Force off my tanks we'll be fine,*" he thought. Diss remembered a few weeks back when one of those new PLA UAV ground-attack planes had torn into his battalion. They'd lost several tanks before the drone had been shot down. The sight of that thing had scared the hell out of them—it was the first time they'd seen the PLA's newfangled weapon.

Diss heard some radio static in his CVC and then the familiar beep as the SINCGAR synced. "Mustang Four, this is Hawk Three. Be advised, enemy armor spotted nineteen kilometers to your front. Enemy armor at least battalion strength. Moving to engage them now. Out."

"Well, at least our gunships found the enemy before they found us," he thought, trying to look at the bright side. Part of him was selfishly upset that the Apaches would get to score some kills before his tanks arrived on scene. His company already had more tank kills than any company in the brigade, and it was a point of pride for his unit.

Depressing his own talk button, he spoke to his tankers. "Heads up, Mustangs! FRAGO follows. Our Hawk element has spotted enemy armor. Roughly battalion-size, nineteen kilometers to our front. They're engaging them now. I want everyone to get ready to move off the expressway in a few more kilometers. We'll approach from the fields to our left."

A few minutes went by as the tankers drove a little closer to the enemy on the smooth surface of the expressway. Then Diss's lead tank bulldozed through the cement barrier on the edge of the expressway, creating a hole for the rest of the company to follow through.

As they approached the outskirts of Gengyang, they saw a handful of black smoke columns drifting skyward, evidence of the Apaches' earlier visit.

"*Damn, those guys were probably setting up an ambush for us in the city,*" Diss thought, grateful that the gunships had made their visit first.

Captain Diss examined his map; they were roughly halfway to their objective of relieving the 10th Mountain Unit. This was the last place they wanted to get bogged down—it was one of the few major cities between them and the soldiers they were supposed to relieve.

A familiar crackle of static echoed in his CVC before the radio beeped. "Mustang Four, Warrior Two. I've got eyes on at least twelve Type-96 tanks intermixed inside a small cluster of multistory apartment complexes. We've also spotted seven Type-11 assault gun trucks. Unknown number of dismounted infantry, but it looks to be at least company strength. How copy?"

The Warrior element was their scout platoon assigned to them from brigade. The combat observation and lasing teams were specially equipped M1200 armored cars that would speed ahead of the armored forces, looking for enemy targets for the armor to engage. In this case, they zeroed in on the targets the Apaches had found and would lead the tanks right to them.

Captain Diss depressed his talk button. "Warrior Two, this is Mustang Four. Good copy. We're eight clicks from your current position. Can you get some steel on those assault trucks?" he asked, hoping they might be able to get some artillery support. He was concerned about the AT trucks in particular—although not heavily armored, they could really damage his tanks if they got within range of their antitank guided missiles or 105mm cannons.

"Copy that, Mustang. Stand by while we see what's available," came the reply.

Diss switched over to his company net. "Mustangs, I want everyone to reform into a wedge formation and slow down to fifteen kilometers an hour. Stay alert. We're approaching Warrior's position."

As their company approached the outskirts of a small village southeast of the major city, their scout platoon spotted movement.

"Mustang Four, this is Warrior Two. We're unable to find a way around this village. Recommend following close behind us as we look to navigate a clear path through the village. We'd sure like some support as we move in. How copy?" asked a very nervous lieutenant on the other end.

Diss snickered before he replied; he knew exactly what the young officer wanted. He wanted him to lead his tanks into the village hot on their heels, in case they ran into trouble. He didn't blame the guy—who wouldn't want a 62-ton tank or a 27-ton Bradley fighting vehicle for backup?

Depressing his talk button, Diss replied, "Warrior Two, that's a good copy. Stand by at the edge of the village while I position a couple of Bradleys to take point."

He then switched over to his company radio and ordered two of his infantry Bradleys to move forward and saddle up with the scout cars. His tanks and remaining Bradleys would follow behind them as they moved through the village.

Standing in the commander's hatch, Diss made sure the Ma Deuce machine gun was ready for action. He saw the other tank commanders popping out of their commander's hatches, doing the same. Then the gunner's hatch opened, and Sergeant Cortez popped up and unlocked the other turret-mounted machine gun, the M240.

Slowly, the scout cars started to advance with the two Bradley fighting vehicles maybe ten meters behind them. The infantry soldiers in the vehicles chose to stay buttoned up inside until a threat materialized that required them to leave their secured cocoons. The armored column made it four blocks deep into the small village before all hell broke loose.

Swoosh...BOOM.

Ratatat, ratatat, zip, zip, zap, crack, BAM.

In dozens of nearby windows, machine-gun crews sprang into action. Then, on the roofs of many of the three-to-six-story buildings, dozens of enemy soldiers wielding RPGs and Molotov cocktails materialized. The wicks on the flaming concoctions were already lit, and they hurled them speedily through the air.

"Ah hell, here it comes," Diss said aloud to no one in particular. He swiveled his M2 toward the roof top of a building and started aiming for soldiers carrying RPGs.

Bang, bang, bang, bang.

The roar of his 50-cal. added to the overwhelming racket assaulting his every sense. He quickly saw the first set of enemy soldiers explode into a cloud of red mist as his projectiles cleared the rooftop of enemy threats.

BOOM.

The lead scout car suddenly exploded as two RPGs slammed into it from opposite sides of the street. The other scout vehicle right behind him pushed the burning wreck aside as they pressed forward to get them out of the village. They only had another four blocks to travel and they'd be out of the urban area and back in a flat open field.

"To the right!" shouted Cortez.

A swarm of enemy soldiers rushed out of a nearby building, running right for the Bradley in front of them. The soldiers inside the vehicle began shooting out of the gun slits as fast as they could at the mob rushing them. Then a massive explosion rocked the vehicle, obliterating all the attackers in one torn and bloody mess. When the dust settled, the Bradley had been blown to the side and its right track had been completely torn apart. The vehicle was dead in the water and immobile right in the center of the road.

The Bradley's back hatch opened and the soldiers inside tumbled out, stunned and disoriented from the blast that had rocked their vehicle. A couple of the soldiers got cut down by a hail of enemy bullets before the others snapped out of it and took cover behind several vehicles parked on the side of the road.

"We've got to get out of here, Captain!" shouted Cortez. He fired a long burst of gun fire at several soldiers along the roof of another building.

Depressing the talk button, Diss called out to his vehicle driver, "Keep moving forward! Push the Bradley out of the way and crush those cars on the right side of the street if you have to, but keep us moving."

The tank lurched forward as the driver moved to get them out of the kill zone. Several of the dismounted infantrymen saw what they were trying to do and got out of the way as Diss's tank crept up to the right rear side of their disabled vehicle and pushed it to the side of the road. Meanwhile, bullets bounced off the tank's armor and whizzed all around Cortez and Diss, who did their best to provide covering fire for the infantrymen and keep the enemy RPG teams from disabling any more of their tanks.

The other Bradleys in their column dismounted their infantry soldiers as well, and the whole scene became a chaotic cluster mess. The gunners in the tanks tried their best to use their heavy machine guns to tear into the enemy soldiers as best they could.

"If we don't get the column moving through this kill zone soon, we'll all end up dead," thought Captain Diss.

In the span of a couple of minutes, they managed to push the disabled vehicle off to the side and were once again on the move. The driver moved them quickly toward the right side of the road, rolling over several smaller vehicles parked on the side of the road, crushing them under the weight of their tank as the tracks tore the metal and plastic composite molding of the car apart.

They moved another two more blocks, past the first ambush, meeting little enemy resistance as their infantrymen did a good job of shooting any enemy soldiers they saw.

Then out of nowhere, a Type-99 tank drove out of one of the alleyways with its turret already turned to meet the American tank. Before Captain Diss or anyone in his tank could react, the Chinese tank fired its 125mm cannon at near point-blank range into the side of their tank.

In the blink of an eye, Captain Diss's mind registered his body being catapulted out of the turret and into the air, floating effortlessly for the briefest of moments before gravity took over and his body tumbled to the ground, landing in a heap. As he lay there on the sidewalk, his mind tried to compute what had just happened. The more he tried to focus, the foggier things became, until everything just went black.

Chapter 27
Endgame

Beijing, China

August First Building

Ministry of National Defense HQ

General Yang Yin placed his notepad in the leather briefcase he planned on bringing with him. His suitcase had already been packed by one of his assistants. Several uniforms, a couple sets of casual clothes, his workout clothes and running shoes comprised the bulk of what he was bringing with him for this short trip. He had hoped to get the Allies to agree to a seven-day ceasefire while they negotiated an acceptable end to the war, but sadly, he had only been able to obtain a three-day cessation in the fighting.

"Perhaps the Allies know I'm just stalling to buy my country more time," he thought.

A major walked into his office. "Sir, your vehicle is ready to take you to the airport," he announced.

Yang nodded, not saying anything more as he grabbed his briefcase. He followed the young man out of the office to the elevator that would lead them to the garage and the waiting car. Walking through the command center,

General Yang still marveled at how they had managed to stay alive in this building for so long, considering how many times the Allies had bombed it. Thus far, none of the bunker-buster bombs had made their way to his command center.

"Perhaps the Allies haven't figured out where the bunker is in relation to the building above it," he thought.

Many of the officers gave him a curt nod as he passed, knowing he was on his way to speak with the Americans. They hoped he'd be able to find some way to end the war without their nation having to endure a prolonged global humiliation or occupation like the Russian Federation had had to accept.

When the elevator arrived at the parking garage level, several additional armed security guards were waiting to meet General Yang. They quickly gestured for him to walk toward another blacked-out vehicle nearby, where a guard opened the rear door and President Xi got out.

Yang smiled at the sight of the President but inwardly felt a pang of fear that his presence might mean something ominous.

Xi quickly grinned, softening his demeanor as he extended his hand to the general, guiding the two of them closer to the wall of the parking lot, away from prying ears, even those of his security detail and especially the general's men.

Leaning in close, Xi said, "Yang, it's important that you secure an end to this war."

Yang looked at him with a bit of surprise. Up to this point, Xi had been adamant that he try to buy more time, find a way to prolong the war until after the American presidential election, when a more amenable government would hopefully come to power. What could have changed that calculus since their last meeting?

Responding in an equally hushed tone, Yang asked, "What if the Allies demand that you step down as the leader of China? What am I to say to those terms?"

Xi had clearly thought about that question. "I will not step down if the Allies plan to replace me with that woman, President Hung Hui-ju. She's an apostate to our form of government and will ruin everything our country has pursued up to this point. No, she would be a puppet of the West. If I have to step down as President, then the People's Republic of China will select a new leader through our governmental processes."

Yang nodded. This was a much better outcome than what they had originally discussed a couple of days ago, when Xi had outlined the parameters of what the PRC would accept to end the war. Still, he pressed the President for more clarity.

"If the Allies don't agree to this option, then how far can I push them? How far are you still willing to push this war?"

Xi thought about that for a second. "You've made the case about further use of nuclear weapons. I agree it would be pointless to try and use them, considering we would still lose. However, if the Allies are not willing to see reason, then tell them that we will continue to arm our populace, that we will encourage and foment a never-ending insurgency across China even after they have defeated our armed forces. Also, let them know that we will look to use every cyber capability we have to turn the lights out in America. If they won't see reason, then we will try to send them back to the Dark Ages." There was ice and fire in his eyes as he spoke.

Yang saw Xi's sincerity. If he was going to have to give up his dream of being the supreme leader of the PRC, the man who would lead the world into the 21st century of Chinese Greatness, then he would have a say in who would take his place, or he would do his best to burn the world to the ground.

Yang nodded, then clasped Xi's hand as he whispered, "I will do my best, Mr. President. I must be going."

The two parted ways.

****

Above Kathmandu, Nepal

As General Yang flew over the Himalayan Mountains, he thought to himself that this was something everyone should get to experience at least once in their lifetime. The expanse of the mountain ranges, many covered with snow, was a surreal scene to take in. Up here, flying over the mountains had given Yang some time to just pause and think, away from all the decisions and pressures of his new position.

Closing his eyes for a moment, he thought back to his time growing up in America. He had grown up living the American dream. Albeit, his father was a wealthy Chinese businessman, but he still went to the malls, movie theaters, beaches, and theme parks many Americans grew up going to. During his time at the Citadel, he had formed some great friendships. He thought about some of those old friends more and more these days, wondering how many of them were currently fighting against his country.

Yang had lost contact with many of them over the years as he'd moved further up the military ranks. It was frowned upon to stay in touch with US military officers once the Americans had taken a more adversarial relationship with China in the mid-2000s. Still, he wondered how some of his old friends were doing. Thinking back to those times at the Citadel made him question what he was doing on this trip, especially after Xi's last-minute conversation with him. Was Xi testing him? Would he really accept peace terms if it meant he had to surrender control of the government? Would the Americans even entertain such an idea? From everything he remembered of his training at the Citadel, the Americans would not willingly accept anything less than complete surrender from a foe they felt they could defeat.

In school, he had studied the terms of surrender presented to the Germans and the Japanese by the Allies; during that war, the Americans had been willing to wipe out those countries' entire populations to achieve victory if they had to. The Americans had had several more atomic bombs sent to the Pacific, ready for use when the Japanese emperor had overruled his military leaders and announced the country's surrender.

Sighing, General Yang opened his eyes and took another drink of his tea. They were nearly to Kathmandu—he'd need to collect his thoughts and begin to focus on the task at hand: obtaining an end to the war.

****

After nearly nine hours flying in a plane, General Yang's back was stiff and sore.

As soon as he landed at the international airport, his advance party was there to meet him. They whisked him away to the secretive location where the peace talks would be held. Because of the nature of these negotiations, the number of staff members involved had been kept to a bare minimum. Neither party wanted protests to form or for any threat to develop that might threaten the talks.

****

Kathmandu, Nepal
Hotel Yak & Yeti

Secretary of Defense Jim Castle, General John Bennet, and Secretary of State Landover sat in one of the executive suites of the hotel they had turned into their temporary operations center. The furniture and bed had been moved out of the room to accommodate the collection of computer monitors, communications equipment, and other odds and ends the senior officials needed to run the war and communicate back to the Pentagon and White House. A handful of Defense Intelligence Agency, CIA, and NSA personnel were also present, representing their own organizations and bringing to bear any capabilities Castle, Bennet, and Landover might need for this all-important meeting.

The three men were in the middle of reviewing the latest battle reports when a major general walked into the room. He snapped to attention before announcing himself. "Sirs, Major General Larry Breedlove reporting as ordered."

General Bennet looked up at the general and waved off his salute. "Take a seat," he said. Then he picked up the man's personnel file while Secretary Castle looked him over.

"You know why you've been asked to join us in Nepal?" asked Castle with a blank look on his face.

Breedlove shook his head nervously. "No, Sir. I had no idea any of you would even be in Nepal," he answered.

Bennet saw the confused look on the man's face and did his best not to smile. Two days ago, General Breedlove had been commanding a division in Shanghai, and now, through a series of cloak and dagger exchanges, he found himself whisked away to a secretive meeting in Nepal.

"*I might be a bit disoriented too*," Bennet thought in amusement.

Keeping a straight face, General Bennet asked, "You graduated from the Citadel, correct?"

Although they all obviously knew the answer, all three men stared at Breedlove, waiting for his response.

"Yes, Sir, I did. I believe you have my military file in front of you. It also lists when I was there and what military schools I've completed since then."

Nodding, Bennet continued, "You were roommates with a foreign student by the name of Yang Yin, correct?"

They all leaned forward. Breedlove shifted uncomfortably in his seat. "I was," he admitted. "Is that a problem?"

Secretary Landover probed, "What are your thoughts on the man? Do you know how he felt about America and his ancestral home?"

General Breedlove sat back in his chair. His eyes shifted up and to the left as he seemed to transport himself to a college dorm room twenty years ago. "I knew Yin to be a very capable cadet. He excelled at everything at the academy. I was actually very surprised when he turned down

489

a commission in the Army to return to China. However, I also knew his father was a very wealthy businessman from China, and his family was only living in America while his father's business worked through some corporate acquisitions. I must say though, I haven't talked to Yin in more than ten years. His opinions of America have probably changed a lot over the years."

"Do you know why all of us are here, in Nepal?" asked Castle.

Breedlove shook his head.

"The Chinese have asked to discuss potential terms to end the war," Secretary Landover explained.

Bennet added, "And the reason you're here, General Breedlove, is because your former Citadel roommate, Yang Yin, is the new head of the People's Liberation Army and the man flying here to discuss that with us. We've asked you here because we'd like any insight we can get that might help us end this war—anything from what he's like, to his character, to possible tactics we might be able to use against him to convince him to agree to a termination of the conflict."

General Breedlove let out a deep breath. "I'll do what I can to help. What more would you like to know about him?"

The group talked for several more hours about Yang Yin. By the end of the conversation, they knew everything about the man they could, from what kind of music he appreciated to what his family was like. In negotiations this important, even the PLA general's favorite American foods could turn out to be important.

****

Following Day

Major General Breedlove examined the room. All appeared to be in order. The table for the meeting had been set, with little American flags adorning the place settings of each of the principal American negotiators, and small Chinese flags sitting along the opposite side. At the opposing heads of the table were seats designated for the American and Chinese notetakers, who would transcribe the talks. Along the ornate walls, additional chairs had been placed for staff members.

Security was tight. A contingent of neutral Nepalese Gurkha soldiers had been assigned to secure the room, and both the Americans and the Chinese had a contingent of their own agents to ensure a peaceful negotiation took place.

At 0830 hours, the American delegation entered the room and quickly sat down before organizing their paperwork and files. Five minutes later, the Chinese delegation joined them and likewise prepared themselves for the first meeting. A few adjustments were requested to the setup of the room from both sides, which took up a few minutes.

When the clock showed 0850 hours, Major General Tom Breedlove, who had been placed in charge of the staff function of the meeting, spoke into a handheld radio. "We're ready to begin," he said. His PLA counterpart did the same.

General Bennet, the five-star general and Supreme Military Commander of Allied Forces in Asia, entered the room, quickly followed by Secretary of Defense Jim Castle and Secretary of State Philip Landover. A minute later, General Yang Yin entered the room, along with the Chinese Foreign Minister, Wang Yi.

When General Yang saw his former roommate, he did a double take. He was obviously caught completely off guard by the sight of the man who had once been his close friend. Then he brushed off the surprise and his face returned to a neutral expression. He took his seat, opposite General Bennet.

With the principles now seated, the meeting could begin. "General Yang Yin, I'm grateful that we are able to meet together to discuss this proposal in person," said General Bennet. "As we have all said previously, it's time for us to find a way to bring about an honorable end to this bloody war that has been consuming our planet."

He paused after his opening remarks, then continued, "You and I are soldiers, General. We don't have time or patience for politics. We demand results of our subordinates, and we execute the orders given to us by our political masters. I hope the two of us can dispense with some of these political pretenses and just get down to the business of ending this war."

General Yang let a slight smile slip. Breedlove was happy to see that his old friend still appreciated the bluntness of the American generals.

Before Yang could respond, Minister Wang spoke first. "General Bennet, Secretary Castle and Secretary Landover—from President Xi, I would like to express his gratitude for agreeing to this private meeting in a neutral country. We agree with you in principle about bringing an end to this war, an honorable end that all parties can agree to. President Xi acknowledges that there are certain demands you're going impose upon us. I'm here to listen to those demands and determine if the People's Republic of China can accept them. If you will, can you please outline to us what the basic terms are for us to bring this war to an end, so we can begin the negotiation process?"

General Breedlove examined the faces of Minister Wang and General Yang. Although Wang had spoken first, he got the impression that he was just a face to the negotiation and that it was his friend who truly held any sway in this meeting.

Secretary Landover looked at his two colleagues briefly before he brought out a list of terms in both English and Chinese for everyone to read. The Chinese representatives quickly scanned the pages, murmuring softly to each other. It was clear from their motions to each other that some points were agreeable while others were going to cause a significant problem.

After they'd had a few minutes to review the bullet points, Secretary Landover said, "I believe the outline of the proposal is both fair and equitable, especially considering that it was China who first invaded Southeast Asia, then Korea, Taiwan and the Philippines."

Minister Wang vigorously shook his head. "The PRC cannot accept some of these terms," he asserted.

"Please elaborate on which terms the PRC is not able to accept," replied Landover. Bennet and Castle stayed silent, but Breedlove could see them eying General Yang for any indication of what *he* thought of the terms.

"The PRC can't accept nuclear disarmament," Wang pronounced. "We've maintained a small nuclear stockpile as a deterrent for generations, and we need that deterrent more than ever right now."

Nodding his head, Landover wrote a couple of notes on the side of the document. "OK, we can come back to that point. Did you have another?"

Looking down at the document again, he added, "The PRC won't give up the territorial gains we've made in Southeast Asia. Several of these nations were already communist countries, and many of them want to remain a part of Greater China."

Major General Breedlove waited for the reaction to this point with interest. It would be difficult to get the PRC to give up control of Laos, Cambodia, Vietnam, Myanmar and Thailand, and he knew from his perspective as a commanding general that the Allies were in no position to evict the Chinese from those countries, either.

"The people of Thailand and Singapore don't wish to remain a part of Greater China," Secretary of Defense Castle shot back. "These were democratically elected countries prior to your invasion, and they wish to return to that form of government." He shot Wang an icy stare.

"*This is getting good*," thought Breedlove, wishing he could sit back with a bag of popcorn and watch this with some friends.

"The Allies are in no position to remove us from these captured lands," Minister Wang said sternly.

General Bennet chimed in. "You're right, my forces are in no position to evict the PLA from those countries," he admitted. Then he leaned forward. "However, *my* forces control Guangdong Province, Shanghai and the surrounding area, along with most of northern China. Even now, our forces are marshaling on Beijing. If you don't want me to divide up your country, then you'll concede some of these positions, Minister Wang."

Bennet sat there staring at the foreign minister for a moment before Wang became uncomfortable and broke eye contact. Then General Bennet turned to look at General Yang, who had not said anything as yet.

Secretary Landover broke in. "You know where the Allies stand with ending this war—what are the terms President Xi is willing to accept?"

Wang smiled as he proceeded to pull a piece of paper out of his own briefcase. He handed English copies to the Americans and a copy in Chinese to General Yang, who quickly read it over. Yang raised an eyebrow at some of the points but still remained silent.

Landover and Castle shook their heads. Castle read the points aloud:

1) All Allied forces must withdraw from Chinese-occupied territory.

2) No Allied military facilities are to be built or leased in what is now formerly North Korea.

3) No Allied military facilities are to be built or leased on the Island of Formosa.

4) The PRC will retain all territorial gains made up to this point in the war.

5) The Allies will accept PRC territorial claims in the South China Sea.

6) All parties will agree to a cyber warfare détente and will not support or condone any state or non-state actors from carrying out cyberattacks against each other.

"Wow, those are some pretty ballsy requests," General Breedlove thought. It was hard to stay quiet during this meeting.

Secretary Landover bristled. "These are the demands of a victor, not a nation that's on the brink of collapse," he said in a voice that verged on shouting. "Obviously, we won't accept these terms."

Minister Wang leaned in. "Tens of thousands of Allied soldiers will continue to die if this war continues. President Xi is committed to fighting the Allies even after our armies have been defeated. The Allies will *never* be able to occupy our country, and we will never accept the legitimacy of President Hung Hui-ju. We know your plans are to install her government at the end of the war—we won't allow that to happen."

The discussion continued on for several more hours. The parties went back and forth over what each side would be willing to consider acceptable. As they neared lunch, the two sides broke for a couple of hours to discuss their positions amongst themselves before returning for more talks and the planned formal dinner that evening.

****

Following lunch, General Yang opted to take a short stroll through one of the inner courtyards of the hotel to clear his head. He'd never been involved in any of these types of talks, so he was completely out of his comfort zone. He'd been happy to let Minister Wang do most of the talking, though it was clear he was asking for more than he was likely to get. Wang was trying to write checks Yang knew the PLA couldn't cash.

Sitting at a chair near one of the fountains in the courtyard, Yang spotted his old friend. He smiled as he made his way over to Major General Larry Breedlove.

Breedlove caught eye contact with him and stood. The two looked at each other for a moment before shaking each other's hands. Then they exchanged some brief pleasantries, catching each other up on their families and talking about life in very general terms. Yang then took a seat in the chair next to Breedlove.

General Breedlove sighed. "I'm not sure an agreement is going to be reached," he said, sounding rather defeated. "It seems like we're going to be doomed to keep fighting this war."

General Yang nodded in solemn acceptance. "It does seem that way," he agreed. "However, what Minister Wang doesn't know is that Xi spoke with me prior to coming here.

He said he'd be willing to step down as President, but he wouldn't surrender or dissolve the PRC. He insisted that the PRC be allowed to hold a new election to replace him as President through our own political process."

General Yang read his old friend's expression. It was obvious that Breedlove was doing his best to conceal the surprise he must have felt at Yang's confession.

Breedlove leaned in. "What about other sticking points, Yin? Do you think he'd agree to return the PRC to its original territory prior to the war? Or denuclearization?"

Yang thought about that for a moment before responding, "I think we'd have a better chance of giving up our nuclear weapons than we would giving up some of our occupied territories. A big part of this was about achieving the dream of Greater China. I believe Xi could accept defeat and allow someone else to lead China if it meant his vision had still been achieved."

"What about Singapore and Thailand? I know those are going to be sticking points with Castle and Bennet," added Larry.

General Yang crinkled his eyebrows a bit as he thought about that. "Singapore wouldn't be a big deal, but getting Xi to give up Thailand might be challenging. I think if he knew the PRC would still retain those other territories, I could convince him to agree to those terms."

"What about Taiwan? If President Hung is not to become the leader of a unified China, then Xi would have to accept Taiwan as a fully independent nation. No more One China Policy."

Yang turned to face his friend. "You know, I was in charge of the capture and then defense of Formosa. Your Marines fought like men possessed. I didn't believe they could liberate the island once my forces had dug in…" He trailed off for a moment, lost in a sea of memories. "As to your question," he resumed, "I don't believe Xi would have a choice. He would have to accept Taiwanese independence."

The two sat there silently for a second, not saying anything. Breedlove looked around the courtyard, as if searching for any potential prying eyes. Then he leaned in. "Yin, if Minister Wang and Xi were no longer a factor, do you believe a unified China under President Hung would be possible? Could it work if the current leaders weren't able to interfere?"

General Yang looked at his friend. He could tell he'd been hoping to ask that question since the moment they'd locked eyes in the negotiation room, and this was a moment in which he was being tested. Yang grunted. "It's not that simple, Larry. Even if Xi and certain bureaucrats were eliminated, President Hung would have a terrible time trying to manage a unified China. We are a very large country that has been used to autocratic communist rule for more than seventy years. Yes, we've loosened up some communist rules and adopted certain aspects of capitalism, but we're still a strictly controlled and monitored populace. Open democracy such as what the West would insist upon under President Hung just wouldn't work—at least not right away. It would take time and patience, something the West, and in particular you Americans, are not known to have in abundance."

Breedlove allowed a half-smile at that comment. Then his voice got even more serious. "Yin, do you think you could think about it though? Maybe figure out if it would be possible and how you would make it work? Imagine if you were in charge—how would you make it work?"

General Yang smiled at the thought of running China. "I will think about it," he replied. "We should probably get ready for the rest of the meeting. Let me think about what you said. Perhaps we can try to meet again away from prying eyes and ears tomorrow and I can give you a more practical response." Then he got up and casually walked away.

****

When Breedlove walked back to his room, he was intercepted by Bennet and Castle, who quickly followed him into his room. Once the door was locked, they pounced on him. "How did the meeting go? Is he the main powerbroker for the meeting? What did he say to our alternative proposal?"

Breedlove held a hand up to stop the flow. "Yes, he's the powerbroker for the meeting," he confirmed. "Wang appears to be the figurehead. He thinks he has all the power, but Yin told me that he spoke with Xi multiple times leading up to this meeting, to include just before he flew here. The terms he gave Yin are dramatically different than the terms Wang is pressing for."

The two of them smiled and looked hopeful.

General Breedlove continued, "As to our proposal, he was less optimistic about it working. He said that despite the communist government loosening some controls and freedoms for the people, they're still a tightly controlled autocratic government. People are used to that, and turning that up on its head may not be possible. He did, however, give me the terms Xi would be willing to accept..."

****

The following morning after breakfast, Major General Larry Breedlove sat at a bench in the garden courtyard, drinking a cup of coffee and just enjoying the peace and tranquility of the garden. This was a major change from the turmoil that awaited him. He knew when this meeting was over he'd be flown back to his command; his division was still in the process of fighting it out with the PLA in Changzhou, northwest of Shanghai. His division had been trying to pacify the area while beating back periodic attacks by the PLA and their militia forces, who had not yet accepted defeat.

Ten minutes into his morning solitude, he noticed a figure walking toward him. It was Yin; he'd managed to find a way to slip away from his bodyguards long enough to talk with him again. The two briefly shook hands, and the Chinese general took a seat opposite his longtime friend.

"We don't have much time to talk, so I'm going to be brief," General Yang said. His eyes darted around the garden, looking for any prying eyes that might spot the two of them talking privately.

"OK, Yin. I'm all ears. Go ahead."

Breedlove did his best to pretend he was ignoring Yang while also scanning the area for those who might snoop on their conversation.

"I've been told by President Xi that if his generous terms of surrender are not accepted, then he is more than willing to continue to arm the populace and wage a hundred-year insurgency war against any Allied occupation or Hung-led government. I need to know if the Allies are willing to accept his terms I told you about yesterday."

Landover and Castle were split on what the President should do. General Bennet was against it and said they should continue the war until they were able to get the outcome they wanted. The President was leaning in the direction of his general's opinion, so that didn't leave a lot of room to accept Xi's initial proposal.

Breedlove shook his head somberly. "No, the President and his military leaders won't accept Xi's proposal. They are willing to accept the principle of Greater China with the exception of Singapore and Thailand; those two countries have to be returned to their people. The President is also adamant about China moving toward some form of democracy. The proposal I was given was that President Hung would take over as head of a caretaker

505

government for two years until a new general election could be held. The President also said he would like you to remain in control of the PLA to help facilitate a smooth transition of power. There would also be no restrictions placed on you either staying as commander of the PLA with the subsequent government or you running for President of China yourself."

"What about occupation? Would the Allies occupy China, and if so, for how long?" Yang asked in a hushed tone.

"There would be a limited occupation," Breedlove responded. "Mostly just in the capital and some of the current occupied territories. It wouldn't be a full-blown occupation like Russia—not if you were to stay on as the head of the PLA and you could reasonably hold the country together while the new caretaker government was formed and elections were organized." He was trying to make sure he ran through all the facts quickly; neither of them knew how long they had to talk before a prying eye would eventually spot them.

Yang yawned and stood, stretching his back casually like two random people who had just met at the hotel garden. As he was about to walk away, he turned slightly. "I will think about what you've said and try to figure out if it's even possible. I'll get back to you later today," he said, speaking in a voice so low it was almost as if he was muttering to himself. Then he walked away, back to the main building.

General Breedlove stayed a few more minutes and then left, heading a different direction into the building.

****

The rest of the day's meetings proved to be utterly fruitless. Foreign Minister Wang wouldn't budge on several of the key issues Secretary Landover was adamant about. Landover insisted that the American people had suffered horrific losses in a war started by China and that some issues were just nonnegotiable.

"America must accept Greater China. We have been clear about that from the beginning," Wang said emphatically.

"OK, let's assume America accepts that," Secretary Landover said, playing devil's advocate. "Then we will hold on to the territorial gains we have made in the war thus far. You can keep all of Southeast Asia, we'll hang on to northern China all the way up to Beijing, along with the rest of Shanghai and the entire Guangdong Province."

Minister Wang's mouth dropped open. Then he pounded his fist on the table and yelled, "Impossible, those lands must be returned!"

After snickering at the exchange, General Bennet locked Minister Wang up with one of his icy stares. "I don't think you understand the present situation, Minister Wang, so let me enlighten you. I have nearly two million soldiers preparing to attack the Beijing capital region. Beijing will be in my hands before the end of the year. By this time next year, we'll occupy more than half of China. If you're unwilling to see reason and agree to terms, then you won't have a country left. Do I make myself clear?"

For his part, Minister Wang looked first shocked, then appalled, and then angry. "You will never be able to subdue China. We have over a billion people."

"And how many of them will die this winter from starvation?" asked General Bennet. "How long do you think your people will support your government when you can no longer feed them, pay their wages, or provide them basic services? We are giving you an opportunity to save face and save your people. This offer won't be on the table for long. When this meeting is over, my overall mission to crush your country into the sands of history will resume. You need to decide what kind of country will be left if I'm given my druthers to destroy you."

Secretary of State Landover held his hand up to stop the bickering between General Bennet and Minister Wang.

"Please, gentlemen, this meeting is to discuss ending the war, not how many more people on both sides we intend to kill."

Pausing for a moment to look at his watch, Landover suggested, "Why don't we break early and get ready for dinner? Perhaps some good food will open us all up to find some common ground we can work from."

****

Later that evening, after the official functionaries had spoken, and again, found little compromise, Major General Breedlove found himself sitting outside on one of the balconies overlooking the garden terrace below. He pulled a cigar out of his specially designed carrying case and lit it up, taking several puffs on it. The fragrance of the tobacco wafted its way through the air around him.

He heard a shoe or boot scuff the tile behind him, and a solitary figure stepped out onto the balcony to join him. When Breedlove looked up, he smiled when he recognized his friend Yang, who had once again managed to slip past his minders and found a quiet place for them to speak. Pulling another cigar out, he handed it over to the Chinese general, who greedily took it. Yang puffed on the cigar to get it up to speed before settling into a seat next to Breedlove, who poured him a healthy-sized glass of some very fine cognac that the hotel had provided.

The two sat there for a moment, sipping on their stiff drinks and enjoying their cigars. Breedlove reminisced about a time many years ago, back at the Citadel, when the two of them had done the very same thing toward the end of their senior year. Yang had just told him that he was not going to accept a commission in to the Army, and that his father was taking their family back to China. Breedlove had been sad to hear the news but even more so concerned when he'd heard Yang was going to take a commission in the People's Liberation Army. He'd hoped that despite them serving their nations in their respective militaries, they wouldn't find themselves adversaries one day.

Yang didn't spend long soaking in the moment; he must have sensed that time was of the essence. "I've given your question some thought, Larry. President Xi won't agree to the terms your side is offering. He will order me to prepare the country to fight a protracted insurgency if necessary. If Xi can't end the war on terms he can accept, then he is willing to make sure this war never ends, I'm afraid." He slumped his body back into his chair, dejected. Yang picked up his drink, drained it, and then poured himself another glass as he waited for Breedlove's response.

For his part, Breedlove had known this was probably going to be the response they would be given. At least, that was the assessment of the CIA and other intelligence groups.

"*I guess it's time to play that final card*," he thought reluctantly.

Turning to face his friend, Breedlove threw back the rest of the brownish liquid in his glass before he made one last, desperate appeal. "Yin, this war has to end. We can't allow our political masters to pursue a policy that will destroy the very people, the very nations you and I've sworn to serve and protect. There comes a time when even a soldier has to decide what is morally right, and what is right for the people we're sworn to protect. If President Xi won't see reason, then is it possible for you to take action yourself? As the head of the PLA, surely the army would follow your orders and this war would be ended, right?"

Yang sat there for a moment, not saying anything. Then he chuckled slightly. "You think it's that easy for a PLA general, even one who is head of the PLA, to simply disobey an order from the President—or worse, lead a coup? It isn't quite that simple. Xi has already liquidated nearly everyone who was in a position of leadership at the start of this war. He has truly consolidated power these past three months. With defeat staring him in the face, he's become more and more paranoid about a coup. I'm afraid you overestimate my power and influence. I'm only in charge of the PLA right now because he's killed off most of my superiors and I've managed to eke out some victories against you Americans." He shook his head disappointedly. "What you're asking is just not possible, Larry."

Not accepting defeat, Breedlove pressed on with the alternative plan. "I know this is putting you into a tough position, Yin. What if the Allies just happened to discover where Xi and some of the individuals you believe would be a problem to accepting peace were, and they were suddenly killed by an Allied stealth bomber using specially designed bunker-buster bombs? *If* that were to happen, do you believe you'd be able to assume control of the country and then pursue a peace that would bring an end to this war?"

Yin stifled a short laugh as he shook his head. "I remember studying Operation Valkyrie our junior year at the Citadel," he retorted. Turning serious again, he whispered, "If I made this happen, you couldn't miss. You couldn't fail. If you failed, then I would most likely be removed, and I can guarantee you Xi would resort to using whatever means necessary to retaliate against you. He wouldn't hold anything back."

"If we have to, we can use a nuclear-tipped bunker-buster bomb to make sure we get him and his inner circle. What we'd need to know is when and where to drop it," Breedlove explained.

"He might actually go for this," he thought in amazement.

Yang thought silently for a moment as he puffed on his cigar. Without looking at Breedlove, he answered, "If I arranged for them all to be at a meeting, I would need certain assurances that once I assumed control of the country, you wouldn't try to go after my generals for war crimes. If we committed any wrongs, they were wrongs we had no choice in. Our military system doesn't have the same moral codes and understandings as America or the West. We can't simply disobey an order because we *feel* it's immoral or illegal. We aren't governed that way." He leaned forward. "If this were to happen, the Allies would demand that we dismantle the communist party, wouldn't they?"

"Yes, the communist party would need to be disbanded in favor of a more democratic form of government," Breedlove explained. "That's why the US would like to see the mainland adopt the form of government currently in place in Taiwan. The Republic of China has a functioning democratic process with political parties, a legislature, court system and president. It would take time to implement that process on the mainland, but that's why a caretaker government would need to be established to work with President Hung until a new election could take place and a new government is established. I won't lie and say it won't be messy. It will be, but with you at the head of the government working with President Hung, I'm confident that China as a country will emerge stronger and better than ever before.

"Yin, imagine China with not just freedom of speech, but freedom of thought. Freedom to innovate and capitalize on that innovation without the government seizing control of it or having a heavy hand in every aspect of life. You lived in America, Yin—surely you can see the benefit of this economic model and the personal freedoms it would provide."

"I don't dispute the benefits—I question the method by which we would achieve that," Yang countered. "It wouldn't just be messy; it could cause the country to collapse into chaos. I would have to maintain a tight grip on the country while it went through this transition period, Larry. This wouldn't be as easy as you may think. There are a lot of wealthy businessmen who have just as much control of our government as your wealthy businessmen do in your own country."

Shaking his head, Yin added, "I never wanted to be placed in this position, Larry. I'm in way over my head right now. I'm a corps commander. I understand tactics and I know how to fight…I was never a politician. I wasn't trained for managing an entire country's military, let alone fighting a global war. I just want it to end, but if I don't do my duty or I screw things up, it's not just me that will be killed—my entire family is at risk, Larry. This isn't America…it's China."

"This is why it has to change," Breedlove asserted. "You've been given a unique opportunity to change China, Yin, and in doing so change the world, the future of humanity."

He slipped a piece of paper to General Yang. "If you can arrange the meeting, log in to this email. Create a new message with the subject line 'Valkyrie.' In the body of the message, state the date, time and location of the meeting. Don't send the message to anyone—just save the draft and close the email. We'll check this email at 0900 hours and 2100 hours your local time each day to see if you've been able to arrange a meeting. If you're unable to coordinate all parties to be together, or there's some other problem, then create an email that explains the issue and just save the draft. We can send a response to your question in a different color and font, using the same draft message. This will be our way of communicating, OK?"

Yang took the paper. He looked at it for a minute, memorizing the login information and password before taking a couple of puffs on his cigar and then holding the paper up to the hot embers until it caught fire, destroying the information written on it. Then he got up. "I'll be in touch, Larry," he said. "Give me at least three days before I can figure something out." With that, he left.

The following day of peace talks dragged on with nothing gained. Minister Wang wanted them to meet again to make another attempt at a peace deal. Secretary Landover agreed but said they would have to get back with him as to when.

In the meantime, the US would not agree to a continued ceasefire. The war would continue until the PRC accepted the Allied terms.

Chapter 28
Operation Valkyrie

Beijing, China
August First Building
Ministry of National Defense HQ

Barely two days had gone by since Yang had returned to Beijing, and the Americans had already resumed hostilities. Even now, the Allies were launching a massive offensive aimed at the Beijing capital region. Thus far, the Allies had been held at the outer perimeter, but that wouldn't last for long. They were less than eighty kilometers from the August First Building—a sobering thought.

The sense among the people at large was one of anger at their government for having gotten them into this position and despair that there was nothing they could do about it. Three years ago, the average Chinese citizen had had money in their pocket, food in their belly and a roof over their head. Now, the Chinese economy was in freefall, inflation was starting to run rampant, fuel and other supplies were in great shortage, and many people, if not everyone, either had a member of their family serving in the military or had a family member killed while serving in the military.

The previous night's Allied bombing raid on the industrial centers in the city of Tianjin had resulted in the death of nearly five thousand civilians. It had also killed more than three thousand soldiers and destroyed yet one more of Yang's desperately needed armor brigades. He had been moving some of their strategic-level units such as heavy armor and mechanized units into heavily populated areas and industrial centers, in hopes that the Allies would not risk killing civilians in an effort to destroy his most prized units. That clearly had not worked.

****

A few minutes went by as the other generals and staff officers waited for President Xi to arrive. One of the colonels stuck his head in the doorway, signaling that the President had arrived before he went back to his duties. The others in the room squirmed a bit in their chairs as they waited for Xi. The last forty-eight hours had been a disaster, and they knew the President would not be pleased.

Without any preamble, Foreign Minister Wang walked into the room, quickly followed by several other ministers and then the President. Yang had to admit he didn't know who half of the other ministers were at this point. Xi had been purging anyone he felt had failed him or the State these past few months. Between his purges and the Allies' assassination bombings, there had been a lot of turnover in senior-level positions.

Taking his seat at the center of the table, President Xi surveyed the faces of the men before him. After a moment, he settled his gaze on the two men sitting opposite him, General Yang Yin and Foreign Minister Wang Yi.

"Gentlemen, you've been back from your peace talks with the Americans and their Allies for less than forty-eight hours, and in that timeframe, the Allies have launched a series of new offensives and even now threaten the outskirts of this very city. Account for yourselves!" he demanded. He fixed each of them with a death stare.

Minister Wang fumbled for a few words as he sought to make sure Xi knew he had done everything in his power to convince the Allies that they had to agree to the terms he'd presented. The others at the table remained silent, almost stoic, as they listened to Wang describe how he had presented the facts to the Allies—that if they didn't agree to Xi's generous terms to end the war, China would pursue a hundred-year insurgency strategy, ensuring there would never be peace in China.

For his part, Xi seemed utterly unconvinced by Wang's assurances. Once the foreign minister had run out of steam, Xi nodded and then turned to General Yang.

"What's your assessment, General? Are future peace talks with the Allies worth it? Will the Allies accept the terms Minister Wang presented?"

Yang thought about his response for a moment. He knew what Xi wanted to hear, but he also knew the truth. He sighed. "Sir, I believe it would be best if I spoke with you in private about my assessment of the meeting."

This response caught the others in the room by surprise. They were probably aware that General Yang's assessment of the meeting would be the more realistic one, given his history of candor. After sitting through Minister Wang's blundering recap, they had expected him to say *something*.

President Xi smiled. "Clear the room," he ordered. "Everyone out but General Yang."

Though no one's comments were loud enough to trace back to any individual, there was a general murmur that swept over the room. All the ministers gathered their papers and got up as directed, though several of them had very sour expressions. They were obviously unhappy with being excluded.

"The general doesn't want to deliver the bad news in front of the others. Good, at least he has the sense to keep the truth to himself and those who actually need it."

Once the room had been cleared, Xi returned his gaze to General Yang. "I've always appreciated your forthrightness, General, but in this instance, I find myself grateful for your discretion. If the rest of those fools knew what bad shape we were in, they'd probably be plotting my demise."

Yang bowed slightly.

"Well, it's just the two of us left," said Xi. "I take it the meeting did not go well?"

Yang tried to appear composed, but he knew the end for the PLA was near. He wondered if this was what the German generals had felt like during the last days of World War II, when the Russians were closing in on Berlin.

"No, Mr. President," he responded. "The Americans would not budge. From their perspective, they are winning. They see no reason to agree to the terms you told Wang to present."

Xi swore a few times as his temper got the better of him. Once he'd managed to calm himself a bit, he asked, "What parts of the proposal would they agree to?"

"In principle, they agreed to our Greater China territorial claims, with a couple of exceptions. They insisted that Singapore and Thailand be returned to their people and that Formosa be allowed to officially declare its independence. They also insist on us denuclearizing," he said, adding that last part almost as an afterthought.

"They want us to yield our nuclear weapons? Why would they think we'd ever give them up?" Xi shot back.

"Because we'll never use them, and because we provided the North Koreans with the missiles that hit them," Yang countered. Had there been anyone else in the room with them, he never would have said that to Xi.

President Xi snorted. "I don't know about *never* using them," he retorted. "We just haven't thought up a good enough plan for how to make them count."

Smiling at the comment, General Yang knew he had gotten Xi to walk into the trap he'd baited. "Sir, *I* believe I have an idea about how we can use them to our advantage, and perhaps end the war, once and for all."

Lifting an eyebrow, Xi asked, "How would we do that? And I thought you were dead set against using nuclear weapons."

"Let's just say I've had a change of heart after my meeting with the Americans," Yang replied.

Over the following twenty minutes, General Yang walked President Xi through a scenario of how they could use their nuclear weapons on the Allied forces and end the war.

****

"I must say, General, I'm impressed," President Xi finally said. "You're more cunning than I'd given you credit for. How soon do you believe you could put this plan together?"

"I need a couple of days, Mr. President. If I may, I'd like to suggest that we hold a final planning meeting to go over the details of the plan prior to execution. Would you be available to meet again, in, say, three days, with the rest of the CMC?" Yang asked.

Before Xi could respond, Yang added, "I'd like for us to meet at the Summer Palace bunker. We've never met there during the war, and it's a bunker facility I'm confident the Allies are unaware of. I get nervous each time we all gather in this building," he said, looking up at the ceiling dramatically. "The Allies have already bombed this building a few times. I fear if we hold more CMC meetings in the same place, they will get wise to it and try to bomb this building a little harder."

Xi also looked up. The building had indeed been bombed its fair share of times. Fortunately, the command bunker and operations center was burrowed deep under the building and had survived a few attempts at its destruction.

He nodded, seeming to accept the suggestion that they'd been tempting fate. "Very well," Xi responded. "We'll reconvene the meeting in three days at the Summer Palace facility." Xi paused for a second, apparently sizing Yang up. "I'm glad you've given some more thought to using our nuclear assets. We all know they're a weapon of last resort, but I fear we are quickly approaching that point."

With nothing further to say, Xi got up to head back to his own building.

As President Xi and the rest of his entourage left, Yang began to compose a message in his head. He'd need to find a way to draft a message, and soon. His opportunity had just arrived.

****

Twenty-Four Hours Later
Washington, D.C.
White House

"Mr. President, we've received the message you've been waiting for," JP announced.

"We're sure this is for real and not some trap?" asked the President nervously. He still wasn't completely confident they could trust this Chinese general.

"I have my concerns, Mr. President, but this is the best option we've got," said Secretary Castle. "I've met General Yang, and I do get a sense that he knows there are no good options left. Either he helps us end the war in a fashion that still saves some of his country, or he oversees the destruction of his nation."

The President sat back in his chair for a moment thinking about the plan. If things went according to plan, then General Yang would assume control of the country and move to end the war. *"But what if this doesn't go according to plan?"* he wondered. Yang could just as easily use Xi's assassination to mobilize the country around himself and continue the war.

Looking back at his advisors, the President asked, "If this plan goes south, what's the alternative? How will we still bring about the end of the war?"

Admiral Meyers leaned forward. "We continue with the current plan, Mr. President. Right now, we have nearly two million US and Allied forces less than 100 kilometers from Beijing, we've got another one and a half million Allied forces in the Shanghai region, and nearly that same number in Guangdong Province in the south. By this time next year, we'll occupy more than fifty percent of the country, and seventy percent of the Chinese population will be under Allied control."

The admiral paused for a second, letting that sink in. "We have another thing going for us as well, Mr. President. General Yang lived in America for ten years—he studied at one of our most prestigious military academies. He knows our capabilities inside and out, and more importantly, he knows we won't stop until we win. He's been given an out, an opportunity to save his country, and I believe he'll take it."

Nodding at the logic, the President finally consented. "Order the strike, but make sure you kill Xi. If he or anyone else from that meeting escapes, it could prolong the war."

With the final order given, the staff went to work on executing what everyone hoped would be the final operation to end the war.

****

Yokota Air Force Base, Japan

The past few months had been horrendously busy for Colonel Fortney and his partner, Major Daniels. They had been putting the B-21 Raider through its paces over the battlefield. Despite the bomber still being "experimental," it had been successfully carrying out bombing missions over mainland China for nearly two months. They had tested the bomber's radar-absorbent material by flying over some of the most heavily contested airspace over China, ensuring their antiradar skin was as good as the manufacturers had advertised.

Other missions had tested the bomber's ability to carry out precision strikes by guiding ten JDAMs to a target, then increasing that number up to the full capacity of one hundred smaller 500-pound JDAM bombs. In each test, the software, flight instruments, and targeting computers performed as good as or better than the manufacturers had said they would.

The B-21 Raider was proving to be the dream stealth bomber the Air Force had hoped it would become and a solid replacement for the B-1 and B-2 airframes. With the essential tests having been completed, the entire B-21 line of bombers started full production. The second test bomber was immediately flown to Yokota, giving Colonel Fortney command of the only two bombers in the service.

Two days earlier, the first day after the temporary ceasefire had ended, both bombers had flown to the city of Tianjin, 115 kilometers southeast of Beijing, and paid the city a visit. In a single bombing run, they'd released one hundred 2,000-pound laser-guided bombs, smashing the city's manufacturing plants, port facilities, and two enemy divisions who'd hunkered down in a heavily populated neighborhood. It was a devastating attack by any standard, and it had been carried out by a mere two bombers.

****

Walking into the briefing room, Pappi could tell this wasn't going to be an ordinary bombing mission they were sending him on. There were several armed guards at the exits to the room, a handful of folks in black suits, and a few uniforms with stars on their collars. Whatever was up, it was big.

Turning to look at the pilot chairs, Pappi spotted his partner in crime and made his way over to her. Plopping down next to her, he leaned in. "What have you heard?" he whispered.

Double D shook her head. "Nothing yet. I got here ten minutes ago to go over some notes when all of these new faces started arriving and the security forces guys locked the room down."

Nodding, Pappi opted to just sit back and relax. Whatever was going on involved them and their bomber, and when the powers that be decided to bring them in on it, they'd be there, ready and waiting.

Ten minutes went by as a handful of additional people filtered into the briefing room, way more than what was required or normal for any of their previous raids. They were, after all, a secretive bomber program that no one was fully aware was operational yet.

One of the men who had filtered into the room was a two-star general. As soon as he walked in, he immediately approached the lectern and silenced the room.

"Everyone, take your seats," he announced. "It's time to get this meeting going." All the attendees quickly followed his instructions.

"There are a lot of people in this room, so I'm going to go over some introductions for our two bomber crews," the general said. "I'm Major General Erik Latrell, from Joint Special Operations Commands. To my right are National Security Advisor Tom McMillan and Ambassador Max Bryant. To my left are Major General Tom Breedlove and Katelyn Mackie from the NSA." He paused for a moment as the two aircrews nodded. A captain handed everyone a small dossier of the mission along with a nondisclosure agreement and a signature form for the Special Access Program this operation was being classified under.

"What I'm about to brief you on is a highly classified SAP program by the name of Operation Valkyrie. Once you all have signed the NDA and the SAP signature page, there will still be less than fifty people in our entire country who will know about this mission and what it entails. Needless to say, if *any* of the mission details leak, there are only fifty of you who know about it, so we will find out who you are, and I guarantee you'll be prosecuted to the fullest extent of the law. Do I make myself clear?" he asked, voice close to a drill instructor's in intensity.

Once everyone had agreed, and the signatures had been collected, General Lattrell continued. "Roughly ten weeks ago, President Xi carried out a purge of his senior military generals and political advisors. This placed a series of much younger, more innovative and aggressive generals in charge of the country. The new head of the PLA is a general by the name of Yang Yin. What's unique about Mr. Yang is his family background. His father is the head of a major Chinese electronics manufacturer, and his family lived in America for ten years while he oversaw the American side of their business. During that ten-year period, Yang's father had his son enrolled in a military preparatory school in America, and upon graduation, his son was accepted into the Citadel as a foreign student.

"During his four years of training at the Citadel, he attended Army basic combat training and advanced infantry training at Fort Benning. The following summer, he attended jump school, and his final summer at the Citadel, he went through the US Army Ranger School. He was offered a commission in the Army following his graduation; however, he declined and instead returned to China with his family. His father arranged for him to join the People's Liberation Army Ground Forces, and when he arrived home, he was taken under the wing of several benefactors his father had within the PLA. With his American military training and extensive time in the US, he quickly rose through the ranks. As one of the youngest division commanders in the PLA, he was instrumental in changing a number of their tactics and offensive plans prior to the war. Several months before the war started, he was promoted again and made the youngest corps commander in the PLA.

"It was his corps that led the invasion of Southeast Asia and the quick capture of Vietnam, Laos, Cambodia, Myanmar, Thailand and Singapore. He was also the military commander who oversaw the invasion and occupation of Taiwan and the Philippines. He's a more-than-capable military commander, and frankly, a dangerous one. He's probably the only reason our forces haven't captured Beijing yet, or completely overrun the country."

General Lattrell didn't pause to take any questions. "While General Yang is China's most capable military commander, he is also a realist and knows the war is lost. Right now, he's trying to manage the loss as best he can, but lately, President Xi has become more despondent and desperate to stay in power. It's that desperation that has Yang most concerned, and it has presented us with a very unique opportunity.

Nodding to Major General Breedlove, he added, "Major General Breedlove here was actually Yang's roommate at the Citadel. During our peace talks last week, he was able to rekindle that friendship enough to offer Yang an opportunity to bring an end to the war in a way that would not see China destroyed or humiliated on the world stage. Approximately eighteen hours ago, Yang reached out to Breedlove via a secretive method we'd put in place and presented us with an opportunity to end the war."

Pappi and everyone else in the room sat up a little straighter and leaned forward, waiting to hear the plan.

"General Yang has asked if Xi would arrange a special meeting with the senior civilian leadership to discuss with him and the rest of the CMC generals a long-shot plan to defeat us. Xi agreed, and they've arranged for this discussion to take place in forty-two hours at a government command bunker just outside of Beijing."

At this point, General Latrell signaled for one of the officers to turn off the light switch in the front of the room and start the PowerPoint presentation. As the screen came into focus, they could all see an aerial image of Xiang Shan Park highlighted with a circle on it. The next image showed a small, unimportant-looking building, denoted as the entrance to the underground command center. This command bunker was cleverly hidden at the base of a low-lying mountain range, roughly ten kilometers from the old Qing Dynasty Summer Palace at the western edge of the Beijing city limits.

"We know very little about this command bunker, other than General Yang said it is connected deep inside the mountain. He said the tunnel entrance travels roughly fifty meters to an elevator that takes you another one hundred meters deeper underground. Inside the bunker is a large enough command center for 500 personnel to effectively run the war without going topside for close to a year. Judging by the specifications he's provided, we suspect this is their equivalent to our Cheyenne Mountain facility."

Pappi looked at his copilot, and she gave him a look that said she had the same question he did. He didn't wait to be called upon. "You want us to hit this thing with a nuclear bunker-buster bomb, correct?" he asked.

The room had been quiet before, but when Pappi said the word *nuclear*, you could have heard a pin drop. Everyone's eyes went back and forth between him and General Latrell for confirmation.

Latrell nodded. "That's correct. It's the only way to ensure we collapse the bunker. You'll be armed with our newest nuclear weapon, the B61-Mod 12 earth-penetrating bomb. Because of the depth of the bunker, it's been determined by the bomb experts that we'll need to hit it with a 50-kiloton yield. Fortunately, because this'll be a deep underground burst, it'll have the same effectiveness of us hitting them with a 1.25 megaton ground burst, with the exception that this bomb will leave little in the way of fallout—the explosion will largely stay contained, deep under the mountain."

A few people whistled at the information. This would be the first time the US, or anyone for that matter, had used a nuclear-tipped bunker-buster bomb.

"I have to ask the question," Colonel Fortney interjected. "What happens if this doesn't work? We'll have just tried to take the President of China and his entire administration out with a nuclear bomb. If we miss...they could launch their own nuclear missiles in retaliation." Concern was written on his face.

The others looked around nervously as well. No one wanted to see the war go nuclear, not when they were so close to achieving victory through conventional means.

NSA Tom McMillan jumped in. "Colonel, the President has thought about that as well and has determined this is the best course of action. This meeting that we're going to bomb is a meeting of the Chinese leadership to discuss their use of nuclear weapons against our military forces in China. *They're* planning on using nuclear weapons on their own cities and territory to destroy our military. If we don't decapitate the government now, not only do we risk losing millions of our soldiers, but tens of millions of Chinese civilians will be killed. It's imperative that this strike succeed. That's why both of your bombers will be going on this mission."

Stepping forward now, McMillan added, "Colonel Fortney, your bomber will drop the first bomb. It will be followed by a second bomb less than sixty seconds after the first detonation. If, for whatever reason, your bomber is shot down or you're unable to release your second bomb, then your partner here will finish the mission.

"This has to succeed, ladies and gentlemen. There's no room for error. Tens of millions of lives are relying on the success of this plan. If our mission goes according to plan, General Yang will assume control of China within hours of the attack and he'll move to end the war. This is it, everyone—the mission that will end World War III."

Pappi nodded. He suddenly felt very much like Atlas, with the weight of the world on his shoulders.

Over the next hour, the mission planners went over the specifics of the flight path, the support aircraft that would be involved, and the backup plans in case the primary bomber got shot down or had an equipment failure.

"*Now it's only a matter of time,*" Colonel Fortney thought as they all left the room. All they could do now was wait for the launch order—one that would make history.

****

Xiang Shan Command Center

The armored Mercedes vehicle made the final turn in the road as it sped toward the nondescript entrance to the command center. This was the location where the end of World War III would be decided. President Xi still couldn't believe the war had turned so decisively against them. It had started out so strong; their armies had rolled across Mongolia, Cambodia, Laos, Vietnam, Thailand, Myanmar, Taiwan and the Philippines. They had even sunk several American supercarriers.

"Where did I go wrong...what could I have done differently?" Xi wondered.

Suddenly, the vehicle jerked to a stop. His security detail quickly fanned out, ensuring there were no potential threats before they opened the door to his armored vehicle and ushered him toward the entrance of the underground complex. The cool November air greeted him, along with the smells of fall. As he surveyed the base of the mountain he was about to enter, President Xi observed that the leaves had fully changed colors, and many of them had started to carpet the ground in a beautiful collage. Standing erect, Xi took in a deep breath, wanting to enjoy the air outside before he went underground.

"They're waiting for us," one of his guards prompted him. They didn't like him appearing in public or standing out in the open for very long. They were paranoid that the Allies would somehow spot him and attempt to kill him.

Nodding slightly, Xi followed his security detail. They led him to a small gift shop and café that sat nestled up against the bottom of the mountain. The busy park nearby was frequented by the residents of Beijing, so this café acted as the perfect cover for the intricate command center that lay beneath the natural earthen fortress.

Xi walked in the entrance followed by his detail, and they escorted him down the hallway toward the kitchen in the back. Once there, they moved to a storage room in the back, where a secret entrance was located. There were two other entrances to the facility, but they were both located at other, more prominent and well-known military facilities used for radar and communications. The Chinese had done their best to make sure that the Americans had only known about those official entrances. That way, if a bomb actually did attack them there, it would have little chance of actually penetrating to the depth needed to get at the complex itself.

Once inside the tunnel, the entourage headed down the corridor until they reached a large service elevator. One of the guards entered a randomized code, then placed his hand on a biometric scanner before placing his eye against another biometric device that scanned and compared his iris image with the image on file. Once all of these checks had been completed and verified, the elevator activated and began its journey from the bunker below up to meet them.

A few minutes went by as they waited, then a soft ding sounded, and the door opened. A handful of additional heavily armed soldiers greeted them at the door, startling Xi's security detail, who pointed their guns at the men.

"We're just here to verify who you are and that you have authorization to be here," the soldiers explained. When President Xi's guards lowered their weapons, the soldiers saw the president. They quickly waved off the standard secondary biometric verifications they normally would have performed on each person entering the elevator.

Xi calmly walked to the center of the spacious elevator, and his security detail and the soldiers filled in the space around him. Xi felt that this was a rather cavernous elevator considering the secretive nature of its location. It wasn't like this was a major supply elevator—but then again, with few entrances and exits in and out of the facility, he suspected they made heavy use of each to ferry in the massive amount of supplies needed to sustain such an operation.

When the door opened, Xi's security detail led the way to the central operations room while the soldiers resumed their guard positions at the elevator entrance. Upon entering the operations room, Xi saw a flurry of activity. Soldiers and civilian contractors scurried around the facility, getting it ready to take over operations of the war from the central command center in the bowels of the Ministry of National Defense HQ in the August First Building.

"General Yang isn't messing around," thought Xi. He realized the general was planning on the Americans going after China in retaliation for their use of nuclear weapons.

Foreign Minister Wang Yi walked up to him with a broad smile on his face. "Mr. President, it's good to see you. Come this way." He gestured for Xi to follow him past the operations center to a large meeting room where many of the CMC generals and other senior cabinet officials were milling about, talking amongst themselves and fixing their tea and food that one of the chefs from the kitchen had just brought in.

Turning to look at Xi, Wang commented, "I'm so glad General Yang has come around to your initial proposal about using our nuclear weapons. I truly believe this is going to turn the war around for us and finally bring the Allies to the negotiating table."

Laughing before he replied, Xi said, "You mean *your* proposal to use nuclear weapons, don't you?"

Wang raised an eyebrow at the reference but smiled as he replied, "I think we all know there isn't really an alternative if we want to end this war without a complete surrender."

"Have the Americans broken through our defenses in the Jinzhou District yet? The last report I received before I went to sleep last night was that they were making another large push."

Wang shook his head. "No, not yet. Believe it or not, they still haven't made it past the Great Wall. They've been somewhat reluctant in blowing new holes through it, so they've been largely focused on trying to air-assault forces across it and behind our lines, in hopes of getting us to give up the defensive line."

Since Xi had liquidated many of his senior staff a few months ago, along with most of the senior generals who had previously been running the Central Military Committee, Minister Wang had taken it upon himself to be as up-to-date as possible on what was happening with the war.

"I wonder if he's positioning himself to take over if I die," mused President Xi. China didn't have a formal line of ascension, and Xi knew that Wang was not particularly fond of General Yang.

As the two of them entered the briefing room, Xi surveyed everyone present. The conversations quickly ended in deference to his presence. Right away, he noticed the absence of one key figure, his Sun Zu—General Yang was not present. Turning to one of Yang's deputies, he inquired, "Where is General Yang?"

The colonel looked a bit nervous. He had obviously been asked the question a few times by the other men in the room. "I just spoke with General Yang about ten minutes ago. He said he was delayed in leaving the August First Building."

Xi crinkled his brow at the news; he had hoped to get this briefing going so they could get the ball rolling. It sickened him to think about using nuclear weapons on their home soil, but he couldn't think of any other way to destroy the Allied armies steamrolling their way across the country.

"Did he say what the delay was or when he'll be here?"

The deputy nodded. "Yes, Mr. President," he answered. "There was an Allied bombing raid hitting the capital just prior to your arrival. He wanted to wait until the enemy bombers had left before he ventured out of the bunker to head here. He told me to let you know that he'd be approximately ninety minutes late, but that General Liang could proceed with the brief in his absence. General Yang said it was more important that everyone get secured here in the mountain before we released the weapons."

"Well I'm glad someone is making sure the military and government are safe before this attack happens," Xi thought. The Americans would surely come after them.

"OK, then tell General Liang to proceed. We have a lot of information to go over," Xi said. Then he moved to take his seat and indicated that the others should as well.

****

G103 Highway, En Route to Xiang Shan Command Center

"Sorry about the traffic, General. Perhaps we should have taken one of the helicopters," said Captain Cho, his head of security. Then he chided the driver for letting them get boxed into the traffic gridlock.

"It's OK, Captain. I called ahead to General Liang, letting him know we've been delayed. I would much rather be late to a meeting and stuck in traffic then risk being shot down by an Allied fighter," he asserted. Everyone instinctively looked up at the ceiling of the armored Mercedes-Benz vehicle.

They had two other vehicles in their little convoy, one in front of them and one behind. Despite having their flashing lights and the occasional siren on, they still found themselves stuck in the tail end of the Beijing morning rush hour.

Of course, the air raid on several military buildings across the city had caused another wave of panic in the metropolis. This was the third such raid on the downtown part of the capital in the last two months. The Allies were clearly tightening the noose on the communist government as the remnants of the Chinese Air Force continued to be hunted down and destroyed.

Sitting in the backseat of the armored luxury sedan, Yang felt nauseous. "*What have I done?*" he thought.

The urge to vomit became uncontrollable, and Yang lurched forward, grabbing at the door handle. Despite the protests of his security detail, he pushed the door open. He only made it one step out of the vehicle before doubling over and puking all over the pavement. His body retched uncontrollably several times until he had fully emptied his stomach of what little contents it had had.

Captain Cho handed him a handkerchief, which he took. He wiped at the spittle and vomit on his chin. He blew his nose, and then he suddenly felt a tremor. The ground shook like a mini-earthquake. A sudden *BOOM* broke through the noise of honking horns and angry shouts of commuters stuck on the road. The sharp crack through the air was then replaced with a low, deep rumbling sound before the noise quickly faded.

Before anyone could react to what they had just heard and felt, a second, louder *BOOM* ripped through the city, nearly knocking them to the ground as the earth beneath them shook violently. As they attempted to steady themselves, a loud rumbling noise grew. A large ominous-looking plume from a blast several kilometers away began to rise into the morning sky.

Yang suddenly felt a pull on his shoulder and a voice shouting at him. He couldn't quite make out what was being shouted or who was shouting it because everywhere he looked, he saw people pointing and screaming, then running. A fraction of a second later, he was pulled into the back of the sedan.

Captain Cho started yelling at the driver. "I don't care if you have to ram the cars in front of you—find a way out of this traffic jam! Head back to the August First Building immediately!"

****

24,000 Feet above Beijing

Colonel Rob "Pappi" Fortney slowly began to go through the arming procedure to release their B61 Mod-12 earth-penetrating nuclear bomb. Twenty-seven years in the Air Force had prepared him for the technical aspect of this task. After all, the B-2 stealth bomber was originally designed to penetrate Soviet airspace to deliver a nuclear first strike or counterstrike against the Russians. What all his military training had *not* prepared him for was the moral argument raging in his mind over what his superiors had ordered him to do.

Having completed the arming process for the first nuclear bomb, Pappi moved to preparing the second bomb. Technically, he could have prepared both bombs at the same time—the targeting computer and onboard weapons system did allow it—but he felt he had a duty to ensure that each bomb was made individually ready. As the flight leader for his two bomber raids, he didn't want the other crew to be burdened with the responsibility of using a nuclear weapon. No, he and Double D would do their best to bear that burden for them.

Breaking the silence, Double D turned to look at Pappi. "Are we really doing this?" she asked. "Dropping not one but two nuclear bombs on Beijing?"

A brief moment of silence ensued as Pappi thought about his response. It should have been automatic, but he hesitated, which caused him to feel both anger for allowing his emotions and thoughts to override his trained response, and shame that he felt anger for not responding right away. It was a valid question, a moral question. But he also knew the answer, and he accepted and understood the justification for why they were doing what they were doing.

"Yeah, Daniels, we are. We're going to do our jobs to end this damn war once and for all," he said.

In that instant, he suddenly felt a surge of adrenaline, of strength, resolve, duty and honor he hadn't felt a few minutes earlier. "*Maybe I just needed to utter the words aloud,*" he thought.

For her part, Daniels just nodded in acceptance. "You really think this will end the war?"

"If we're successful, I think it will. If we fail, well, then I guess we'll probably be dropping a few more of these bad boys before the war is over."

"How do you stay so calm on a mission like this?" asked Daniels. "I feel sick to my stomach. I mean, I know we train for these types of missions, but really—when's the last time a bomber crew dropped a nuclear bomb?"

Pappi chuckled at the question, eliciting a dirty look from his copilot. "I'm sorry. I forgot this is your first airframe you've flown in combat. The last time we dropped a nuke was the first day of the Second Korean War, remember?"

"Oh man, I completely forgot about that. Now I feel like an idiot," she exclaimed. Her cheeks flushed red, and it was obvious she was grateful that only the two of them had heard her question.

"It's OK, Daniels," Pappi assured. "I was still recovering at Walter Reed when it happened, but I knew the crews. That was a tough day, but they got through it, just like we will. As to how I stay calm…who says I'm calm? I'm still nervous, Daniels, I've just been doing this longer than you."

The two of them rode a little while longer in silence, the soft hum of the engines and the electronic sounds of the aircraft the only noise present.

"Why did you name our bomber Black Death?" asked Daniels. It seemed like she'd been saving that question up for some time.

"It's actually pretty simple when you think about it. I named it after the color of our bomber and the fact that wherever we travel, death follows. From the day this bomber was ready to fly, we've been test-flying it over enemy skies, dropping bombs. Unlike my previous bomber, this airframe has never known peace. It's been an instrument of destruction from its very first mission," he replied.

Before either of them could say anything further, several warning systems began to blare a danger signal.

"I'm showing dozens of enemy radars lighting up across the city," Daniels said nervously.

"It's OK. They're going after the Viper pilots. Let them do their job; they'll suppress the radars before they become a possible problem for us," he gently reassured her.

Leading the charge ahead of them were three dozen F-16Vs or Vipers, specially equipped to go after the enemy's air defense systems. Attacking Beijing was always a risky venture, since it boasted the most layered and integrated air defense system in the world. Following the Vipers were fifty F-35s, which were slated to target dozens of government and defense buildings throughout the city. The large raid prior to their nuclear attack was part of the elaborate ruse that would ensure General Yang would be late in arriving at the Xiang Shan Command Center. It was imperative for him to have a valid reason in being delayed so his cover would hold, and so he wouldn't be exposed to this elaborate and desperate gamble to end the war.

"Crap, that's a lot of enemy SAMs," Daniels commented. They watched their radar screen light up with enemy missiles being firing at the raiding party.

"Yeah, they're really throwing the kitchen sink at them, aren't they?" asked Pappi.

They watched as dozens of missiles sped quickly toward the Vipers. It looked like even a few of the F-35s were taking evasive maneuvers. Steadily, they watched as many of the missiles missed their marks. Unfortunately, they also saw more than a handful of the Vipers disappear from the radar screens. Even three of the F-35s went offline, indicating they'd been shot down as well.

"This is turning into a costly raid," Pappi thought. Nine Allied fighters had been downed so far, and they were only halfway into the raid.

"Five minutes until we're over the target," Daniels said, doing her best to stay focused on the mission and not the inordinate number of enemy missiles being fired at the raiding party flying ahead of them.

Pappi started getting the bomber ready to release their deadly cargo. He pressed a few buttons on the weapons system, completing the arming sequence on the nukes as Daniels descended to their optimal drop altitude and speed.

Seeing that they were now ready for weapons release, Pappi said a quick prayer for luck as he depressed the bomb release button on the first bomb. Instantly, the aircraft lifted; dropping 800 pounds of ordnance certainly made a difference. With their first 50-kiloton nuke away, they continued their cruising speed and altitude for another thirty seconds before Pappi released the second bomb.

He quickly closed the outer bomb doors, and once the lights showed green, he gave a quick thumbs-up to Daniels, letting her know to increase their speed and get them out of the area.

"Raider One to Henhouse. Bombs away. Both bombs successfully released. Stand by for detonation," he radioed in to their headquarters.

This was the first time they had ever broken radio silence during a bombing mission. Normally, they'd carry out their bombing mission and not let anyone know their status until they were out of enemy airspace. In this case, however, their superiors needed to know if they'd made it to the target and released their bombs.

Anxiously they waited, hoping their targets had hit home and were successful. Then again, when dropping a 50-

kiloton bomb on a target, they didn't necessarily need to hit it spot-on like a precision-guided strike. Still, they needed to get the bomb in close enough proximity to the hidden entrance so it would have the best chance of punching through the hundreds of feet of rock before detonating its warhead. Once the first warhead went off, the second would sail right in through the newly created hole before it had a chance to collapse in and would make it further into the core of the mountain before detonating. This would ensure that no matter how deep or reinforced this bunker system was, it would be destroyed, and with it, the leaders of the People's Republic of China.

Having already turned the bomber back toward home, Pappi and Double D made sure the window curtains were fully closed to block out the blast light. Given this nuclear strike was happening during the day, even though it was underground, there would still be some light leakage, especially from the second detonation.

Suddenly their radar screen went fuzzy for a second and their radio communications cut out before returning, letting them know the first bomb had successfully gone off. Seconds later, their instruments let them know a nuclear flash had just occurred, as once again, their radar and comms blacked out for a second before returning to normal.

Pulling the curtains back, Pappi demanded, "We need to turn the bomber, so we can look back at the city." He needed to see what had happened with his own eyes. Looking out to the west, he saw a rising plume from the side of a mountain—the kind of plume that only a nuclear bomb could create.

"Man, would you look at that," he said. "I've seen videos of what a nuclear bomb looks like after it's gone off, but I never thought I'd see one in real life and know that I was responsible for it."

Daniels fought back her emotions, wiping her face to hide her crying.

Looking at his partner, Pappi replied, "It's OK to shed a tear, Daniels. I never thought I'd drop a nuclear bomb either. Let's just hope this was successful and the war will now come to an end."

Chapter 29

End of an Era

Beijing, China
August First Building
Ministry of National Defense HQ

General Yang Yin stared at the remaining PLA generals of the Air Force, Army, Navy, and Rocket Force as he finished reading over the final terms of the surrender. The looks on the faces of these generals indicated that many of them were not happy with the terms. Several looked like they wanted to openly challenge him for leadership of the country.

General Zhao Keshi, the general in command of the Eastern theater of operations, shook his head and then slammed his fist down on the table. "This is unacceptable! This humiliation is not something I can accept. We must fight on if these are the terms of the agreement."

General Sun Jianguo blurted out, "I will not accept these terms! My army group will continue to fight if you agree to these terms!" He stared daggers at Yang.

Many of the generals seated before him were senior in age and time served with the military, especially in comparison to Yang. They had resented that President Xi had promoted him to Head of the PLA ahead of them, despite the fact that he was one of the few generals to bring China any military victories. General Yang became concerned over the possibility that the generals before him might openly revolt over the proposed deal.

He took a deep breath and let it out. While he was formulating a response, General Du Hengyan, the head of the PLA's strategic rocket forces, spoke up. "I have to disagree, General Sun. These are generous terms, and in light of what has happened to President Xi and the rest of the CMC, I don't see that we have a choice." As the general in charge of China's nuclear weapons, General Du held a lot of sway within the PLA. He was also the oldest general in the army. Despite his age, he had taken a liking to General Yang and, like Xi, had seen him as the future of the PLA.

General Sun responded, "You of all people should want to retaliate against the Americans, Du! This is the second time the Americans have used a nuclear weapon against China."

"And we have already obliterated Oakland and San Francisco, Sun," Du countered. "Do you not realize that to retaliate further would only invite further nuclear catastrophe on our people? Even now, the enemies are at the gate to this very city. They have us encircled. With the loss of Shanghai, and Guangdong, the war is lost."

"The war is not lost until we accept defeat!" shouted General Sun. "I, for one, do not accept defeat. We have already been arming the populace, and we've formed nearly three million of them into newly created militia battalions. We can continue to create militia battalions until we've wiped these invaders from our land." His eyes smoldered.

General Zhao nodded. "Even now, I'm readying an offensive that will push the enemy back from the capital. You have to let me launch my attack, General Yang. At least give me the chance to try and win," he said, pleading for one more offensive.

General Yang sighed deeply. He'd personally reviewed the defenses of the city, and they were solid, the best defensive network he'd ever seen. He knew it would be difficult for the Allies to break through, but he also knew with no real way to stop the Allied air forces, it was only a matter of time until they bombed those positions into oblivion.

"They still can't see that we are defeated?" Yang thought. He wondered how many more lives would need to be lost before they would accept that they couldn't win.

Sitting forward, Yang looked each general in the eyes. Then he replied, "Zhao, let's assume your offensive is successful and you push the enemy back from Beijing. Then what? What happens next?" He paused long enough for them to think about that question before continuing, "Our air force has fought valiantly, but they have been defeated and can no longer stop the Allies from attacking us at will. If we have no air cover, the enemy air forces will pound our forces into the dirt. If every armored column is attacked before it can even reach the battlefield, how can we mount a counteroffensive?

"What do we do about Shanghai? Or Guangdong? How are we going to liberate those cities and provinces if our rails and roads are constantly being bombed? How do we supply our forces with bullets when our factories are constantly being attacked?" Shaking his head, he concluded, "No, gentlemen, we have been defeated. Now it's time to end this war and rebuild our nation."

"Traitor!" shouted General Sun. He stood and immediately made his way to the door. Several of the generals looked a bit startled at his sudden departure. A few of the guards looked at Yang as if asking for instructions.

Shaking his head, Yang said, "Let him go. Let him cool down. This is clearly an emotional moment for us all.

That's why we must think carefully about our next move—tens of millions of our fellow citizens may die. We have already lost millions of people...can we truly justify continuing the war, knowing that millions more will die with no chance of victory?"

Having built up some more resolve, General Yang stood up, placing both of his hands on the table in front of him as he leaned forward slightly, allowing himself to look down on the remaining military leaders of China.

"Our nation has always held the long view when it came to policy, economics, and our military. We deviated from that view when President Xi led us into this war. Our nation was not only on track to be the dominant economic power in the world—we would have become the dominant military in a couple more decades."

He paused to let some of that sink in. "We acted too soon," he explained. "We rushed our plans and deviated from our long-standing policy of thinking long-term. The war is over. The sooner we can accept that, the sooner we can begin to rebuild our nation. This defeat has also given us the opportunity to reshape our country. To reshape our economy and remodel our military. It's time we threw off the shackles of Maoism and Marxism and learned to fully embrace our own unique Chinese version of capitalism. We can't let the economic revival of the last thirty years be lost by returning to the old order. It's time we look to the future."

It took a few minutes for his words to sink in, but once they had, many of the generals at the table nodded in agreement. They knew change was coming, and if they jumped on board with Yang, at least they'd have a guiding hand in where the country would go next. After another hour of talks, it was settled. They would accept the terms of surrender and bring an end to the Third World War and the Communist People's Republic of China.

The official end of the war and surrender would take place in a ceremony at the Forbidden City on November 11, 2019, just two days away, exactly one hundred and one years after the end of the Great War, the War to End All Wars. Following the official signing, General Yang Yin would detonate a charge that would destroy Mao's tomb, figuratively and symbolically ending China's 70-year communist government and ushering in a new era.

Chapter 30
Characters' Fates

Command Sergeant Major Luke Childers eventually went on to become the Sergeant Major of the Army six years following the end of World War III. He officially retired from the Army with thirty-four years of service as the most decorated Sergeant Major of the Army in history with the following awards: Distinguished Service Cross, Distinguished Service Medal, three Silver Stars, four Bronze Stars with a V device, four Purple Hearts, Meritorious Service Medal, four Commendation Medals and three Achievement Medals. Childers retired to his native home, Dallas-Fort Worth, Texas.

****

Lieutenant Colonel Tim Schoolman retired with twenty-one years of service following the end of the war. With the loss of his family at the outset of the war, he returned to an empty home and fell into a deep depression and alcoholism. Two years after retiring, he decided he could no longer go on with the loss of his family and no further war to fight. He committed suicide on the second anniversary of his retirement.

****

Captain Jack Taylor left the Army as a major after ten years of service, once his student loans had been fully forgiven. He went on to lead a quiet life with his family in Pittsburgh, Pennsylvania, as a certified public accountant.

****

First Lieutenant Ian Slater rose to the rank of major before leaving the Army after ten years of service. He did eventually complete his mechanical engineering degree and went to work at Tesla like his older brother. He would eventually retire from the California Army National Guard as a colonel twenty years later. A year after the war ended, the Silver Star medal he had been awarded in Korea was upgraded to the Medal of Honor for his gallantry during the battle of the Yalu River and subsequent escape from capture the following day.

****

Brigadier General Micah Tilman went on to become a four-star general and eventually became the occupation commander for Allied forces in Asia at the end of the occupation term. He was a Marines' Marine and went on to work for many veterans' organizations following his retirement after thirty-four years of service to the Corps.

****

Lieutenant Colonel Tim Long continued his distinguished career in the Marines, eventually rising to the rank of four-star general and becoming the Commandant of the Marines. He retired after thirty-six years of service as the most decorated Marine in the Corps's history. Six months following the end of the war, he was awarded the Medal of Honor for his actions during the Battle of Fei-ts Ui Reservoir during the liberation of Taiwan.

****

Captain Bennie McRae rose to the rank of Lieutenant Colonel before he retired. The day after he retired, he won $3 million dollars on a scratch-off lottery ticket. He took his money and military retirement and moved to a quiet ranch in Wyoming, where he worked on perfecting his hobby of fly fishing.

****

Lieutenant Colonel Rob "Pappi" Fortney had a wild and tumultuous marriage to his copilot, Double D, which lasted all of three months. Though they truly were the only people in the world to have had the same unique experience, they processed it very differently. Daniels' nightmares haunted her, and she fell into a deep depression, which she self-medicated with booze and excessive shopping. Fortney faced his demons head-on. He found support groups, attended therapy, and eventually received a specially trained dog to help him cope.

After getting out of the military, he felt that he needed to do something to give back to humanity, so he became a high school football coach in the inner city. Helping others gave him a deeper purpose and made it easier to get out of the prison of his own mind. Although he was never completely free of the dreams that pervaded his sleep, his life during waking hours helped him to find new meaning and move forward.

****

President Wally Foss felt elated that the war had finally ended, but utterly spent as a man. While he had taken over as President when Gates had been assassinated, Wally had never actually wanted to be President. He had been happy to be the Vice President, working his connections in Congress to help move the President's agenda through the halls where he had once walked and worked himself. The immense pressure of leading the United States of America and knowing that fate of humanity hung on many of the decisions he made was more than he could shoulder. When the war ended, he made the decision that rocked his supporters and political party, and he opted not to run for reelection. Just like Lyndon Johnson during the height of the Vietnam War, the thought of four more years as President was just too much. He didn't feel he possessed the strength to lead the nation and the world through the reconstruction and peace years that lay ahead.

When his term ended on January 20, 2021, he retired to his native state of Indiana and a much quieter, reclusive life where he would focus on doing what he could to help the veterans of the greatest war the world had ever seen learn to reintegrate back into the society they had sacrificed so much to protect.

****

Secretary of Defense James Castle was determined to make sure the politicians didn't screw up the peace deals or the much-needed reconstruction period that would be pivotal to holding the world together. Just as General Marshall and President Truman had known Germany and

Japan would need to be rebuilt following the end of the war, Castle was determined to make sure Russia and China were cultivated and brought back into the fold of peaceful nations.

When President Foss announced that he would not seek reelection, Castle knew this was his chance to lead the nation and the world into a bright new future. He quickly submitted his resignation as Secretary of Defense and the following day announced his candidacy for President. Despite having no prior political experience, his popularity and high approval rating from his handling of the war led to a massive electoral win.

As the new President, he vowed to lead the world and the country into a new era of peace and economic prosperity.

For the Veterans

I have been pretty open with our fans about the fact that PTSD has had a tremendous direct impact on our lives; it affected my relationship with my wife, job opportunities, finances, parenting—everything. It is also no secret that for me, the help from the VA was not the most ideal form of treatment. Although I am still on this journey, I did find one organization that did assist the healing process for me, and I would like to share that information.

Welcome Home Initiative is a ministry of By His Wounds Ministry, and they run seminars for veterans and their spouses for free. The weekends are a combination of prayer and more traditional counseling and left us with resources to aid in moving forward. The entire cost of the retreat—hotel costs, food, and sessions—are completely free from the moment the veteran and their spouse arrive at the location.

If you feel that you or someone you love might benefit from one of Welcome Home Initiative's sessions, please visit their website to learn more: https://welcomehomeinitiative.org/

We have decided to donate a portion of our profits to this organization, because it made such an impact in our lives and we believe in what they are doing. If you would also like to donate to Welcome Home Initiative and help to keep these weekend retreats going, you can do so by visiting the following website:

https://welcomehomeinitiative.org/donate/

From the Authors

Miranda and I hope you've enjoyed this book. We always have more in production; our current project is finishing the last book of The Falling Empires Series, and then we will be working on two new series. So get ready for The Monroe Doctrine, another riveting military thriller series, and The Rise of the Republic, our first venture into military science fiction.

While you are waiting for our next book to be released, we do have several audiobooks that have recently been produced. All six books of the Red Storm Series are now available in audio format as is our entire World War III series. *Interview with a Terrorist* and *Traitors Within*, which are currently standalone books, are also available for your listening pleasure.

If you would like to stay up to date on new releases and receive emails about any special pricing deals we may make available, please sign up for our email distribution list. Simply go to http://www.author-james-rosone.com and scroll to the bottom of the page.

As independent authors, reviews are very important to us and make a huge difference to other prospective readers. If you enjoyed this book, we humbly ask you to write up a positive review on Amazon and Goodreads. We sincerely appreciate each person that takes the time to write one.

We have really valued connecting with our readers via social media, especially on our Facebook page https://www.facebook.com/RosoneandWatson/. Sometimes we ask for help from our readers as we write future books—we love to draw upon all your different areas of expertise. We also have a group of beta readers who get to look at the books before they are officially published and help us fine-tune last-minute adjustments. If you would like to be a part of this team, please go to our author website: http://www.author-james-rosone.com, and send us a message through the "Contact" tab. You can also follow us on Twitter: @jamesrosone and @AuthorMirandaW. We look forward to hearing from you.

You may also enjoy some of our other works. A full list can be found below:

Nonfiction:

Iraq Memoir 2006–2007 Troop Surge

Interview with a Terrorist (audiobook available)

Fiction:

Monroe Doctrine Series

Volume One (available for preorder, estimated release November 30, 2020)

Volume Two (release date TBD)

Volume Three (release date TBD)

World War III Series

Prelude to World War III: The Rise of the Islamic Republic and the Rebirth of America (audiobook available)

Operation Red Dragon and the Unthinkable (audiobook available)

Operation Red Dawn and the Siege of Europe (audiobook available)

Cyber Warfare and the New World Order (audiobook available)

Michael Stone Series

Traitors Within (audiobook available)

The Red Storm Series

Battlefield Ukraine (audiobook available)

Battlefield Korea (audiobook available)

Battlefield Taiwan (audiobook available)

Battlefield Pacific (audiobook available)

Battlefield Russia (audiobook available)

Battlefield China (audiobook available)

The Falling Empires Series

Rigged (audiobook available)

Peacekeepers (audiobook available)

Invasion (audiobook available)

Vengeance (audiobook available)

Retribution (available for preorder, audiobook to be produced after release)

Children's Books:

My Daddy has PTSD

My Mommy has PTSD

Abbreviation Key

1RGR	1st Royal Gurkhas Regiment
ANZAC	Australian and New Zealand Army Corps
BCT	Brigade Combat Team
CAG	Commander, Air Group
CIWS	Close-In Weapon System
CMC	Central Military Commission
CO	Commanding Officer
COP	Combat Outpost
CP	Command Post
CVC	Combat Vehicle Control
DARPA	Defense Advanced Research Projects Agency
DDoS	Distributed Denial of Service
DIA	Defense Intelligence Agency
DoD	Department of Defense
DZ	Drop Zone
FOB	Forward Operating Base
GDP	Gross Domestic Product
GEO	Geostationary Orbit
GP	General Purpose
GPS	Global Positioning System
HE	High-Explosive

HEAT	High-Explosive Antitank Munition
HIMARS	High-Mobility Artillery Rocket System
HQ	Headquarters
HTS	High-Throughput Satellite
IBA	Individual Body Armor
IFV	Infantry Fighting Vehicle
JLTV	Joint Light Tactical Vehicle
JWICS	A Top Secret/SCI network run by the Defense Intelligence Agency
LAV	Light Amphibious Vehicle (Hovercraft)
LCU	Landing Craft Utility
LP/OP	Listening Post/Observation Post
LZ	Landing Zone
MCD	Missile Countermeasure Device
MP	Member of Parliament
NDA	Nondisclosure Agreement
NSA	National Security Advisor OR National Security Agency
PEOC	Presidential Emergency Operational Center
PLA	People's Liberation Army (Chinese Army)
PM	Prime Minister
PRC	People's Republic of China
QRF	Quick Reaction Force
ROK	Republic of Korea (South Korea)

Ro-Ro	Roll-On, Roll-Off
RPA	Russian Provisional Authority
RPG	Rocket-Propelled grenade
RTO	Radio Telephone Operator
S3	Operations Officer
SAM	Surface-to-Air Missile
SAP	Special Access Program
SINCGARS	Single Channel Ground and Airborne Radio System
SNCO	Senior Noncommissioned Officer
TACP	Tactical Air Control Party
UAV	Unmanned Aerial Vehicle (drone)
XO	Executive Officer

Printed in Great Britain
by Amazon

77342498R00325